OUTA LUCK?

Ben and his team looked like something out of a space movie as they gathered near the door of the C-130 transport plane. They were dressed all in black, with faces enclosed in Plexiglas helmets to give them oxygen until they fell far enough to be able to breathe on their own. Harley had said they would be at terminal velocity, 120 miles per hour, for several minutes prior to their chutes opening.

"It's almost impossible to breathe at that speed, so leave your helmets hooked up until your chute opens. After that, if the shock of the sudden deceleration doesn't knock you out, you can jettison your helmets and get your weapons ready to fire. We don't know what we're gonna find when we land."

"What if we get hung up in the jungle canopy too far to drop from our chutes?" Ben asked.

Harley pointed to Ben's chest. "That's what that nylon cord on the front of your HALO suit is for. Just attach it to your harness, hit the release button, and climb down the rope to the ground."

"And if the rope doesn't reach the ground?" Corrie asked.

"Then you're SOL," Harley replied with a grin.

"SOL?" she asked.

"Shit outa luck," he replied, and turned to watch the lights at the front of the transport, waiting for the jump light to turn from red to green.

BOOK YOUR PLACE ON OUR WEBSITE AND MAKE THE READING CONNECTION!

We've created a customized website just for our very special readers, where you can get the inside scoop on everything that's going on with Zebra, Pinnacle and Kensington books.

When you come online, you'll have the exciting opportunity to:

- View covers of upcoming books

- Read sample chapters

- Learn about our future publishing schedule (listed by publication month *and author*)

- Find out when your favorite authors will be visiting a city near you

- Search for and order backlist books from our online catalog

- Check out author bios and background information

- Send e-mail to your favorite authors

- Meet the Kensington staff online

- Join us in weekly chats with authors, readers and other guests

- Get writing guidelines

- AND MUCH MORE!

**Visit our website at
http://www.pinnaclebooks.com**

TYRANNY IN THE ASHES

William W. Johnstone

Pinnacle Books
Kennsington Publishing Corp.
http://www.pinnaclebooks.com

PINNACLE BOOKS are published by

Kensington Publishing Corp.
850 Third Avenue
New York, NY 10022

All Kensington Titles, Imprints, and Distributed Lines are available at special quantity discounts for bulk purchases for sales
promotions, premiums, fund-raising, educational, or institutional
use. Special book excerpts or customized printings can also be
created to fit specific needs. For details, write or phone the office
of the Kensington special sales manager: Kensington Publishing
Corp., 850 Third Avenue, New York, NY 10022, attn: Special
Sales Department, Phone: 1-800-221-2647.

Pinnacle and the P logo Reg. U.S. Pat. & TM Off.

First Printing: September, 2000
10 9 8 7 6 5 4 3 2 1

Printed in the United States of America

In every tyrant's heart there springs in the end
This poison, that he cannot trust a friend.

Aeschylus (525– 456 BC)

No government power can be abused
long. Mankind will not bear it . . .
There is a remedy in human nature against
tyranny, that will keep us safe under
every form of government.

Samuel Johnson (1709–1764)

Prologue

If a war had not engulfed the entire world, plunging every nation into bloody chaos, the theory was the government of the United States would have collapsed anyway. Personal income taxes had been going up for years, and the hard-working, law-abiding citizens were paying well over half their income to the government. The left wing of the Democratic party had taken over and passed massive gun-grab legislation, effectively disarming American citizens—except for the criminals, of course, and about three quarters of a million tough-minded Americans who didn't give a big rat's ass what liberals said, thought, or did. Those Americans carefully sealed up their guns and buried them, along with cases of ammunition. When the collapse came, those Americans were able to defend themselves against the hundreds of roaming gangs of punks and thugs that popped up all over what had once been called the United States. The great nation would never again be accurately referred to as the United States of America.

Slowly, an ever-growing group of people began calling for a man named Ben Raines to lead them. But Ben didn't want any part of leadership. For months he disregarded the ever-increasing calls from people all over the nation, until finally he could no longer ignore the pleas.

Months later, thousands of people made the journey to the northwest part of the nation and formed their own nation out of three states. It was called the Tri-States, and those who chose to live there based many of their laws on the Constitution of the United States: the original interpretation of that most revered document. Basically, it was a commonsense approach to government, something that had been sadly lacking for years with liberals in control of the old United States of America. But after only a few months in their new nation, Ben knew that only about two out of every ten Americans could—or would was more to the point—live under a commonsense form of government. Under this form of government, everyone, to a very large degree, controlled his or her own destiny. The Rebels, as residents of the Tri-States were named by the press, took wonderful care of the very old, the young, and those unable to care for themselves. But if a person was able to work, he worked . . . whether he liked it or not. There were no free handouts for able-bodied people. If they didn't want to work, they got the hell out of the Tri-States. Very quickly.

The first attempt at building a nation within a nation failed when the federal government grew powerful enough to launch a major campaign against the Tri-States. The original Tri-States was destroyed and the Rebel Army was decimated and scattered. But the federal government made one major mistake: They didn't kill Ben Raines.

Ben and the few Rebels left alive began rebuilding their Army, and then launched a very nasty guerrilla war against the federal government that lasted for months: hit hard, destroy, and run. It worked.

But before any type of settlement could be reached, a deadly plague struck the earth: a rat-borne outbreak, the Black Death revisited.

When the deadly disease finally ran its course, anarchy reigned over what had once been America. Gangs of punks and warlords ruled from border to border, coast to coast. Ben and his Rebels began the long, slow job of clearing the nation of punks and human slime and setting up a new Tri-States.

This time they settled in the South, first in Louisiana, in an area they called Base Camp One. Then they began spreading out in all directions as more and more people wanted to become citizens of the new nation called the Southern United States of America: SUSA.

Ben and the Rebels fought for several years, clearing the cities of the vicious gangs and growing larger and stronger while the SUSA spread out.

In only a few years, the Rebel Army became the largest and most powerful army on the face of the earth . . . with the possible exception of China. No one knew what was going on in China, for that nation had sealed its borders and cut off nearly all communication with the outside world.

A few more years drifted by while the Rebels roamed the world at the request of the newly formed United Nations, kicking ass and stabilizing nations as best they could in the time allotted them.

But back home, the situation was worsening. Outside the SUSA, the nation was turning socialistic with sickening speed. The old FBI was gone, in its place the FPPS: Federal Prevention and Protective Service. It was a fancy title that fooled no one. The FPPS was the nation's secret police, and they were everywhere, bullyboys and thugs. Day-to-day activities of those living in the USA were highly restricted. The new Liberal/Socialist government of President for Life Claire Osterman and her second in command, Harlan Millard, was now firmly in control.

There were border guards stationed all along major crossings in every state. But now many of them had been moved south, to patrol along the several-thousand-mile border of the SUSA.

A bloody civil war was shaping up between the USA and the SUSA. Rewards had been placed on the head of Ben Raines: a million dollars for his capture, dead or alive. But Ben was accustomed to that. He'd had rewards—of one kind or another, from one group or another—on his head for years.

Anna, Ben's adopted daughter, had been kidnapped by the FPPS. She was to be tried as a traitor against the Liberal/Socialist government and executed. A very highly irritated Ben knew the taking of Anna was intended to draw him out, for the FPPS was certain Ben would come after her . . . which he damn sure did, with blood in his eyes. That abortive move cost the FPPS several dozen agents and accomplished nothing else for Osterman and her henchman. But it further heightened the already monumental legend of Ben Raines . . . and made Claire Osterman and her government look like a pack of incompetent screwups . . . which they certainly were.

After Claire completely lost her temper and what little rational judgment she had, she started a civil war with SUSA, using hired mercenaries when half of her own USA troops refused to fight their neighbors. All along a battle line that stretched for thousands of miles, from Texas to Georgia in the Old South, federal troops faced Rebel forces across no-man's lands.*

Once again the SUSA, led by Ben Raines and his team, kicked her federal troops' butt in battle after battle, driving her into a fury that knew no bounds.

When Sugar Babe Osterman got word from her field commanders that Raines had killed Commanding General Walter Berman, head of her entire Army, in a hand-to-hand combat, she almost had a stroke. In a fit of pique, she notified Cecil Jeffreys, President of the SUSA, that if he and his leaders, especially that bastard Ben Raines, didn't surrender, she was going to launch an all-out missile attack against the SUSA at 0600 hours. The missiles were to contain a highly effective, ancient strain of anthrax bacteria developed by a USA scientist, Yiro Ishi. The vaccinations the SUSA had given their troops against anthrax would be useless due to the ancient nature of this new strain.

Standoff in the Ashes.

However, Ishi double-crossed Claire Osterman and gave the formula for an effective vaccine to Ben Raines and a fake formula to Osterman's government. As the plague began to decimate the USA, Otis Warner, one of Claire Osterman's cabinet officers, conspired with General Joseph Winter to have Claire Osterman killed in a plane crash.

When the plane went down, Warner and Winter, sure Osterman was dead, took over the government of the USA, then contacted SUSA president Cecil Jeffreys and began to discuss a peace accord.*

However, Claire Osterman survived the plane crash and was taken in by a family in the Ozark Mountains of Tennessee . . .

Crisis in the Ashes.

One

Claire Osterman looked up into the inky blackness of the night sky as the plane she'd just jumped out of exploded in a fiery ball of flame. The cold air rushed past her face and she flailed her arms, falling at 120 miles an hour toward the Tennessee mountains below.

She opened her mouth and began to scream . . .

"Wake up, lady," a voice said, pulling her from the depths of the nightmare she'd had every night since her plane crash four weeks ago.

Claire Osterman looked up into Bettye Jean Holt's face, fighting to come fully awake and put the horrible dream behind her. She glanced around at the small bedroom where she'd been staying since hobbling through five miles of wooded Ozark mountain forest with a broken jaw, broken left arm, and severely sprained left ankle to finally find refuge in the Holts' small wooden shack a month before.

Bettye Jean Holt was carrying a bowl of what could only be described as gruel. She'd told Claire it was oatmeal, that being the only thing Claire could manage to eat as her broken jaw healed, but if there were any oats in it, they were few and far between.

"What time is it?" Claire mumbled sleepily, rubbing her eyes to erase the picture of General Willford Hall being blown to bits above her.

"Heck," Bettye Jean said in her thick backwoods accent,

"h'it's almost five in the mornin'. Billy Bob's gone out to feed the chickens an' hog." She grinned, exposing yellowed teeth with several black gaps where malnutrition had caused them to fall out.

Claire reached for the oatmeal, wincing as pain shot down her left arm, restricted by the crude splint Bettye Jean had taped on it after setting the broken bones.

"He said to git yore lazy butt up an' fer me to git his breakfast 'fore he came back, Mary," Bettye Jean said, using the fake name Claire had given them when she found out they hated Claire Osterman and the entire government of the USA.

"He said it was about time you started earnin' yore keep around here, but"—and Bettye Jean's voice changed to a conspiratorial whisper as she continued—"I tole him yore arm weren't healed enough jest yet."

As Claire took the oatmeal from her, Bettye Jean pulled a folded-up newspaper out of her apron pocket. "I also brung you a paper Billy Bob got when he drove the ol' pickup into town yesterday. H'it's a couple'a weeks old, but I figgered you'd like to know what was goin' on in the world since you fell outta that tree."

"What . . . oh, yeah," Claire said, remembering she'd told the Holts that she'd received her injuries when she climbed a tree to get her bearings after getting lost in the woods. Billy Bob had said he thought she looked like Claire Osterman and if she was, he was going to shoot her. Her cover story had been a quick attempt to save her life until the search party from USA headquarters could find her.

Claire took the spoon and bowl and began shoveling the soupy mixture into her mouth, wondering why they hadn't already come for her.

As she left the room, Bettye Jean lit a small kerosene lantern on a table next to the door. The cabin had no electricity or running water, and the bathroom was in a small shed fifty yards down the path.

Claire's face flushed and her heart pounded as she read the headlines of the two-week-old paper: "President Warner and President Jeffreys Make Progress toward Peace Agreement."

President Warner? *Why that backstabbing son of a bitch, Claire thought. When I get back I'll show him who's President! I'll personally put a bullet in the bastard's mouth!*

She finished the cereal and struggled out of the bed, hobbling on a still-sore left ankle toward the kitchen. She had to get to a phone so she could let them know at government headquarters she was still alive. She'd be damned if she was going to let this peace proposal go any further!

"Bettye Jean," she said from the door to the kitchen.

Bettye Jean looked over her shoulder from the sink where she was washing dishes. "Oh, you scared me, Mary."

"Bettye Jean," Claire said, handing her the bowl and spoon, "I've got to get to a phone. How far is it to the nearest one?"

Bettye Jean pursed her lips, thinking. "Oh, 'bout five mile down the road. There's a gas station there that has a phone on the wall." She shook her head. "Course, they don't often have any gas to sell, since that crazy Osterman lady done started this here war."

"But she had to," Claire said, exasperated that this simple country woman couldn't understand the dangers the country faced from Ben Raines and his Rebels. "She had to protect the country against the Rebel Army."

Bettye Jean put her finger to her lips. "Shhh, don't you let Billy Bob hear you takin' up fer that bitch. He's liable to take a switch to you, or worse," she said, naked fear in her eyes.

"Do you think he'll take me down to the gasoline station in your pickup?"

"I doubt it, Mary. He says we don't got no gas to waste on foolishness, what with it costin' five dollars a gallon now, when they got any."

Claire was getting awfully tired of the crap this hillbilly

named Billy Bob was always spouting. She sighed. It was time to take matters into her own hands before it was too late and Otis Warner and his crowd screwed everything up beyond repair.

"Okay, Bettye Jean. You go on back to your dishwashing and I'll go out back and ask him myself."

" 'Member now, don't go sayin' nothin' 'bout that Osterman woman, or you'll git a beatin'."

Claire's lips curled in a sneer. "Oh, I think Billy Bob's beating days are over."

She left the kitchen, Bettye Jean staring at her back with a worried look on her face. Claire went down the hallway to the Holts' bedroom and opened the closet door. Leaning in a corner was a double-barreled shotgun. Bettye Jean had told her Billy Bob always kept it loaded with 00-buckshot.

Claire picked it up, broke open the barrel, and checked the loads. Both barrels full. She clicked it shut, put it over her shoulder, and headed out back to where the hogs and chickens were.

"Here, chick, chick, chick," Billy Bob was saying as he scattered a few meager handfuls of grain for the hens. A bucket of slops was next to his feet, intended for the rather skinny hog in a makeshift pen a few yards away.

"Billy Bob," Claire called to his back. "I need a ride down the road to the gas station. I need to make a phone call."

Without turning around, he answered, "I ain't got gas to waste on you and yore foolishness, woman. Now git back to the house and hep Bettye Jean with her chores."

Claire's face flushed in anger. No one had talked like that to her in ten years, and she wasn't about to let this inbred idiot do it now.

"I don't think so, Billy Bob," she said in a low, dangerous voice.

"You sassin' me, woman?" he said as he turned around, eyes widening as he saw the long-barreled shotgun cradled in her arms.

"What you doin' with my scattergun?" he asked.

"Thanking you for your hospitality, you dumb son of a bitch," she said, her eyes sparkling with excitement as she pulled the trigger.

The shotgun exploded, twisting her half around as the heavy load blew Billy Bob backward to land half in the hog pen.

"You'll have something special to eat tonight, hog," she said as she turned and walked up the hill toward the house.

Bettye Jean came running out of the door, her hands to her mouth when she saw what Claire had done.

"Oh, Mary," she screamed, tears running down her cheeks. "What'd you do that, fer?"

"I'm sorry, Bettye Jean, but I can't let you tell anyone I'm here until my people have a chance to come get me. It would be too dangerous with the attitude you mountain people have towards the government."

"Huh?" Bettye Jean asked.

"I'm truly sorry, Bettye Jean. You were really nice to me, but you had the misfortune to become involved in things more important than your miserable life."

The shotgun exploded again, knocking Bettye Jean backward through the screened-in rear porch, dead before she hit the ground.

Claire took the keys to their battered pickup truck off a nail on the kitchen wall. She reloaded the shotgun, just in case, and started toward the gasoline station down the road. It was time to call in the troops.

Two

Virgie Malone, Otis Warner's new secretary and "gal Friday," stuck her head in the door to the President of the United States' office and called, "Mr. President!"

Otis glanced up from the latest communiqué from President Cecil Jeffreys, surprised at the urgent tone in Virgie's voice. He was interested to see what could make the usually unflappable Virgie so excited.

"Yes, Virgie? What is it?" he asked.

"There's someone on line one," she said, a little breathless since she'd run the twenty feet down the hall from her office to give him this message personally rather than trusting the interoffice intercom.

"Who is it?"

"She says she's Claire Osterman."

"Shit!" Otis exclaimed, sweat popping out on his brow and his stomach feeling as if someone had kicked him in the balls.

"Should I put her through?" Virgie asked, watching his reaction carefully.

"Uh . . . yeah, sure, just give me a minute to . . . collect myself. Oh, and get General Winter down here immediately!"

"Sir," Virgie said, "I thought she was dead."

Otis pulled a rumpled handkerchief from his pocket and wiped his forehead. "So did I, Virgie, so did we all."

She pulled her head out of the doorway like a turtle going

back in its shell, and a few moments later the phone on his desk buzzed.

His hand hesitated just a few seconds as he reached to pick up the receiver, as if he were afraid to touch the instrument lest some venom from the bitch on the other end leak through the plastic and eat his flesh away.

Finally, he picked the phone up. "Hello, this is Otis Warner."

"I'm surprised you didn't call yourself the President, Otis," the sarcastic voice on the other end snarled in a tone he remembered so well.

"Claire, is it you? We thought you'd been killed."

"No doubt," she replied drily. "Well, as you can see, or rather hear, I'm alive, and I'm ready to get back to headquarters."

"Uh, sure, okay," Otis stammered, playing for time as he frantically tried to think of what to do next.

"I want you to send a pickup team immediately, Otis."

"All right, Claire. Just where exactly are you?"

"I'm at a little log cabin in the woods about seven or eight klicks north of the crash site. You can't miss it. There's nothing else around for miles. There'll be a rusted-out red pickup truck parked in front."

Otis nodded at the phone, forgetting she couldn't see him. "Okay. I'll have an extraction team there in a couple of hours."

"You'd better," she snapped. "Oh, and Otis?"

"Yes?"

"When I get back, we're going to have a very serious talk about this bullshit peace protocol you've been trying to push through."

"Yes . . . uh, Madame President."

He winced at the loud click as she slammed the phone down.

General Joseph Winter knocked lightly on his door, and entered without waiting for his answer.

"Good morning, Mr. President," he said formally, as was his wont when addressing his old friend.

"Can the shit, Joe!" Otis said. "We've got trouble."

"Oh?"

"Yeah. Claire Osterman just called me on the phone."

"What? But . . . she was confirmed dead."

"No, she wasn't. Evidently the plane went down without her on it. She's at a little cabin just north of the crash site. She wants an extraction team ASAP."

Winter paused to stare out of Otis's window, thinking.

"We're royally fucked, Joe," Otis said, wiping more sweat from his face.

Winter's eyes found his. "No we're not, Otis. Just because we missed once, doesn't mean we can't try again."

"You mean . . ."

"Sure. We've got her location, so instead of an extraction team, we send a hit team. I'll send an Apache gunship and blow the cabin all to hell."

"Have you got men you can trust to do this?"

"Absolutely. As I told you, I've weaned out most of the men sympathetic to Osterman's ideas."

He got to his feet. "Just leave everything to me, Otis. Remember, don't sweat the small stuff, and . . ."

"I know, it's *all* small stuff," Otis said, finishing the joke between the two men who had engineered a takeover of one of the most powerful governments on earth.

"Let me know when it's over, will you?" Otis asked.

Winter nodded as he put his cap on his head and pulled it down tight. "Hang in there, Mr. President," he said as he walked out the door.

Otis swiveled in his chair so he could stare out his window. It was all so close to becoming reality. The war with the SUSA was days away from being history. Now was no time for that bitch to show up and put a monkey wrench in his plans.

* * *

Claire Osterman drove back to the cabin in the Holts' truck, parked it in front, and went inside. She walked around the cabin, but found nothing she wanted to take with her.

She made a pot of coffee, using the last of the grounds in the Holts' cupboard. *Ha,* she laughed to herself as she emptied the can. They wouldn't have need of it any longer.

After she had been waiting for an hour, her stomach began to cramp from the four cups of coffee she'd downed. *Damn,* she thought, *one more trip to that misbegotten outhouse.*

She walked the fifty yards down the path through the woods to the small shed and went inside. As she sat on the wooden bench with the two holes in it, she thought, *Why in the world do they make these things with two holes? Surely people don't sit here next to each other and use them at the same time.*

She was only half-finished when she heard the unmistakable *whoop-whoop* of helicopter blades overhead. *Damn,* she thought, *wouldn't you know it. The goddamned Army never comes at an appropriate time.* She was in the process of pulling up her pants when the sound of the helicopter blades changed, becoming higher in pitch and much louder as it roared by less than twenty feet over her head.

She jerked the door of the outhouse open just in time to see the tiny log cabin virtually disintegrate under the onslaught of thousands of rounds of ammunition from the Gatling guns of the attack ship. She ducked back inside the outhouse as the Apache warship made a sweeping bank to the left, lined up on the cabin, and fired two Hellfire missiles into the roof.

The shock wave from the explosion hit the outhouse like a mighty fist and knocked it over on its side. This probably saved Claire's life, as the outhouse was now flat among a row of bushes at its rear and covered from sight.

As the flames from the explosion died down, the helicopter landed and two men jumped to the ground, automatic rifles cradled in their arms.

They walked into the smoldering wreckage of the house, and Claire could see them stirring a smoking lump of charred flesh with their boots. One of them turned and gave a thumbs-up to the pilot, and both men ran back to the helicopter.

After it took off, Claire pushed broken boards off her body and struggled out of the bushes, finally getting to her feet. She ran to the house to see what the men had been looking at. She held her nose as she stood over Mrs. Holt's still-burning corpse. *Those bastards were making sure a female had been killed in the attack!* she thought. *The sons of bitches were sent to kill me!*

The realization stunned Claire as nothing else ever had. She stumbled from the burnt-out shell of the cabin, thinking furiously. She had to clear her mind and be sharp, or else she'd never survive this.

She walked around the ruins of the cabin and found the pickup on its side, flames licking the rusted red paint from the metal. *So much for transportation,* she mused.

She ran back to the outhouse, picked up the shotgun she'd carried with her, and began to walk toward the gas station. She figured she had a couple of hours' walk to figure out her next step. But one thing was sure. She was going to make that son of a bitch Otis Warner rue the day he fucked with Claire Osterman.

Three

Ben Raines, Commander in Chief of the Rebel Army of the Southern United States of America, threw the rubber ball as far as he could. His malamute puppy, Jodie, took off in a lumbering run after the ball, her tongue hanging out as she panted from the workout Ben was giving her.

Cooper, Ben's driver and friend, squatted on his haunches nearby. "That's a pretty good throw for an old man, Ben. You missed your calling. You should've been a major-league pitcher."

Ben glanced at the young man as he sleeved sweat off his forehead. "I don't know who's getting the best workout here. Me or the dog."

Jersey, Ben's female bodyguard who was never very far from his side, said, "It's a shame you don't have two balls, Ben. Then you could throw one for Coop to fetch, too."

Coop glared at Jersey. "Ben, what's another word for female dog?"

Jersey pointed her finger at him. "Don't *even* go there, Coop, or you'll be wearing those little ornaments hanging between your legs on your head."

Coop snickered. "Hell, might as well be wearin' 'em for all the use they've gotten lately."

As Jodie brought the ball back to Ben and dropped it at his feet, he leaned down and petted her head. "That's enough, girl. You're wearing Daddy out."

Jersey, unwilling to let Coop off the hook, observed, "Well,

Coop, now that the war with the USA is on hold, maybe you can find some undiscriminating females at a local bar who'll consent to go out on a date with you."

"Unlike some of the female members of this team who haven't had any dates since reaching puberty, I won't have to look too far. The babes are lined up waitin' for me to ask 'em out."

Jersey turned to follow Ben into their offices in SUSA headquarters. "That's gotta be the shortest line in the country," she muttered.

"Hey, I heard that!" Coop said, falling in behind her and Ben. "And if I hadn't been so busy this past year pulling your butt out of the fire, I'd've had plenty of chances to score."

Jersey's heart fluttered at the words, and her mind flashed back to the night Coop was referring to . . .

The jump master and his helpers shoved large wooden crates out the door, alternating equipment drops with the jumps of Ben's team so the matériel would land within easy reach of the Rebel forces. Finally, only Coop and Jersey were left in the big C-130.

Coop gave a low bow, sweeping his hand to the side. "After you, my pet," he said with a sardonic leer, glancing at the way Jersey's battle fatigues fit snugly over her buttocks.

"Pervert," she said, noticing where his eyes were fixed. "Have a good look, 'cause that's all you'll ever get!"

She hooked her chute cord on the overhead line and bent to step out of the doorway. Just before she jumped, the Big Bird hit an air pocket and suddenly lurched and dropped fifty feet straight down.

Jersey was thrown out the door, tumbling uncontrollably in the updraft as the plane plummeted earthward. Her chute deployed and was immediately snagged on the tail fin of the airplane, ripping to shreds and streaming behind her as she fell.

"Shit!" screamed the jump master, leaning out the window to watch her fall. He turned an ashen face to Coop. "She's a goner."

Coop whipped out his K-Bar and slashed his chute line. "Uh-uh, pardner, nobody dies tonight," he said, and dove out of the door after her.

He tucked his chin onto his chest and put his hands tight against his sides to minimize drag, and blinked his eyes against the hundred-mile-an-hour-wind as he arrowed downward, desperately trying to catch sight of Jersey's black silk against the darkness.

Jersey's body tumbled, her arms loose and flopping like a rag doll's, unconscious from the jolt she'd received when her chute was ripped apart.

This saved her life, as she fell much more slowly than Coop did, and he caught up with her in a matter of seconds. When he came up to her, he spread his arms and legs to slow his fall, and grabbed the tangled shreds of her chute, wrapping his hands around the silk.

He took a deep breath, grabbed the D-ring of his chute release, and jerked. When his parachute opened, the jolt nearly took his arms off, and he felt as if both his shoulders were dislocated by the force of the sudden slowdown.

Even though the Ranger parachutes were specially made for low-level drops, they weren't designed to hold two people at once. Coop and Jersey fell with alarming speed through the night.

Coop gritted his teeth and bent his knees slightly, hoping he'd be able to hit and roll without breaking a leg, or even worse, his neck. "Mamma always said there'd be days like this," he muttered to himself.

In a stroke of great good fortune, Jersey and Coop plummeted into the outer branches of a giant sugar maple tree, the limbs slowing their fall enough to cause them to suffer only minor bruises and cuts.

As soon as he could untangle himself from the lines of his chute, Coop took a quick inventory of his body. No major bones seemed to be broken, and other than a deep gash on his left thigh, which he wrapped with a piece of silk from his chute, he seemed in fair condition.

When he was satisfied the bleeding from his leg was controlled, he scrambled through the darkness to where Jersey lay, still unconscious.

He gently unwrapped her from the shroud of silk covering her, and spread her out on the ground. He was running his hands over her limbs and body, checking for major wounds or broken bones, when she opened her eyes and stared angrily at him.

"Just what the hell do you think you're doing?" she asked, propping herself up on her elbows.

Coop sat back on his haunches. "Just coppin' a quick feel, darlin'," he answered, more relieved than he cared to show that she was all right.

"Well, unless you want to pull back a nub, keep your hands to yourself, Coop."

He grinned. "Yes, ma'am," he said, holding his hands out palm up. "Whatever you say, Jersey."

"What happened?" she asked, and tried to stand up, collapsing when she put her weight on her right ankle, which was already swollen to almost twice normal size.

He leaned forward and took her leg in his hand, untied her combat boot, and pulled it off, causing her to shout in pain.

"Hold on there, big boy," she said. "What're you trying to do, pull my foot off?"

He gave a low whistle when he saw her ankle. It was black and blue and grossly misshapen. Slowly, he moved it through a complete range of motion, again bringing tears of pain to her eyes.

"I don't think it's broken, but you're not going to be walking on it anytime soon," he said.

As she stared at him, her eyes glistening with moisture in the half moonlight, he explained what had happened, and how her chute had fouled on the tail fin of the C-130.

"Damn!" she exclaimed, looking heavenward.

"What is it?" he asked.

She shook her head. "Now I owe you my life, and I can't think of a worse thing to have happen."

"Oh, things could be worse."

"How?"

"I could be scraping your body up with a spatula about now," he answered.

She snorted. "I don't know if that would be worse or not."

He leered at her. "Oh, don't make such a big thing of it," he said. "I figure you did this on purpose, so we'd be marooned alone out here in the woods, like we were in Africa."*

He shook his head. "Hell, you didn't have to go to all this trouble to be alone with me . . . all you had to do was ask."

She kicked at him with her injured ankle, then moaned in pain. "Don't flatter yourself, pervert. I'd sooner be alone with a snake than with a lecher like you."

"Speaking of being alone, why don't you try to bump Corrie on your headset? Mine got ripped off when I sky-dove to catch up with you."

Jersey reached up to trigger the speaker on her headset, only to find it smashed to pieces, hanging uselessly around her neck.

"Damn, no can do, Coop. Looks like we really are alone. Do you have any idea where we are, or where the rest of the team is?"

"Don't have a clue. After the plane hit the air pocket, we could have turned in any direction. There is no way of telling where we are, at least not until daylight."

---

*Triumph in the Ashes.

Jersey glanced at the chronometer on her wrist. "It's about one A.M. now, so that gives us at least five hours until dawn."

Coop got to his feet and dusted his pants off. "I'll cut some branches and make us some sort of shelter against the cold. We can use the silk from the chutes to form a windbreak, and maybe we won't freeze to death before the sun comes up."

After he'd fashioned a lean-to from maple branches and strung pieces of their parachutes around them, he scraped together a mound of pine needles into a makeshift bed underneath, out of the wind.

He helped Jersey to her feet, putting his arm around her to support her weight.

She took his hand where it lay against the side of her breast and moved it down on her ribcage. "And don't try that old standby about using our body heat to stay warm," she said.

He shrugged. "It worked in the jungle, didn't it?"

She glared at him. "I seem to remember you promised never to mention that night again," she said with some heat.

"That was before I knew what lengths you'd go to in order to spend another night with me," he answered as he lowered her into the lean-to.

She lay on the pine needles, her back to him as he gently covered her with a piece of parachute silk. "Wake me when it's dawn," she mumbled, already almost asleep.

"Women," he whispered as he lay next to her, "can't live with 'em, and can't kill 'em."

Later, just as he was dozing off, he felt her turn and wrap her arms around him, spooning against him to get warm, her breath stirring the hairs on the back of his neck and causing thoughts he knew he'd never dare mention to her.

She moaned once, and her breathing slowed as she fell asleep, leaving him wide awake and acutely aware of her breasts pressing against his back.*

Crisis in the Ashes.

* * *

Jersey stopped and turned, her hands on her hips, pushing the memory of that night from her thoughts. "Look, Coop. I told you thank you for saving my life already. What more do you want?"

He grinned and waggled his eyebrows. "Well . . ."

"In your dreams, mister!" she exclaimed, and whirled around, her mood of thankfulness evaporating like ice on a hot stove.

"More like my nightmares, you mean," he rejoined as they entered Ben's office complex.

When they walked through the door, they found Dr. Lamar Chase, Ben's team doctor, waiting for them.

"Howdy, Doc," Coop said.

"Hello, Lamar," Ben added.

"Hi, guys," Doc said.

"What brings you to visit?" Ben asked. "Time for more inoculations?"

"Please say no," Coop begged. It was a well-known fact that Coop, who feared almost nothing else on earth, was deathly afraid of needles.

Doc Chase held up his hands. "No, Coop, no more shots." He grinned. "And it's a good thing, too. Last time I had to give you an injection, you used up my entire supply of smelling salts."

"Sissy," Jersey whispered under her breath.

"Bitch," Coop replied, his face flaming red, continuing the constant game of sarcastic rejoinders the two played on a daily basis. Ben had often said they ought to get married, as much as they fought. Both Coop and Jersey acted aghast at the very idea.

"Actually it's to tell you the plague in the northern states is on a rapid decline," said Doc. "With our shipments of antibiotics and the new vaccine Yiro Ishi gave us, the citizens of the USA are healing and very few new cases of anthrax are being reported."

"No thanks to Sugar Babe Osterman, God bless her memory," Ben said sarcastically.

Doc Chase nodded. "You're right there, Ben. Her . . . uh, untimely death probably saved more lives than anything she'd ever done in life."

Ben bent and rubbed Jodie's head as he took his seat at his desk.

"How are the peace negotiations going with Otis Warner?" Doc asked.

Ben shrugged. "Okay, I think. Cec Jeffreys says Warner and his new cabinet are much more reasonable to deal with than the Osterman regime was." He grinned. "Warner at least seems to have the citizens' welfare uppermost in his mind, rather than some misguided feelings of revenge against me personally as Sugar Babe did."

"What are the latest terms?" Coop asked.

"Warner has agreed to reset the boundaries between our two countries back to their status at the time Osterman began her attacks against us."

"What about reparations?" Jersey asked.

Ben wagged his head. "There are to be none. There wouldn't be any use anyway, 'cause the treasury of the USA is just about empty."

Beth, the statistician on Ben's team who was responsible for keeping track of resources and matériel during times when they were at war, nodded. "It's just as you predicted, Ben. The hideously high taxes they've been collecting all these years have been used to support the vast bureaucracy of their government and their stupid welfare programs instead of for the good of the working citizens who are paying them."

"Maybe they'll finally glom onto the fact you simply cannot pay people not to work and expect workers to keep propping up the system. It goes against all human nature," Ben said.

"Well, folks, politics is your bailiwick," Doc said. "I just came to tell you about the plague, so I'm off."

"Headin' for the golf course?" Coop asked with a smile. He was always kidding Doc about his quest to break 100 on the golf links around the base.

Doc smiled. "Yeah. I've got this new driver that is guaranteed to let me hit the ball three hundred yards."

"That just means you'll have to trek that much farther into the woods to find it," Coop said.

"Ain't that the truth," Doc said as he waved good-bye and headed out the door.

Corrie, the team's communications expert, looked up from one of the portable headsets she was fiddling with. "What are you going to do now that peace is threatening to break out, Ben? Take up golf like Doc Chase?"

Ben smirked. "Oh, I wouldn't worry too much about us warriors being out of a job, Corrie," he answered. "If I remember my history correctly, there haven't been too many years since man crawled out of the primordial muck that warriors weren't much in demand. It seems human beings just can't seem to get along for any length of time with each other. If it's not the color of their neighbors' skins that causes them to go to war, it's the fact that one nation has something another wants and doesn't want to work to get it. It's always easier for politicians to send us in to do their dirty work rather than have the courage to pass laws that are painful to the voters who keep them in office. So, no, I'm not going to take up golf. I'm going to keep my .45 cleaned and oiled and be ready for the next hot spot to pop up, as one always does."

Four

Claire Osterman was sweaty, exhausted, and covered with mosquito bites by the time she'd walked the five miles to the service station and the nearest phone.

She stood the shotgun in a corner and walked into the office. "I need to make another phone call," she said.

The proprietor, a tall, skinny man with several days' growth of whiskers on his face, looked up at her from under the brim of a large, black, flop-brimmed hat as he cut a piece of tobacco off a plug with a pocketknife.

"You got money? Long-distance calls ain't exactly cheap, ya know."

Claire felt in the pockets of the pants she'd appropriated from the Holts. Damn, she thought, she'd forgotten to take the stash of money Bettye Jean Holt had squirreled away in her sugar bowl, hidden from her husband.

"Listen, I'm calling a friend to come pick me up. I'll tell him to bring the money to pay you back for the call."

The man grinned, exposing teeth yellowed by years of chewing poor-grade tobacco. "That ain't gonna cut it, little lady," he drawled in the soft accent of south Tennessee. "No money, no call, It's as simple as that."

Claire tried to put a seductive smile on her face, in spite of the swelling that still remained in her broken jaw. "How about I pay another way, handsome," she purred, unbuttoning the top two buttons of her shirt. What the hell, she thought, it'd been over a month since she'd had any loving, and there was that old saying, any port in a storm.

The owner of the station stared at her body, thinner than before due to the near-starvation rations of the Holts, but still twenty pounds overweight, and her sagging, lifeless breasts.

"That might git ya some food, but yore not near pretty enough for a long-distance call, lady."

Claire's face blushed red and her heart hammered in anger. *Why, that lousy no good son of a bitch,* she thought, humiliated at the rejection.

"Okay, have it your way," she said quietly through teeth gritted tight.

She turned around, picked up the Holts' shotgun, and opened the door. After making sure no one was around, she whirled and pointed the barrel at the man.

"What's your name, mister?" she asked.

He looked up, eyes widening at the sight of the scattergun pointing at his face. He held up both hands, as if he could stop the buckshot if she fired. "Uh . . . I didn't mean no disrespect, ma'am. Go ahead an' use the phone."

"I said, what is your name?"

"Kyle, Kyle Truman. Why do you want to know?"

She grinned, feeling better suddenly. " 'Cause I make it a practice to know the names of men I kill," she growled, pulling the trigger.

The shotgun exploded, kicking back against her shoulder as the buckshot took Kyle Truman's head almost completely off at the neck, blowing his body backward to land spread-eagled on his desk behind the counter.

Claire walked around the countertop and punched the No Sale key on the cash register. When the drawer opened, she pocketed the two hundred dollars in bills and as much of the change as she could stuff in her pockets. When the register was empty, she walked to Truman's cooler, took out a couple of beers and three Butterfinger candy bars, and carried them to the phone. As she dialed, she tore the wrapper off the chocolate bar and popped the top on the beer.

She drank half the bottle down in one long gulp, thinking she hadn't tasted anything so good in a long time.

The operator at USA headquarters answered, "United States Capital Services."

"I need to speak to BuPers, please," Claire said, asking for the Bureau of Personnel.

After several clicks and some static from the satellite connection, Claire was finally connected to the correct department.

"Can I help you?" a feminine voice asked.

"Yes. I need to talk to Herb Knoff. He used to be assigned to President Osterman's staff."

There was silence for a moment, then the voice came back. "Military personnel aren't allowed to receive personal phone calls."

"This isn't exactly a personal call," Claire replied, wanting to strangle the bitch on the other end of the line. "This is Nurse Jenkins at Baptist Memorial Hospital. Mr. Knoff's mother has had a heart attack and she's requested that we notify her son."

"Oh . . . in that case, I'm sure it'll be all right. Lieutenant Knoff has been assigned to the motor pool. I'll connect you."

Motor Pool? Claire thought. *So that bastard Warner is getting rid of anyone who might still be loyal to me.*

After another series of annoying bursts of static, a surly voice came on the line. "Motor pool, Knoff speaking."

"Herb, don't say a word . . . this is Claire."

There was a long pause, "Oh . . . uh . . . hello. This is quite a surprise."

"I suspect it is," Claire replied drily. "How are you liking your new job?"

"Oh, I just love being a grease monkey," Knoff replied sarcastically.

"Are you open to another more attractive offer?"

"What do you think? Of course I am."

"Good. Here's what I need. Find as many men as you think you can trust and commandeer a couple of HumVees and as much small arms and ammunition as you can get your hands on."

"That won't be too hard. The . . . recent changes have left a lot of men unhappy with the new order of things."

"I thought it might be that way. Who's staying in my old apartment?"

"Harlan Millard and his wife took it over after your . . . accident."

"Can you get to Harlan and talk privately?"

"Sure. Why?"

"I need him to open the safe I have hidden in the wall, behind a picture of the Capitol buildings. I've got some cash and a black book with the account numbers and bank locations where I've stashed enough cash to finance my return to power."

There was a pause of a couple of minutes, and Claire added, "And Herb. Don't even think of taking it for yourself. The book is in code and you won't be able to get your hands on the real money without me."

"I wasn't . . ."

"I know you weren't, but I thought it prudent to remind you of what's at stake here. You can stay a mechanic, or you can join forces with me and be my second in command."

"Sounds good to me. Nothing is more boring than the prospect of peace to a soldier."

"When you talk to Harlan, offer him a job with us. He should be ready to do anything to get rid of that bitch of a wife of his."

"And if he refuses?"

"Wait until you get the book from the safe, and then kill the son of a bitch."

"Yes, ma'am. Where do I meet you?"

Claire gave him directions to the service station and arranged to meet him there in one week's time. She figured she could find a local farmhouse to hide out in for the time it would take him to get the vehicles and make the journey to Tennessee.

"You won't have any trouble getting passes for the checkpoints, will you?" she asked.

"Naw, one of the men I intend to bring with us is a sergeant in the Intel division. He was demoted from a warrant officer for insubordination, so he'll do whatever I ask to get the chance for some payback."

"Just the type of men I need. I also want you to get Harlan to give you the file on Perro Loco."

"Perro Loco? You mean that crazy rebel down in Nicaragua who calls himself Mad Dog?"

"Yeah. I was in negotiations with him to attack Ben Raines from the south just before my plane went down. I think he's moved his headquarters to Belize, and we're gonna need some help to finish what I started and get my old job back."

"Will do. Anything else?"

"Yeah, hurry up. I'm hornier than hell and can't wait to see you."

"Give me a week and I'll be there with bells on."

"Don't worry about the bells. Just bring me some hard sons of bitches and some guns. I'll do the rest."

Five

Claire's first job after talking to Herb was to find a safe place to wait for him to gather his men and equipment and come to her. Figuring the authorities, if there were any in this godforsaken state, would check out Kyle Truman's house and then leave it alone, she took his driver's license and keys and went out the back door.

"Uh-huh," she mumbled to herself upon seeing a large, four-wheel-drive pickup with huge knobby tires on it parked in the back. *Just the type of car I'd expect a bubba like Kyle to have,* she thought as she climbed up into the driver's seat and put the key in the ignition.

The motor started immediately, and the engine had a deep, throaty growl to it. Now she had to find out if he was married. There'd been no way to tell from the papers in the station, but at least there were no pictures of a little woman and rug rats on his desk.

She glanced at his driver's license, and headed for what passed for the nearest town, Harveyburg. As expected, there were only a couple of streets, so she had no difficulty finding Kyle's. She parked his car around the corner and walked to the house with his address on it. Walking around to the back of the house, she carefully peeked in a window. The place was a mess. Beer cans, cardboard pizza containers, and garbage of every type littered the table, and even some areas of the floor. If Kyle was married, his wife was an even bigger slob than he was. So, now that she had her hidey-hole, all she had to do was wait for the police to come and make their routine check of the premises; then she could move in. She planned to pass the time at a local restaurant, since the beers and candy bars had done little to curb her appetite.

Sure enough, after she'd finished eating a greasy fried-chicken steak and french fries at a nearby diner named Bell's Place, she returned to Kyle's house and found the front door sealed with tape bearing the sheriff department's logo. She quickly put Kyle's truck in his garage and slipped in the back door. After cleaning up the worst of the mess, she discovered the refrigerator was at least stocked well enough so she wouldn't have to go out to buy groceries for a while.

Claire spent the week and a half waiting for Herb Knoff to make the trip from USA headquarters to Tennessee working on her weight and physical conditioning. The remark from the gasoline station owner had stung her more than she cared to admit.

When she was the leader of one of the two most powerful countries in the world, no one had ever dared to speak to her in such a way, and she had become complacent both with her body and her conditioning. She now knew she was going to be in for the fight of her life, against both her former comrades and Ben Raines, so she needed to get in fighting trim.

She had a head start on the weight loss, since the Holts' food supply had been meager and Billy Bob was anything but generous with the helpings. At Kyle's, she threw out all the fatty foods, cooked only low-fat, nutritious meals, and exercised three times a day until she was covered with sweat and her muscles ached and knotted with cramps.

Claire Osterman had a lot of faults, but lack of resolve had never been one of them. When the time came to go meet Herb, she'd lost all of her excess weight and was beginning to get some muscle definition in her arms and legs. Her belly, while still not flat, no longer hung over her belt, and she could run in place and do situps and pushups for long periods of time without becoming winded. She was ready to face her adversaries.

Claire drove to the gasoline station outside of town at ten o'clock, after it was closed for the night by the new proprietor. She didn't want any witnesses to her meeting with Herb. He wasn't supposed to make his appearance until midnight, but she wanted time to search the vicinity and make sure there was no one hanging around.

When Herb's small caravan finally arrived two hours later, Claire was sitting in the station, calmly drinking a beer.

He walked into the room, a .45 in his hand and a surprised expression on his face.

"Claire?" he asked, with upraised eyebrows, clearly unsure of whether this thin, muscular woman was the one he'd known previously.

She got to her feet and walked over to him. Seeing there were men watching them through the plate-glass window, she didn't take him in her arms as she wanted to, but stuck out her hand. "Yes, Herb, it's the new me. I'll give you a proper welcome later, when we're alone," she said as he shook her hand formally.

"Now," she said, "show me what we've got to work with."

"Yes, ma'am," he answered, and with a grin whispered, "and I can hardly wait until later."

He took her outside and showed her what he'd brought with him. "I've got three HumVees, all four-wheel-drive with diesel engines. Twenty-two men joined me, including one you know very well," he said, pointing to the lead vehicle.

Harlan Millard opened the door and stepped out, a weak grin on his face. Claire smiled, relieved he'd been willing to come. Herb was a great bodyguard, and not too bad in bed, but she needed someone with brainpower and cunning at her side, and Harlan was a natural-born conspirator who knew all the tricks of the trade when it came to wielding power and making the most of it. She hadn't realized how much she'd depended on him until she thought she might lose his services.

She stepped to his side quickly, her hand outstretched. "Harlan, I'm so glad you came," she said, giving him a quick wink.

"Yes, Madame President," he replied, smiling more broadly now that he saw he wasn't going to get his ass chewed out by her. "I welcome the chance to do everything in my power to see that you get your Presidency back."

As he spoke, his eyes roved freely over her body. He was clearly happy with what he saw. Claire knew she would no longer have to threaten him to make him go to bed with her. There were definite benefits to this new body she was sporting, she thought, as a tiny tingle started between her legs. Yes, she was most certainly looking forward to working very closely with both Herb and Harlan.

Herb lined the men up in front of the HumVees for Claire's inspection. "These are all ex-Blackshirts," Herb explained.

"Ex-Blackshirts? What do you mean?" she asked.

"That fool Otis Warner has disbanded the Blackshirt Units," Harlan said with a sneer. "It's all part of his kinder, friendlier administration. He says there's no place for Gestapo tactics in a free nation."

Claire wagged her head. "The man is even more of a fool than I thought he was. How does he expect to keep the citizens in line without a show of force?"

Harlan smiled. "He's dumb enough to think if he does what the people want him to, like end the war with Ben Raines, they'll suddenly jump up and do what is right."

"The fucking people don't have a clue as to what's right," Claire observed. "But enough about Warner, his time is limited anyway. Have you found a place for us to use as our base?" she asked Herb.

He nodded. "Yeah. There's an old base at Gatlingburg that was downsized after the plague killed most of the troops there. About all that's left is a small contingent of ex-Blackshirts who were left in place 'cause Warner didn't know what else to do with them."

"Will they be a problem?"

"I doubt it. They're as pissed as these men were to have their jobs and their rank taken away from them." He shrugged. "And if any do object, we're more than capable of taking them out."

"Has it got what we need?"

"Oh, yeah. The communications gear was left in place and is up to date, with all the scrambling equipment and satellite connections still usable. We should be able to talk to just about anyone in the country without Warner knowing about it."

"Then, what are we waiting for? Let's get moving to our new home."

They arrived at the Gatlingburg base just before dawn, and were delighted to find several helicopters and some half-tracks and armored personnel carriers still in the hangars. There were no men present at the guardhouse at the entrance to the base, so Claire and her men just drove onto the base.

Herb led the caravan to the barracks area and parked in the middle of the street. Bradley Stevens, Jr., a third-generation soldier and the man Herb had picked to be in charge of Claire's new order, got out of the second HumVee, followed by six men carrying automatic rifles.

In a running crouch, Bradley led them toward the barracks. He stopped, squatted in front of the door, and with a wave of his hand sent his men in a sweeping circle around the building. Once they were in place before the windows, he stood up and walked through the door.

After five minutes, when there were no shots fired, Claire and Herb entered the building. They found Bradley standing before a line of twenty men in their underwear, some still trying to wipe sleep from their eyes, but all standing at strict attention.

"I'm Major General Bradley Stevens, Jr.," Bradley said, pacing back and forth in front of the line of men, two of his soldiers standing at port arms with their M-16's locked and loaded.

"I understand you men were once part of a Blackshirt Unit."

A soldier on the end of the line nodded.

"Speak up, son, I can't hear a nod," Bradley barked.

"Sir, yes, sir!" the man yelled back.

"That's good. That means you know the meaning of the word discipline."

"Sir, yes, sir!" the men all hollered in unison.

"Well, boys, here is your Commander in Chief, President Claire Osterman."

As Claire stepped up to the men, they all stared at her as if they were seeing a ghost.

"Yes, boys, I *am* alive," she said, stopping to stand directly in front of them. "The present so-called leaders of this country tried to assassinate me and take over the government illegally. My question to you men is, are you going to work with me to regain my Presidency and carry on the war against the Southern United States of America?"

As if they were robots, all programmed with the same responses, the men shouted, "Ma'am, yes, ma'am!"

She nodded, looking them each in the face for a second. "Good. General Stevens, will you see to the disposition of the men while my associates and I go to the Admin Building?"

"Yes, ma'am," he answered, giving Claire a smart salute as she and Herb and Harlan walked out of the barracks.

"I told you, Claire, once a Blackshirt, always a Blackshirt," Herb said. "I believe we'll be able to get as many men as we need if we scour the countryside for ex-Blackshirts and ex-FPPS men."

Claire stared at him as she climbed into the HumVee. "Don't tell me Warner has disbanded the Federal Prevention and Protective Service, too."

Harlan answered from the backseat. "No, but he's severely curtailed their authority. Now they are subject to the same laws and restrictions as the regular police are."

"You mean they have to get search warrants and let a suspect talk to a lawyer and things like that?" Claire asked incredulously.

"Yes, ma'am."

She shook her head. "The way that idiot's running the country, I won't have to do anything and he'll be overthrown in six months."

"That's what I mean, Claire. If we tell people we're going to reinstate the old order and give them back their jobs and their authority over the citizens of the USA, we'll have plenty of soldiers and Blackshirts and FPPS men clamoring to join us."

She nodded, thinking. "Yes, I can see that. But we've got to keep a very low profile until we're strong enough to repel any attempt by Warner and his minions to kill us. Now, get me to the Admin Building so we can get started on my plan."

Claire moved right into the old base commander's office and gathered her administrative staff around her, which consisted at the moment of Herb and Harlan and General Bradley Stevens.

"Did you bring me the file on Perro Loco?" she asked Harlan, leaning back in the chair and putting her feet up on the desk after removing her shoes.

"Yes, ma'am," Harlan answered. "It's complete up to the last time we had contact with him, but hasn't been updated in several months."

So," Claire said, leaning forward and massaging her swollen feet. "We don't have current radio frequencies on him?"

"No, ma'am."

"General Stevens, I want you to pick two men you can trust and we'll send them down to Belize to make contact with Loco. He's a crazy bastard, but he's got lots of men to throw at Raines and keep him busy and out of our hair while we work on getting rid of Warner and the rest of those traitors he's got with him."

"I know just the two men, Madame President. Both speak excellent Spanish and know the southern areas well. They shouldn't have any trouble crossing Mexico and getting to Belize."

"How long do you think it will take them to get there and make contact?"

He shrugged. "In one of the HumVees with all the necessary papers and passes, if they're lucky enough not to get caught by the Rebels before they cross the border into Mexico, they should be able to make the trip in less than two weeks."

"Good. Get them what they need and give them the scrambler codes and frequencies we're going to use here and get them on their way. Make sure they take a portable satellite transmitter and keep in touch with us so we'll know their progress. The sooner we find out if he's willing to help us, the sooner we can take steps to regain my Presidency."

"Yes, ma'am," the general replied.

"And Bradley," she called to his back as he was leaving the room.

"Yes, ma'am?"

"Don't waste any time. While they're on the way to Belize, I want you and a team of men to go out into the surrounding countryside and see if you can recruit some more men for us from the other bases in Tennessee and the adjoining states. We're going to need all the men we can scrape together if we're going to succeed."

"You got it, Madame President."

Six

Randy Grimes pulled the HumVee off the road into a stand of mesquite trees after he crossed the border at Reynosa, Mexico. The only signs of life he and Arnold Mendoza had seen for the past two hundred miles driving across the backcountry of Texas had been a few scraggly cattle, some javelinas, and a family of white-tail deer.

Arnold, whose real name was Arnoldo, climbed in the back of the HumVee and cranked up the portable satellite transceiver. As it warmed up, he activated the Unitel Model 602 scrambler attached and dialed in the code numbers to the matching scramblers at the base in Gatlingburg.

Grimes, who had carrot-colored red hair, stood outside the HumVee applying sunblock to his freckled, fair skin. "I tell ya, Arnold, if I don't git skin cancer from all this here sun it'll be a flat miracle," he said in his deep grits-and-gravy southern accent.

Arnold shook his head, smiling. He liked Randy, even though he was a cracker from Georgia and about as hick as they come. Arnold, who'd grown up in a household where English was rarely spoken, could speak better English than his bubba friend Randy could.

"Well, Randy, why don't you get back in the Hummer and out of the sun then, you redneck idiot?"

"I'm damn shore gonna be a redneck 'fore this here assignment's over, that's fer sure."

As the satellite transceiver hissed and crackled with static, trying to connect to the TelStar Satellite overhead, Arnold pulled out a cigarette and stuck a match to it. "Say, Randy I never asked before, but how in the hell did a nice southern boy like you learn to speak Spanish?"

Randy's face blushed even redder than it already was. "My papa, after he divorced my mama, married a Mexican. She'd been our maid, an' was twenty year younger'n my daddy, but he up an' married her anyways. I's only four or five at the time, so I jest kinda naturally picked it up over the years."

Arnold took a deep drag of the cigarette, letting the smoke trickle from his nostrils as he replied, "It's a damn shame you didn't pick up English the same way."

"Huh?" Randy said, a puzzled expression on his face.

"Never mind," Arnold said, turning to the radio. "It's time we checked in."

"You tell 'em we made it through Texas an' now we're headed for Monterrey and then Sautillo. We can pick up what passes for the Mexican freeway, the Camino Real, at Monterrey, an' then it's clear sailin' all the way down to Costa Rica."

Arnold shook his head. Randy was always trying to tell him what he already knew. Still, the boy had a good heart and he wasn't too bad to travel with, other than the fact he snored like a buzz saw. Arnold had taken to stuffing his ears with cotton so he could get some shut-eye.

Ben Raines was jogging down one of the roads around headquarters, Jodie running alongside him, when his personal SUV pulled up.

He stopped, leaning over with his hands on his knees blowing air, while Coop stuck his head out of the window. "Hey, Bossman, you're gonna kill yourself, running at your age."

Between breaths, Ben managed to say, "You think you young studs can keep up with me, come on out next time and give it a try."

Coop smiled, shaking his head. "Some men just don't know when it's time to hang it up and sit by a fire and clean their false teeth."

Ben straightened up and held up his hands. "Okay, you've got your digs in. Now what's so important that you interrupted my quality time with Jodie?"

Coop's face sobered. "Corrie's intercepted some radio transmissions she thinks you'll be interested in."

"Oh? From the USA?"

Coop shook his head. "No, but a couple of names cropped up that might just get your attention."

"What names?"

"Claire Osterman and Perro Loco."

"Get in the back, Jodie," Ben said, opening the rear door to the SUV. "We gotta go home."

Ben found his team gathered in the main meeting room of his headquarters suite of offices. Corrie was rewinding a tape recording she'd made of the transmissions.

"How did you manage to intercept these?" Ben asked as he sat at a desk and wiped the sweat off his face with a towel.

Corrie grinned. "I patched into the old NSA computers that are still in use up north, the ones the old USA used to spy on everyone around the world. Those dumbbells in the present USA either don't know they're there, or aren't smart enough to use them properly. They can hear virtually every radio transmission around the world."

Ben nodded. "I know that, but so do most of the other governments, so they all scramble their transmissions."

"These were scrambled."

"Then how did you manage to understand them?"

"The idiots were using the old Unitel Model 602 scrambler. It has a distinctive whistle to its interference, so I managed to find one in a closet and hooked it up." She grinned.

"Hell, that model's ten years old and I didn't even know there were any around, much less still in use."

Ben pointed at the tape recorder. "Okay, genius, let me hear what you got."

As he and his team listened to the recording, Ben's heart began to beat faster and he felt sweat pop out on his forehead. He realized he wasn't yet through with that bitch Claire Osterman, and the thought chilled him to the bone.

When the recording was over, Ben got up and began to pace around the room, as he often did when he was thinking a problem through.

"First, get Mike Post in here," he said, referring to his Chief of Intelligence and second in command of the Rebel Army. "He needs to hear this."

Corrie picked up a phone and began dialing.

"What do you think it means?" Jersey asked. She was sitting on the edge of Ben's desk, slowly running the edge of a K-Bar assault knife over a whetstone. Jersey was part Apache Indian, which may have explained her penchant for killing with a knife when silence was required.

Ben stopped walking. "Obviously, Claire Osterman is not dead, as we were told."

"Do you think the transmission could be a fake, one designed to make us think she's still alive?" Beth asked.

Ben shook his head. "There'd be no point in that. No, I think someone in Warner's administration tried to take her out, and failed. Now she's out there working to get control of the government back."

"What about this Perro Loco they keep mentioning on the tape?" Coop asked.

Ben shrugged. "I don't know. I've never heard the name."

From the doorway, Mike Post said, "I have."

"Oh, hi, Mike," Ben said. "Glad you could make it."

Mike smiled wryly. "Oh, the mention of Claire Osterman and Perro Loco got my attention right away."

"We know Claire. Why don't you tell us about this Loco guy," Ben said.

Mike Post sauntered into the room, moving in his usual manner as if he hadn't a care in the world. In his job as Ben's Chief of Intelligence, or Intel, it was his job to know everything there was to know about the leaders of the opposition to the Rebel forces. Which included not only the USA but most of the other governments around the world. The SUSA form of government was extremely unpopular with most other countries, since it concentrated power in the people instead of in the hands of a few dictators or kings or sultans, or whatever they happened to call themselves nowadays.

Mike grabbed a seat in front of Ben's desk, pulled out a battered, scorched pipe, and began filling it with a tobacco that was so strong it was almost black.

Corrie glanced at Coop, who nodded, walked to the window, and pulled it up in anticipation of the clouds of foul-smelling smoke that would soon be produced.

Once Mike had his pipe going to his satisfaction, he leaned back, crossed his legs, and began to talk in the manner of a college professor giving a lecture to undergraduates.

"Perro Loco was born Dorotero Arango in a small village in Nicaragua twenty-five years or so ago. Like so many of the places down there in those times, the area was under the sway of one of the local 'rebel' leaders, a man named Santiago Guzman. Guzman was more like a tribal warlord, exacting tribute from the villagers in the form of food, money, and sometimes the young men of the village when he needed them to join his forces. Guzman was known as 'El Machete,' The Knife, because he always carried a long machete he used to execute those who disobeyed his orders."

"This is beginning to sound like a bad opera," Coop said as he turned a chair around and straddled it, his arms folded across the back and his chin on his arms.

Mike nodded. "You have to understand the times, Coop. The world was going through the adjustment to the holocaust of the Third World War, with very few governments able to function at all. There were literally thousands of El Machetes around the world, and no one to keep a check on them."

"We remember," Ben said. "Go on, Mike."

"Well, the story goes that one day when Dorotero was just entering his teens, El Machete came to his village and called his father out of their hut. He said he needed the boy to come with him. Dorotero's father declined, saying the boy was needed at home to take care of his mother and sister while the father worked the fields. El Machete didn't argue, he simply walked over to the boy's mother and sister and beheaded them with one swipe of his long knife. When the father fell to his knees, cradling his dead wife in his arms, El Machete killed him too. Then he turned to the boy and said, 'Now you have no reason to stay in this miserable pigsty of a village.' "

"Oh," Beth said, her eyes sympathetic, "that's terrible."

Mike shrugged. "Those were terrible times."

"So the boy went with El Machete?" Coop asked.

Mike smiled. "Not exactly. He told the man he needed to go into their hut and gather his things. When he came out, he walked up to El Machete, pulled a sickle his father used to cut ribbon cane from beneath his shirt, and buried it in El Machete's chest. Guzman had time for one swipe with his machete and he laid Dorotero's face open with it before he died."

"Jesus!" Jersey said, glancing down at the K-Bar she was sharpening, the Apache in her appreciating the tale of revenge and death.

"Dorotero then went on a killing spree, grabbing El Machete's long knife from his hand and killing three of his men before they could draw their weapons. As he stood there in the clearing in the middle of his village, one of the neighbors is said to have whispered, *'Perro loco,'* meaning mad dog. Dorotero took that as his name, and vanished into the jungle, where he began recruiting his own gang, which soon became known for their ferocity and viciousness and utter lack of mercy towards their enemies."

Ben nodded. "Now I remember some of the story," he said. "Didn't you bring his name up to me a few months back?"

Mike smiled. "I thought you'd remember. At that time, we had intel that Osterman was trying to contact Perro Loco to try and make some arrangement with him, the details of which we never learned. We suspected at the time she was going to use him to open up a second front against us, but her plane went down before they could finalize their plans."

"So you think she's alive and well and trying to take up where she left off?" Coop asked.

Mike shrugged. "I don't know, Coop. One radio transmission isn't much to go on, and Perro Loco has been keeping a pretty low profile down in Belize somewhere."

Ben picked a letter opener up off his desk and began to fiddle with it as he thought. After a few moments, he pointed it at Coop. "In any event, I think we should nip any attempt to stir up trouble on our southern border in the bud. Coop, I want you and Jersey to head down there and make sure Perro Loco, or Mad Dog, or whatever he calls himself, doesn't live to give us any problems."

"But Ben—" Coop started.

"I know, you don't exactly fit in down there, but Jersey knows Spanish, and with the right makeup can pass as Hispanic. You won't be able to get close enough to do the job personally, so you'll have to hire it done."

Jersey tested the blade on her K-Bar with her finger, finally satisfied with its edge. "That shouldn't be too difficult. Every leader in South America has plenty of rivals or enemies who want his job. It shouldn't take us too long to discover some who'll take Perro Loco out if we give them the right equipment to do it with."

"Exactly," Ben said. "Take what you need, a couple of

good sniper rifles, some explosives and car-bombs, you know the drill."

"Come on, Coop," Jersey said, a glint in her eye. "I'm gonna teach you how to work undercover."

Coop let his lips curl in a smart-ass smile. "Oh, is that a promise?"

Jersey glared at him, then smiled back. "On second thought, I'll just introduce you to a couple of babes down there. Those women all carry knives and know how to use them, and they just *love gringos.*"

Coop strutted across the room. "One night with me, an' they'd forget all about their knives."

As they left the room, Ben heard Jersey mutter "pencil dick," followed by Coop growling "slut." He shook his head. "If those two don't kill each other on the mission, I think our worries about Perro Loco are over."

"Yeah," Mike said, tapping his ashes into the trash can next to Ben's desk. "But what about Claire Osterman?"

"I want you to get in touch with Otis Warner and let him know we have information she may still be alive. And try and figure out if he knows it already when you talk to him. We don't need anything getting in the way of this new peace proposal."

"Will do," Mike said.

Seven

In the seedy underbelly of Belize City in Central America, in a dark seaside bar named the Gray Gull, a heavy-faced, thick-muscled native of Nicaragua sat nursing a Belikin beer. His given name was Dorotero Arango. A long scar crossed his right cheek. Since the wars began raging all over the world, he'd become known as Comandante Perro Loco. In Spanish, the term simply meant Commander Mad Dog. He liked the nickname. It fit his temperament, his style. His closest associates called him "Loco."

He was feared throughout Central America for his ruthlessness, his blood lust, his penchant for killing. He commanded a mercenary army, more of a marauding bandit gang than a group of organized soldiers. Today, at the Gray Gull, he had begun to plot one of the boldest moves in his life with his second in command.

He spoke to Paco Valdez, a Belizian assassin with a fearsome reputation of his own. Perro Loco spoke English. Belize was an English-speaking country since its days as British Honduras so long ago. "To the north all is chaos. Ben Raines and his Tri-States forces have all but crushed President Osterman's USA—what is left of it. Now is the time to reap the spoils. Raines is far to the north. We can gather a huge army from all over Central America, for many men here are hungry, desperate. I'll promise them riches . . . whatever we can take as we move northward across Mexico. I can make them rich men. With Raines and his forces occupied thousands of miles away, no one has the military capability to stop us."

"It is a good plan," Paco said, gazing out a window at the gulf. He was tall, powerfully built, with an old bullet wound in his forehead. "Thousands of hungry men will join us. Former soldiers from Guatemala and Nicaragua have no money, no food, no jobs, no hope. They will listen. I have heard reports that there are twice that many jobless men in Costa Rica and El Salvador. Most of them will be willing to fight for our cause. Food, and the promise of a small amount of money, will bring them to us. They will be ready to die for a chance to make money and to get food for their wives and children. And do not forget the starving men in Honduras. There are food riots in the streets of Tegucigalpa. Women and children are starving to death in the jungles."

Loco nodded. "There is military equipment all over Costa Rica and Mexico. The government treasuries are virtually bankrupt. Now is the time for us to strike, before they grow any stronger north of the Mexican border. It is the Rebel Army of Ben Raines that we have to worry about. He will be a formidable adversary."

"We have five thousand men now," Paco said. "But most of them are poorly armed. We need guns and ammunition. Trucks to carry our soldiers across Mexico. Starving men cannot march more than thirty miles a day. Trucks and gasoline will be of the greatest importance."

"Air support also will be crucial," Loco said, tipping back his beer. "We have nine of the American-made helicopter gunships, Apaches, and two of the more advanced Comanches, as well as the older UH-1's. Eduardo is working on the captured Blackhawk, a good fighting machine."

"Striking from the air will save us hundreds of casualties when we cross Mexico," Paco said.

Loco shrugged. "Who will be counting bodies? If we lose a few thousand soldiers, it is the price to be paid for victory over the Martinez government in Mexico and this Rebel General Ben Raines."

"I agree," Paco said.

"Fuel is a problem. And we have so few trained pilots who know how to fly these killing helicopter machines."

"We will find new recruits in Mexico, *comandante*," Paco said. "During the drug wars thirty years ago, the Americans were kind enough to train Mexican pilots in the use of their helicopter gunships in order to battle the drug lords.

"There is still the matter of fuel. Since the final war began, many of the refineries have closed or been blown to pieces by Rebel bombs."

Loco agreed silently, thinking. "We can capture fuel tank trucks in Mexico City. The Federales have been reduced to a few hungry soldiers who have not been paid in months, even years. They will not put up much of a fight . . . In fact, many of them will probably join us."

As Loco was speaking, a lanky soldier in a khaki uniform came through the back door of the bar. An AK47 on a leather strap dangling from his right shoulder, he walked toward the table where Paco and Perro Loco sat.

"*Comandante*," the soldier said, giving Loco a lazy salute. "We have two prisoners outside in the alley. They say they are from President Osterman of the USA. We found them trying to cross the border at Corozal."

"What are their names?"

"One of them is a *gringo* whose name is Grimes. The other is a *latino* named Mendoza."

"What do they want with us?" Loco asked.

"Mendoza says they have a message for you, *comandante*. We surrounded them in a jeep in the Orange Walk district, only a few miles from the Yucatan."

Loco looked at Paco. "Why would the President of the USA send messengers to me now? It has been many months since we last spoke and she has not contacted me since."

Paco shrugged, as if the question mattered little. "We can

find out very quickly, *comandante*. I will kill one of them now. The other one will tell you the truth when he sees his friend die."

Paco drew a long pointed dagger from a sheath inside his boot, admiring the blade. "I will cut his throat and let the other one watch him bleed to death. He will speak true words when he sees his companion die slowly."

Loco stood up, fisting his beer. "Let us see what they have to say."

Paco followed Perro Loco to the rear door of the Gray Gull with his knife beside his pants leg, tapping the cloth as if it were impatient for the taste of blood.

Two young American soldiers sat against a wall of the bar, bound hand and foot. One of them, a boy with red hair, had a deep gash across his forehead and he appeared to be only half conscious, his eyes vacant and staring.

Four of Loco's uniformed soldiers stood around the pair, rifles aimed at the prisoners.

Loco leaned over them, examining their faces. Paco was beside him, grinning, his eyelids drawn into narrow slits as he stared at the prisoners.

"Who sent you?" Loco asked. "Who gave you my name, and told you where to find me?"

The latino named Mendoza spoke. "President Osterman told us where to find you, *comandante*. She has an offer she wants to make you, and she wouldn't risk trying to reach you on a shortwave radio transmission unless it was scrambled. We didn't know what frequency to use."

"An offer?"

"Yes, *comandante*. We have been driving across the Southwest and Mexico for two weeks, trying to reach you."

"And what is this . . . offer?"

Mendoza swallowed. "Our President would like to arrange a meeting with you."

"A meeting? What kind of meeting?"

"As you must know by now, General Ben Raines and his SUSA forces have attacked us. Our casualties have been very high. We lost valuable equipment . . . airplanes and helicopters and tanks, to General Raines' armies."

"What does this have to do with me?" Loco asked.

"President Osterman believes that the war has been costly for the SUSA as well. Despite the fact that Ben Raines has won, his arms inventory is seriously depleted. Our intelligence sources tell us that he is pulling his men back. He apparently does not intend to occupy the territory he has conquered. The President feels that if a strong attack came from the south, from Mexico, Raines would be unable to defend two fronts. She would like to talk to you about an alliance."

"Why has she waited so long to contact me again?"

Mendoza hesitated, as if he knew nothing about the past negotiations. "President Osterman was in a plane crash, *comandante*. She has only recently recovered from her injuries enough to resume leadership of our country."

"So, now the female *presidente* needs the help of Perro Loco to win her war, eh?"

"You are considered to be one of the most powerful leaders in Central America, she told us. President Osterman wants to talk to you in person about the details, for even a scrambled radio message might be intercepted by the SUSA, but she believes there would be enough spoils of war if Raines was defeated to divide between the USA and your armies. She thinks the alliance would be good for everyone. She intends to offer you everything south of Texas if you agree to join us in our war with the SUSA."

"Why should I believe you?" Loco asked. "Maybe you are only SUSA spies trying to trick me . . ."

"I have a radio frequency in my pocket. You can contact the President yourself if you have any doubts. She asks that you send a scrambled message. I have the encoding information with me. I also have it memorized. I can send your reply myself, if you wish. President Osterman will only discuss the details of an alliance with you in person. She does not trust the radios or our codes. There have been spies among us. Most of them are dead now, or gone into hiding."

"Shall I kill him?" Paco asked while Loco was thinking. "He may be a spy, as you said."

"Not yet," Loco replied, piercing the captive soldiers with an icy stare. "Take them to our headquarters at San Ignacio. Drive through the mountains so no one will see you. Bring them to my *hacienda*. I will stop at the airstrip to see about repairs to our captured Blackhawk helicopter. Make certain neither one of these men escapes."

Paco's grin had no humor behind it. "Do not worry, *comandante*. They will not escape." He held up his dagger. "My blade is hungry for blood. It has been weeks since I killed anyone with it. For a man to have a good day, he should kill someone before breakfast."

"The smell of fresh blood is good," Loco agreed, "but an alliance with the colossus to the north might taste even sweeter." He turned to go back in the bar. "I will inspect the helicopter first. I should be at San Ignacio in a couple of hours."

Paco knelt down and placed the tip of his knife against Mendoza's neck near his windpipe. "Get up, *gringo,*" he spat. "I will take you to our jeeps."

"My partner can't walk," the American protested. "When one of your guards hit him over the head with his rifle butt, he was knocked out. You can see the cut on his forehead. If you'll untie my hands, I can help him to the jeep."

Paco was angry over missing the chance to kill an American soldier. It had been over a week since he'd murdered anyone and he was getting impatient, as an alcoholic does when denied the chance to drink.

"My men will carry him," he snarled. "Now get up and follow me down this alley . . ."

Mendoza struggled to his feet, wishing like hell someone else had been sent to talk to these crazy men.

Eight

"Are you still sulking?" Jersey asked Coop as they bounced across the Yucatan Peninsula.

Coop took his eye off the rutted, potholed, miserable excuse for a road they were on long enough to raise his eyebrows and plant an innocent look on his face. "Who, me? Sulk? Why would I do that," he said, speaking loudly so he could be heard over the coughing, sputtering engine of the fifteen-year-old Ford Falcon they'd bought in Campeche, Mexico.

Ben had put Jersey in charge on this mission, and it'd been her plan for Coop to fly them to Mexico City in one of the SUSA's small jets, then take a military HumVee to Campeche. There they would purchase an inconspicuous automobile with a trunk big enough to hold the sniper rifles, car-bombs, and the handheld Stinger antiaircraft missile they had with them. After they had their cover in place as two ex-soldiers of the Mexican Army now out of work, they would drive across the peninsula to the small town of Chatumal, just across the border from the Belizian city of Corozal.

Ben's contacts in the friendly government of Mexico had identified some men in Corozal who wouldn't be averse to seeing Perro Loco have an unfortunate accident, or so they'd been told.

Jersey grinned. "Go on, admit it, Coop. You're pissed off 'cause Ben put me in charge on this mission."

"Bullshit!" he exclaimed, his fingers tight on the steering wheel and his gaze straight ahead.

"Hey, lughead, it's only because I speak better Spanish than you do. It's no reflection on your vaunted manhood."

He finally turned to look at her. "What makes you think I'm pissed?" he asked.

She threw back her head and laughed. "Oh, Coop. You've been puffed up like a toad for the past two days. And when you didn't even make a cursory pass at that cute little secretary in the Mexican Counsel's office, I knew something was seriously wrong."

"She wasn't my type," he said sullenly, putting his eyes back on the road.

"Ha! She was under thirty, female, and had huge . . . well, her measurements were enough to wake you from a dead sleep."

Coop's lips curled in a small grin, the first Jersey'd seen in several days. "She *was* amazing, wasn't she?" he asked dreamily.

Jersey folded her arms and leaned back against the seat. "Good to have you back, Coop."

Coop glanced over at Jersey, noticing the heat from the desert and their lack of air-conditioning was making Jersey sweat through her Army T-shirt, and the wet cloth was clinging to her breasts like a second skin, her nipples plainly visible through the thin cloth.

"Speaking of amazing measurements," he said, letting her see where he was staring.

She quickly pulled the cloth away from her breasts and sat up. "Coop, don't you start on me now . . ."

He shook his head. "Don't worry, Prudence," he said. "I was just warning you to cover 'em up. We're almost to Chatumal an' if you go to our meeting with these rebels lookin' like that, they ain't gonna be thinkin' about Perro Loco."

Jersey reached over the seat and grabbed an old, threadbare Army shirt and pulled it on. They'd gotten the clothes from the Mexican government to fit their cover story. "Okay, point taken. Now, when we get into town, see if you can find a bar named La Gazapera. That's where we're supposed to meet our contacts."

"La Gazapera? What's that mean in Spanish?"

She grinned. "It has two meanings. One is Warren, as in rabbit warren."

"What's the other?" he asked.

"Den of Thieves," she replied with a shake of her head. "Not very subtle, but then Mexicans have never exactly been known for their subtlety when they're planning a revolution."

"And the man we're gonna be meeting?"

"He calls himself El Gato Selva."

"Which means . . . ?"

"The Jungle Cat."

"Jesus!" Coop laughed. "The Mad Dog, The Knife, and now The Jungle Cat. Don't any of these guys use real names down here?"

Jersey looked at him, her face serious. "Coop, you've got to remember. We're here in southern Mexico, the land of Macho, spelled with a capital M. Most of these leaders and their followers are less than one generation away from being peasants, fighting for enough food to keep from starving. It's the motivation that's driven countless revolutions over the years."

"So, they take some crazy macho name, convince a few starving peasants to follow them around the jungle waving stolen rifles and guns that are ten years out of date, and suddenly they're all Pancho Villa?"

She shrugged. "That's about the size of it. Now, when we meet this guy, he's bound to have a couple of tough bodyguards watching our every move. They don't trust anyone down here, and if we make one false move, they'll kill us without batting an eye."

He glanced at her. "So, you're telling me to be on my best behavior?"

"Exactly, I'm telling you not to let your *macho* get in the way of their *macho*."

"Okay, okay. What's the word for pussycat?"

"*Minino.*"

He grinned at her. "Then you can just introduce me as El Minino."

She shook her head. Sometimes she wondered if all Coop's brains were in his nether regions, down below his belt. At least it seemed as if that was what controlled his thinking.

Coop took a left turn just past the city-limits sign, which read Chatumal, and drove down the main street, which was made of dirt and just as potholed and rough as the cross-country road had been.

"Not exactly Mexico City, is it?" he asked, glancing at the chickens and dogs and cats that seemed to outnumber the people in the town.

Jersey followed his look. "Yeah. You can see why the people down here are ready to follow anybody who says they can deliver them from this squalor."

"There it is," Coop said, inclining his head toward a seedy building made of soiled and blackened adobe with a sign over the door, *La Gazapera,* and a crudely drawn picture of a rabbit going down a hole.

He pulled the Falcon to a stop in front of the doorway. "You think it's safe to leave the car unattended?"

She nodded. "Yeah. We might come back to find the tires missing, but they won't be able to get in the trunk where the interesting stuff is."

Coop grabbed his Colt .45 and stuck it in the back of his belt while Jersey slipped her K-Bar assault knife inside the front of her pants. "Remember," she said, "let me do all the talking."

"Of course," Coop replied sarcastically. "After all, you're in charge."

Jersey shook her head, mumbling "asshole" under her breath.

Coop replied with "arrogant bitch" as he followed her into the darkness of the bar.

Both wrinkled their noses at the heavy smell of stale beer,

old smoke, and marijuana and the stench of open toilets in the rear of the place.

"Nice ambience," Coop whispered to the back of Jersey's head as he followed her toward the bar.

A heavyset man with a shiny gold tooth in the front of his mouth grinned at Jersey. "Welcome, *señorita,*" he growled in Spanish, his eyes roving freely over her body.

Jersey didn't answer as she took a seat on a tattered bar stool and swiveled around to check out the occupants of the room. Coop didn't sit, but stood next to her, his fingers flexing in anticipation of grabbing his .45 at the first sign of trouble.

Several of the tables were occupied by middle-aged men, all of whom looked beaten down by life and seemed to be trying to drown their misfortunes in large beakers of beer.

At the very rear of the room, in a corner even gloomier than the rest of the place, Jersey spied three men at a table. The one in the middle was younger than the others and had the look of danger about him. *That's our man,* she thought, and pushed off the stool and walked to approach their table, letting a little swagger enter her gait.

The man at the table glanced at her, then directed his attention to Cooper. *Typical Hispanic attitude,* Jersey thought, *thinking the male has to be the one in charge.*

"El Gato Selva?" she asked, letting him know she was the one to discuss business with.

"Si," he answered.

As he spoke, the two men with him stood and flanked him, their hands inside their coats, ready to draw if they saw any threat to their leader.

Jersey sat down, while Coop remained standing behind her chair, his eyes on the bodyguards, letting them know he too meant business. She studied El Gato, letting him see her examine him. It was time to set the ground rules of their relationship, and she had no intention of playing second-fiddle. He was short, as most of his people were, and his face showed scars of adolescent acne and some other rather interesting scars. Either he'd been severely abused as a child, or he'd spent considerable time being questioned by someone who didn't much care if he survived the ordeal. Probably a little of both, Jersey concluded, considering the man's present occupation and hatred of Perro Loco.

Finally, Gato smiled, though it didn't change the overall impression of danger he exuded like some exotic aftershave. "If you've quite finished, perhaps we can begin our conversation?" he asked in slightly accented English. Evidently he didn't want the other patrons of the bar to be able to understand their talk.

Jersey nodded and also spoke in English. "I am told we have mutual interests," she said.

"Concerning?"

"A certain man nearby," she said. "A man we both would like to see disappear."

"Does this man have a name?" he asked, picking up the glass in front of him and swirling the amber-colored liquid in it around.

Jersey leaned her head closer and whispered, "Perro Loco."

El Gato grinned. "Sí. Your information is correct. I would not shed too many tears if I learned of his . . . demise."

"I was told, if the price were right, you might take a more active interest in seeing that Perro Loco contracts a fatal illness."

El Gato shrugged. "I am a businessman. Tell me of your offer."

"I have one thousand dollars American in gold coins, and all the equipment you'll need to get the job done."

"What equipment?"

"Two Heckler and Koch model G3 SG/1 sniper rifles, two car-bombs for attachment to his automobiles, and an S-11 Stinger antiaircraft missile to use on his helicopter if need be."

El Gato's eyebrows raised in surprise at the wealth of armament she'd brought. "That is indeed a lot of equipment."

He glanced at his guards, then back at Jersey. "But, *señorita,* what is to prevent me from taking your money and your guns and not providing the service you request?"

Jersey smiled, and the look in her dark eyes made El Gato lean back in his chair and visibly pale.

"Then my next visit to your country will be for you, El Gato. And the offer will concern not only you but your wife, your children, your friends, and everyone who has ever known you. Do I make myself clear?"

Even though they could not understand her words, El Gato's guards took a step forward at the threat in Jersey's voice, only to stop when Coop's .45 suddenly appeared in his hand, pointed at their boss's face. El Gato licked dry lips and held out his hands when Coop eared back the hammer.

"Of course, *señorita.* I was just joking, for it is as much to my benefit as it is to yours to see that *bastardo* Perro Loco killed."

"Good. Then we understand one another," Jersey said in a soft voice, all hint of the hardness of a moment before gone. "Where can we make the exchange of equipment?"

"I have a truck parked in the rear of the bar. Just pull around the corner and you can follow us into the jungle. There are too many prying eyes in town to make the switch here."

As they climbed into the Falcon, Coop grinned. "Charming character. In my high school he would have been called Pizza Face."

Jersey looked at him. "Did you see his eyes? I have a feeling anyone who called him that would wake up minus important parts of their anatomy."

"Yeah, he did look kinda mean at that."

"You can bet on it, Coop. Anyone who lives down here and has the *cojones* to go up against the local bandit leader is plenty tough."

They drove around to the rear of the bar, and saw a large

four-wheel-drive pickup with large knobby tires on it parked there. As it drove off, they followed, bumping and bouncing over the ruts in the road.

"What do you think, Jerse?" Coop asked, his face serious for once. "You think they're gonna try and hijack our weapons and gold, or do you think they'll play straight?"

She shook her head. "I have no friggin' idea, Coop, so let's make sure we're ready to dance if that's what they want."

She reached under the seat and brought out a .45 of her own, jerked back the ejector slide to put a bullet in the firing chamber, and stuck it in the front of her pants, letting her shirt fall down over it. Then she felt under her inside left pants leg to make sure her K-Bar was loose in its scabbard and ready for action.

Coop watched her with interest as she went through these motions. As much as he teased and kidded, and at times lusted after Jersey, there was absolutely no one he'd rather have at his side if there was going to be serious trouble. She was a stone killer when need be, and if she ever felt the slightest fear, she'd never shown it to him.

The truck they were following turned left at the end of the alleyway, and followed a road that soon deteriorated into not much more than two ruts in the red dirt of the jungle. As bushes, elephant-ear plants, and trees closed in on both sides of the trail, brushing the sides of the Falcon, sweat began to pop out on Coop's forehead.

"I don't like this, Jerse, I don't like it at all," he said.

"Me neither, Coop. Me neither," she answered, her eyes flicking back and forth, watching the thick foliage on both sides of the car, her hand resting on the butt of her .45.

Nine

"It is an older model, this Blackhawk," Eduardo said as he cleaned his hands with a rag. "But it has many advantages. It has two turbine engines. If a SAM missile takes out one of the turbines, a good pilot can still fly it in safely." Eduardo had been working on the Blackhawk for weeks, scavenging abandoned British bases in Belize for parts.

Since the British pulled out many years ago, there had been no protectorate agreement for tiny Belize and the country was all but lawless. Small bandit gangs had roamed the streets of Belize City, looting stores, taking whatever they wanted. But that was before Comandante Perro Loco came from Nicaragua with his armies. His best *soldados* slaughtered leaders of the gangs during a nationwide manhunt. Order was restored. In spite of the bloodshed, often including the killing of innocent bystanders, Comandante Perro Loco was a Belizian hero to the masses. The streets of Belize City were quiet now.

Loco examined the dark gray aircraft. "Only four missiles in the launching tubes," he said, his pox-scarred face a mass of lines when he frowned.

Eduardo shook his head. "The fifty-caliber machine guns have plenty of ammunition, *comandante,* but as you say, there are only four missiles. They will have to be used sparingly. They are small air-to-ground rockets of a special type. They will be very hard to find, although they have very powerful warheads, or so we are told."

"We may find them in Mexico. Will this machine fly the way it is?"

"*Sí, comandante.* But there is little fuel. A helicopter such as this requires large amounts of fuel and has very limited range."

"Fuel is always a problem. The Mexican government has big underground storage tanks close to Mexico City. One of our first objectives will be to capture those fuel reserves and the tanker trucks to haul them. It won't be a problem. The Martinez government is weak and corrupt. We should take their military bases easily. We will march through Michoacan to take the capital in a few weeks, but we will need this Black-hawk and the other helicopter gunships to give our grand troops and armored divisions air support for the attack."

"It is almost ready for battle, *comandante,*" Eduardo said. "I only have a few more minor adjustments to make with the tail turbine and the targeting devices. I need less than a week to make the changes. It will fly now, but there are prob-lems with the Heads Up Targeting. I can fix it, but I will require a few more days."

"Can you fly me to my *hacienda* at San Ignacio? I wish to see how well it flies."

"Now?"

Loco nodded, his gaze still roaming across the sleek lines of the aircraft.

"Of course, *comandante.*"

"I'll tell my driver to take the jeep back. Let me know as soon as you are ready to leave."

"The gunship will be ready to fly in five minutes. Is there a landing pad close by?"

"Only a small opening in the jungle. My men keep the vines and grass cut away."

"Give me five minutes," Eduardo said, tucking the red rag in his back pocket as he hurried off toward an empty aircraft hangar at the end of a shell-pocked runway where Soviet-made missiles had landed during the big war, the war to end all wars that went around the globe in a deadly, world-wide holocaust ending in political and military mayhem.

Loco strolled toward his battered military Jeep, a vehicle captured in Honduras when the bombs began to drop, wondering about the two soldiers from President Osterman. Was it wise to form an alliance with a weak government? Radio reports said that General Raines had crushed most of the USA's forces in North America.

"Drive to San Ignacio," he told the driver. "Radio the *hacienda.* Tell them I'll be arriving in a helicopter in half an hour. And tell them to make certain the landing place is well guarded."

"Sí, comandante." His aide started the jeep and backed away from the landing strip.

Loco was still puzzled by the unexpected appearance of the two American soldiers, and President Osterman's offer. He made up his mind that he would use it to his advantage. If conditions were right he would meet with Osterman and agree to join forces with the USA . . . without telling her that his plans were on a far larger scale. He intended to control the former United States himself.

When the time was right he would crush the weakened armies of the USA and take control of the entire North American continent. All he needed was time, and a small amount of luck when they marched across Mexico looking for fuel, armored equipment, and ammunition.

The rhythmic thump of huge rotor blades filled his ears as the old Blackhawk took off. Eduardo, a trusted helicopter pilot and chopper flight instructor, was at the controls. Loco watched the ground fall away beneath the helicopter's skids as the craft rose above the jungle canopy outside of Belize City, its prop-wash swirling the palm leaves below.

These powerful American gunships could quickly turn the tide in any conflict, he knew. Strafed from the air by heavy machine-gun fire, enemy ground troops made easy targets, and with enough rockets even an armored division could be taken out in a single pass with well-armed helicopters.

Good, he thought. *Air power will take us across Mexico in short order. The Mexicans have few SAM batteries and only a handful of radar installations still working. Taking Mexico, using the element of surprise, should be relatively quick with low casualties.* One of the major elements in their attack would be the Comanche and Apache helicopters his men had captured from the Mexican government.

Loaned to the Mexican authorities initially by the American DEA agents to fight the drug lords of the south, they'd been abandoned when the big war started and were now in the hands of Perro Loco.

One of the major advantages of the Comanche helicopters was their invisibility on radar screens. Made from a synthetic material, they created no blips on conventional radar screens. With the Comanches flying in front of the Apaches and the Hueys, Loco's strike force would sweep across Mexico virtually undetected.

"It seems stable," Loco said into the mouthpiece of his headset.

Eduardo nodded. "It operates very smoothly, *comandante.* I can have it ready to fight in five or six days, if all goes as well as it should."

Flying westward, Loco glimpsed the dim outlines of jungle mountains ahead. San Ignacio lay in a valley near the Guatemalan border, sheltered by huge palm trees. "You will be rewarded for your dedication to our cause, Eduardo," he said. "Very soon we will empty the treasuries of Mexico. You will be well paid for what you have done."

"*Gracias, comandante.* As you must know by now, I am only loyal to you."

Loco leaned back in his seat, watching the Toledo District of Belize pass below them. He paid no attention to the whine of the twin turbines or the clatter of the main rotor, thinking about the bold move he was making.

All of Central America was in chaos. No leader had emerged to take control . . . not yet. Since he was a boy, the oldest son of Manuel Arango, he had known that he was destined for leadership of some kind.

The time was at hand. The *norteamericanos* were fighting each other. General Raines was expending his military might in conflicts all over the world, depleting his arsenals, losing men and precious war matériel to crazed fanatics like Bruno Bottger in Europe and Africa. Raines had battled countless others over the years since the final devastating holocaust.

It was curious that Ben Raines had not met his match in wars around the globe. Some said he was a military genius, while his detractors called him brash, foolhardy, a risk-taker. Loco had decided long ago that General Raines was simply lucky. Lady Luck would smile on some men and shit on others.

Perro Loco had always been lucky.

The Blackhawk settled slowly toward a patch of bare jungle floor near Loco's mountain *hacienda,* rocking and bucking against the prop-wash. It had required only fifteen minutes for the gunship to take him close to the Guatemalan border east of San Ignacio.

Half a dozen armed guards stood at the edges of the landing pad. Radio communications had indicated that all was clear for them to land.

Loco had maps to study before Paco brought the two Americans to the *hacienda*. There was much to be done to prepare for an invasion of Mexico and the splintered remnants of what had once been the United States.

* * *

A blast of machine-gun fire came from one side of the jungle road. Bullets thudded into the jeep caravan commanded by Paco Valdez. Three jeeps with mounted machine guns in the rear came to a halt as Paco jumped out with his Remington Model 870 shotgun cradled in his arms, dashing for the protection of jungle undergrowth.

"Bandidos," Paco hissed, scanning the jungle with practiced eyes, searching for muzzle flashes or wisps of gunsmoke in the canopy shadows.

"Sí," said Juan Medina, Paco's driver for many years during the bandit wars. "Only two. I will take Rudolfo and get around behind them."

"Make it quick," Paco snapped. "Tell Arturo to make sure nothing happens to the two *americanos*. El Comandante wants to question them or I would have already killed them."

"Sí, jefe," Juan said, moving off into the jungle.

Paco's gaze stopped where a banana plant stalk moved in an unnatural way.

There, he thought, raising the Remington to his shoulder. "I send you to meet your ancestors," he said quietly.

The explosive blast of the shotgun ended the silence gripping the rain forest as the load of needle-sharp flechettes was fired. The flechettes, finned one-inch-long razor-sharp projectiles, had a velocity of two thousand feet per second and could penetrate a flak jacket at four hundred yards. A muffled scream came from the banana plant as its leaves were shredded like confetti.

A dark-skinned Caribe toppled forward among the stalks with blood pouring from multiple wounds, his flesh ripped from his body. He clutched a machine gun to his chest as he fell.

"Die, *bastardo,*" Paco whispered, moving quickly to another spot in the vines to keep from making a target of himself for the other bandits.

He slipped quietly through the undergrowth, toward a spot where he had heard gunfire when the caravan was attacked.

Paco knew the jungle. His boots made no sound as he closed in on his enemy, a dagger in one hand, his Remington in the other. Paco's heart beat rapidly and his breath came in short bursts at the prospect of an up-close kill. The thrill of anticipation and his blood lust was almost sexual in its intensity for him.

Armando Diaz held the M-16 to his shoulder. He was afraid now. Paulito was dead. It had been Paulito's idea to capture a jeep so they could form the beginnings of a revolutionary army in the Orange Walk District. Armando was alone, and he knew he was in serious trouble.

He backed away from a breadfruit tree, using all the stealth a lifetime in the Belizian jungles had taught him. It was time to retreat, for there were too many jeeps and too many soldiers to fight.

As Armando suspected, these were soldiers in the service of the infamous Perro Loco. It had been a deadly mistake to shoot at them so soon, before he and Paulito could identify them as murderous henchmen loyal to Comandante Perro Loco, the mad dog killer. Armando was only fifteen, too young to match wits with experienced soldiers. He barely knew how to fire the automatic rifle he carried.

He heard a soft noise behind him. He glimpsed a quick flash of sun on metal as something sliced across his throat. He felt excruciating pain, glancing down at a fountain of red pouring across the front of his shirt.

Armando sank to his knees, dropping his rifle, wishing for all he was worth that he could be with his mother now.

The jungle went dark around him.

Paco stood over the fallen boy, his eyes glittering in the soft light of the jungle as he licked the blood off his blade.

"Nothing tastes as good as the blood of a traitor," he mumbled to himself.

Ten

Finally, after what seemed to be hours, the pickup truck leading them through dense jungle stopped when it suddenly broke into the clear on a pristine beach.

Coop and Jersey got out of the Falcon and walked up to the truck as El Gato Selva got out. "Beautiful, isn't it?" he asked, as if he were a real estate agent trying to sell them beachfront property.

"Yeah, great," Coop growled, stretching and trying to get the kinks out of his spine from their trip over trails more suitable to goats than fifteen-year-old automobiles.

"Is this the Caribbean?" Jersey asked, pulling her shirt together as she noticed Gato's bodyguards giving her chest the eye.

"No. This is Chetumal Bay," Gato said in English. Then, in Spanish too rapid for Coop to follow, he barked an order to his men.

They walked a short way into the jungle, moved some ground brush aside, and uncovered a Zodiac inflatable boat lying there. The two men each grabbed a side, and they dragged the boat out to the beach. It was equipped with a five-horsepower electric engine, which was attached to the rear board.

Gato held out his hand. "This is the only safe way to cross the border into Belize. All of the border guards are either totally loyal to Perro Loco, or so afraid of him they will not stay bribed."

"Don't his men patrol the bay?" Jersey asked.

Gato shrugged. *"Sí.* But we will only be exposed for a very short time, a matter of minutes. It is a chance we must take, for otherwise we will never be able to smuggle in your equipment."

Coop stepped into the jungle and opened the trunk of the Falcon, checking to make sure his .45 was still secure in the back of his belt.

While Gato's men transferred the guns and bombs to the Zodiac, the rebel leader held out his hand. "I believe there was also a mention of one thousand dollars American?"

"Uh-uh," Jersey said, shaking her head. "I don't hand over the money until I see the men picked to do the job."

"But . . . but that is impossible," Gato objected.

Coop stepped up next to Jersey, his face set. "No show, no dough, pal."

Gato pursed his lips in thought, then another shrug. "Okay, it is your funerals if you are caught. Perro Loco will have no mercy with those who hire assassins."

They all got in the boat and sat back against the rubberized side cushions for what turned out to be a ten-minute ride down the beach. After they'd pulled the boat ashore and wiped all trace of its presence off the sand, Gato's men transferred the equipment into yet another large four-wheel-drive truck.

He gave Coop and Jersey an apologetic smile. "I am afraid you two will have to ride in the back. We were not expecting to have additional passengers."

"No problem," Coop said as he vaulted into the bed of the pickup, then stuck his hand out and hoisted Jersey up also.

"Hold on, my friends," Gato said. "The trip will be rather rough."

"Where are we going?" Jersey asked.

"Up into the mountains," he replied.

* * *

After another four hours spent bouncing over rutted paths and trails, they came to a dirt road on the outskirts of a small village high in the mountains as the day changed to dusk and the sun was disappearing in the west.

"Jesus," Coop said as he jumped down out of the pickup, "hasn't anyone in Belize heard of paved roads?"

Gato stepped out of the truck, a smile on his face. "The trip would have been shorter but we had to go around Corozal. The sight of two *americanos* would have surely been reported to Loco's men."

"Is this your headquarters?" Jersey asked, rubbing the small of her back.

"Oh, no," Gato replied. "This is merely a small village where some men live who work at Perro Loco's *hacienda*. It is they who will kill him for us."

They left the truck at the edge of the village and walked to one of the small houses, shacks really, nearby.

As they approached, a short man emerged from the door and waved at Gato.

"That is Reynaldo Soto. He is one of the guards at Loco's place."

Reynaldo greeted Gato and his bodyguards by name, and then turned a questioning glance on Jersey and Coop.

"These are friends who also wish Perro Loco dead," Gato said. "No names are required."

Reynaldo nodded as he stepped to the rear of the truck and peered in at the equipment they'd brought. "Do they have what we need?" he asked.

"*Sí.*"

"Good. Let me go get Jose and we will go over the plan," Reynaldo said.

As he walked to a nearby house, a woman stood in his doorway, a small boy and girl at her side, staring out at them.

"That is Esmeralda, Rey's wife, and his son Carlos and his daughter Rosita," Gato explained.

"Do they know what we're doing here?" Jersey asked,

wondering how they would be able to maintain security with so many people in on the plot.

"No. They are aware of our . . . friendship to Reynaldo, but they know nothing of our plan to assassinate Loco."

Reynaldo reappeared with another man, who had a worried look on his face.

When they leaned over, peering in the back of the truck, Esmeralda and the children disappeared back into their house.

Coop picked up one of the Heckler and Koch G3 sniper rifles and held it out to Reynaldo. "The PSG uses a six-power telescopic sight adjustable up to six hundred meters," Coop explained. "It has a precision aiming tripod, fires a 7.62-caliber slug at eight hundred sixty meters per second, and is extremely accurate up to four hundred meters and fairly accurate at six hundred. I've brought a twenty-round magazine and two extras, so you'll have a total of sixty shots to get our man."

Reynaldo gave a mirthless smile and said in heavily accented English, *"Señor,* if the first one or two do not do the job, I will not get another chance."

Coop nodded. "How about the car-bombs? Any chance of planting one of them in his automobile?"

Jose shook his head. "No. Loco always has someone else start the car before he enters it, and the underside and engine are always checked before a trip."

Reynaldo, still checking out the Heckler and Koch, added, "It is the same when he flies in his helicopter. He is a very careful man."

"Then I guess you're gonna have to rely on the sniper rifle." Coop stared at Reynaldo and the clumsy way he was handling the Heckler and Koch. "Have you ever fired a high-powered rifle before?" he asked.

"Oh, *sí,*" Reynaldo said, nodding his head. "Perro Loco has us carry machine guns when we patrol the jungle near his *hacienda.*" He grinned. "Sometimes, when we get bored, we shoot the wild pigs that live there."

Coop sighed. He knew shooting a machine gun that sprayed bullets like a water hose was very different from lining a man up in the sights and squeezing off a single round or two from a precision instrument like the Heckler and Koch. "Come on, guys, let's get this thing adjusted to your grips."

He had both men each grip a rifle and lean over the rear of the pickup as if they were going to fire. Once they were comfortable, Coop adjusted the cheek pad and the stock and grips on the rifles to suit their shorter arms and thicker necks. Since they didn't want to give the mission's goal away, he was just going to have to hope the telescopic sights were still accurate, as there would be no chance for the men to fire the weapons in practice.

As Coop worked on the rifles, Jersey looked at El Gato. "When do they plan to try the hit?"

"Tomorrow morning when Perro Loco returns from Chatumal. They will only get one chance, when he gets out of the helicopter. It is the only time he is not surrounded by guards."

"Is there any chance they can do the deed and get away?"

Gato shrugged, a grim smile on his thick lips. "There is always a chance, *señorita.*"

"But not a very good one?"

"No. They will most probably die."

"Then why are they willing to go through with this?"

"It is a very poor village. Reynaldo's little girl, Rosita, is very sick and needs an operation that can only be done in a large city. Your gold is to pay for that operation for his child."

"What about Jose?"

"Jose's brother once was heard to say Perro Loco was not good for the country. Loco's guards cut off his head and put it on a pole in the center of his village to remind the peasants what it meant to oppose him. Jose has never forgotten."

At the mention of gold, Jersey reached in her pack and pulled out a small canvas pouch. She handed it to Gato.

"Make sure their families get their share if they don't come back."

"Of course, *señorita*. It will be an honor to reward them if their husbands succeed in ridding the country of Loco."

Coop appeared at Jersey's side, shaking his head. "Well, I've showed 'em all I can about how to use the rifle. Now it's up to them."

Jersey asked Gato, "Is there someplace nearby we can stay until we know the job's been done?"

Gato turned to Reynaldo, who was standing behind him cradling the sniper rifle in his arms like a newborn baby, and spoke in rapid Spanish.

Reynaldo nodded and grinned, exposing teeth made narrow and sharp from gnawing on the sugarcane that grew wild in the region. *"Sí.* There is a small hut off to the side of the village. The couple who once lived there built a bigger house and this one is still empty." He shrugged apologetically. "It is not so nice, but it will keep you dry if the rains come during the night."

"One bedroom or two?" Coop asked.

Reynaldo looked confused. *"Señor.* The entire place is but one room."

"Just kiddin'," Coop said, glancing at Jersey and winking.

"Asshole," she muttered before turning to Reynaldo and saying, "That will be just fine, Señor Soto."

"Would you like to have supper with my family?" Reynaldo asked.

"No, thank you," Jersey replied before Coop could say anything. "We're really tired from our journey and need to get some sleep."

After they'd been shown to the small hut at the very edge of the village and were finally alone, Coop asked, "Why didn't you want to eat with them?"

Jersey pulled a Meals, Ready to Eat out of her pack and popped the tab on the side that would cause a chemical reaction and heat it up. As she bounced it from hand to hand, she answered. "Look at this place, Coop. These people barely have enough food to feed their kids. I didn't want you sitting down to the table and eating up a week's worth of groceries."

"Okay, I see your point. It's just that I can't stand these MREs. They taste more like warm sawdust than"—he paused to read the small print on the side of his food container—"ham and navy beans."

"They weren't designed for taste, Coop. They were designed to keep you alive and healthy in the field."

"Alive maybe, healthy I doubt," he answered, tentatively tasting his MRE with a grimace.

After they'd finished eating, Jersey began to unroll a sleeping bag from her pack in the corner of the room.

"You know, it gets pretty damned cold up here in the mountains. Maybe we'd better share one of those to conserve body heat."

Jersey looked back over her shoulder to see him staring at her behind as she bent over. She straightened up and faced him, hands on hips. "We're on a mission here, bozo. And that doesn't include fooling around."

Coop smiled. "Oh, and if we weren't on a mission, does that mean you'd fool around with me?"

Jersey rested her hand on the butt of her K-Bar assault knife in the scabbard on her belt. "Sure, Coop," she answered sarcastically. "I'd be glad to fool around with you. Of course, then I'd have to scalp you to keep you from bragging about it all over the camp."

He pursed his lips thoughtfully. "Hmmm, it might be worth it."

Jersey shook her head. The man was impossible. "Go to bed. I have a feeling we're gonna be up early tomorrow."

She climbed in her bedroll and pulled the edge up to her chin. "Coop, seriously, do you think those men stand a chance of killing Perro Loco?"

He glanced back at her from his own bedroll across the room. "Honestly? I think they've got two chances, slim and none."

Eleven

"The flying machine is coming," Reynaldo said.

"I see it. I hear it," Jose replied.

"It will be very dangerous to kill the *comandante* here at the *hacienda*," Reynaldo whispered.

"Think of the money," Jose told him.

"I have been thinking about the money. I am also thinking about death . . . about dying today if we do not escape into the jungle," Reynaldo replied, gripping with sweaty palms the Heckler and Koch sniper rifle the *norteamericanos* had given him.

The clatter of a helicopter's blades grew louder from the east.

"We were promised to be paid in gold," Jose muttered, jacking a shell into the firing chamber of his carbine. "There is no gold in Belize. We will be rich men if we follow the instructions the *americana* gave us. All we have to do is kill the mad-dog Nicaraguan who oppresses our people, calling himself a soldier. Think of the gold, Reynaldo."

"If we live long enough to spend it," Reynaldo said in a quiet, deliberate voice as he removed the plastic covers from the telescopic sights on his sniper rifle.

"What about the others guarding the landing place?" Jose asked.

"They will not shoot us. If one of us can kill Comandante Perro Loco when he gets out of the flying machine, the others will not know what to do."

"Where is Paco Valdez?" Jose wondered. "He is the one to be feared."

"In Belize City. Some of our soldiers captured two *americanos* at the Yucatan border. Capitán Valdez had them brought to him at the Gray Gull."

"I hope this works," Jose said. "If it does not, we are both dead men."

"Our families are starving. We have no money. It is a chance worth taking," Reynaldo reminded him. "All we have from Comandante Perro Loco is empty promises and empty bellies. We have no choice." He added to himself, "And my Rosita needs the money for her operation."

Jose knew that Reynaldo was right. When the offer came to assassinate Perro Loco, it had sounded too good to be true. But when the soft-spoken *americana* who made them the offer gave them each a pair of gold coins, with the promise of much more if they could kill Perro Loco, he was listening closely. To a Belizian jungle farmer like Jose, it seemed like a fortune, more money than he had ever seen in his life.

"The black machine is coming down," Reynaldo said. "Wait until you are certain of your target. The radio message from Belize City said that Perro Loco would be aboard this dark helicopter."

"I will not miss," Jose promised, shifting the butt-plate of the fancy gun to his right shoulder, glancing around him to be sure none of the other soldiers guarding the landing pad was suspicious.

Jim Strunk, a transplanted Englishman with a Belizian wife and four children, crept outside the *hacienda* walls with a Glock 9mm pistol, a silencer screwed into the muzzle. A houseboy for the *comandante* had said he'd overheard two of the guards talking as they surrounded the landing space hacked out of the jungle near the *hacienda*. As Chief of Security at Comandante Perro Loco's headquarters, Strunk knew what was expected of him. Killing two green recruits was a far safer bet than waiting to see if Tomas, the houseboy, was right about what he'd heard when Reynaldo and Jose whispered to each other.

Strunk was an ex-SAS sergeant from the British Army. The Special Air Service units were specialized forces used for much of the British Army's undercover work, which would range from operating behind enemy lines to the surveillance and infiltration of terrorist groups. They were so well trained and deadly, the Americans had copied their training methods for their own special forces. The Americans' 1st Special Forces Operational Detachment Delta was created with SAS as a model, the SFOD-Delta intended as an overseas counterterrorist unit specialized in hostages rescue, barricade operations, and specialized reconnaissance.

When Strunk infiltrated Perro Loco's band of terrorists, he realized he could go much farther and get much richer if he switched sides and allegiance to the man known as Mad Dog. He also got many more chances to use his specialized training in killing, which he enjoyed almost more than the money he was paid.

Strunk entered the rain forest canopy leading to the landing space, his senses keened. The *comandante* would not care if he shot a couple of men suspected of being traitors, or assassins. It would make Strunk look like he was doing his job, even if he was wrong.

There would be no one left alive to dispute him.

The heavy Blackhawk lowered slowly and settled onto the grass, its turbines making enough noise to deafen anyone who was close by. Palm branches swayed fiercely until the rotor mast began to slow.

Reynaldo knelt down to steady his aim, keeping his sights on the pilot's head. The pilot would be Eduardo. A helmeted figure in front of him was unmistakable as the *comandante*.

Reynaldo's arms trembled with fear. What he was about to do would make him a fugitive, or a hero. The gold coins he'd hidden in a deep hole behind his hut were enough to convince him that what he was doing was right, worth the risks.

The turbines grew softer, slowing, as the blades began to stop.

Now, he thought, glancing sideways to see if Jose was ready to fire.

Jose held the Heckler and Koch to his shoulder, unaware that Reynaldo was watching him.

Good, Reynaldo told himself. *The Mad Dog of Central America will not escape a bullet this time.*

Jim Strunk saw a uniformed Belizian aiming for the helicopter at the edge of the jungle with a large, unfamiliar rifle in his arms. Tomas had been right to say that an assassination attempt would take place.

"You ignorant bastards," Strunk whispered, jacking a shell into his Glock pistol, winding his way through the forest until he was only a few yards behind the soldier.

A look to the right showed him another soldier aiming for the helicopter, a slender youth all but hidden by vines and brush.

I can kill both of them, Strunk thought, calculating the range.

He aimed for the first soldier's back and pulled the trigger. A soft, puffing sound came from the Glock when it jumped in his hand.

Before the first soldier fell, Strunk aimed for the second assassin and fired off another quiet round.

The Belizian closest to Strunk folded over on his hands and knees with blood pouring from his mouth. His rifle tumbled from his hands. A bullet through a lung sent a fountain of crimson away from his face . . . He began choking as he slumped to the ground on his belly.

The second soldier did a curious dance, like a ballet move away from the tree trunk where he was hiding, embracing the stock of his carbine as if he held a beautiful woman. He made a half circle on one foot and staggered to keep his balance, his eyes bulging.

"Drop, you bloody son of a bitch," Strunk muttered in his crisp British accent, checking to see if any of the other men guarding the landing pad had seen what was going on. Sound from the Blackhawk's turbines would have hidden the soft puff of his silenced bullets.

The second soldier collapsed on his rump and sat there with his rifle against his ribs, staring off at the jungle. A bloody hole in the front of his khaki shirt was proof that Strunk's aim was good.

Impatient, Strunk aimed for the soldier's forehead and put a bullet between his eyes. The back of his skull ruptured, sending bits of brain tissue and plugs of hair flying into the bark of the palm tree behind him.

The Belizian's head jerked backward and he fell against the tree, his eyes still open, frozen in death while he stared up at the branches above him.

"Some are harder to kill than others," Stunk said to himself as he picked up the rifle from the dead man's arms and turned to go back to the *hacienda*. He'd lost count of the men he'd killed a long time ago. At fifty, after following a career as a British Special Forces sergeant, the body count had ceased to be important. The global war had given him so many chances to take another man's life that it no longer mattered. Dead men told no tales.

Reynaldo crawled across a carpet of thick grass and weeds to reach Jose. He could not breathe. It was important to tell

Jose where he'd hidden the gold coins, since he had not told his wife what he was planning to do, or about the money.

"Jose," he croaked, reaching for his seated companion's left arm.

Jose would not look at him.

"Jose!"

Jose seemed to be studying the treetops. And there was blood on the front of his shirt.

"Listen . . . to . . . me, Jose," Reynaldo pleaded as a wave of dizziness swept over him. "The gold . . . is buried . . . behind my house . . . underneath the clay pot. Give it . . . to Esmeralda, and tell . . . her that . . . I love her."

Jose remained motionless. Only then, as Reynaldo was losing consciousness, did he realize that Jose was dead.

Two gold coins lay buried behind his thatched hut, and his wife did not know where to find them, or why he had them at all. At first, he wanted to keep his role as an assassin a secret from her. Somehow, he must get a message to Esmeralda before he lost consciousness . . . or before he died.

He struggled up on his elbows with a strange ringing in his ears, trying to focus on the clearing where the helicopter sat near the wall of the *hacienda*.

"Dios," he croaked, strangling on blood.

Six soldiers stood near the flying machine. Two men got out of the cockpit. One of the soldiers was pointing toward the spot where Reynaldo lay beside Jose.

"No!" The sound of Reynaldo's voice was wet, unnatural.

One of the men aboard the helicopter started toward him as he drew an automatic pistol from his belt. The soldiers were following him.

The only thing Reynaldo could think about was the gold, a fortune, enough to feed his wife and children for many years to come. But how could he tell Esmeralda where he had hidden the coins?

The sounds of heavy boots moved closer to him. He rested

his head in the grass, gasping for breath until a deep voice spoke to him.

"Who paid you to kill me?"

Reynaldo knew he was dying. "A woman and a man. *Americanos.*"

"Who were they? Who sent them?"

Reynaldo's eyes closed. He heard the cocking of a gun and then a loud crack as his skull was split in half. After that, he heard nothing at all.

Twelve

Jim Strunk spoke softly, meeting alone with Comandante Perro Loco in a cellar, an underground command room beneath the *hacienda,* a fortified space surrounded by maps on the wall and a bank of green radar screens.

"Their names were Reynaldo Soto and Jose Villareal," he said. "They had their rifles aimed at you when you got out of the helicopter. I killed them. One of the houseboys overheard them plotting to shoot you. He told me about the plot only a few minutes before you arrived."

"Someone got to them. We have to find out who, and why. I suspect the *bastardo* rebel commander El Gato Selva is behind this assassination attempt."

"Both men were poor Belizian farmers," Strunk said. "I have squads of men out picking up their families so we can question them, but I do not think we'll find out anything. I suspect they did this on their own . . . for money, of course. Someone had to pay them to take this kind of risk. They were simple men who would not concoct such a scheme on their own. Someone paid them. I'm sure of it. Someone with ties to the American government."

Perro Loco's eyebrows raised. "Why do you say that, Comander Strunk?"

Strunk held up the Heckler and Koch rifle he'd been holding in his hand. "This is a very advanced, very expensive piece of equipment. Both of the assassins had one. I do not think El Gato Selva could acquire two of these weapons unless he had help from someone in America. Hell, I've never even seen one before, and I've handled just about every type of rifle there is."

"They may be tied to the pair of USA soldiers my men captured crossing the Yucatan border," Loco said, a thoughtful expression on his face. "One of them says they are from President Osterman. They want to make a deal with an alliance of some kind between us and the government of the USA."

"Why do we need a deal with a defeated government?" Strunk asked. "According to all radio reports, the Rebels smashed all the major military bases in the USA, and there is another report that President Claire Osterman is dead. How do we know who is telling the truth about Osterman? Is she dead, or alive? How do we find out?"

"We shall see," Loco replied. "When the two Americans get here, we will question them."

"Where is Paco?" Strunk asked.

"He is bringing them here, to the *hacienda*. One of them claims to have a code, a way to scramble a message to the USA if we agree to help them."

"I don't trust any of these fucking Americans," Strunk said with heat in his voice.

"Neither do I," Loco muttered. "I will kill one of the soldiers, to see if the other one will tell us the truth when he sees his companion die."

"Good," Strunk grunted, turning for the stairway. "Killing one of the Americans will make the other one tell us the truth about President Osterman. Maybe she is trying to play both sides of the fence, sending two men to talk to you of an alliance while simultaneously giving El Gato weapons with which to assassinate you."

Strunk climbed the steps and went to the ground floor of the *hacienda* to await Paco's arrival.

* * *

Paco Valdez had both American soldiers tied to chairs in an adobe room behind the *hacienda* where farm tools were kept. The chairs were bolted to the floor. Each prisoner had his hands and feet strapped to the chairs. The chairs were bolted to the floor in the dark, windowless room.

Jim Strunk and Paco Valdez stood on either side of the prisoners as Loco entered the adobe. Two more armed guards were flanking the doorway with AK-47's cradled in the crooks of their arms.

"Tell me again," Loco began, "about this offer you bring me from President Osterman. I am very curious, for all our reports indicate your President is dead."

"She survived the crash," the dark-haired prisoner named Arnoldo Mendoza said in a hoarse voice.

"Yeah. That's right," the redheaded soldier said, barely conscious after the blow to his scalp. Blood ran down his neck to his shirtfront.

Loco pulled a gleaming bayonet from a sheath on his belt and moved closer to the red-haired soldier. "What is your name, *americano?*"

"Randy. Randy Grimes."

"Are you ready to die for what you told me, Señor Grimes?" Loco asked. "Do you believe that strongly in what you just told me about your President?"

"It's the truth. President Osterman is alive. She wants to form an alliance with you." Randy's words were slurred, hard to understand.

"Do you know the scrambling code for the radio?" Loco kept on.

"No. Only Arnold knows it."

"Then what do we need with you?" Loco demanded.

"I am the driver. I knew the way across Mexico so we could tell you about President Osterman's offer. I have papers that let us pass through Mexican guard posts."

"Only papers? Then we don't need you now, do we?" Loco demanded.

Randy looked up at Loco, blinking away waves of unconsciousness. "I'll need to drive the HumVee back," he said. "I know who to talk to at the checkpoints . . . and where to go."

"But if your vehicle is not going back, then what purpose do you serve?"

Randy glanced down at the blade in Loco's hands, his eyes filled with terror. "I'm the only one who can get us back across Mexico. Arnold doesn't know this country."

Loco placed the tip of his blade against Randy's throat and gave it a gentle nudge. Blood trickled from the pinprick where the point of the bayonet pierced his skin.

"You ain't gonna kill me, are you?" Randy asked, tears streaming from his eyes to trickle down his sunburned cheeks. "I'm part of the team sent to contact you. President Osterman wants us to join forces with you."

Loco smiled. "If I do kill you, it will send a message to President Osterman . . . if she is still alive, that I will not tolerate bullshit."

"Please don't kill me. I've got a wife an' kids back in Macon."

"Don't kill him," Arnoldo said quickly in fluent Spanish. "I'll never find my way out of here."

"Who said you were leaving?" Loco asked Arnoldo. "What makes you think I'd let you leave here alive? You know where my headquarters is now. You could radio coordinates and before the sun comes up, bombs would be falling on my roof."

"We were sent to offer you an alliance," Arnoldo insisted, his dark face turning pale. "Why would you kill us when we came here with peaceful intentions?"

"I only have your word that your intentions are peaceful," Loco replied, pressing the long knife blade a little harder into Randy's throat.

"It's the truth," Randy protested as more blood came from his neck. "Why would we come here otherwise?"

"To spy on us," Jim Strunk said, his brow knitted into a web of lines. "You could be handing us some bullshit story about the alliance. President Osterman is dead. We got confirmation on it a few days ago."

"She is alive," Arnoldo croaked. "All you have to do is contact her on the radio frequency and use the right scramble. I have the codes in my head . . . memorized, and the frequency is in my shirt pocket."

"How will we know it is your President who answers us?" Paco wanted to know.

"It's part of the code. I swear she's still alive. Herb Knoff is her second in command. He'll vouch for us and tell you everything you need to know to satisfy you as to who we are, and that we're here on an official mission from the USA."

"Perhaps," Loco said. "But in order to be sure, I am going to kill this soldier named Randy. Unless you are telling us the truth, Arnoldo, you will be the next to die."

"No!" Arnoldo cried, glancing over at his companion.

"There is no other way to be sure," Loco told him. "This way, you will know how serious I am about finding the truth in what you've told us."

Loco sent his knife plunging into the throat of Randy Grimes, and a stream of red came spitting forth from the jugular vein, squirting over Loco's shirtsleeve. Grimes's windpipe fell down on his chest, making a wet, whispering sound.

"No!" Arnoldo cried.

Loco laughed, the scar on his face twisted in an odd sort of way, like the wriggling motions of a snake.

"Die, *bastardo!*" Loco shouted, pulling his bayonet out of Grimes's neck.

"Oh, no," Arnoldo sighed, turning the other way.

Loco stared at him. "Is it hard to watch a friend die?" he asked. He leaned closer to Arnoldo, his eyes riveted on the young soldier's face. "What will be much harder, *compadre,* is to feel your own lifeblood leaking down on your belly."

"Kill the son of a bitch," Paco said, licking his dry lips when he scented blood. "Kill both of the American motherfuckers now!"

Loco straightened up, examining the expression on Arnoldo's face. "Not yet, Paco," he said.

"Why not?"

Loco grinned, wiping the blood off his bayonet on his pants legs. "Because now, this one will tell us the truth. He knows we mean business."

"I . . . swear . . . I'm telling the truth," Arnoldo stammered as his companion slumped lower in the chair. "We were not lying to you in the first place."

Loco regarded him for a moment. "But how were we to know you were telling the truth?" he asked.

Arnoldo Mendoza swallowed as Randy Grimes stopped breathing through his severed windpipe. "Because we came all the way down here. Why would we come at all, unless we were ordered to?"

Jim Strunk pushed away from the wall where he'd been watching the proceedings. "Ask him about the rifles, Loco."

Perro Loco held out his hand and Paco Valdez handed him one of the Heckler and Koch sniper rifles. He showed it to Arnoldo. "Is this how your President offers an alliance? By giving rebels in our jungle these weapons with which they can kill me?"

Arnoldo shook his head. "I do not know what you are talking about," he said. "I've never seen a gun like that before."

"This could only come from America," Loco persisted. "Are you saying that your President did not try to have me assassinated?"

Arnoldo shook his head again. "No, *comandante!* I do not know anything of that. We, Randy and I, were only ordered to come here to offer you a partnership with President Osterman. Why would she want you killed? She needs you to help defeat Ben Raines."

"He's probably right, *comandante*," Strunk said, watching the American's eyes closely to see if he was telling the truth. "Why would they come into our territory . . . unless somebody ordered them to?"

"I don't give a shit about their reasons," Loco spat. "I want to know if they are spies."

"I'm not a spy," Arnoldo said, turning away from Grimes's dead body. "I'm only following orders. I swear it."

Loco gave Strunk a glance. "Prepare the radio. We shall see if the man is speaking true words. If he is not, I will kill him myself. Take the other one outside and bury him. Remove any papers he has in his pockets and bring them to me."

Thirteen

Esmeralda Soto heard them coming, the sounds of gasoline motors grinding through the jungle. She came out of her palm hut to see who was driving the jungle road to their village. It was never good when a motorized vehicle came this way, for it was almost always soldiers who were looking for someone, or bandits coming to loot the village of what little they had in the way of food and clothing. Or to take away the young women who had no children.

Reynaldo had been acting strangely since the American man and woman came, the woman who appeared to be *una india* by her facial features. She and Reynaldo and Jose whispered among themselves too often while she was here, and even Anna noticed the change in Jose after she and her companion went to their hut at the edge of the village.

"Come inside," Esmeralda said to her five-year-old son as he was playing in the dirt not far from their hut. Carlos had his father's eyes. When she looked at little Carlos she saw Reynaldo when he was younger.

Carlos looked up. "But why, Mama?"

"Someone is coming up the mountain. I need to tell Anna we have visitors. Take your sister and go inside. It may be the soldiers."

Carlos got up and dusted off his knees. "Come, Rosita," he said to a tiny naked girl playing in the mud beside him. "Mama says it is time to go."

Esmeralda watched the jungle trail, shading her eyes from

the sun with a hand. The noises made by the engines grew much louder. It would be soldiers coming, for the village was too far off main roads to be visited by anyone else.

In the past, rebel soldiers from Nicaragua and Guatemala and El Salvador had come to loot Belizian villages, looking for wild pig meat and fruit gathered by the mountain tribes. The tribes had so little and yet the soldiers came anyway, often shooting down tribal elders and anyone else who voiced a protest to the banditry.

But when Comandante Perro Loco took charge in Belize, most of the bandit gangs were killed off, or sent into hiding. The Mad Dog, as his name implied, killed anyone and everyone who stood in his way when he took command of the country. Some saw him as a Belizian hero . . . Esmeralda was not so sure. She wished with all her heart that Reynaldo had not become a guard at the Mad Dog's headquarters in San Ignacio. He had changed so much in the months since he went to work as a *hacienda* guard. He hardly spoke to her now. They needed the money from his job, especially if they ever hoped to pay for Rosita's operation, but Esmeralda worried that harm might come to her husband if he had a job guarding the *comandante*.

Anna, a slender Caribe Belizian girl with three children, came running from the jungle with an armload of breadfruit as she cast a worried look over her shoulder. She was only eighteen, too young to understand the political things going on in the capital city. And she was pretty, making her vulnerable to the soldiers' demands.

"Who comes?" Anna asked, stopping in front of Esmeralda's hut.

"Soldiers, or *bandidos,*" Esmeralda replied, still watching the jungle road. "Take your children inside and keep them there until we know who it is. Do not come outside for any reason until they are gone."

"Why have Jose and Reynaldo not come home?" Anna asked. "I expected them last night."

Esmeralda continued to stare at the road. "I do not know. Something may be wrong."

Anna dropped the sack of breadfruit and raced for her hut to grab her children. Down deep, Esmeralda had a feeling that the motor sounds meant trouble for the villagers.

Coop stuck his head out of the hut he and Jersey were sharing as soon as he heard the growling of engines from the jungle.

He whirled and ducked back inside the hut. "Pack our shit as fast as you can, Jersey. Sounds like company's on the way."

Jersey quickly rolled up her bedroll and stuffed it in her pack as Coop did the same with his stuff. "You think it could be El Gato coming to tell us the hit went okay?" she asked.

"Uh-uh. Those motors sound like jeeps, an' Gato drives a pickup. I'm very much afraid the shit's hit the fan, an' if we don't get a move on, it's gonna splatter all over us."

"What about the villagers?" Jersey asked as they pulled their packs on, picked up their weapons, and melted into the jungle.

Coop shook his head. "Whatever happens to them, it'll go a lot worse on 'em if the soldiers find us hiding here. Get a move on!"

Sergeant Felipe Garza directed his driver toward the center of the village. A tripod-mounted fifty-caliber machine gun bolted to the rear floor was manned by Lupe Ozaro.

Garza signaled the drivers of the other vehicles to remain on the periphery of the village to guard their backs until they saw what they were up against. Loco had said there might be some foreigners stationed here and to be careful.

More than two dozen grass huts stood in the clearing on a high jungle mountainside. Garza saw no evidence of armed resistance, so he had his driver proceed further into the village.

"Alto!" Felipe shouted.

The jeep ground to a halt.

Sergeant Garza jumped to the ground with his pistol drawn.

"Where is the wife of Reynaldo Soto?" he cried. "The wife of Jose Villareal?"

A small woman in a tattered cotton dress came slowly from the doorway in one of the huts.

"Who are you?" Felipe demanded.

"Esmeralda. Esmeralda Soto."

Felipe strode across the clearing with his gun pointed at the woman. "Your husband? Where is he?"

"He . . . is a guard at the *hacienda* of Comandante Perro Loco in San Ignacio."

Felipe smiled. "Yes. I know that. He is dead! He tried to assassinate the *comandante.*"

Esmeralda shook her head, her hands to her face and sudden tears springing to her eyes. "No. Reynaldo would not do such a thing."

The tears streamed down her cheeks. Sergeant Garza found her tears amusing. "He was a traitor! So was his friend from this village, Jose Villareal. They were killed when they tried to kill our commander. Tell me, bitch, why they would do something like this?"

"It is not true . . . it cannot be true."

"It is *la verdad.* They are both dead. Now tell me . . . who would pay them to do such a thing?"

"No one," Esmeralda whispered. "Reynaldo was a good father and a good husband."

"He was a murderer!" Felipe snapped.

"No. He has never killed anyone in his life."

Felipe glanced around him. "Where is the wife of Jose Villareal?"

Esmeralda's eyes flickered to the front door of Jose's hut. "There," she said softly.

Felipe turned to Corporal Lupe Ozaro. His eyes were hard, flat and uncaring. "Fire into the hut. Kill them!"

Before Esmeralda could scream a warning, the heavy chatter of machine-gun fire echoed across the village. Palm fronds erupted from the walls, tossed into the air by the power of lead slugs, shredding coconut leaves into pulp.

A child screamed as the hut was being cut to pieces by the hail of bullets.

Esmeralda sank to her knees, covering her face with her hands, sobbing uncontrollably.

The shooting ended. Sergeant Garza grinned. "Now do you believe me, bitch?" he snarled. "Unless you tell me who paid your husband and his friend to assassinate Comandante Perro Loco, you and the others in this village will die."

Esmeralda sobbed. "I do not know. I swear it. There was this woman . . . *una india,* only she spoke English. She came here with a man, *un americano.*"

"These *americanos* . . . who were they?"

"They did not give their names. They talked to Reynaldo and Jose in private," she said, not even considering adding that El Gato Selva had also been there.

"What did they talk about?" Felipe demanded.

Esmeralda peered through her fingers when Anna came crawling out the door of her hut with blood covering her tattered dress. Her leg dangled behind her at an odd angle. Inside the hut the sounds of children crying filled the village.

"I do not know," Esmeralda cried.

"You lying bitch!" Felipe hissed, his teeth clenched when he spoke. "Tell me the truth or I will blow a hole through your head."

"I swear I do not know!" she screamed, looking around her as if she might find help from the other villagers. She saw no one. Everyone else in the small village was hiding behind closed doors.

Felipe cocked his automatic pistol, aiming down at the cowering woman. "This is your last chance to tell me what the woman said, and who she was."

"She . . . gave Reynaldo something. Later on that night he went out and buried it behind our house. This is all I know. I swear it on the lives of my children."

Anna Villareal rolled off the steps into her hut and landed on the ground. Felipe turned his gun on her and fired a thundering round.

His bullet split Anna's skull in half. Her limbs jerked with death throes. Her broken leg thrashed helplessly behind her.

A small boy, no more than ten or twelve months old, came crawling to the door of the hut, staring down at his dying mother.

Sergeant Garza fired at the boy. The bullet went through his spine, flipping him over on his back as a shrill scream came from his lips.

"Now do you believe me?" Felipe asked, aiming his weapon down at Esmeralda. "Tell me who the *americana* bitch was, or you will die . . . and all your children will die!"

"She did not say her name!" Esmeralda pleaded. "I swear I am telling the truth!"

"Lying bitch!" he whispered. "What did your husband bury behind your house."

"I do not know."

"Show me where it is buried."

Anna Villareal strangled on blood and lay still as Esmeralda got to her feet.

"It is beneath a clay pot where we boil our sugarcane and yam roots. Please do not kill my children . . ."

She led him to the pot behind the hut, where a bed of ashes surrounded the base of a bowl.

"Are you sure it was here?" Felipe demanded.

"Yes. Yes. Reynaldo did not know I was watching him that night when he dug the hole."

Felipe walked over to the fire-blackened clay pot and gave

it a closer examination. "I will have Corporal Ozaro dig it up," he said. "If there is nothing under it, I will kill you."

Sergeant Garza motioned for Lupe Ozaro to climb down from the Jeep.

Esmeralda crept backward, resting on her knees.

"Dig here," Felipe instructed.

Esmeralda closed her eyes.

Lupe Ozaro found a handful of gold American coins wrapped in a cloth at the bottom of the firepit. He gave them to Sergeant Garza.

Felipe turned abruptly and fired a bullet into Esmeralda's chest, slamming her over onto her back in the jungle grass.

"Let us go now," Felipe said, pocketing the coins. He would have to tell the *comandante* that the story about Reynaldo and Jose working for the Americans to assassinate him was true, but he would not mention the gold.

The gold would remain in Felipe's pocket. After all, it was more than he could make in several years in the service of Perro Loco, and the gold would buy the favors of many *señoritas*.

He stopped, looking down at Esmeralda.

"Por favor, do not kill me," she begged as bloody froth bubbled from her lips.

"I have no choice," Felipe said. "You saw me dig up the gold."

"I did not see anything."

"I wish I could believe you," Felipe told her. "I do not like killing women."

"I saw nothing," she stammered, coughing and holding her chest. "I have two small children who need me . . . now that I know Reynaldo will . . . not be coming home to us."

"As you wish," Felipe said, turning as if he meant to return to the jeep.

"Gracias, señor," Esmeralda replied, trying to get to her

feet, swaying from the pain in her chest where the bullet had entered. "There would be no one else to care for my children."

"I understand," Felipe remarked.

As he was rounding a corner of the hut, he wheeled and aimed his pistol at the woman. The bark of his weapon ended the quiet in the clearing.

Esmeralda Soto fell over on her back with a dark red hole in her forehead. The secret of the location of the gold coins was now between Felipe and Lupe Ozaro and their driver.

Just as Lupe climbed into the jeep, two more gunshots rang out in the forest.

Sergeant Garza did not intend to share his fortune with anyone else. He pushed Lupe's and the driver's bodies out of the jeep and drove off, already making plans on how he would explain the deaths of his companions to the others waiting in the jungle.

He would blame the *americanos,* saying they attacked them from hiding. He would order a search of the village in order to prove to Perro Loco that he was thorough in his assignment and that he had tried his best to avenge the deaths of Lupe and his driver.

Who knows? he thought. *They might even find evidence of the* americanos' *presence in the village.*

Fourteen

Coop had to physically restrain Jersey when the fat sergeant ordered his man to fire into Jose's hut. She put her M-16 to her shoulder, and would have blown the shit out of him if Coop hadn't stopped her.

"What's the matter with you, Coop?" she demanded angrily. "There's only three of them in the village. We can take them easily."

He shook his head. "I heard at least four or five jeeps, Jersey. The rest are covering the sergeant's back. We wouldn't stand a chance."

"But . . ." she started to say as the sound of machine-gun fire shattered the quiet in the jungle, causing a flock of fruit bats to take wing over their heads.

"Goddammit!" she whispered hoarsely. "That son of a bitch is gonna kill them all."

Coop gritted his teeth until his jaws ached. It galled him to stand by and do nothing, but it would do no good for him and Jersey to be killed and it certainly wouldn't protect the villagers.

"Hang on, Jers," he said, his voice tight. "We'll get our time at bat and we'll make the bastards pay, but now's not the time."

After Sergeant Felipe Garza shot his men, he jumped in the jeep and spun his tires, fishtailing in the soft dirt of the jungle floor as he raced out of the village.

He slid to a stop when he got to where the rest of his command was waiting just inside the thick foliage of the surrounding forest.

Corporal Beto, his second in command, stood up in his jeep, his hands on the fifty-caliber machine gun mounted on a post in the vehicle.

"What happened, Felipe?" he asked. "We heard shooting but got no call on the radio requesting help."

"Americanos!" Garza shouted. "They ambushed us. There was no time to radio."

Beto saw the blood on the seats of the jeep Garza was driving. "And Lupe and Jose?" he asked, referring to Garza's driver.

"Killed," Garza answered shortly. "I managed to drive the *americanos* back, but they may still be in the village. I want a complete search of every hut. Spare no one if you find evidence they were helping the *americanos.*"

Beto waved his arm, and the other four jeeps pulled into the village, just in time to see the last of the villagers fleeing into the jungle. No one was left behind.

The search didn't take long; the buildings were all too small to hide anyone. When they came to the hut Coop and Jersey had been in, Garza stooped and picked up two empty MRE packets, holding them aloft for the others to see.

"The *americanos* were here, just as I said. I will radio Comandante Loco to see if he wants us to search the jungle or to return to base."

After informing Loco of the presence of Americans in the jungle, Garza was ordered to return to base. Loco said other men better equipped for a jungle search would be sent to apprehend the traitors. He needed Garza to bring the aircraft fuel they'd picked up on their way into the jungle as soon as they could, for it would be needed in the upcoming offensive against the Mexican government.

* * *

Sergeant Felipe Garza rode at the front of the procession as they crossed jungle mountains toward San Ignacio and Loco's *hacienda*. Five trucks with men loyal to the *comandante* drove the vehicles. The trucks loaded with aircraft fuel would be a star in his crown, a way to earn a promotion, as would his finding out that Americans were indeed involved in the recent assassination attempt on Loco's life. The airplanes, especially the helicopters Comandante Perro Loco had, were in good mechanical shape, but they lacked the fuel to fly across Mexico to achieve the objectives the *comandante* wanted as he led his forces north to conquer the North Americans.

Corporal Beto spoke, still gripping the fifty-caliber machine gun with both hands while they moved through the jungle. "The *comandante* will be pleased," he said. "The fuel will be very important."

Felipe knew the *comandante* would be more than pleased to have the fuel he sought so desperately. "Yes. When we get to San Ignacio to show him what we have found, he may give us all a small bonus. He was very pleased that we chased the *americanos* into the jungle."

"I could use the money," Beto said. "My family is almost starving."

"Many people are hungry in Central America," Garza said as the jeep rolled over a hillside. "We are among the lucky ones who have jobs."

"But this . . . job," Beto argued, "it does not pay much and we don't get our money very often."

"Silencio!" Garza said, glancing down at the driver, a Salvadoran named Julio Corte who spoke very little English. "If someone close to the *comandante* hears you say this, you will be executed by his bodyguards."

"I know," Corporal Beto murmured, keeping an eye on the jungle. "It is *muy estupido* to say anything against the *comandante*. A wise man keeps his mouth shut in all matters when you are around him."

"Verdad," Garza replied.

A moment of silence passed.

"Tell me, Sergeant . . . what was at the bottom of the hole under the clay pot? It looked like small pieces of gold wrapped in the cloth."

"How did you see that?" Garza asked. "You were supposed to be back in the jungle awaiting my command to enter the village."

Beto shrugged. "I walked forward to make sure everything was all right after I heard your machine-gun fire. When I saw you dig up the small pouch, I returned to my men."

Good, Garza thought, *he didn't see me shoot Lupe and Jose.* Garza knew, however, it was still necessary to silence the only witness to what he had done.

"You think you saw gold?" he asked, letting his right hand slide down near his pistol.

"I saw something yellow . . . It glittered in the sun when you opened the cloth."

"You saw too much," Garza answered. "You should have been looking the other way."

"What do you mean, Sergeant?"

Garza pulled his weapon. "You saw something gleaming in the sun," he said. "It was a mistake to be looking at what I took from the cloth."

Beto saw Garza lift his pistol, aiming for Beto's head as the jeep moved over bumpy ground.

"No, Sergeant!" he cried.

"But you saw the gold."

"No! I saw nothing!"

Private Corte looked up with both hands gripping the steering wheel . . . He knew something was wrong.

Felipe knew he would have to kill the driver as well as Beto, since Private Corte had overheard what was being said between them. He'd just have to blame it on the *americanos* again.

Garza was tightening his finger on the trigger, when the

roar of automatic-weapons fire came from both sides of the jungle road.

A series of molten bullets ripped through Sergeant Felipe Garza's chest. He fell back in the seat of the jeep with his mouth full of blood.

Private Corte was torn out of his seat by the incessant pounding of machine-gun fire as it swept him off the driver's seat in a hail of lead.

Corporal Beto fired at the muzzle flashes he saw in the jungle, moving the barrel of his fifty-caliber tripod-mounted weapon back and forth.

The recoil of the machine gun made his arms tremble, and for a moment he wasn't sure he'd hit anything.

Then he felt a stabbing pain in his chest, as if someone had buried a knife below his ribs.

"Dios!" he cried, his trigger finger locked on the firing mechanism. The hammering sound of machine-gun fire filled the forest.

Bullets sprayed the jungle canopy above the caravan as more shots came from drivers in the trucks, single bullets fired by pistols and carbines.

Felipe saw and heard what was happening without being able to lift a finger to help his men. All he could think about were the drums of fuel in the trucks, and the few gold coins in his pocket.

"Kill them, Beto!" he croaked. "Don't let them take the gold or the fuel!"

The jeep sputtered and came to a halt without a driver at the controls.

"What the hell?" Felipe Garza asked, his chest filled with fiery pain.

He noticed that the driver's seat was empty. He cast a glance back at Corporal Beto.

Beto's mouth was a fountain of blood. He continued to fire the machine gun.

"Beto!" Garza shouted. "Kill these sons of bitches before we all are all killed!"

Corporal Beto's eyes had a glazed look to them, although he continued to fire into the jungle in a blind way, spraying the treetops with lead.

"What the fuck are you shooting at?" Garza cried, holding his chest with both hands as if he could stop the crimson blood from leaving his body. "There is no one in the trees!"

It was then that Garza saw the bloody bullet holes in the front of Corporal Beto's shirt. Blood leaked down over his belt and into his pants pockets.

"Keep shooting!" Garza ordered, trying to get up from the seat of the jeep in spite of the pains in his chest and deeper in his belly.

"I ordered you to shoot, Corporal Beto!" Garza bellowed as more bullets came from the jungle, shattering the windshield he gripped with his right hand.

A stinging pain entered his right armpit and it slammed him back into the seat of the jeep. For a moment he was stunned by the blow, not knowing what it was.

He glanced down at his khaki shirt and saw blood streaming from his sleeve. He stared at it for a time, unable to think clearly.

"They shot me, Beto," he said. When he saw the front of his shirt, he knew he'd been wounded several times.

"Drive away from here!" he said, his voice muted by blood crossing his tongue.

He saw the driver, Private Corte, lying beside the jeep with a bullet hole through his head.

Garza cast a look at the jungle. Two dark shapes were moving toward him and the precious cargo some of the trucks carried.

"The gold," he whispered, losing consciousness.

His final thoughts were of the coins hidden in his pocket. Then he went to sleep.

* * *

Coop and Jersey stood over the bodies strewn about the jungle path. Jersey reached over with her foot and kicked Garza in the mouth. "That'll teach you to kill innocent women and children, you bastard!" she growled.

Coop glanced at her. He'd never seen her so furious. "You want to scalp the son of a bitch, too?" he asked.

She started to give a sarcastic answer, then hesitated, a thoughtful look on her face. "You know, Coop. Every now and then you come up with a pretty good idea, even if it is by accident."

Jersey took out her K-Bar and squatted over Garza's body.

"Hey, wait a minute, Jersey. I was just kidding . . ."

She looked up at him. "I'm not." She bent and with a quick slash of the K-Bar made a circular incision around the top of Garza's skull, then grabbed his hair and yanked a full scalp lock off in one squishy jerk.

"Damn!" Coop said, almost gagging at the horrible sight.

"Listen, Coop," Jersey said, pausing to wipe her bloody hands on Garza's shirt. "We're stuck out here in the middle of a jungle, surrounded by hostiles, with no transportation and no way to 'phone home.' "

"We can take one of these . . ." Coop started to say, pointing to the jeeps in the path, until he saw bullet holes in all the hoods and steam coming from each and every motor.

"Good thought, Sherlock. Wanta try again?" Jersey asked.

"So, what does that have to do with scalping our enemies?"

"The only chance we have to survive is to put some fear in our opposition. The more barbaric and crazy we can seem, the fewer men who are going to be willing to come into the jungle after us."

"You really think taking a few scalps will scare off men like these?" he asked, pointing to the dead lying around them.

"Not *just* scalping, but I have a few more ideas. Remember, I'm part Apache."

Coop took a deep breath as he pulled out his own K-Bar. "Okay, Pocahontas, show me the way."

Fifteen

Mike Post, Ben's Chief of Intelligence, entered the office to find Ben and his team waiting for him.

"I hear there's been some word from Belize," Ben said.

Mike nodded, frowning. "Yes. Unfortunately, it's not good news."

"Let's have it, Mike."

"El Gato Selva, the intermediate between Jersey and Cooper and the assassins, radioed to say the entire mission was a bust. The assassins were killed, but not before they talked. Evidently, they gave away Jersey and Coop's position and a hit team was sent in to take them out."

Ben felt his chest tighten and his mouth go dry at the words. "Do we know what happened?"

Mike pulled up a chair and set down. He reached into his coat, pulled out his pipe, and began filling it as he talked. "Our intel is not one-hundred-percent reliable. Jersey and Coop were staying in a small village in the jungle. The hit squad killed six or eight of the villagers and reported back to Perro Loco that they were after two Americans who'd paid the assassins. Later that day, radio contact with the hit squad was lost, so we don't know what's gone on since then."

Ben leaned back in his chair, a small smile on his face. "I can tell you what happened, Mike. Those soldiers made the mistake of messing with a buzz saw when it was busy cutting wood. Jersey and Coop took the hit team out."

"That's possible, but we won't know for several hours.

This is all happening in a very remote part of the country and communications are difficult because of the mountains."

"Well," Ben said, "I'm not going to wait. I'm going to take a scout team in after Jersey and Coop."

"But Ben," Mike said, "you can't leave. You're right in the middle of negotiations between President Otis Warner and Cecil Jeffreys about the peace protocol."

"That's gonna have to wait. Two members of my team are in trouble, and I intend to see that they make it back."

Mike fired up his pipe, sending clouds of blue smoke toward the ceiling. "Who's going with you?"

Ben nodded his head at Anna, Corrie, and Beth, sitting across the room. "My usual team along with a couple of my best scouts." He got to his feet. "They're waiting outside."

He crossed the room and opened the door. "Harley, Hammer, come on in."

Two men entered the room, each seeming as big as a house. Ben put his hand on the shoulder of a six-foot-four-inch man with blue eyes and red hair in a single braid hanging down to the middle of his back. "This is Harley Reno," Ben said. "He's gonna take us in and bring us out. He's the best scout in the Army."

Reno nodded at the team as Ben stepped to the next man. Only marginally smaller than Reno, he stood six feet three inches and had coal-black hair and icy green eyes. "This is Scott 'Hammer' Hammerick. He's our weapons expert, and also happens to be fluent in Spanish and knows Belize like the back of his hand."

Hammer stepped forward. "The country we're gonna be fightin' in is high mountain jungle. Lots of thick foliage, not too many open spaces. That means we're gonna make some changes in the weapons you carry. Your M-16s won't be much use up there, an' they're much too heavy to carry up and down mountain passes."

He reached down and unslung a small machine gun from the strap over his shoulder. "You women will be carrying these Mini-Uzis. Fully loaded, they weigh only four kilograms, have forty-round detachable box magazines, and can fire six hundred fifty rounds per minute on full automatic."

He nodded at Harley, who held out a shotgun with a pistol grip on it. "Ben, you and I and Harley will be carrying the SPAS Model 12. SPAS stands for Special Purpose Automatic Shotgun. It's twelve-gauge, weighs 4.2 kilograms, has a seven-shot tubular magazine, and on full automatic can fire two hundred forty rounds per minute."

"Wait a minute," Corrie said. "Don't shotguns have a very limited range?"

Hammer shrugged. "Depends. We have a variety of slugs available, from light bird shot to heavy metal slugs that'll penetrate steel plate at a hundred yards."

Corrie nodded and sat back.

"Now, as far as handguns, the old Colt .45's are out of date. I prefer the Beretta Model 93R. It fires a 9mm Parabellum bullet, has a twenty-round magazine, and can fire single-shot or in three-shot automatic bursts. On automatic fire, a small lever drops down in front of the trigger guard for the left hand to grab and steady your aim."

Anna got to her feet. "This is all well and good, but while we're standing here talking, Jersey and Coop are in trouble. When are we leaving?"

Harley Reno smiled at Anna. Evidently, she was his kind of woman—no bullshit, ready for action.

"As soon as you get suited up and pick up your weapons," he said. "We're going to make a HALO drop over the mountains in six hours."

"HALO drop?" Corrie asked.

"High Altitude, Low Opening," Harley said. "We'll go out of the plane at ten thousand feet but we won't open our chutes until we're a few hundred feet off the ground so we won't be picked up on radar."

"Isn't that cutting it awfully close?" she asked.

Harley smiled. "Yeah. A tenth of a second late an' you're hamburger."

Hammer added, "But don't worry, the chutes are fitted with automatic pressure gauges that open 'em automatically . . . most of the time."

Ben got to his feet. "Okay, team, let's go. We're burnin' daylight and we've got an appointment with some friends to keep."

Paco Valdez entered the main room of the *hacienda* to find Perro Loco and Jim Strunk discussing new security arrangements in light of the recent assassination attempt.

Loco glanced up from a map of the grounds when Paco entered. "What news have you of the squad with the aircraft fuel?"

Paco shook his head. "There has been no radio contact for some hours now, *comandante*."

Loco slammed his hand down on the desk, making even the imperturbable Jim Strunk jump. "I want to know what is happening, and I want to know it now!"

"*Sí, mi comandante,*" Paco answered hastily. "I will have the helicopter fly over the area immediately. The good news is there has been no signs of smoke in that region, indicating the fuel was not exploded."

Loco turned to Strunk. "Jaime, go with Paco and make sure that the fuel is found and delivered back here safely. If it is lost, it will seriously delay my offensive against Mexico City."

An hour and a half later, Strunk and Paco Valdez climbed out of the helicopter they'd landed in the center of the village where Felipe Garza had been when he'd last made contact. They were followed by fifteen handpicked troops who'd ridden in the big Huey with them.

Strunk grabbed his AK-47 and led the way down the jungle path, following the tire marks of Garza's caravan. Valdez strolled at his side, a short-barreled shotgun in his arms loaded with 00–buckshot.

They'd traveled only two miles when they saw the remains of the convoy. The jeeps were sideways in the trail, crippled by hundreds of bullet holes, motors still smoking and sending up steam.

"Mary Mother of God," Paco whispered, and unconsciously crossed himself at the sight of the bodies of Garza and his men.

Sergeant Felipe Garza had been scalped and was sitting spread-eagled with his arms tied outstretched to a tree. His abdomen was sliced open and his entrails were in a circle around him.

Corporal Beto was tied down over an army-ant bed and was systematically being eaten by the hungry insects—his eyes and most of his face already gone.

Another man was strung upside down from a tree, his head only inches above a bed of coals, which was cooking his brains.

Several of the soldiers with Strunk and Valdez bent over on the trail and vomited on their boots; others just turned their heads, mumbling quiet prayers to themselves as they stared into the surrounding jungle with fear in their eyes, gripping their weapons so hard their knuckles were white.

"Who would do such a thing?" Valdez asked.

Strunk gave a lopsided grin of admiration. "Someone who wants to put fear into our troops . . . someone very smart. I've done the same thing a time or two, back in Africa when I was with the SAS. It's very effective if done right."

"I will inform the men they are not to discuss what they have seen here," Valdez said.

Strunk gave a short laugh. "You can tell 'em anything you want, Paco. They're still gonna talk about this."

"At least they weren't smart enough to destroy the aircraft fuel," Paco said.

Strunk's face became troubled. "Yeah, that was a mistake." He shook his head. "I don't understand why they didn't . . ."

"You men," Paco interrupted, pointing at a group of men standing near the jeeps. "Start unloading the drums of fuel. I will radio for additional trucks to come haul it away while you stand guard."

As two of the men walked to the nearest jeep and took hold of a drum, Strunk suddenly said, "Hold it! It's a trap!"

He was too late. The men tipped the drum up on one edge to roll it off the jeep, and a hand grenade that had been wedged beneath it popped free, its pin already removed.

Strunk grabbed Valdez and dived to the ground behind a large banyan tree just as the grenade exploded, igniting the fuel drums in a giant fireball.

Trees were leveled for a hundred yards and every one of Valdez's squad was incinerated into ash in a split second of intense heat.

Strunk woke up a half hour later, blood streaming from both ears and his nose. It took him another twenty minutes to free his legs from the banyan tree trunk where it'd fallen on him and Valdez.

Paco Valdez was conscious but incoherent, and both men were still deaf from the explosion. By the time they got back to the helicopter, it was almost dark.

"Loco is going to be very angry," Paco said in a loud voice so Strunk could hear him.

Strunk nodded. "We'd better come up with a good explanation for why we didn't check the fuel drums for booby traps before we tried to move them."

"But Señor Strunk, we didn't try to move the drums," Paco said with a sly grin as he sleeved blood off his face. "We were about to examine them when one of my clumsy men stumbled over a trip wire and set the explosion off." He spread his hands, an innocent look on his face. "There was nothing more we could have done."

Strunk nodded. "Yeah, that's the way I remember it, too, Paco."

They climbed into the helicopter and the pilot started the engines.

"I believe I will radio the *comandante* and tell him the bad news over the air," Paco said, reaching for the microphone. "I am very much afraid if I tell him in person, he will shoot me before I can make my excuses."

"Good idea, Paco. That way he'll have plenty of time to calm down before we get back to camp."

"You, my friend, had better use the time to come up with a plan for capturing these *americanos* before they do more damage to our forces, or no matter what excuses we come up with, Loco will have our heads."

Sixteen

Ben and his team looked like something out of a space movie as they gathered near the door of the C-130 transport plane. They were dressed all in black, with faces enclosed in Plexiglas helmets to give them oxygen until they fell far enough to be able to breathe on their own. Harley had said they would be at terminal velocity, 120 miles per hour, for several minutes prior to their chutes opening.

"It's almost impossible to breathe at that speed, so leave your helmets hooked up until your chute opens. After that, if the shock of the sudden deceleration doesn't knock you out, you can jettison your helmets and get your weapons ready to fire. We don't know what we're gonna find when we land."

"What if we get hung up in the jungle canopy too far to drop from our chutes?" Ben asked.

Harley pointed to Ben's chest. "That's what that nylon cord on the front of your HALO suit is for. Just attach it to your harness, hit the release button, and climb down the rope to the ground."

"And if the rope doesn't reach the ground?" Corrie asked.

"Then you're SOL," Harley replied with a grin.

"SOL?" she asked.

"Shit outta luck," he replied, and turned to watch the lights at the front of the transport, waiting for the jump light to turn from red to green.

* * *

Perro Loco paced the main room of his *hacienda* cursing and asking God why He had forsaken him on his glorious quest to save the poor working peasants from the overlords of capitalism. Paco Valdez and Jim Strunk sat across the room watching him. Both were thinking the same thing. *Horseshit!*

Finally, when Perro had exhausted his vocabulary of curse words, he stalked over and sat at his desk. He pulled a Cuban cigar out of a humidor, lit it, and he leaned back with his feet on the corner of the desk.

Pointing the cigar like a pistol, he asked Valdez, "Paco, have you got our commanders in Nicaragua and Costa Rica moving toward Mexico?"

"Sí, mi comandante," Valdez answered. "All of our battalions are massing on the border as we speak. The Mexican *presidente* has protested strongly to the United Nations, but we have told them it is merely military exercises."

"By the time the Secretary General of the U.N., Jean-François Chapelle, gathers the courage to act, we will be well on our way to Mexico City," Strunk said, grinning.

"And have you figured out a plausible excuse for the attack on Mexico?" asked Valdez, peering at them through blue clouds of aromatic cigar smoke.

Strunk laughed out loud. "That's the best part. One of our squads has stolen a Mexican Army helicopter. When you give the order, we'll have one of our own men pilot it and attack the Presidential Palace in Nicaragua, giving us the perfect reason to join the oppressed people of Nicaragua when they arise and retaliate against the Mexican aggressors."

Perro Loco nodded, smiling for the first time since he heard about the loss of the aircraft fuel. "Good. Very good. And one of the first orders of business for our troops will be to capture the fuel dumps south of Mexico City. Without that aircraft fuel, our attack will be short-lived. We need our attack helicopters to lead the way to Mexico City."

Valdez cleared his throat and leaned forward in his chair. *"Comandante,* I know the United Nations will fail to act—

they always do—but what about this Ben Raines of the SUSA? When he hears we are advancing on Mexico City, he will surely come to their aid."

"That is why I am going to accept Osterman's offer of an alliance. She says she can keep Raines busy by resuming an attack on the SUSA from the north while I move from the south." He shrugged. "Even if she only delays his actions a few weeks, it will be enough. We will be in Mexico City and will have declared ourselves the rightful government by the time he finishes her off and turns his attention to us."

"And once we have Mexico, it is but a short step to the United States," Strunk added, rubbing his hands together.

"*Sí.* Now, bring me the *americano* who has the scrambler codes in his head. I wish to speak to Presidente Osterman at once."

Seventeen

"Goddamnit, Harlan, quit sniveling," Claire growled at Harlan Millard as she finished her twenty-fifth situp. She was proud of her "new body" and in her enthusiasm for fitness, had decreed that all of her new cabinet members would also get in shape.

Harlan, after only ten situps, was holding his groin and moaning. "I swear, Claire, I have a hernia and this exercise is aggravating it," he cried.

Herb Knoff, in the other corner, was doing pushup after pushup and barely working up a sweat. Claire noticed the way his arm muscles were bulging, and had to force her mind back to business and off his magnificent body, and the things he did to her with it.

Claire grabbed a towel off the counter and sat behind her desk. "All right, gentlemen, let's have a status report."

Harlan breathed a silent sigh of relief and crawled to his feet, wincing as he stretched muscles tight and sore from the exercise. He collapsed into a chair across from Claire and Herb sat next to him.

"Mr. Secretary of State," she said to Harlan, "what progress are we making in our negotiations with the U.N.?"

"Jean-François Chapelle has agreed to take the matter up with the Security Council, but he did state that he felt the answer would be not to interfere in the governmental process of a sovereign nation."

"That's bullshit!" Claire said, slamming her hand down

on her desk. "Those bastards tried to assassinate me and then they took over my country."

Harlan nodded. "You're right, of course, Madame President, but if we can't get Chapelle to push it for us, we stand little chance of any help from the U.N."

Claire turned angry eyes on Herb Knoff. "Mr. Vice President?"

In a confident voice, Herb said, "I don't think it's gonna matter, Claire. We're getting stronger every day. More and more of the old Blackshirt and FPPS squads are joining us, and even a lot of the regular troops that hate the prospect of losing their jobs with the new peace proposals."

"What about equipment and supplies?" she asked.

"Also no problem. Every man that comes has to bring something with him to get in. We now have over ten helicopters, five battle tanks, and even a couple of older-model jet fighters."

"Are we strong enough to go up against Otis Warner and his Army yet?"

"No, but if we can survive another month, I think it'll be possible."

Harlan cleared his throat. "Uh, Herb, why haven't they tried to attack us here at our home base? They must know what we're doing by now."

"Oh, they know, all right, and I'll bet it's got them plenty worried. Their problem is they don't know where we are. I've kept the original men who were stationed here on the communications gear, so as far as they know, all is well here. Warner and his crowd know we're out here, and they know we're actively recruiting and stealing men and equipment. They just don't have a clue as to where we are."

"All right, men, I think it's time we upped the ante in this game. Herb, I want you to work with General Bradley Stevens and have him send out some teams to begin a campaign of sabotage against the bases still controlled by Warner. Nothing too severe—I don't want to cripple too much equipment we might need when we go up against Raines and the SUSA later—but concentrate more on killing key personnel—officers and men who have shown their disloyalty to me."

"Got you," Herb said. "It shouldn't be too difficult since we can forge passes for the assassination teams that will allow them to pass freely through the countryside."

"I also want a team of your very best men to see if they can get close enough to Warner to take him or General Winter out," she added. "If Warner were to be executed, it would make it that much easier for me to resume my previous position as head of the government."

Herb frowned. "That's gonna be awfully difficult. Since he's become aware of your survival, my intel tells me he's doubled his normal security and no one is allowed even near his quarters unless they're known to be loyal to him."

She nodded. "I'm well aware it won't be easy, Herb, but see what you can do. He's got to stick his head up sooner or later if he's going to meet with Raines and Cecil Jeffreys to discuss the peace protocol. He'll be most vulnerable when he's traveling."

"Yes, ma'am."

Before she could continue, General Stevens knocked and entered the office, a look of excitement on his face.

"Claire, Perro Loco's on the horn, calling from Belize."

"Is it scrambled?" she asked.

"Yes. He's using the codes our men gave him."

"Put him on."

Stevens flipped a switch on the phone on Claire's desk, putting the call on a speaker-phone.

"Perro Loco, this is President Claire Osterman speaking. How are you?"

"I am fine, Madame President. I have received your offer of an alliance and wish to discuss the terms."

Claire was a bit surprised at how well the *bandido* spoke English. She had figured him for some South American clown who was barely literate, and now could barely discern an accent to his speech.

"Well, Perro Loco, the terms are simple. If you agree to attack Mexico immediately, I will agree to let you keep everything south of the Rio Grande River as your country."

"But Madame President, I will already have that without your assistance. What are you offering to do for me?"

Claire cocked an eyebrow at Stevens. This jungle idiot was smarter than she thought. "In the first place, Perro Loco, under the present status quo, you won't stand a chance of succeeding by yourself. If the USA and the SUSA are not at war, Ben Raines and his Army will be free to help Mexico, and with Raines on their side, Mexico will kick your butt all the way back to Nicaragua."

There was a pause, and Claire wondered if she'd gone too far. She knew these Latin types were very proud and wouldn't accept a slur on their macho manhood.

Finally, he came back on the line. "That may well be true. Mexico aligned with the SUSA would be a formidable opponent. Do you think you are in a strong enough position to keep that from happening, considering your . . . ah, recent problems?"

Claire had to bite her lip to keep from shouting back at the arrogant bastard. "Don't you worry about that, Perro Loco. Even now we are in the process of planning attacks against SUSA which will stop the peace process in its tracks. Once Raines has to worry about a possible resurgence of the hostilities between the USA and the SUSA, he will be forced to keep a large portion of his troops stationed on the borders up here and won't be able to send them against you."

"That is comforting, Madame President. If that turns out to be the case, then I am sure we can come to a mutually agreeable arrangement later. For now, on my part, I will agree to move my troops against Mexico immediately. If you *can* manage to keep Ben Raines out of the fight, then we have an agreement."

"Thank you, Perro Loco. I will be in touch."

After General Stevens pushed the button terminating the call, Claire growled, "That arrogant bastard. Who does he think he is to give ultimatums to me?"

Stevens took a seat across from Claire. "He's right on one point, Claire. We may not be strong enough at the present to keep Raines from helping Mexico."

"Bullshit!" She turned to Knoff. "Herb, you said we had a couple of fighter jets?"

"Yeah."

"I want them loaded to the gills with as much armament as possible and I want them to attack someplace in the SUSA. If they can manage to get past Raines's defenses now that they're not expecting an attack, it should get his attention."

"He's got a couple of battalions in Arkansas," Stevens said. "They're mostly infantry and won't have a lot of air defenses set up now that they think peace is at hand. We might be able to do a quick hit-and-run there."

"Then let's do it," she said. "It'll serve two purposes. Raines won't know for certain if Warner ordered it or I did, and Perro Loco will see that we can do our part to freeze Raines's troops in their present positions."

Stevens stood up. "I'll get right on it, Madame President."

"Herb," she said, pointing her finger at him, "I want those assassination teams on their way by the end of the week. Okay?"

"You got it, Claire."

Eighteen

Several thousand miles away, Perro Loco leaned forward and pushed the disconnect button on his phone. He took a deep drag on his Cuban cigar, blew dark smoke toward the ceiling, then looked at his companions across his desk.

"Paco, what do you think?"

Paco Valdez shrugged. "I think the lady may have some trouble doing all that she says she can. My information is that she is barely hanging on to her present position. She may sometime be able to take her government back, but not for a while yet."

"Mr. Strunk?"

"I agree," Jim Strunk said. "Even if she does manage to create some tensions between the SUSA and the USA, and Raines is forced to keep his troops on the border, that still leaves him with several battalions in Texas he can send against us. I think we'd better figure on having to fight both Mexico and Ben Raines."

"What do we know about him and his tactics?" Perro asked.

Strunk leaned over and pulled a thick sheaf of papers from a briefcase on the floor. "That American you killed, the one sent by Osterman, had these in his knapsack. They're copies of some journals kept by Raines during his African campaign, along with some article written by a newspaper correspondent who accompanied him during his fight down there. They seem to give some good insight into how he thinks and the strategy he employs in certain situations."

Loco held out his hand and took the papers from Strunk. "Good. I will study Mr. Ben Raines. I have learned, the more one knows of one's enemies, the easier to defeat them."

"Comandante," Valdez said, "do you want to begin the attack on Mexico?"

Loco nodded. "Yes. It is time to unleash our troops against our neighbors to the north. Send some air strikes to disable their radar and begin to move our men forward on all fronts. Meanwhile, I will read about Ben Raines to learn how he thinks and to see how he can be beaten."

The Apache helicopter gunship hugged the desert terrain of southern Mexico, flying at less than a thousand feet across the Guatemalan border near San Felipe where a Mexican radar installation swept the skies.

Captain Raul Rosales kept both hands on the controls, the yoke and the collectives, his feet applying just the right amount of pressure on the rotor pedals to keep the ship stable at low altitudes.

Captain Roque Vela sat in the gunner's position in front of the pilot.

"I have the radar signal on my HUT," Vela said, reporting what he could see on his Heads Up Targeting, a projection of a target signal that appeared to be displayed on the windshield of the gunship.

"Wait a moment longer," Rosales replied. "Comandante Perro Loco insists that this radar site must be taken out before the campaign to move northward across Mexico begins. San Felipe is the only radar installation the Mexicans have in this sector of the Yucatan."

"If they have missiles, we can't wait much longer," Vela said into his headset. "If we are to be sure of our safety, I should fire a missile soon."

"We have no missiles to waste, Roque. Wait until you are certain of your target."

"They may be tracking us on radar at his very moment," Vela replied. "It could be dangerous to wait much longer. They may be able to shoot us down from here. I say we should fire one missile and let it track the radar beam."

"This gunship is more important than the missiles we carry," Rosales said, dropping lower, to eight hundred feet, when his altimeter sounded an alarm. "This is a dangerous mission, Roque. We cannot fail . . . We must not fail. The radar installation at San Felipe has to be taken out."

"I understand, Captain."

"What do you see on your HUT?"

"Only the radar beams."

"We have to get closer. We must be sure."

The rhythmic churn of the rotor blades filled a moment of silence.

"What do you see now?" Rosales asked again.

"Only the signal, and it is weak."

"Do nothing," Rosales said. "We are below their targeting . . . even if the stupid Mexicans are awake so early in the morning to see that we are coming."

The altimeter read 750 feet as they flew across the southern fork of the Rio Candelaria, a dry riverbed this time of year. Below, there was nothing but rolling desert hills and flats. The Mexican military outpost at San Felipe was only a few miles away.

"I see something," Vela said.

"What is it?"

"I do not know. A spot on the display. It is moving toward us."

"A SAM," Rosales whispered into the microphone. "Find the target and fire a rocket. I'll drop down to five hundred feet and we'll see what happens. It won't be able to track us at low altitude."

Rosales slowed the rotor and tail turbine, losing altitude

as beads of sweat began to form on his brow. This was the tricky part . . . shooting down an enemy missile while avoiding a rocket fired from the ground. The older American-made Apaches were all but invisible to many radar screens. Only a few Soviet radar posts had the capability of seeing an incoming Apache above a thousand feet.

"I do not know how they spotted us," Vela said, fixing his targeting display.

"It will not matter *how* they did it," Rosales said. "Fire a rocket. Take the installation out or we will both be killed by their SAMs."

Captain Vela did as he was instructed. He pulled the trigger on one air-to-ground missile mounted on the belly of the Apache.

A trail of rocket vapor darted away from the craft. The Sparrow rocket traveled at speeds too fast for the naked eye to see.

Desert sands swirled upward from the prop-wash of the rotor blades.

"What do you see?" Rosales demanded, holding the ship at four hundred feet.

"Only the spot on the screen. It is headed straight for us."

Captain Rosales knew he had to take evasive action. He let the gunship drop lower . . . three hundred feet, and then two hundred feet.

Directly below them, from a grove of mesquite trees, he heard the stutter of machine-gun fire.

"Who the hell is shooting at us?" Captain Vela shouted, as the floor of the chopper rattled with the impact of bullets. *"Dios!* My left foot . . ."

A tuft of lint swirled away from the rear of Captain Vela's seat, followed by a stream of blood.

A change occurred in the sounds made by the helicopter, a clanging noise from the rear of the craft. Suddenly the ship began to swing in a circle.

"They shot out the rear turbine!" Rosales cried, trying to steady the chopper with the collectives.

Vela did not answer him . . . his head was lolled back against the seat, his hands free of the firing controls, resting in his lap.

"Son of a bitch!" Rosales roared when the Apache did not respond to the yoke or rotor pedals.

The heavy gunship plummeted downward at an odd angle, its nose pointed toward the ground while the tail made big looping circles.

"Shit!" Rosales spat, fighting the pull on his yoke, making every adjustment he had been trained to make when a helicopter lost its tail rotor.

The earth rushed toward him and Raul Rosales knew he was about to die.

"Dios," he screamed, then he began saying Hail Marys as fast as he could mouth the words, a prayer he knew from his childhood.

A shuddering crash sent him forward in the cockpit and his head slammed into the rear of Captain Vela's seat. He smelled fuel . . . and fire.

The main rotor chewed into the desert sands until it broke apart; then the main turbine stopped.

Rosales slumped forward upon impact and wondered about the silence around him.

His eyes batted shut.

Perry Osborn examined the wreckage, an M-16 dangling below his shoulder on a leather strap.

Justin Law approached what was left of the aircraft with his automatic rifle aimed in front of him. "You need to radio Ben. There are no markings on this Apache, so we don't know who it belongs to."

"I'm fairly sure it's part of the Nicaraguan's fleet," Perry replied.

"Then there may be something to all this bullshit about Mad Dog forming an army . . . Comandante Mad Dog."

"General Raines says our intelligence is good. The bastard calling himself Perro Loco is planning to move north. He'll take Mexico. Unless we stop him."

"Where do they come up with helicopter gunships like this?" Justin wanted to know.

"Captured after the drug wars in Colombia," Perry said, a keen eye on the chopper before they moved away from the mesquite thicket. "The old United States government sent dozens of these things down to help with the cocaine problem. Then all hell broke loose and nobody was left to keep track of where the Apache and Comanche gunships were."

"Then we're basically fighting our own technology," Justin remarked.

"It's technology from the past," Perry said. "But it still can be effective. Ben was right to send us down here after he heard what was going on."

"We need to let him know he was right about Perro Loco starting to move on Mexico."

Perry shook his head. "We can't. He's on a secret mission someplace to rescue one of his team."

"The woman . . . what was her name?"

"I heard it was Jersey, but no one's saying for certain. I do know she's very close to General Raines, whoever she is. Since General Raines is out of pocket, we'll inform Intel about the raid; they'll get the message to him."

"Let's make sure the sons of bitches aboard this thing are dead," Justin said.

"Nobody could have lived through this crash," Perry said in a low voice. "But like you say, we need to make damn sure there are no survivors."

"I'll come in from the other side," Justin whispered as they left the grove.

"Shoot anything that moves," Perry instructed. "We'll take any identification papers we find off the pilot and the gunner.

Damn lucky that this thing didn't explode when it hit the ground as hard as it did."

Raul woke up by degrees. At first he saw nothing but fog before his eyes. He heard voices . . . faint, far away, and his nostrils caught the strong scent of aircraft fuel when he came closer to consciousness.

"What happened?" he asked aloud, expecting an answer from Captain Vela.

Vela did not reply. Raul could see his helmet lying against the back of the gunner's seat.

"Roque?"

Raul became increasingly aware that his flight jacket and pants were doused with helicopter fuel. It was rare to survive a crash in a chopper, and even more unlikely that the ship had not exploded upon impact.

"Roque?" The voices were louder now, and Raul was sure he heard them distinctly . . . but Roque was not moving. Who was talking to him?

The enemy, he thought. A squad of Mexican machine-gunners had shot them down and now they were coming for him. There was no other explanation for the voices.

Numbed by the impact of the crash, he reached for his Luger 9mm pistol belted to his side.

"Be careful," a voice said in English.

Raul drew his pistol.

"One of them's still moving. I can see his head bobbing up and down."

And now Rosales knew he was surrounded by the enemy. But why were they speaking English?

He lifted his weapon and aimed through a splintered side window of the Apache.

"Look out!" a voice cried. "One of them's alive and he's got a gun!"

Rosales blinked. He tried to find a target in the blur of brush and trees outside the helicopter.

"Don't waste a shot," another, deeper voice said. "A match will do a better job."

Rosales heard a match being struck. Then he saw a billowing cloud of flames.

"Ayiii!" he shrieked as his flight suit erupted in a ball of fire.

The crackle of spreading flames was the last sound Captain Raul Rosales heard. He was consumed by an inferno, and when he opened his mouth to scream, he inhaled a mouthful of fire that made his lungs feel like burning cinders.

Nineteen

Harley Reno walked down the belly of the C-130 checking each member of the drop team's oxygen masks and rigging for the HALO drop.

"Remember," he shouted to be heard over the roar of the four big engines of the aircraft, "watch your altitude gauge on your wrists. If the automatic pressure release doesn't work, you've got about five seconds to do it manually; otherwise it's *adios, amigo* and we'll be picking you up in a sponge."

Anna glanced at Ben, standing next to her. "That's a cheerful thought," she said.

Ben nodded, his mind already on the planned meeting with their contact in Belize, El Gato Selva. Gato had radioed them coordinates for the drop, and promised to meet them and hopefully lead them to the area where Coop and Jersey had disappeared. Ben hoped they weren't dropping into a trap, for he knew little about Gato other than he hated Perro Loco and wanted him dead.

Reno stepped to the open cargo door of the big airplane and stood next to Scott Hammer Hammerick, who would be the first to jump. All eyes in the plane were on the twin lights at the front of the cabin, waiting for red to change to green signaling a go.

When the green light began flashing, Reno tapped Hammer on the shoulder and he dove out of the door. Anna was next, then Corrie and Ben. Reno went last, dipping his head in a dive that was to last almost five miles.

As he arrowed down through air that was seventy degrees below zero at that altitude, Ben wondered briefly if he was crazy to be doing such a stunt at his age. *Who says they can't teach an old dog new tricks,* he thought as he gripped his chute-release button in his right hand and stared fixedly at the altitude meter on his left wrist. He didn't dare look at the green jungle rushing up at him at almost two hundred miles an hour. Reno had said more than one sky diver had been killed when so mesmerized by the sight of the onrushing ground that he failed to open his chute in time.

Just as Ben started to punch his release button, thinking his altitude sensor had failed, his chute deployed, almost jerking his head off.

He hit the ground going twenty miles an hour, and tucked and rolled as he'd been taught years before in paratrooper school. As he came to his feet, he whipped his SPAS 12-gauge assault shotgun around his body and cradled it in his arms, crouching and looking around for enemies.

The coordinates Gato had given them were for a large, open field, to minimize the danger of injury from attempting to land in the rain-forest canopy. Ben squatted and glanced around him. He was standing in a field of poppies. Evidently, growing the plant that heroin was made from was one of the ways Gato financed his insurrection attempts against Perro Loco.

Ben shook his head, a dark smile on his face. He wasn't crazy about teaming up with a man who grew and presumably sold heroin, but he knew war made for strange bedfellows. Besides, Ben was a nihilist about such things as drug control. He figured if a person wanted to ruin his life for a temporary high, that was his business, as long as they didn't try to finance their habit by robbing other people. Drug use was the mark of a stupid person, and Ben had no use for stupid people.

Within ten minutes, the team had gathered in a loose-knit

group, not standing too close together in case they came under attack.

Reno stepped to Ben's side. "We'd better get out of the open and under cover, Boss," he said.

Ben shook his head. "Harley, on this mission, you're the boss. This is your neck of the woods and you and Hammer are the resident experts in scouting, so take the point."

Reno nodded and waved his hand over his head, leading the others toward the safety of the thick jungle ahead. Just prior to reaching it, a man in khaki BDUs (Battle Dress Uniform) stepped from the forest, his hands over his head to show he was not a hostile.

"Welcome, General Raines," El Gato said.

Behind Gato they could see several men, all of whom looked thoroughly dangerous in their jungle cammies carrying Russian-made AK-47's in their arms.

Ben nodded and shook hands with Gato. "This is Harley Reno, my team leader. He's familiar with this country and he will be leading my team until we're extracted," Ben said.

Gato spoke a couple of sentences in rapid Spanish to Reno, and grinned when Reno answered him in an equally fluent manner.

"*Bueno,*" Gato said, then waved his arm and added, "*Vamos!*"

As Gato's men led the way down barely discernible jungle trails, Reno asked him, "Do you have a probable location for our people?"

Gato smiled. "Yes. A convoy carrying considerable amounts of airplane fuel was destroyed a couple of days ago, and all of the men in the convoy were not only killed, but mutilated."

Reno nodded. He knew it was the work of Jersey, using a well-known scouting technique to spread fear and terror among natives.

"Not only that," Gato continued, "but the fuel was . . . how you say . . . booby-trapped. The explosion came within inches of killing two of Perro Loco's most important men, and did manage to wipe out the entire force sent to rescue the fuel."

Ben laughed. "I knew Coop and Jersey wouldn't go quietly into the night. Leave it to them to kill a bunch of the enemy to let us know where they are."

Gato cut his eyes at Ben. "Then you also believe this attack was a deliberate attempt to advise us of their position in the jungle?"

"Of course," Ben answered. "If they wanted to stay under cover, all they had to do was avoid the patrols." He shook his head. "No. The communications equipment they have is only useful up to a distance of about five miles, maybe less in this mountainous region. They knew we'd be coming after them and had to give us an approximate location to start our search."

Gato nodded approvingly. "Your people are very well trained to be able to anticipate your moves."

"We've been together a long time and been through a lot together. They knew I'd never leave a member of my team hanging."

Gato pointed. Up ahead Ben could see several vehicles covered with camouflage paint parked under a canopy of trees so they wouldn't be visible from the air. They looked to be vintage World War II jeeps.

"There is our transportation. We should be at the approximate location within two hours," Gato said.

"Good. The sooner the better," Ben replied as he climbed into the back of a jeep.

Coop slapped at his neck and softly cursed as he and Jersey walked through jungle as thick as any he'd ever seen in Africa. "Damn bugs think I'm a walkin' buffet," he said.

Jersey, who was in the lead, glanced back over her shoulder. "Quit whining, Coop. It could be worse."

"Oh? And how is that?"

She smiled wickedly. "There could be snakes," she purred, referring to Coop's well-known phobia of snakes. In Africa, during the campaign against the Neo-Nazis, he'd been attacked by a snake, and in his terror fallen into a river and gotten washed downstream and lost in the jungle. Jersey had vowed to never let him forget that episode.

He stopped and pointed a finger at her. "You promised not to mention that again."

She kept walking, shaking her head. "No, I didn't. You asked me not to, but I didn't say I wouldn't."

"Bitch," he muttered as he scrambled to catch up with her.

"Asshole," she replied without turning around.

Both were smiling.

Sounds of a motorized vehicle up ahead caused Jersey to hold up her hand and duck down behind foliage. Coop followed suit, swinging his M-16 around and slowly cocking it.

Crawling on hands and knees through thick underbrush, Jersey made her way forward until she could peer out from behind a giant elephant-ear plant. They were on the outskirts of a small village—only half a dozen grass-covered huts in a circular clearing.

A road that wasn't much more than a footpath led off to the side, and two jeeps were standing empty at the edge of the clearing.

Angry voices could be heard coming from the village, but from where they sat they couldn't see anything. Suddenly a woman screamed and a gunshot rang out.

Jersey turned an angry face toward Coop. "You ready to dance?"

He nodded. "Damn right, podna."

They eased out of the brush and made their way toward the sounds, keeping a hut between them and the soldiers they knew were on the other side.

As they looked around the wall, they saw six soldiers standing in front of about fifteen natives. One of the women was trying to hold the torn remnants of her dress together as she wept hysterically and stared at an older man lying dead on the ground next to her.

"He should not have interfered," a soldier with sergeant markings on his sleeve said. He stepped forward and forced her hands down, letting her dress open and expose her breasts.

He grabbed them with both hands and roughly kneaded them, as if he were trying to make bread dough. "How you like this, bitch?" he snarled. "Now that your man is dead, maybe I come back and show you good time, huh?"

Another man stepped forward, holding his hands out. "We told you, *señor,* we have not seen any *americanos.* We are but a poor village. We have done nothing wrong."

"Let's go," Jersey whispered. "I'll take the one on the left."

"Got'cha," Coop answered.

They stepped out into the open, M-16's leveled in front of them. Of the six soldiers, only two had weapons drawn and ready.

Coop and Jersey's rifles barked, sending the two men to Hell as slugs ripped them apart.

As the other soldiers reached for their weapons, Coop raised his carbine and yelled, "Freeze!"

One didn't; instead he clawed at a pistol on his belt. Coop shot him in the face, snapping his head back and throwing him spread-eagled in the dirt.

The other three slowly raised their hands, fear-sweat covering their faces and staining their khaki BDUs.

"Who is in command here?" Jersey asked.

The men looked at each other; then the one with sergeant stripes said, "I am."

"What is your name?"

"Sergeant Miguel Hernandez."

She looked at the woman holding her dress. "Is this the man who shot your husband?" she asked.

The native woman nodded once, her eyes glittering with hate at the sergeant.

Jersey looked back at Hernandez. "Are you currently at war with these people?"

"Huh?"

"You heard me."

"Uh . . . no."

"Then you've committed murder, and I sentence you to death."

"What?"

Jersey pulled her K-Bar and glanced at the crying woman, her eyebrows upraised as she held out the knife.

Without a word the woman grabbed the knife and plunged it into the gut of the sergeant, twisting and jerking it as he screamed and doubled over in pain. He looked up at the woman and she spat in his face. Then he fell to the ground and died.

"Muchas gracias," she whispered to Jersey, before leaning over her dead husband and cradling his head in her arms.

Jersey bent over and pulled her K-Bar from Hernandez's stomach, wiping the bloody blade on his shirt.

Coop picked up one of the soldiers' AK-47's and handed it to the villager who'd spoken up earlier. "We'll leave these two in your care."

When the man gave him a questioning look, Coop added, "You know you can't let them go back alive after this."

The man nodded, a slow grin on his face. "The jungle is a very dangerous place. There are many big animals."

Coop grinned back. "We'll take both of the jeeps and get rid of them a long way from here."

"Gracias, señor."

As Jersey and Coop climbed in the jeeps, one of the soldiers yelled, "Please, don't leave us here with them!"

Jersey glanced at Coop. "I always say, let the punishment fit the crime."

Coop nodded and picked up the handset to the radio in

the jeep. He thumbed the microphone and said, "Hey, Perro Loco. This is the man you're lookin' for speakin'. If you want me, you're gonna have to send better men than this, you stupid son of a bitch."

Jersey grinned as she climbed in the other jeep and started the motor. "Oh, that ought to get his attention."

"You think so?" Coop asked, starting his jeep. "I'll race you to the river."

Jersey looked puzzled. "What river?"

He shrugged. "This is a jungle, Jers, there's always a river."

Twenty

When he was told of the loss of yet another patrol to the *americanos* and of the taunting message sent by one of them over the radio, Perro Loco flew into a rage.

He called General Juan Dominguez, the head of his forces in Belize, into his office. "General," he said, his eyes bright with anger, "why is it your troops are unable to capture two Americans who are lost in the jungle?"

"But *comandante*," Dominguez began.

Perro Loco pulled a Colt .45 pistol from his belt and stuck it against the general's forehead. "No excuses!" he screamed. "If your men continue to fail, I will be forced to accept your resignation, General, and I am quite sure your family will mourn your sudden death as well."

Sweat poured from the general's forehead as he quickly nodded. *"Sí, mi comandante.* I will take personal charge of the search from now on."

Loco holstered his pistol and turned away, dismissing the man with a curt wave of his hand.

Jim Strunk and Paco Valdez, sitting across the room, both breathed a sigh of relief. They knew Dominguez was a good soldier and were glad Loco hadn't killed him.

"Comandante," Strunk said, holding up a sheaf of papers in his hand. "These Americans are capable fighters. I have here some journals and articles written by a newspaperman during Ben Raines's campaign in Africa a couple of years

ago. Some of the journals are said to have been written by Raines himself."

"Where did you get those?" Loco asked.

"They were in the possession of the *americano* sent by President Osterman. An accompanying note from her says they are for you to read to learn how Raines thinks, how he plans his battles." Strunk shrugged. "They might be useful."

Loco took the papers and set them on his desk. He walked to the corner bar and poured himself a drink, then lit a cigar and sat down to read. "I will see just how formidable an opponent this Ben Raines is," he said, picking up the papers.

"The first part there is a series of articles outlining how Raines and his Rebels came to power," Strunk said. "It was written by a war correspondent for the United Press, Robert Barnes."

"As North America began to slowly pull itself out of the greatest economic and social collapse in world history, Ben Raines found himself to be the most hated man in all of America. That really didn't come as any surprise to Ben, for right after the collapse, Ben had gathered together a small group called the Rebels—a mixture of political/militia/survivalist-oriented men and women—and told them, 'We're going to rebuild. Against all odds, we're going to carve out our own nation. And we're going to be hated for our success.'

"As it turned out, hate was not nearly a strong enough word. Ben and his Rebels first went to the northwest and settled what would be forever known as the Tri-States, developing the Tri-States form of government. The philosophy was based on personal responsibility and common sense. It soon became a hated form of government for those living outside the Tri-States, for liberals and other left-wingers don't want to be responsible for anything they do and they don't appear to possess any common sense.

" 'Of course, that isn't entirely true,' Ben once said in one of his rarely granted interviews with the press. 'But that's the way it seems to those of us who believe that government should stay out of the lives of its citizens as much as possible.'

"In the Tri-States, if you got careless and stuck yourself in the face with the business end of a screwdriver, you didn't sue the manufacturer of the screw driver for damages . . . You learned to be more careful in handling tools.

"Common sense.

"Ben Raines realized that not everyone could, or would, live under a system of law that leaned heavily on common sense and personal responsibility. From the outset he estimated, correctly, as it turned out, that no more than two or three out of every ten Americans could live under a Tri-States form of government. People who came to live in the old Tri-States did not expect something for nothing . . . and that was wise on their part, for they damn sure weren't going to get something for nothing.

"In the Tri-States, everybody who was able worked at something. No able-bodied person sat on their ass and expected free handouts from the taxpayers . . . That just wasn't going to happen. You might not like the job that would be found for you, and it would be found very quickly, but you worked it, or you got out.

"Criminals discovered almost immediately that in the Tri-States, they had very few rights. All the rights belonged to the law-abiding citizens. If a criminal got hurt during the commission of a crime, he or she could not sue for damages. If they got killed, their family could not sue for damages. And in the Tri-States, a lot of criminals got killed during the first years. The Tri-States was not a friendly place for criminals . . . and it didn't take criminals long to discover that. The residents of the Tri-States didn't have a problem with drugs; the penalty for selling hard drugs was death; when caught, and after a very brief trial, the criminals had a choice, hanging or firing squad. Consequently, very soon drug dealing in the Tri-States dropped off to zero.

"Life was so good in the Tri-States, the central government, once it got back on its feet after only a few years, couldn't stand it and moved against the Tri-Staters. It was a terrible battle, but in the end the old Tri-States, located in the northwest, was destroyed.

"But Ben Raines and his dream lived, and Ben gathered together the survivors of the government assault, and declared war on the government . . . a dirty, nasty, hit-and-destroy-and-run type of guerrilla warfare.

"Eventually, the entire United States collapsed inward and Ben and his Rebels, now hundreds and hundreds strong, were able to move into the South and set up a new government. This time it was called the SUSA: the Southern United States of America.

"It was a struggle for a few years, and one time the SUSA was overrun by rabble from outside its borders. But the Rebels beat the attackers back and rebuilt their nation, larger and stronger and more self-sufficient than ever before.

"The Rebels are now the largest and most powerful and feared fighting force in the free world, so much so that the Secretary General of the newly reorganized United Nations met with Ben Raines and made a bargain with him: You deal with a few trouble spots around the world, especially with Bruno Bottger and his band of Nazis, and we'll recognize the SUSA as a free and sovereign nation.

"The two men shook hands, sealing the deal, and Ben took his Rebels and sailed off to Africa. Ben and his Rebels were ready for the big push southward. The hundreds of replacement troops, all fresh from the SUSA and green as a gourd when they deplaned weeks back, were now combat-tested and hardened. In the weeks they had been in Africa, they had seen sights that toughened them mentally; they had learned what every experienced combat soldier learns: You shove the bloody, awful sights into a secret part of your brain and close and lock the door . . . and keep on doing your job."

* * *

Loco glanced up from his reading. "I do not understand why Raines would take his army halfway around the world to fight a man who posed no threat to his country."

Strunk shrugged. "Raines is something of an idealist. He is always ready to fight what he thinks is evil, whether it benefits him or not."

Loco's eyes narrowed. "Such men are dangerous. They do not always act in ways which are logical, and thus their moves are harder to predict, and to counter."

Twenty-one

Loco looked back down at the papers in his hand.

"The next part is a combination of journals written by Raines and notes kept by the war correspondent who accompanied his Army on its move through Africa," Strunk said.

"Good. I want to see how Raines thinks in battle," Loco said as he began to read . . .

"Ben's 501 Brigade was halted on the Cameroon/Gabon border, just north of Bata. The other brigades were stretched out across Africa, all the way over to Mogadishu, Somalia. They waited for Ben's orders to move out.

"Ike's 502 Brigade was just to Ben's east, on the Congo's west border. Thermopolis's 19 Batt, which kept up with everything going on, and not just concerning the Rebels, was in the center of the ten brigades. Pat O'Shea's 510 Brigade was on the coast of the Indian Ocean, almost twenty-five hundred miles away from Ben. Doctor Lamar Chase, the Rebel Army's Chief of Medicine, was traveling with Ben's brigade. The brigades had traveled several hundred miles since reforming and so far had seen only limited action, most of it coming from gangs of thugs.

"All that was about to change.

"For the past week, Ben and the Rebels had made good time, considering the condition of the roads, in some cases, almost nonexistent. Ben and his 501 Brigade had traveled south through the western portion of Cameroon and found very little resistance. They had seen thousands of human skeletons, their deaths brought on by war, sickness, starvation, and Bruno Bottger's deadly laboratory-concocted virus that he'd unleashed on the population.

"But the animals had made a miraculous comeback. The Rebels saw dozens of prides of lions. They saw leopards and hyenas and wild dogs and what appeared to be thousands of different species of birds. Scouts reported all sorts of animals ahead of the main force.

" 'Gorillas,' Cooper, Ben's driver, said. 'I want to see some gorillas.'

" 'Go look in the mirror,' Jersey, Ben's diminutive bodyguard, told him.

"Beth, the statistician, looked up from the tattered travel guide she was reading and smiled at Ben, then returned to her reading.

"Corrie, the radio tech, was busy yapping with somebody about something, her headset on, and didn't hear the exchange. She probably wouldn't have paid any attention to it anyway, for Jersey and Cooper had been hurling barbs at one another for years.

"Anna, Ben's adopted daughter, squatted in the shade of a large bush, sharpening one of her knives, which was already razor-sharp. The young woman, taken in by Ben during the Rebels' European campaign, was in her late teens, and deadly. She had been orphaned while just a child—when the Great War swept the globe—and had fought for every scrap of food while growing up. Ben had seen something worthwhile in the dirty face of the waif, and taken her in to raise during her formative teenage years.

"And that was Ben's personal team. They had been together for a long time, through both good and bad times.

" 'Bruno's people have pulled back, Boss,' Corrie announced, removing her headset. 'All the way across Africa. They packed it up and headed south.'

" 'They didn't do it because they're afraid of us,' Ben said, rolling a cigarette. He looked at her. 'Were they in a hurry when they hightailed it out of here?'

" 'Didn't seem to be. Scouts report they left nothing usable behind.'

"Corrie paused for a moment. 'Except a lot of dead people,' she added.

" 'Is anyone reporting any action at all?' Ben asked. 'Anywhere?'

" 'Nothing, Boss.'

" 'This will slow us down to a crawl," Ben said. 'I want every bridge, every mile of road, checked for mines. If the village or town is deserted, it's probably filled with explosives. Do we have anybody left in South Africa . . . or what used to be called South Africa?'

" 'Not any more,' Beth told him. 'The last batch of our people that we'd sent in about eighteen months ago just got out alive a few weeks ago.'

"Ben nodded in understanding. He lit his hand-rolled cigarette and frowned, silent for a few heartbeats. 'Bruno's going to bug out,' he finally said. 'Bet on it. He's going to buy some time by sacrificing his troops and then bug out through the southernmost ports, taking his top people and his best troops with him. That's the only thing that makes any sense. He knows he's finished here in Africa . . . He can see the end in sight. He's anything but a stupid man. Arrogant as hell, but brilliant in his own right.'

" 'Where in the hell's he going to bug out to, Boss?' Cooper asked.

" 'My guess would be South America,' Ben replied. 'The last word we got was that there wasn't a stable government in any country down there. Corrie, tell Mike Richards to send some people into South America. See what they can dig up.'

" 'Will do.'

" 'No point in pulling out until we've got a few miles of

road cleared. Have the Scouts or any flybys found any usable railroad tracks?'

" 'Negative, Boss. Bruno's people destroyed miles of track and blew the railroad bridges.'

" 'We can expect the same all the way down,' Ben said. 'And for the roads to get worse. We're in for some slow going.' Ben opened his map case and pulled out a map of Gabon, studying it for a moment.

" 'We'll avoid Libreville,' he said. 'We don't need to use the port and all we'll find is trouble there. Place is filled to overflowing with sick and dying people.' Ben shook his head. 'Doctor Chase and his people say there is nothing we can do for them. Nothing at all. Except let them die in peace,' he added softly.

" 'Bruno's virus?' Anna said, standing up and sheathing her long-bladed knife.

" 'Not so much that,' Ben replied. 'But that is certainly a part of their trouble. Chase's people say just name a disease, they've got it.'

" 'When are the Israelis going to join us?' Cooper asked.

" 'They're not,' Ben said. 'They're fighting on three fronts. We just got word that a dozen or more Arab resistance groups formed up and began attacking. The Israelis have their hands full. I wished them good luck and told them we'd handle this. Corrie, radio everyone to stand down and relax. We'll make this push south slow and careful.'

"The Rebels pushed off two days later and advanced thirty miles. Then they waited for two more days before pushing off again, and again they advanced thirty miles. They met no resistance anywhere along the 2500-mile front, running east to west. Bruno Bottger's troops had definitely bugged out to the south . . . how far south was still up for grabs.

" 'But we've still got hundreds of gangs roaming around,' Ben cautioned. 'Ranging in size from twenty to a thousand.'

" 'You think a small bunch of punks would attack us?' Ben was asked by a young sergeant. The sergeant was fresh from the SUSA and his combat experience was sparse. 'It would be suicide for a small gang to attack a full brigade.'

"Ben's XO, John Michaels, opened his mouth to tell the young sergeant to get back to his squad and don't bother the CG with stupid questions.

"Ben held up a hand. 'I didn't say they were smart gangs, Sergeant,' Ben told him. 'Although we don't ever want to underestimate their intelligence . . . Many of them are very cunning. Just like criminals in every country in the world. If they would use that intelligence for something constructive, they would be useful and productive, helping out their country and the people. But they never do that. They think they're smarter than everyone else. If they hit us, and I think they probably will, very soon, they'll come at us with ambushes and sneak attacks, hit and run. So, heads up, son.'

" 'Yes, sir,' the young sergeant said, and got the hell out of that area.

"The hundreds and hundreds of men and women in the miles-long column mounted up and moved slowly on to the south.

" 'Boring,' Anna said, looking out the window of the big wagon as they proceeded on, at about fifteen miles per hour. The roads were in terrible shape. In many areas of the sprawling continent, roads were no more than a faint memory.

" 'Scouts report the bridge is out about five miles ahead,' Corrie said.

"Ben lifted a map, studied it for a moment, and then cussed. 'There are no highways at all to the west, and it would put us fifty miles out of the way to head east to the next crossing. And on these miserable excuses for roads, it would take us two or three days to travel that distance.' He sighed. 'Get the engineers up here, Corrie.'

" 'Right, Boss. They're on their way.'

" 'It'll take some time, General,' the officer in command of this detachment of combat engineers told Ben. 'The rest of the day and part of tomorrow, at least. That's a hell of a section blown out.'

"Ben nodded. 'Fix it.'

" 'Yes, sir.' The combat engineer started yelling orders to his people.

"Ben glanced at his watch. thirteen-hundred hours. The column had made lousy time since pulling out that morning. At this rate it would take them several months to reach the south part of the continent. And that would give Bruno more than ample time to throw up a front that would be tough to punch through.

"Ben sighed and shook his head as he looked around him. The terrain would be perfect for an ambush. 'Corrie, no one moves more than a few yards away from this cow path they call a road until the area has been checked out.'

" 'Right, Boss.'

" 'Scouts out east and west.'

" 'Done, Boss.'

"Ben smiled as he leaned up against the big wagon and began rolling a cigarette. Corrie always stayed about two steps ahead of him. The team had been together for so long, each member knew how the other would react and in most cases, orders were merely routine, given out of long habit.

" 'Any towns or villages close by?' Cooper asked.

" 'Why?' Jersey asked. 'You planning on going in and checking out the night life?'

" 'I thought I might buy you a nice present,' Cooper said, coming right back at her.

" 'The best present you could get me would be to lose your voice for about a year or so.'

" 'Oh, my little desert flower,' Cooper said, feigning great personal pain. 'You know you don't mean that. Just the thought hurts my heart. You'd miss me like the flowers would miss a gentle rain.'

" 'Blahh! Yukk! Barf!' Jersey said. 'That's disgusting, Cooper.' She made an awful face, and moved around to the other side of the vehicle, muttering, 'Guy gets worse every month.' But out of Cooper's sight, the awful face vanished and she smiled. She and Cooper were good and close friends . . . They just liked to stick the needle to each other.

"The first section of the Bailey Bridge was hauled up and off-loaded. The engineers were laying it out when the mortar rounds began falling. Two of the combat engineers were killed and half a dozen wounded in the first barrage.

"Ben and his team left the road and jumped for the cover of thick brush that lined both sides of the old highway. 'If they hit that new wagon, I'm gonna be really pissed!' Cooper said, setting up his SAW (Squad Automatic Weapon).

" 'You better hope one of those rounds doesn't land on your ass,' Jersey told him.

" 'That would irritate me too,' Cooper replied.

" 'But only very briefly,' Jersey replied.

"The first span over which the engineers had to build a new temporary bridge was about fifty yards wide . . . but it was right in the center. The second section that had been knocked out was on the other side, the connecting span.

" 'I figure about a hundred meters from our position,' Ben said. 'Give that to the tank commanders, Corrie.'

" 'Right, Boss,' she replied.

"A minute later the main guns of the battle tanks began howling and roaring. The first few rounds were short, the range quickly corrected, and then the tanks began laying down a field of fire that virtually destroyed everything on the other side of the sluggish river.

" 'Cease fire,' Ben ordered, looking up into the sky. 'Here come the gunships.'

"The gunships began strafing the other side of the river bank with machine-gun fire and rockets. They worked back and forth for a couple of minutes. Ben bumped the flight commander on his two-way and gave orders for them to back off. 'Scouts, find a place to get across that river and check it out,' he said.

" 'Chopper pilots reporting no signs of life over there, Corrie said. 'But plenty of dead bodies.'

" 'Good,' Ben said. 'Throw them in the river and let the crocs have them.'

" 'Are there crocodiles in that river?' Cooper questioned.

" 'Probably,' Ben told him. Ben didn't know if there were any crocs in the river or not . . . but if he had to make a bet, he'd bet there were. Either way, the river was certainly going to be ordered off limits for swimming.

"About five minutes later, after the firing had stopped and the area was quiet once again, Dr. Lamar Chase, the Rebels' Chief of Medicine, came walking up. His driver had brought him as close to the head of the column as she could; then Chase had hoofed the last several hundred yards. Chase and Ben had been together since the very beginning; their friendship spanned many years. The doctor stood for a moment, watching his doctors work on the wounded, then turned to Ben.

" 'You think those troops that ambushed us were Bruno's men, Ben?'

"Ben shook his head. 'No. It would really surprise me if they were. Probably just one of the many hundreds of gangs that prowl and slither around this continent. Scouts are checking it out now.'

" 'I certainly hope you cautioned them not to fall out of the damn boats,' Chase warned. 'There are probably crocs in that river.'

"Ben cut his eyes, grunted a noncommittal reply, and continued to watch the scout teams as they cranked the outboards and headed for the opposite shore.

" 'One of the wounded just died,' Corrie said. 'The others are going to make it.'

" 'Who died?' Ben asked.

" 'Major Larsen.'

" 'Shit,' Ben muttered. He sighed. 'Bury them off the road

in the brush. Deep and well. I don't want animals digging them up. Get a chaplain up here.'

" 'OK, Boss.'

"Major Larsen had been with Ben for years, starting out with the Rebels when he was just an enlisted man in his teens and working his way up through the ranks. He was well liked by everyone and would be sorely missed.

"Chase looked at Ben's face for a moment and said, 'Watch your blood pressure, Ben. These things happen.'

" 'My blood pressure is fine, Lamar.'

" 'Then what's wrong?'

" 'This damn country.'

"Chase grunted in response, frowning as Ben began rolling a cigarette.

" 'Of course, wait until we hit South America,' Ben said. 'Then we'll really get bogged down in certain areas.''

" 'Is that where we go next?'

" 'Probably. You can bet that's where Bruno's heading . . . if he makes it out of Africa alive, and he will. The bastard has more luck than a leprechaun. He can't go back to Europe, that's for sure. He's the most wanted man on the continent.' "

Perro Loco looked up from his reading. "Paco, I want you to check with our contacts in South America. Evidently this man Bottger had resources there that might be useful to us in our upcoming battle against Raines and the SUSA."

Paco Valdez nodded, making a note in a small notebook he carried in his shirt pocket.

Loco got up, stretched, refilled his drink, and resumed his reading . . .

"Chase waited for Ben to continue, sensing there was more. He was right.

" 'The Secretary General warned me that we might go to South America when we finished here.' Ben shrugged. 'It was all part of the deal we made.'

" 'A deal that isn't worth the paper it's written on or the handshake that sealed it,' Doctor Chase said. 'You don't believe for a minute the federal government outside the SUSA will keep their end of the bargain. Do you?'

"Ben smiled. 'Of course not, Lamar. I wouldn't trust a liberal out of my sight. But it bought us some time. Much-needed time.'

" 'They don't believe you'll use nuclear and germ weapons against them, Ben.'

" 'Then they don't know or understand me at all, Lamar. I will personally push the buttons that lets the birds fly if they invade us. Those crybaby assholes had damn well better understand that. And don't think for a second Cecil won't do it . . . because he damn sure will.'

"Chase studied Ben's face for a few seconds. 'Yes. Cecil will push the buttons. I'm sure of that. But do you think the SUSA will be invaded? Do you believe the federal government will really take that chance?'

"Ben lit his hand-rolled cigarette and was silent for a few heartbeats, letting a very slight breeze slip the smoke away.

"When he spoke, his words were low. 'Yes, I do, Lamar. But I'm still undecided as to whether it's going to be an all-out assault or a guerrilla, hit-and-run attempt.'

" 'What do Mike's people have to say about it?'

"Mike Richards was the Rebels' Chief of Intelligence.

" 'That some type of action against us is being planned. But they're unable, so far, to break into the inner circle and pin anything down.'

" 'Doesn't leave us much to go on, does it?'

"Ben smiled. 'Not a whole lot, Lamar. Except we know it's coming. But not when or how.'

"The two men stood in silence as the wounded combat

engineers were transported back to a clearing to be worked on in a MASH facility.

"One of the medics walked back to Ben and Lamar. 'One is going to lose a leg, I think. The others will be back on limited duty before long.'

"Lamar thanked the medic, and the young woman nodded and walked away. No one saluted in a combat zone.

" 'I am beginning to truly hate this place,' Ben said. 'I know I shouldn't, but I do. Not the people, at least not most of them, but the place.'

" 'If it'll make you feel any better, Ben, the country doesn't thrill me all that much either. Even though much of it is quite beautiful.'

" 'Scouts found several alive over there,' Corrie said. 'They're bringing three of them across now.'

" 'Do they speak English?' Ben asked.

" 'Oh, yes, sir," Corrie replied. 'They sure do. They're Americans.' The three men had suffered only very minor wounds and their wounds had been attended to. They were all in good physical shape, strong and certainly very healthy-appearing. Ben studied the trio for several moments before speaking. He did not like what he was thinking.

" 'How'd you boys get to Africa?' Ben finally asked.

" 'Greyhound,' the bigger of the three popped back.

" 'Oh,' Ben said with a smile. 'A sense of humor. That's good. You're damn sure going to need one. Now, I'll ask again: How did you boys get over here?'

" 'Plane,' the oldest of the three volunteered.

" 'When?' Ben asked.

" 'Six, seven months ago,' the same man replied. 'I'm not sure. Time sort of runs together over here.'

"Ben silently and certainly agreed with the man about that. 'Go on.'

" 'What do you mean, sir?'

" 'Who paid you to come over here? How many of you came over? And why?'

" 'Keep your damn mouth shut, Leon,' the first man to speak said.

" 'Screw you, Jimmy,' the oldest man said. He looked back at Ben. 'Two battalions.'

" 'Mercenaries,' Ben said.

" 'Yes, sir.'

" 'All Americans?'

" 'Most of them, yes, sir. But other nationalities mixed in there, too. A few Canadians, half a dozen or so Germans and Russians. Some English.'

"Ben again studied the three for a moment. They were dressed in cammie BDUs. Because of the way they were dressed, he couldn't threaten them with being spies, and they probably were well aware of that. 'Who's paying you?'

"This time, the bigger man spoke. 'That we don't know, General. You can believe it or not, but it's the truth.'

"Ben believed him. But he also had a damn good idea who was paying the men. 'More mercenaries coming over?'

" 'Yes, sir,' the third man said. 'I can tell you for a fact that recruiting has been going on for a long time.'

"Ben nodded. 'And a long time is . . . how long?'

" 'Over a year, General.'

"There were a lot more questions Ben wanted to ask, but he would save it and turn the man over to Intelligence for more interrogation. He hoped they would be honest with Ben's Intel team, for if they sensed the men were lying, it could get very nasty when they hauled out the drugs. Not painful, not physical torture, but the men would tell the truth . . . Bet on that.

" 'What happens to us now, General?' the youngest of the trio asked.

" 'You'll be turned over to our Intelligence section for further questioning. I urge you to cooperate with them.'

" 'In other words,' the big one said, 'here come the needle and the drugs.'

" 'In other words,' Ben replied, his smile rather grim, 'you're right.'

" 'We're over here fighting for money, General. Not for any political philosophy or cause. They won't need to use drugs on us. We'll tell them what they want to know . . . as much as we can. Which isn't much.'

"Ben believed that. He was reasonably sure the men had been recruited by a third party; that was the way it was usually done. The money men (in this case, he was sure it was the fast-growing and decidedly socialistic government outside the SUSA) stayed anonymous in the shadows.

"Ben waved for the guards to take the prisoners away, and then shifted the camp chair around and stretched his long legs out in front of him, away from the field desk in his tent.

"Before the team from Intelligence could start their work on the three American mercenaries, the men decided to tell all they knew . . . or so they insisted. Intel believed they were holding a lot back, but what they did say was enough for Ben to fit another piece of the puzzle in place. There were still gaps in the overall mystery, but Ben felt he should talk to Cecil Jefferys back in the SUSA and warn him that the government outside their borders was planning some sort of move against the SUSA.

" 'We're just beginning to get whispers about that, Ben,' Ben's longtime friend and the President of the SUSA said. 'I was going to give you a bump in a few hours. Of course, we both knew it was coming eventually.'

" 'Yes, that we did, Cec. I think it might he best if you had a little chat with somebody in power.'

" 'I'd do just that, Ben. But nobody really knows who makes up the shadow government.'

" 'Everything is really still all that screwed up in the new capital?'

" 'It's a mess, and that's being kind. To be blunt, it's a royal fuckup. The people we felt we could trust are out of the loop . . . or just out, period. And I mean all the way out.

There have been half a dozen little power plays since you left. Sometimes it's weeks before we learn of the full magnitude. And here is something we learned just hours ago, and it's unbelievable; the announcement just came down the line: The upcoming national elections have been postponed.'

" 'Postponed?' Ben questioned. 'For what reason?'

" 'The bottom line seems to be security concerns.'

" 'Oh . . . that's bullshit!'

" 'Of course it is. But that's the word—the party line, you might call it—the central government is putting out. And you know who they're blaming . . .'

" 'The SUSA.'

" 'Right. Those in power are claiming the SUSA is planning to move against the New Democracy . . . as it's being called by the press. Bless their little pointy heads.'

" 'The New Democracy?'

" 'That's it. Really catchy phrase, isn't it?'

" 'Sounds like something a bunch of silly-assed liberals would dream up.'

" 'You got it.'

" 'Next we'll have a chicken in every pot and a car in every garage.'

" 'I'm sure.'

" 'Where are we heading, Cec?'

" 'Well . . . the military outside our borders is just not strong enough yet to tangle with us . . . but they're slowly building to that strength. Now that the main force of the Rebels is out of the picture—so to speak—thousands of miles away. I think the people—a certain type of person, that is, and you know the breed as well as I do—living outside our borders will be used for cannon fodder.'

" 'Those give-me-something-for-nothing, I-want-the-government-to-take-care-of-me, cradle-to-grave, politically correct, I'll-sue-you-for-the-slightest-slur types will attempt a swarm across our borders and mercenaries will be right behind them, with the new military backing up the second wave.'

" 'You nailed it right on the head.' Cecil laughed. 'Of course, I had no doubts that you would. I'll keep you up to date. You take care now, Ben, and I'll see you.'

" 'Do that, partner.'

"Cecil Jefferys was the President of the SUSA, the first black man elected to such a high office in America . . . and it took the separation of the nation and the men and women of the South to accomplish it.

"Cecil and Ben had been friends for many years. Cecil had left the grueling life in the field to enter politics after a heart attack nearly killed him during a campaign.

"Ben walked outside and stood for a moment. His mind was already busy adding up the troops he could take back to the SUSA when it was time to go . . . if the job here wasn't finished. Ben had guesstimated this campaign might take anywhere from a year to as much as five years. Ben now felt he would be leaving Africa with his 501 Brigade, and several other brigades as yet unchosen, in a matter of weeks, not years.

"He walked to his tent and opened a map case. He spread the map out on a table and began studying it. He found a port in the country of Congo, just south of where the Rebels were now stalled. The small city had an airport that would be just large enough for the planes coming over from the SUSA to use. He put the map away and stepped outside to stand in silence for a moment.

"The shadows were beginning to gather and soon it would be dark, and in Central Africa, when night falls, it does just that . . . in a hurry.

"Down by the river, huge portable floodlights had already been set up so the combat engineers could work through the night laying down the Bailey Bridge.

"Ben did not expect another attack by Bruno's people or by any of the many roaming gangs that were terrorizing the land, but he was taking no chances. He had ordered the guard doubled and there were choppers in the sky, the gunships slowly moving in a huge circle.

" 'What you doing over here, Lamar?' Ben questioned. 'Aside from irritating me, that is?'

" 'You need irritating, Raines. What is the word from back home?'

" 'How would I know?' Ben asked innocently, but with a very sneaky smile.

" 'Because I know you've been talking with that other old rooster, Cecil Jefferys, that's how I know. Now give.'

" 'How do you know that?'

" 'A little bird landed on my shoulder and told me, Raines. Now what's going on?'

"Ben held nothing back from his team, never had, never would. As a matter of fact, Corrie usually knew what was going on before Ben did.

" 'Things have taken a turn for the worse back in the States, Lamar. As we knew they would.'

" 'That bad, Ben?'

" 'I think it might be even worse than Cec is telling me.'

"Lamar nodded, looking up as a very sweaty and very dirty combat engineer came walking up.

"Ben turned to face the engineer.

" 'We've just about got everything wrapped up. We'll be ready to take vehicles across in a few hours, General.'

" 'Good deal. You're in command of this detachment now, Captain. I'll put the paperwork through promoting you to major.' *Just as soon as one of my team tells me your name, that is,* Ben silently thought. There was a time when he knew the name of every officer in his command. But those days were long ago and far away. Where once there were a few hundred men and women in the Rebel Army, now there were thousands.

" 'Thank you, sir,' the engineer said.

" 'You earned it,' Ben replied.

"The man walked away, and Ben turned to Beth. He opened his mouth to speak and she said, 'Adam Matson, Boss.'

"Ben smiled. 'Thank you, Beth. See that the paperwork on his field promotion gets through pronto, will you?'

" 'Will do, Boss.'

" 'What next, Ben?' Lamar asked.

" 'We secure a port and an airport. Probably in a few weeks. Then we'll start the drive that will end Bottger's reign of terror once and for all.'

" 'And a new reign of terror, if that's the right word, will be about to erupt in America?'

" 'I'm not sure if terror is the right word, Lamar. Millions of people want to live under what the leaders outside the SUSA are calling the New Democracy. But the rub comes into the picture when other millions say they don't want any part of it and by God they won't live under it.'

" 'Are you about to give me a lecture, Raines?' Lamar asked, a smile playing on his lips. 'If you are, kindly save your breath and my ears.'

"Ben laughed at the expression on his old friend's face. 'I wouldn't dream of doing that, Lamar. What would be the point? You haven't changed your mind about anything in fifty years.'

"Lamar did his best to work a hurt expression on his face. He couldn't pull it off. 'I don't have to stand here and be insulted by you, Raines. I'm leaving. Good night.'

" 'Be careful, you old goat,' Ben told him.

" 'Blow it out your ass, Raines,' the doctor called over his shoulder.

" 'That isn't very professional, Lamar. Not coming from a man of your stature and advanced age,' Ben called.

"The chief of medicine flipped him the bird and kept on walking.

"Ben's team laughed at the exchange between the two men. They'd seen and heard it all before, dozens of times.

"Ben's eyes caught a shadow of movement at a corner of a parked vehicle. He blinked a couple of times. Stared at where he was sure he'd seen movement. Nothing. But he was certain he'd seen something out of the ordinary.

"A monkey that slipped into camp? That would be about the only thing that could slip through the Rebels on guard. Unless . . . Pretty far-fetched, he thought, minutely shaking his head. But certainly possible, if someone had done some careful planning, and that was something to be considered.

" 'Gang,' Ben said in low tones. 'I think we're about to be hit and hit hard. Corrie, pass the word to the troops.' He deliberately turned his back to the shadows and faced his team. 'Do it quietly. No one gets in a hurry.'

" 'OK, Boss,' she replied in an even voice. 'Will do.'

"Cooper got up and stretched nonchalantly, scratched himself, then wandered off a few yards to the bed of a truck. Ben knew that was where he kept his SAW and extra two-hundred-round containers of 5.56 ammo.

"Beth placed a hand on her CAR and continued sitting on the tailgate of a truck. Jersey was staring into the darkness that had dropped over them as suddenly as death . . . and probably bringing a lot of that with it. Jersey stiffened just a bit, and Ben felt certain she had seen something moving in the darkness.

"Anna had not moved from her crouch beside a HumVee. But her CAR was held in a position that she could bring to ready in an instant.

" 'Tunnels,' Anna whispered just loud enough for Ben and the team members close to hear her. 'The bastards used tunnels and holes in the ground. This was carefully planned out by someone with some sense.'

" 'The first ambush failed, so they waited until dark,' Ben said. 'They must have been nearly roasting in those holes and tunnels.'

" 'Too bad they didn't,' Corrie remarked. 'That would have saved us a lot of trouble.'

" 'I heard that,' Cooper said from a few yards away. He was standing close to his SAW, ready to grab it and hit the ground when the action started.

"Ben shifted positions, walking over to the bed of the truck to stand close to Anna. He had left his CAR in the tent and carried only his holstered 9mm.

" 'There can't be more than a handful of them,' he whispered. 'Not unless they've been digging tunnels and holes for days. Which is certainly possible,' he added.

" 'They must've hidden when our choppers came close, then crawled out of the brush and started digging the instant they left,' Beth whispered.

" 'That's got to be what happened,' Ben said. 'This is going to involve a lot of grenades and very close work on their part. Pass that word, Corrie.'

" 'Right, Boss.'

" 'We're going to take some casualties,' Ben said. 'It's going to get real nasty in a hurry.'

"The moments dragged by. Five minutes passed with nothing happening. Ben began to wonder if he had been wrong; had he really seen movement? Was an attack imminent? Or was his imagination running wild?

" 'Intelligence on the horn, Boss,' Corrie whispered, breaking the silence. 'One of those mercs finally broke. The jungle on both sides of the road is filled with hostiles. Several companies at least.'

" 'Shit,' Ben muttered.

" 'The camp's as ready as it can be,' Corrie added after a few seconds' pause.

"Ben thought about walking over to his tent to retrieve his CAR, then rejected that idea. This fight was going to be eyeball-to-eyeball and a pistol would be easier to handle. In short, it was going to be a real bloodbath.

" 'All patrols in?' Ben asked.

" 'Everybody's in camp,' Corrie answered.

" 'OK. Everyone holds their position. No moving around. If it moves, shoot it.'

" 'Orders given, Boss, Corrie said, ten seconds later.

"A few heartbeats afterward, the huge encampment erupted in gunfire and the screaming of the wounded.

"Enemy troops began pouring out of the ground on both sides of the camp like ants out of a rotting tree. The darkness was filled with running shapes. Ben did not have to give the orders to fire; that would have been superfluous. The Rebels had a horde of screaming enemy troops right on top of them and literally in their faces. Hundreds of Rebels began firing, at very close range, most of them using pistols, one in each hand. Machine guns and grenades were useless to both sides this close.

"Ben had dropped down to a kneeling position and was picking his targets; not a difficult task, for the enemy was bunched up all around him.

" 'They're after the boss,' Cooper yelled. 'Has to be. The attack is too concentrated.'

" 'Get those fuckin' flares up,' Ben shouted.

"Cooper was right: The main thrust of the attack was at the center of the encampment, where Ben had his CP. Only lighter probes were being conducted north and south of his location.

"The night skies suddenly sparked into harsh light as flares were sent up and popped into illumination. Ben lifted his 9mm and shot an enemy soldier in the face. The man was so close Ben could smell his body stink.

"He shifted his boots to face another soldier, and put three rounds of hollow-points into the man's belly and chest. The soldier screamed and fell against Ben, dead, almost knocking Ben off his boots.

"Anna jumped onto the back of an enemy soldier and grabbed the man's hair, jerking his head back. She cut the man's throat with one hard swipe of her knife and rode him down to the ground. Rising to her boots, the young woman drove her knife into the belly of another of Bottger's soldiers and twisted it savagely. The man howled in pain, his scream silenced when Anna kneed him in the balls and ripped her knife from him. The man fell forward on his face, his legs jerking as agony tore through his body just before death claimed him.

"Cooper had left his SAW and was taking a deadly toll of the enemy, a 9mm in each hand.

"If that one enemy soldier had not gotten careless, Ben thought later, as he banged away with his pistol, the sneak attack might have turned into a disaster for the Rebels.

"Then Ben had no more time for any thoughts other than staying alive. The enemy soldiers came in another rush, and everything was confusion as the Rebels battled hand-to-hand with knives, clubs, entrenching tools, pistols, and their bare hands.

"For a few moments, it was a wild, savage, deadly scene in the African night. The enemy troops had, for the most part, ceased their yelling, and the battle was silent except for the grunting of men and women locked in combat and the moaning of the wounded.

"The intensity of the battle began to wane as the enemy troops began to realize their sneak attack had failed. Many faded back into the jungle's hot, humid thickness and slipped away. Those who stayed and fought, died.

"For those caught up in the deadly brawl, the attack seemed to last for hours . . . In reality, it lasted only a few minutes and was over.

"Every Rebel involved in the quick and savage fight, and there were many camped a couple of miles to the north of the river who took no part in the battle, suffered bruises, scratches, cuts, and gunshot wounds.

" 'Keep those flares up and going east and west of us,' Ben ordered. 'I don't think they'll try again, but they might.'

" 'They sure might, General,' a medic called, kneeling beside a wounded solider. 'They're popped up on something.

Some sort of speed, I think. This man is incoherent and his vital signs are racing . . . His heartbeat sounds like an M-16 on full auto.'

" 'We've taken casualties,' Corrie reported. 'Mostly wounded. So far, the death count is low.'

" 'Any other brigade get hit?' Ben asked.

" 'Negative, Boss. Not so far. I'm still checking on that. But I think we're the only ones who were attacked.'

" 'They were after you, Ben,' Ben's XO, John Michaels, said, walking up. 'This was very carefully planned on their part. No advance teams were hit, and they were all over this area. It was well planned, all right.'

" 'We captured lots of their wounded, Boss,' Cooper called. 'Fifty and counting. What do you want done with the really seriously wounded among them . . . those that the docs are sure aren't going to make it?'

" 'Give them a shot to ease their suffering and help them along their way in peace. We'll scoop out a hole for them in the morning. Turn the rest over to Intelligence.'

"Ben turned to his XO. 'We'll probably be doing some shifting around very soon, John. I haven't set a date for it yet, but I'm pretty sure I'll be heading back to the States with my brigade.'

"The XO arched an eyebrow in surprise, but Ben could not see it in the darkness.

" 'Conditions are getting a little rocky outside the SUSA,' Ben added.

" 'I knew they weren't good,' his XO replied. 'Do we fight again over there?'

"Ben sighed. 'We might, John. We just might have to do that. I hope not, but it's looking as though we'll have to fight for our nation.'

" 'Again?'

" 'Yes. Again. Those bastards outside the SUSA can't say I didn't warn them.'

"The brigades mounted up and moved out the next morning, after engineers scooped out a hole for the dead soldiers and dumped them in. A much more dignified service was held for the Rebels' own dead. Intelligence had told Ben, just before the brigade moved out, "White officers commanded the troops that hit us last night. Americans, for the most part. A few Europeans. They're all being readied to ship back to the SUSA . . . including the three we took prisoner yesterday.'

" 'Good. I want to be able to hold them up and point them out to the powers-that-be outside the SUSA. I want to see the expressions on their faces when I do that . . . especially after the prisoners have spilled their guts about who hired them. And they will tell us everything they know,' Ben added, a deadly grimness behind the words. 'Bet on that.'

"The miles-long column pulled out, heading south, and hit no more trouble as they crossed the bridge and stretched out. Advance patrols and eyes in the sky reported no signs of the enemy. Flybys indicated the port where Ben was heading appeared usable and the small city itself looked to be almost deserted.

" 'I still haven't seen any tigers,' Cooper bitched as they rolled along . . . crawled along might be a better way of putting it, for if the column could average twenty miles an hour, they were doing well.

" 'For the umpteenth boring time, you halfwit ninny,' Jersey told him from the second seat in the big wagon. 'You're not going to see any tigers. Lots of lions, no tigers.'

" 'Tarzan fought tigers over here in his movies,' Cooper said right back.

" 'Give it up, Jersey," Corrie told her. 'It's hopeless. Hell, Cooper's hopeless.'

" 'I think he needs professional help,' Jersey said. 'Of course, I've thought that for years.'

"Beth looked up from her reading of old travel brochures and smiled. 'I know we've got a long way to go before we get there, but Point-Noire used to have a population of over half a million. But flybys say it's almost deserted. What happened to the people?'

" 'Bottger probably killed them all,' Cooper said.

" 'Half a million of them?' Jersey questioned. 'I don't think so, Cooper.' Then she frowned. 'Well . . . maybe you are right, Cooper. As much as I hate to admit it.'

" 'He might have used the gas on them,' Ben said. 'Or a form of experimental gas while his scientists were working all the bugs out of it—so to speak. We'll know when we get there, I suppose.'

" 'I don't understand why he's killing off all the people,' Jersey said.

" 'Cuts down on the resistance problem, Jersey,' Ben told her.

" 'And damn sure helps to keep the rest of the people in line.'

" 'I can see where that certainly would,' Jersey replied.

" 'Says here that there are over forty ethnic groups each with their own language,' Beth said, reading from the travel brochure. She winked at Anna and added, 'And Cooper, here's something for you: Watch out for the Gaboon viper.'

" 'The what?' Cooper asked.

" 'It's a snake, Coop. The largest and heaviest viper in all of Africa. Grows to a length of about eight feet long and can weigh up to twenty-five pounds. It's very deadly. Likes to crawl into sleeping bags at night and snuggle up to the sleeper.'

" 'The son of a bitch wouldn't snuggle up to me for very long,' Cooper said. 'I'd be out of that sleeping bag before it could open its mouth.'

"Cooper shuddered and made a terrible-looking face. Cooper hated snakes of all types, sizes, and descriptions. 'Jesus, I don't even like to think about that.'

" 'Relax, Cooper,' Beth told him. 'This snake is found in central Africa, in the tropical rain forests.'

" 'Of course, Coop,' Ben said, 'there are all types of poisonous snakes here in Africa. For instance, the one you really better look out for is the spitting cobra.'

"Cooper shook his head and cut his eyes to Ben for a second. 'I read all about those nasty things. They spit venom that can blind you.'

" 'Always keep your sun shades on, Cooper,' Jersey told him.

" 'Protect your eyes.'

" 'If I do that, how the hell am I supposed to see at night?'

" 'Carefully, Coop,' Jersey told him with a straight face. 'Very carefully.'

"After a moment, Cooper slowly held up his right hand and gave Jersey the bird.

"Beth covered her face with the travel brochure to stifle her giggling as Jersey and the others burst out laughing. The laughter lasted only a few seconds. Corrie suddenly held up a hand as her headset began crackling with transmissions.

" 'Scouts report the town just up ahead is populated. Lots of sick and dying. No apparent gunshot wounds. The interpreter is trying to make some sense of it all now.'

" 'How many people?' Ben questioned.

" 'Several thousand. They're not unruly. Just sitting and waiting to die. The scouts' words, Boss.'

" 'Are the scouts in protective gear?'

" 'Gas masks only.'

" 'Halt the column, Ben,' Doctor Chase's voice popped over a speaker. 'If the scouts haven't dropped dead or started showing some signs of sickness in thirty minutes, we'll proceed into the town . . . the advance party of medical people wearing full protective gear.'

" 'You're the boss on this, Lamar,' Ben replied. 'It's your call from here on in.' Ben then gave orders to halt the column.

" 'Some of Bottger's gas?' Cooper wondered.

" 'Probably,' Ben said. 'But it might be starvation or some natural disease. It's all up to Chase's people now. Corrie, tell the troops to un-ass their vehicles and stretch. Double the guards.'

" 'Now we wait,' Anna said.

"Ben nodded. 'Now we wait.'

"Chase's bio/med team entered the town and got their equipment ready. Several of them took the scouts into their mobile lab to check them out, while the others began inspecting the town and the residents, checking the air and the water and the soil.

"It did not take the bio/med team long to determine that the air was fine to breathe, but the water had more germs in it than a city garbage dump . . . but they were nature's bugs, not man-made. The people were not contagious and posed no threat to the Rebels.

"The bio/med team gave the column the okay to enter the town.

" 'Bottger's gas cause this?' Ben asked, stepping out of his vehicle and looking around.

" 'We're running analyses now, General. But if I had to make a guess, I'd say yes.'

" 'What has the interpreter been able to find out?'

" 'Just that one day everybody felt fine, the next day people were getting sick and dying all around them. Whatever it was, it touched everyone with violent nausea, uncontrollable diarrhea, and high fever . . . Breathing became very difficult, and then death to most. Those who survived are very weak, but we think they're going to make it.'

" 'Bottger's crap,' Ben said.

" 'Probably.'

" 'What can you do for the people?'

" 'Well, actually, very little, sir. Give those who are dying a shot to ease them on their way out. That's about it.'

" 'Do it,' Doctor Chase said, walking up and catching the last part of the report.

" 'Yes, sir.'

"Chase turned to face Ben, then grimaced and said, 'Why

should I tell you, Raines; you'd just turn around and tell Corrie. I might as well start giving all orders to her from the outset. Besides, she's a lot easier on the eyes than you are.' He turned to face Corrie. 'You know the drill, dear: no drinking of the water, no petting of animals, no fraternization with the locals. See that those orders are passed up and down the line promptly, please.'

" 'Certainly, sir.'

"Chase smiled. 'It's so nice to see that someone in this team knows something about military courtesy.' He turned and strolled off before Ben could retort, chuckling as he walked.

" 'Somebody must have put thumbtacks in the old goat's oatmeal this morning,' Ben said. 'Feisty old bastard.'

"Lamar Chase was definitely too old for the field . . . Ben knew it and Lamar knew it. But he was in excellent health and showed no signs of slowing down. As long as he could keep up, he would stay in the field. Like Ben, when it came time for him to leave the grinding world of combat campaigns, he would know and would do so voluntarily . . . He would not have to be told. Both Ben and Chase knew that day was coming for them, but neither of them liked to dwell much on it.

" 'Let's see what we've got in this town,' Ben said. 'As if we didn't know," he added.

"*Death, suffering and hopelessness,* Beth wrote in her journal as the team walked along. And: *Nearly all of Africa is the same. No matter where we go we see the same thing. Bruno Bottger is not responsible for everything that has happened to these poor people, but he is certainly to blame for most of it. He is an evil, immoral man, probably insane, who must be destroyed . . . no matter the cost.*

"She carefully noted the name of the town, dated the page, then closed the journal and tucked it away in her rucksack and buckled the flap.

"Ben was also keeping a journal, and in content, it was surprisingly very similar to the one Beth was keeping.

"The other members of the team felt the same way as Beth and Ben about Bottger . . . as did the entire Rebel Army. They had all been pursuing the rotten bastard for too long . . . over thousands of miles and two continents.

"It was time to bring it to an end.

" 'Gas masks on,' Ben ordered. 'The smell is going to be tough.'

"That order did not have to be repeated, for the odor was very foul.

" 'Corrie,' Ben said, after only a few minutes of walking through the human suffering. 'Get the engineers up here with their equipment. We've got to get these bodies in the ground. Many of the dead are rotting. We've got to get these dead buried . . . and do it damn quick.'

"No matter where the Rebels looked, there were rotting, maggot-covered bodies. It wasn't a matter of the living not caring: The survivors were just too weak to bury their dead. They just did not have the strength.

"Wild dogs and hyenas had made their way into the town to join the birds of prey in dining on what appeared to be hundreds of bodies . . . and there was plenty of dead and rotting flesh to satisfy even the most indiscriminate of appetites, and hyenas and vultures were neither picky nor dainty eaters.

"The birds of prey did not seem to mind the Rebels walking among them as they ripped and tore off strips and hunks of flesh. The hyenas were another story: The savage animals with their bone-crunching jaws presented a clear menace to the Rebels.

" 'Try to chase them off,' Ben ordered. 'They're only doing what they were put on earth to do . . . as disgusting as it is. If they won't back off, shoot them.'

"After a dozen of the hyenas were shot, the rest began backing away, reluctantly, from the dead, long enough for the Rebels to toss the bodies into the beds of trucks . . . if the bodies didn't fall apart when they were picked up; then it got really interesting for the Rebels, interesting being a totally inadequate word in describing the procedure.

" 'Jesus Christ, Ben,' the XO, John Michaels, said after a few moments. 'We came over here to fight, not to be subjected to this.'

" 'I know, John. I know. I'm not real thrilled about it either, I assure you.'

" 'Then why are we doing it, Ben? We sure as hell don't have to.'

" 'Because there is no one else to do it, John. If there were no living watching us—many of them relatives of the dead, I'm sure—I'd have the bodies scraped up into a pile and use the town for a funeral pyre.'

"The XO shook his mask-covered head. 'Sorry, Ben. I'm just blowing off steam.'

" 'I know you are, John. And I understand your frustration. I feel the same way. Believe me, I do.'

" 'What a fucking thankless miserable job for these young men and women," John replied, his eyes on the Rebels struggling with the rotting bodies.

" 'It wasn't all that thrilling an experience for the dead either, John. Especially when you take into account they didn't know why it was happening to them . . . or even what was happening to them. But as long as my Rebels are handling the dead, their officers are going to stay with them and witness all the horror of it. I want us all to understand what manner of men we're fighting.'

" 'I believe they will all know that, Ben, to the fullest extent.'

" 'So they shall, John. I want them to know the stink and the rot and the total evil of Bottger and his dream, so when they move against that son of a bitch and his men, there will be damn little pity or compassion shown.'

" 'I think we can both be sure of that, Ben.' John looked

into Ben's eyes and inwardly shuddered. He felt as though he were gazing through the fiery, smoky gates into Hell itself.

" 'This last leg of the campaign is going to be a brutal, bloody bastard,' the XO said. 'There won't be a survivor left from the other side . . . not unless they give it up right now and beg for mercy.' John had been with Ben for a long time, and he had witnessed firsthand how low-down and mean Ben could be when he got pissed . . . and right now he was plenty pissed."

Perro Loco put down the transcript of the expedition written by Robert Barnes, war correspondent for the United Press, and the journals written by Raines and the female member of his team. Ben Raines was part madman, he concluded, making him a far more formidable adversary.

Ben Raines and his men were tough, apparently unafraid of a madman like Bruno Bottger or any of his Nazi weapons, even chemical and germ warfare. It would be a test of Loco's fighting men to face a general like Ben Raines. Loco could only hope that Raines's battles with the forces of the USA had weakened him.

It was a gamble worth taking, a chance to control all of the American continent. What difference would it make if he lost a few thousand men? Fighting men were expendable. Central and South America were full of men who were willing to risk their lives for the promise of money.

Twenty-two

Harley Reno and Hammer Hammerick were riding in the lead jeep with a couple of Gato's men as they headed deeper into the jungle. The second jeep contained Corrie and Beth, and the third held Gato, Ben, and Anna, who refused to leave Ben's side when Jersey wasn't around to guard him.

Ben was talking to Gato about what he thought Perro Loco's plans were when he saw Reno suddenly reach over the driver of his jeep, grab the wheel, and steer the vehicle off the trail into the brush.

Ben grabbed his driver's shoulder and yelled, "Stop!"

As the others jeeps slid to a stop, Reno and Hammer vaulted out of the lead one and jogged back to meet them.

"What's going on, Harley?" Ben asked.

"I saw light reflecting off a glass up ahead," Reno said as he checked the loads in his SPAS shotgun. "It was either binocs or a telescopic sight."

Gato started to speak, "But, Señor Reno, there is no—"

Ben interrupted, "Believe him, Gato. If Harley thinks there's an ambush ahead, there is. He and Hammer are the best in the world at what they do."

Gato shrugged, but he clearly still did not believe there was any danger.

"Give us ten minutes, Chief," Reno said. "Then you can come up the trail."

Ben nodded and Reno and Hammer split up, each disappearing into the jungle on opposite sides of the road.

"Gato," Ben said, "have one of your men open the hood of that jeep and act like he's having trouble with the engine so if anyone is watching, they'll know why we stopped."

Gato shook his head as if all this was unnecessary, but he gave the order.

Harley Reno, in spite of his size, moved through the jungle like a big jungle cat, making no sound whatever as he slipped through the dense undergrowth.

Within minutes he could smell the acrid scent of cheap tobacco ahead. He shook his head in disgust. If men under his command dared to smoke while on patrol, they'd have their heads handed to them on a platter.

He silently pushed the leaves of a banana tree aside and saw the trap. There were four men waiting just off the road, hidden in the bushes. Three were armed with AK-47's, while the fourth manned an old Browning Automatic Rifle on a tripod. Even though the weapon dated from World War II, it would have made short work of the jeeps had they continued down the trail.

Reno glanced at his watch. Five minutes. Hammer should be ready on the other side, he thought as he laid his SPAS on the ground. He pulled his K-Bar assault knife from its scabbard and eased forward.

He grabbed the man in the rear, placing his left hand over his mouth as he pulled his chin up and back, exposing his throat. There was no sound as the razor-sharp blade of the knife sliced through his carotid arteries and trachea. The soldier died without ever knowing what hit him.

Reno slowly laid his body to the ground, his eyes on the other three in front of him. As he moved toward them, one must have sensed something for he turned and looked back over his shoulder. Reno moved quickly, swinging his left fist and crashing it into the soldier's face, smashing his nose flat and sending teeth and blood spraying into the air as his head snapped back and he fell to the ground.

The other two whirled around, the barrel of the AK-47 swinging toward Reno. He blocked it with his left arm and slashed backhanded with the K-Bar while simultaneously lashing out his right leg in a swinging side-kick. As the K-Bar severed one man's neck, almost decapitating him, Reno's size-twelve combat boot took the other soldier in the chin, fracturing and dislocating his jaw. In one continuous motion, Reno whirled and slipped the K-Bar under his ribcage at a forty-five-degree angle upward. The soldier grunted once as the knife point penetrated his heart, stopping it in midbeat. He hung there a moment, impaled on Reno's fist, his eyes wide and surprised, until Reno jerked the knife out and let him collapse to the ground.

Reno crouched, letting the adrenaline wash out of his system for a few minutes, watching to see if there were any more men hiding in the jungle. When he found none, he leaned his head back and whistled, the sound of a sparrow hawk coming from his lips. It was the signal the scouts of the SUSA used to signify a successful attack.

Moments later, the sound was repeated from across the road, and Reno and Hammer stepped out of the jungle to greet each other.

Hammer glanced at the blood splatters on the front of Reno's shirt and pants, shaking his head. "Sloppy, podna, awful sloppy," he growled, a grin on his lips.

Reno shook his head. "I know. I must be gettin' slow in my old age," he answered as they walked back up the trail toward Ben and the others.

Gato's eyes widened and his mouth dropped open when he saw the two men walking up the trail, Reno's clothes covered with fresh blood.

"Dios . . ." he muttered.

Ben smiled. "How many were there?"

Reno held up four fingers, Hammer three.

"Weapons?"

"Three AK's and a BAR," Reno said.

"Two AK's and an M-16," Hammer added.

"Any survivors?"

Hammer shook his head. Reno said, "I left one alive. I figured Gato might want to ask him a few questions."

Gato looked puzzled. "Questions?"

Reno shrugged. "Sure. Like how they knew where we were gonna be. It might just be you got a mole in your outfit, Gato."

"A mole?"

Ben explained. "A spy, Gato. Someone who's reporting your plans to Perro Loco."

Gato's face turned dark. "Pedro, Jose," he said to two soldiers standing nearby. "Go and find out what the *bastardo* knows."

In a few minutes, harsh screams of terror and pain could be heard from the site of the ambush as Gato's men questioned the survivor about the possibility of a spy in Gato's group of rebels.

Trying to ignore the yelling and begging for mercy coming from the nearby bushes, Ben asked Gato, "How much farther is it to the site of the ambush of the fuel caravan?"

Gato shrugged. "Only about five kilometers, but it is through a winding trail so it will take us a couple of hours to get there."

Ben nodded. "Good. I know my people and they'll probably stay within radio range of their original firefight. The sooner we get there, the sooner I can have my people home."

Minutes later, there were two closely spaced gunshots and the screaming abruptly stopped. The two soldiers appeared on the road, their BDUs covered with splatters of blood and mucus.

"Did you find out who the traitor is?" Gato asked, his eyes glittering with anticipation.

The taller of the two men shook his head. "No, *mi comandante*. They were merely *soldados* who did not know who gave their leader the information about our position."

"Well, no matter," Gato said, disappointment showing on his face. "Now that I know there is a leak, it will not be long before I find out who is responsible."

He waved his arm in a circle, and the men all piled into their jeeps to continue the journey through the jungle toward the ambush site.

Twenty-three

Private Porfirio Negra rode his Yamaha motorcycle for all it was worth toward San Ignacio, squeezing the twist-grip throttle on the handlebar until it hurt his hand. The noise made by the two-stroke motor filled the jungle around him, louder when he shifted to a lower gear.

What he had seen while traveling through the jungle only added to his haste.

"Madre," he said to himself, crossing a vine-clogged ridge south of the *hacienda*.

The slaughter in the jungle near the Guatemala border was still fresh in his mind, the ambush by soldiers no one could identify. They wore black paint on their faces and camouflage uniforms. It was as if they had come from nowhere. The rest of the squad lay dead in the vines and undergrowth. Porfirio was the only survivor of the surprise attack.

Sergeant Felipe Garza and Corporal Beto had been among the first to die. Five truckloads of airplane fuel and ammunition had fallen into enemy hands . . . only Porfirio did not know who the enemy was. The ambush had come so suddenly. There had been no warning.

When he knelt beside Sergeant Garza, with bullets flying around him, Porfirio found the pair of gold coins in the sergeant's front pocket. He was searching for orders rather than wealth.

"I must tell the *comandante* about the ambush," he said above the throb of the Yamaha engine. "But I will say nothing about the gold." His wife and infant son would be able to live for many years with so much money.

Porfirio had always liked Corporal Beto . . . He'd wanted his job as gunner for the sergeant. But after what he saw today, he felt much better about his low rank. Tipping his motorcycle over in jungle vines when the shooting started had certainly saved his life.

As he'd sped away from the attack on his motorcycle, he'd glanced back over his shoulder, surprised to see only two soldiers appear out of the jungle—one of them a woman!

He considered putting the gold money in his boot, just in case Comandante Perro Loco knew about it. Porfirio understood that if he was searched he would lose the gold, and perhaps even be executed as a traitor. How could he explain having so much wealth on a private's pay?

"I should stop near the *hacienda* and bury it," he said, changing to a higher gear where the road was level. Two gold coins would be enough to make him a rich man, although he didn't know how much they were actually worth in Belizian dollars with the world in so much turmoil.

The attack near Guatemala against the villagers friendly to the Salvadoran rebels led by El Gato had been a short-lived success. Whoever the soldiers were who came at them in the jungle, they must have known about the bullets and aircraft fuel. Maybe, he thought, they knew about the gold in Sergeant Garza's possession.

"But how did they know about the gold in Sergeant Garza's pocket?" he asked himself, wondering whom the money had belonged to before the attack.

It was unlikely that Felipe Garza had come by the gold by honest means. Gold was as scarce in Central America as teeth in a fighting rooster. Since the global war, everyone was dirt-poor, and a man only had what he was strong enough to keep by force.

Porfirio sighted the walls around the *hacienda* in the distance. He had to be careful of a search by the deadly Englishman, Jim Strunk. Strunk was perhaps the most ruthless man on Perro Loco's staff, if you did not count Paco Valdez.

Valdez was truly crazy, even more so than the *comandante* himself.

Private Porfirio Negra saw an unusually tall palm tree to the left of the road. He decided this was where he should hide his money until he gave his report to the *comandante*.

He slowed the Yamaha and steered off the trail.

Jim Strunk heard the high-pitched sound of a motorcycle and when he did, he was certain that something was wrong.

He left the *hacienda* by a wrought-iron gate in the back wall after nodding to a pair of armed guards.

"I'll be back," he said softly. "Don't let anyone in unless you know them."

He crept into the jungle, drawing his 9mm pistol, making sure of the loads in the clip before he jacked a round into the firing chamber.

The motorcycle engine was quiet now.

Porfirio dug furiously with his hands at the base of the palm tree. A parrot whistled from a nearby branch and somewhere deeper in the rain forest, a spider monkey called to its mate, a chattering noise.

He thought about the money he'd taken from Sergeant Garza's pocket. Felipe Garza was a confidant of Paco Valdez, and Valdez was seldom wrong when he placed trust in his officers and the men who served them.

"But no one has any gold," he said under his breath as the hole he dug went deeper, near a thick root of the coconut palm above him. "Where did it come from?"

Porfirio heard a click.

"What? Who is there?"

No one answered him.

"I know I did not imagine it . . ."

Even the parrot was silent now. Porfirio's eyes swept the rain-forest shadows around him. He sensed a presence, yet no one was there.

"I am imagining it," he told himself, returning to his slow digging, damp earth buried beneath his fingernails, clinging to the palms of his hands.

"Nice hole you've got there," a voice said, a voice thick with a British accent.

Porfirio froze. His rusting Colt .45 automatic was in a holster tied to his belt.

He searched the forest for the source of the voice. "Who is there?" he asked.

"What do you intend to put in the hole?" the same voice asked.

His mind raced. "Nothing. I am digging for fishing worms, *señor.* Who are you?"

"You know who I am."

"No. I am Private Porfirio Negra, a soldier in the service of Comandante Perro Loco."

"Why are you digging that hole?"

"Worms. Worms, so I can go fishing at the river after I give my report to the *comandante.*"

"What do you have to report?"

"An ambush in the mountains near Guatemala. I was assigned to Sergeant Garza's command. We captured five trucks full of ammunition and fuel for airplanes. Someone attacked us in the jungle near the border. Everyone was killed, including Sergeant Garza and Corporal Beto."

"Who led the attack?" the Englishman asked, and now Porfirio was certain who he was. Jim Strunk, the executioner for Perro Loco, was asking the questions.

"I do not know. They had black paint on their faces and we could not see them clearly. There were two of them, a man and a woman."

Strunk's face showed his disbelief. "You mean only two soldiers were able to take out an entire convoy?"

"Sí," Porfirio said, nodding his head rapidly up and down.

Strunk shook his head. "Then your Sergeant Garza must have been criminally negligent. It is a good thing he died in the attack, or Perro Loco would skin him alive for his carelessness."

Strunk stared at the ground at Porfirio's feet. "What are you putting in the hole?" he asked again, this time with more emphasis.

"I was only digging for worms, *señor.*"

"A strange place to dig for fish bait. Stand up and put your hands over your head."

"But why?" Porfirio asked, fear making his heart hammer in his chest. "I need to give my report to the *comandante* at the *hacienda.*"

"You weren't in too big a hurry to stop to dig for worms," the man said. "It seems odd, if you have an important message for your commander."

"My wife . . . my family is hungry," Porfirio said, coming to his feet. "We need fish. The river is not far away."

"Too damn far for you to be digging here. Keep those hands high while I search you."

Porfirio knew the henchman would find his gold and then he would be killed. It was better to take the only chance he had of coming out of this encounter alive.

As the Englishman leaned close to pat his pockets, Porfirio grabbed desperately at the hand holding the pistol, twisting with all of his might and spinning to throw the man over his hip.

Strunk dropped the pistol, his face grimacing with pain as he hit the ground and rolled quickly to his feet.

Porfirio dropped to his knees, frantically searching for the gun, which had disappeared in the tall pampas grass.

He looked up when he heard the snick of a knife being drawn from a scabbard.

Strunk was grinning now, his teeth flashing in the sunlight as he walked slowly toward Porfirio.

Porfirio got to his feet, his hands out from his side. He'd never liked knife fights, even as a teenager. He pulled his knife from his own scabbard on his belt and crouched, knowing his life depended on being quicker and better at this than the Englishman.

They circled each other in the dappled shadows of the jungle, both keeping their eyes on the chest of the other man in the traditional knife-fighting technique.

"I'm going to kill you," Strunk said, "but it's not gonna be quick. I think I'll gut you like a hog and watch you bleed to death slowly."

Porfirio grinned, though fear almost made his heart stop its ceaseless hammering. "Don't be too sure, *gringo*," he muttered. "I was raised fighting with the knives. What does an Englishman know of such things?"

"Oh, you might be surprised, you cocky bastard," Strunk answered as he continued to circle the native. "My instructor in the SAS could cut off your ears and give you a shave at the same time before you could shit."

When Porfirio opened his mouth to answer, Strunk made his move, feinting with his knife hand toward the soldier's groin.

As Porfirio lowered his knife in defense, Strunk whirled in a spinning side-kick, his combat boot taking Porfirio in the side of his face, smashing his jaw and spinning him in a full circle to land on his hands and knees in the grass.

Quick as a jungle cat, Strunk pounced onto his back, his right boot stamping down on Porfirio's knife hand, crushing the knuckles and breaking three of his fingers.

"Aiyee!" Porfirio screamed, letting go of the knife and rolling to the side in a desperate attempt to dislodge the much larger and stronger man.

Strunk wrapped his left arm around Porfirio's neck and

rolled with him until the soldier was on top and Strunk on the bottom.

With a calm, deliberate motion, Strunk reversed his hold on the K-Bar in his hand and stabbed it into Porfirio's abdomen, just above the pubic bone.

With a grunt, Strunk jerked upward, slicing Porfirio's stomach open from pubis to rib cage. As his victim screamed again, Strunk kicked him off and jumped to his feet, standing over the wounded man and grinning again.

"I told you it would not be quick," he said in a low voice, his eyes sparkling as he watched the native slowly bleed out. "I love the smell of blood in the morning," Strunk whispered, copying a line from one of his favorite movies.

Twenty-four

Coop drove their stolen jeep down narrow jungle trails while Jersey held their M-16's pointing forward, ready for trouble. They'd laid the jeep's windshield down flat so they would have a ready-made rifle rest should the need arise.

When they came to a fork in the trail and Coop took a right turn, Jersey glanced in his direction. "Do you have any idea where you're going?" she asked.

"Of course not, dear," he replied cheerfully.

"Don't call me dear!" she snapped, forcing her eyes back onto the road.

"Why not?" he asked. "You're acting like a typical wife with your backseat driving and questions about my ability to get us where we want to go."

"If I were your wife, I'd've already committed suicide, Coop."

"If you were my wife, you wouldn't have to commit suicide, 'cause I'd've already killed you."

"In your dreams."

"No, in *your* dreams, dear," he rejoined. Then both laughed, enjoying the game they played on a constant basis.

They rounded a sharp turn in the jungle trail and Coop slammed on the brakes to keep from hitting an oncoming vehicle. As his jeep slewed sideways on the trail, it came to rest radiator-to-radiator with another similar jeep.

The four soldiers in the other vehicle stared wide-eyed at Coop and Jersey, still dressed in their jungle cammies. Jersey acted first, thumbing off the safety on her M-16 and spraying the soldiers with a quick burst on full automatic.

The twenty rounds in the M-16's magazine tore into the troops, making them jump and wiggle in a grotesque dance of death as the molten lead shredded their bodies. They barely had time to scream before it was over, the small clearing filling with smoke and the acrid smell of cordite as the echoes of the M-16's explosions still echoed through the afternoon gloom of the jungle.

Coop grabbed his M-16 from the seat next to Jersey and pushed her from the jeep, just as the front of their hood exploded under the impact of hundreds of 9mm bullets fired from the four vehicles behind the one they'd shot up.

"Hit the bush!" Coop screamed to Jersey as he followed her into the surrounding jungle in a running crouch, bullets pocking the dirt at his feet and riddling leaves over his head.

He and Jersey both hit the dirt at the same time, diving behind a fallen tree just as its bark was shredded by a fusillade of slugs.

Coop grabbed a fragmentation grenade off the harness on his chest, pulled the ring with his teeth, and lobbed the grenade over the tree in a sidearm throw.

Jersey raised her eyebrows at him. "Your teeth?"

He shrugged, his face flaming red. "I saw John Wayne do it in *Sands of Iwo Jima.*"

Jersey's whispered "Jesus . . ." was drowned out by the explosion of the grenade and the subsequent screams of dying and wounded men pierced by the several hundred shards of razor-sharp iron it threw out.

Jersey quickly raised her head up, aimed the M-16 at the sounds the men were making, and triggered off another burst on full auto.

As soon as her clip was empty, Coop popped his head up over the log and did the same thing, laying down covering fire as she jumped to her feet and took off at a dead run farther into the jungle.

Coop scrambled after her when his clip emptied, hearing screams and shouts in Spanish behind him as he followed Jersey deep into the thick overgrowth around them, looking for a hole to crawl into.

When she stopped abruptly, he almost ran into her back before he could slide to a halt.

"What the hell's the matter?" he whispered hoarsely, until he saw she was standing on the mossy bank of a river.

"Uh-oh," he muttered.

"You said it," she replied as she looked up and down the bank, searching frantically for a place to cross.

There was no place where the swirling waters of the river looked calm enough for them to wade across without being drowned, or eaten by whatever critters swam in the murky water.

Coop shook his head and stepped away from the bank to squat behind the bole of a large banyan tree. "Looks like this is it, Jers," he said in a low voice. "Those soldiers'll be here in a few minutes."

Jersey's shoulders slumped as she turned. "Damn, never a bridge when you need one," she said in a light voice.

"Listen," Coop said, "there's not time for both of us to cross, but I can keep 'em off you long enough for you to make it."

"Bullshit, Coop," she replied, squatting next to him and aiming around the other side of the tree. "There's no way I'm gonna take off and let you play hero."

"I can't believe you're so selfish," he said. "I've always wanted to go out like John Wayne in *The Alamo.*"

She grinned back at him. "How about we both go out like Butch Cassidy and the Sundance Kid?" she said, jerking back the loading lever on her M-16.

He shrugged. "Okay, as long as I can be Sundance."

She laughed. "Are you saying you always pictured me as a Butch?"

He smirked. "You said it, Jers, not me."

Vague shapes could be seen moving silently through the underbrush toward them fifty yards away.

Jersey put her M-16 to her shoulder and aimed, squeezing off a single shot. She was rewarded with the sound of a guttural scream from her target as he disappeared from sight.

"Good shot, Butch," Coop whispered, firing rapidly three times from the other side of the tree.

He ducked back just as his shots were answered with hundreds of rounds fired into their tree. "Great idea, Sundance," Jersey said sarcastically. "All you managed to do was draw their fire."

"That's my plan, Bitch . . . uh, I mean Butch. Draw their fire and make them use up all their bullets. Then we walk out of here and capture 'em."

"That's really smart, Coop, except I'm down to my last clip. How about you?"

Coop checked his pockets. "Half this one and one more. That's about thirty rounds, plus the eight in my .45."

She got serious. "Save the last two rounds, podna. Trust me, we don't want to be captured by these bastards!"

He too became serious. "Got ya, Jers."

He handed her one of his last two grenades, then turned and jerked the ring out and threw his as far as he could. He heard a frightened shout as the soldiers saw the grenade sailing toward them; then his ears rang with the loudness of the explosion as it blew bits and pieces of two men skyward.

Jersey slapped him on the shoulder. "Two down, about twenty to go," she said.

Coop pushed her down and fired his M-16 from the hip over her shoulder as a soldier rushed at them from the side, screaming cuss words in Spanish.

He choked on his words as Coop's burst of slugs tore his throat out and ripped his chest open, sending his body spinning into the river.

"Looks like the crocs are gonna have Mexican food for lunch," Coop drawled.

The bark on the tree they were behind erupted under an onslaught of bullets from several AK-47's as several men charged through the jungle, firing from the hip and yelling in Spanish.

Both Coop and Jersey leaned around the tree and opened fire, spraying 9mm slugs into the men. Their bodies stopped and were thrown backward as if they'd been kicked by a mule, their arms flung wide, their shouts drowning in gurgles and screams as their lives were torn from them.

Jersey glanced at Coop as her M-16 clicked on an empty firing chamber. Her eyes glittered as she slowly drew her K-Bar from its scabbard, and her lips drew back from her teeth in a savage grin. Coop shivered, knowing now what cowboys had faced when confronted by Jersey's Apache ancestors.

He jerked his clip out—two slugs left. Switching his firing pin to single-fire, he pulled his Colt .45 out and handed it to Jersey. "Here ya go, Butch. You got seven in the mag and one in the chamber. Use 'em wisely."

He peered around the tree, and could see ten to fifteen men slowly advancing on their position through the jungle, spread out so they'd make tough targets. He figured they had about ten minutes to live.

Suddenly a redheaded giant appeared in the brush behind the advancing soldiers, holding a funny-looking rifle in his arms.

"Goddamn," Coop muttered, "it's Eric the Red."

Jersey looked around the tree in time to see the red-haired man grin as he pulled the trigger. A rapid succession of booming explosions came from what they now could see was a shotgun. It bucked and jumped as it fired faster than any shotgun they'd ever heard of, sending 00-buckshot loads spreading through the soldiers, cutting them down like a scythe, shredding them and sending bodies and body parts flying through the air.

In seconds it was all over, and the giant walked toward

them through clouds of cordite and gun smoke as if out of a fog of death.

"Jersey, Coop," he yelled. "We've come for you."

Coop and Jersey stepped out from behind the tree, shaking their heads. "Jesus," Coop whispered, glancing around at the bodies scattered like cordwood on the jungle floor.

The giant grinned. "No, actually, it's Reno. Harley Reno, at your service," he said, giving a small bow as Ben Raines and the rest of his team came running into the clearing.

More gunshots could be heard in the distance as Hammer Hammerick took out the sentries left behind to guard the soldiers' jeeps.

Coop grabbed Reno's hand. "Thanks, podna, you saved our bacon back there."

Reno shrugged. "That's what they pay me for."

"Can I see that cannon you were using?" Coop asked, reaching for the SPAS assault shotgun. "The sumbitch sounded like a machine gun."

"You two okay?" Ben asked as Corrie, Beth, and Anna ran to Jersey and embraced her.

"What? No hugs for me?" Coop said, looking up from examining the shotgun, a hurt expression on his face.

Jersey looked at the Mini-Uzis and Beretta pistols the women were carrying and raised her eyebrows. "Hey, nice ordnance," she said. "New toys?"

"Yeah," Anna replied, glancing at Harley Reno as he talked with Hammer Hammerick. "Harley got 'em for us."

Jersey noticed the adoring look in Anna's eyes when she stared at Reno. "Harley, huh?" she asked, a smile curling her lips. "Do I sense more than a professional interest in the red giant?"

Anna's face flamed bright red and she stammered, "I . . . I don't know what you mean."

Both Corrie and Beth laughed and nodded. "I'm afraid Harley is causing our girl some sleepless nights," Corrie said.

"Is not!" Anna replied, looking away as she blushed even more.

"Okay, guys," Ben said. "Tell me what you two have been up to while we've been slaving away in the States."

As Coop and Jersey filled Ben in on their recent activities, El Gato and his men hung back, keeping watch on the jungle in case more soldiers showed up.

Twenty-five

Sam Gentry was at the wheel.

Billy Bob Collins, Nick Lewis, and Bob Madden sat quietly in the battered Subaru station wagon as they reached the checkpoint outside of Indianapolis, driving empty roads from Tennessee in the dark to carry out their assignment. They were ex-Blackshirts who'd been handpicked by Herb Knoff and General Bradley Stevens, Jr., to carry out what they'd been told was the most important assignment of the war. To kill the men who'd deposed President Osterman and ordered the disbanding of their Blackshirt units.

It had been difficult to find gasoline in places, but Sam had a crew with him who knew how to find things when they were scarce. Showing a gun often made gas station owners less reluctant to part with their precious stores of fuel, now that the country was in chaos after the bombings and raids by soldiers from the SUSA.

Gentry slowed when he came to the perimeter fence, a maze of razor wire and electrically charged chain link around what had been called the War Room, a heavily guarded military compound that had once been President Osterman's underground headquarters before Ben Raines and his Rebels struck, sending Osterman into hiding in Tennessee.

Armed soldiers came out of the guardhouse. Gentry braked to a halt in the light from a pair of mercury vapor lamps. The rest of the compound was cloaked in darkness.

"What's your business?" a uniformed soldier asked, peering into the car window, his eyebrows raising at the sight of their black uniforms.

Gentry took out his false papers, a good forgery even in bright light. "We're here to see General Joseph Winter and Mr. Otis Warner. A Code Seven. They're expecting us."

The soldier glanced at his identification, then at the other three passengers. "I thought all the Blackshirt units had been disbanded."

Gentry smiled. "Most of 'em have, but we're on special assignment. That's what we're hear to report about."

"What's this Code Seven?"

"You're supposed to know about it."

"I'll have to check," the soldier said. "Can't let you in without authorization. Stay put while I call down to the command center. I never heard of Code Seven."

The guard walked away. Gentry spoke softly over his right shoulder. "This may not work. President Osterman said a Code Seven would get us in."

"I say we just kill these sons of bitches," Bob Madden said, his fist wrapped around a Glock .45 with a silencer, hidden inside his coat. "We can cut the phone lines and bust their radios."

"I agree," Nick Lewis said. "This is bullshit. If we keep sittin' here, they can kill us real easy."

"Five guards," Gentry observed. "We'll have to take 'em fast and quiet."

"Let's do it," Billy Bob Collins said, a strange glint in his eyes. "The way we are now, we're sittin' ducks."

He jerked a silenced Colt .45 automatic from his belt and opened the door on the Subaru. "I've got the electronic pass-key Osterman gave us. We kill these sumbitches an' drive in. Then we kill Warner and Winter and get the hell out of here before they know what hit 'em."

Lewis was not waiting for further encouragement. The

money President Osterman was paying them to assassinate General Joseph Winter and Otis Warner was enough to be worth taking a few chances, not to mention the opportunity to have their Blackshirt units reinstated. As a hit squad, Sam Gentry's group had never failed to carry out an assignment.

"Hey, there!" Lewis shouted to the soldier inside the guard station. "I've got somethin' else I want to show you."

The others got out slowly, as though with no real purpose in mind.

"Stay in the car!" a soldier commanded. "You've gotta wait until Sergeant Drake gets clearance for you."

Bob Madden walked up to the guard. "Fuck you," he whispered as he stuck the barrel of his silenced Walther against the soldier's belly.

A puffing noise followed. The guard's eyes bulged as his knees gave way. Blood poured from a huge hole in his back where the shell exited. Pieces of his spinal column jutted through his camouflage shirt.

Billy Bob Collins fired three whispering bullets into a guard slouched beside the gate.

The soldier collapsed in a heap beside the chain-link fence and groaned, letting his rifle fall to the damp ground where he sprawled, bleeding.

Gentry shot the guard in the guardhouse. The other soldiers were killed instantly when Bob Madden turned his gun on the remaining men.

"Open the gate, Billy Bob," Gentry said. "Nick, you cut the phone lines and take out that radio. We'll pull the bodies out of sight and close the gate behind us. That way, it'll look like it's supposed to look."

Gentry fired his Glock at a soldier still squirming beside the guardhouse. The thump of molten lead entering flesh was muted by the quiet throb of the Subaru's engine.

"Let's go," Lewis said after he pulled the guard's body

out of sight behind the guard station. Lewis was the last man to climb back into the car when the gate was closed.

"I cut the phone lines and smashed the radio," Madden said as Gentry put the car in low gear. "With any luck at all we'll be out of here in ten minutes."

"We gotta kill both of them," Gentry said, aiming for a bunker a quarter of a mile away where two more guards stood at the top of a stairway leading underground. "And we've gotta kill these two guards without any noise."

"Give 'em the Code Seven bullshit again," Billy Bob said from the backseat.

"Yeah," Lewis said. "While you're tellin' them about Code Seven, I'll climb out this back door and blow their fuckin' heads off."

Billy Bob chuckled softly. "That's what a Code Seven really is, Nick. It's a death sentence, an' we're the ones who are here deliverin' it."

"Keep your guns out of sight," Gentry warned, drawing closer to the underground compound. "Smile the prettiest smiles you've got and act natural."

Tommy Davis had been expecting trouble for weeks. Rumors that President Osterman was dead couldn't be verified. He watched the yellow Subaru station wagon approach the entrance to the underground command center where General Joseph Winter and Otis Warner were trying to control a war-torn country.

"Something smells like shit," Davis said. "I don't like the looks of this car. We didn't get any clearance from the gate, so be ready. I'll call the front gate to see who these people are, and what they're doing here."

Herbert Faust readied his Uzi, jacking back the loading mechanism. "You give the word, Captain, an' I'll blow that little yellow car to bits."

Davis keyed the mike on his radio. "Main Gate One. Who is in the yellow station wagon?"

He got no answer. Davis picked up the telephone connecting the guardhouse with the bunker. "Sergeant Drake?" he asked into the mouthpiece.

Again, he got no reply.

"What did Sergeant Drake say?" Faust wanted to know.

"He didn't pick up the phone," Davis replied.

"These motherfuckers broke through," Faust snarled, rising above the concrete wall in front of the entrance with his Uzi in both hands. "I'll kill them."

"Wait until we hear their story. The communications lines could be down," Davis said.

The Subaru ground to a stop in front of the entrance into the War Room. Four men got out.

"What are you doing here?" Captain Davis asked, his hand resting on his own Uzi.

"We're here to see General Winter and Mr. Warner," the driver said. "It's a Code Seven."

Faust grunted. The old entry codes were no longer valid. General Winter had changed all the old signals when he took over command of the USA forces after President Osterman was reported killed.

He rose up and aimed his machine gun at the strangers. "Code Seven has been discontinued," he said. "Put your hands where I can see them or you're dead meat."

The slender one, the driver, came out with a pistol. It was all the prompting Herbert Faust needed.

He sprayed the Subaru and the newcomers with a hail of bullets, the hammering of his Uzi ending a quiet around the compound at Indianapolis.

Two men went down with his first burst of gunfire, blood spattering all over the yellow station wagon as their bodies danced and jigged under the onslaught of the molten lead ripping into them.

A shot was fired by a man behind the Subaru, his bullet

tearing a chunk of meat out of Captain Davis's shoulder and spinning him half around. Faust directed his fire across the luggage rack of the car, ripping the man's head off when a string of bullets crossed his throat.

The last man to go down was killed by Captain Davis with a short burst of automatic-weapons fire fired one-handed, his left arm hanging useless by his side.

"We got 'em," Faust said.

Captain Davis nodded, his face screwed up in pain from the wound in his shoulder. "Make sure they're all dead," he growled. "Then go through their pockets and find out who they are . . . who they *were*. I'll inform President Warner there's been an attempt on his life."

Twenty-six

Comandante Perro Loco stood by a window of the *hacienda* while a radio operator, Sergeant Manuel Ortiz, adjusted the dials on a shortwave set sitting on a desk against a far wall. The dark-haired American prisoner stood by to give the operator instructions for the frequency Ortiz would need to contact President Osterman.

Manuel looked up when he found a garbled speaker's voice on the dial. Radio transmissions across most of Central America were subject to weather conditions and the strength of the signal.

"Someone just said an announcement was forthcoming from the military headquarters of General Ben Raines," Manuel said. "It is a special broadcast given by General Raines. It is being relayed all over the North American continent. The speech will be translated into Spanish as well as English. Do you want to hear it, *comandante?*"

Perro Loco's jaw jutted unconsciously despite being preoccupied with other matters. He stared blankly out the window while static crackled from the radio's speaker.

"Yes. Let's hear what the mighty general from the colossus to the north has to say."

"We have a message from General Raines," a deep voice announced. "A reading of the Tri-State Manifesto, which the general says will govern policies all across North America from now on. Here is General Raines."

A deeper voice began speaking.

"As advocates and supporters of the Tri-State philosophy, we believe that freedom, like respect, is earned and must be constantly nurtured and protected from those who would take it away. We believe in the right of every law-abiding citizen to protect his or her life, liberty, and personal property by any means at hand, without fear of arrest, criminal prosecution, or lawsuit. The right to bear arms is essential to maintaining true personal freedom.

"We believe that politicians, theorists, and socialists are the greatest threat to freedom-loving peoples and that their misguided efforts have caused grave injustices in the fields of criminal law, education, and public welfare.

"Therefore, in respect to criminal law, an effective criminal justice system should be guided by these basic tenets: Our courts must stop pampering criminals.

"The punishment must fit the crime.

"Justice must be fair, but also be swift and, if necessary, harsh.

"There is no perfect society. Only a fair one.

"Therefore, in respect to education, education is the key to solving problems in any society and the lack of it is the root cause of a country's decline.

"An effective system of education must stress hard discipline along with the arts, sciences, fine music, and basic skills in reading, writing, and mathematics. It must teach fairness and respect. It must teach morals, the dignity of labor, and the value of the family.

"Therefore in respect to welfare. Welfare—we prefer workfare—is reserved only for the elderly, infirm, and those who need a temporary helping hand.

"And the welfare system must also instill the concept of honest work for honest pay. Instill the concept that everyone who can work must work, and be forced to work if necessary.

"It must instill the concept that there is no free lunch and that being productive citizens in a free society is the only honorable path to take.

"And that racial prejudice and bigotry are intolerable in a free and vital society. No one is worthy of respect simply because of the color of their skin. Respect is earned by actions and by deeds, not by birthright.

"There are only two types of people on earth . . . decent and indecent. Those who are decent will flourish, and those who are not will perish. No laws laid down by a body of government can make one person like another.

"A free and just society must be protected at all costs even if it means shedding the blood of its citizens. The willingness of citizens to lay down their lives for the belief in freedom is a cornerstone of true democracy. Without that willingness the structure of society will surely crumble and fall into the ashes of history.

"Therefore, along with the inalienable right to bear arms, and the inalienable right to personal protection, a strong, skilled, and well-equipped military is essential to maintaining a free society.

"A strong military eliminates the need for allies, allowing the society to focus on the needs of its citizens.

"The business of citizens is not the business of the world unless the rights of citizens are infringed upon by outside forces.

"The duty of those who live in a free society is clear, and personal freedom is not negotiable.

"In conclusion, we who support the Tri-State philosophy and live by its code and its laws pledge to defend it by any means necessary. We pledge to work fairly and justly to rebuild and maintain a society in which all citizens are truly free, and are able to pursue productive lives without fear and without intervention."

A pause. Perro Loco turned his face to the radio.

"This is the manifesto by which the continent of North America will be governed," Raines continued. "For too long, the people in parts of this country have been dominated by a woman named Claire Osterman and a political system in which she proclaimed herself President. As of this date, President Osterman's armies have been crushed. President Osterman is reported to be dead. This period of Nazi-style government has come to an end. Elections will be held, and the people of North America will be free to govern themselves. President Osterman has been defeated. You have nothing to fear from her now. She has been driven from power, if she is still alive, and most of her soldiers are prisoners of the Tri-States government."

Perro Loco glared at the American prisoner. "Can this be true? Is your President dead?"

"No," Arnoldo Mendoza said. "You spoke to her yourself not two days ago."

Loco regarded him through narrowed eyes. "I spoke to a voice on a radio claiming to be President Osterman. Now, this general from the SUSA says she is dead." He shrugged. "Who is to know what is true?"

Mendoza shook his head back and forth. "I'm telling you, sir, she is alive. She sent me here to find you."

Loco held up his hand for quiet as a final message came from the radio. "Rulers like Osterman are the root of all evil on this planet. And we pledge to hunt them down, as well as all others who oppose the freedom of mankind. North America is free, and we intend to make sure it remains that way forever."

Jim Strunk shook his head. "It's bullshit, *comandante*. I believe Osterman is still alive. After all, the woman you talked to knew all about our previous conversations before she was reported dead."

The radio transmission ended.

Perro Loco grimaced. "What you say is true, Jim. For now, we will proceed as if the woman we are speaking to is in fact the President as she says. After all, if she is not, we have risked nothing we have not already planned to do in any case. However, we will be careful not to let her know too much of our plans."

Loco walked to his desk and picked up his cup of coffee, cold now, as his thoughts turned to General Ben Raines, the man he was soon to face in battle. *Raines feels sure his victory was complete,* Loco thought. *I will prove him wrong.*

"When we meet on the battlefield, Raines," Loco snarled, "you will face total annihilation. Enjoy your brief moment of triumph, you arrogant bastard. When I march north across Mexico it will be with one purpose . . . to destroy you. And I will!"

He gave Ortiz a chilly stare. "Find the frequency for this President Osterman. Tell her that I will agree to form a military alliance with her . . . but under my conditions."

"Sí, comandante," Ortiz replied, twisting a dial on the shortwave set.

Arnoldo Mendoza cleared his throat. "I fought Raines before over in Africa, while I was with Bruno Bottger. Raines is clever as hell. I was lucky to escape with my life."

"Tell me about it . . . about Raines," Perro Loco said. "What is it that makes him so hard to kill?"

Mendoza thought for a moment, then looked up at Loco. "He's smart as hell, and he seems to have an instinct for what an enemy is going to do next." The American shook his head. "I've never heard of him being caught by surprise . . ."

Twenty-seven

Arnoldo Mendoza began the story of the months he'd spent in Africa under the command of Bruno Bottger, speaking softly as Ortiz twisted his radio controls.

"General Conreid came into Bruno's subterranean office, his face a ghostly white. He saluted smartly and stood at attention until Bruno spoke to him.

" 'What is so important that you told Rudolf you had to see me right away?'

"Conreid took a deep breath. 'I have bad news, General Field Marshal.'

" 'I guessed as much. It has to do with your armored division tracking the Rebel bitch, Commander Malone. I use the term loosely.'

" 'I'm afraid so,' Conreid replied. 'I sent one of our best field armored commanders, Major Schultz, and almost fifty of our Minsks and Bulldogs. Three hundred men from the Pretorian Guard went along as infantry support . . .'

" 'And?' Bruno was growing impatient, although he had already guessed what Conreid came to tell him.

" 'We engaged the enemy in southern Angola . . .'

" 'It does not matter where! Get on with it!'

"Conreid swallowed hard, and his hands pressed to his legs were shaking. 'They destroyed us. Every tank was immobilized or blown to bits. Five men escaped on foot in the jungle. One of them just radioed me with a full report. They had antitank rockets and heavy mortars. Major Schultz is dead and so is everyone else; however, I was told the Rebels captured Captain Klaus, commander of the Pretorian Guard unit. I suppose they intend to question him.'

"Bruno momentarily closed his eyes, fighting back the urge to use his Steyer on General Conreid. Incompetence could not be tolerated. 'They will torture Klaus, wanting to know about our fortifications here at Pretoria so the information can be sent to General Raines. It is quite clear this bastard Raines intends to storm our headquarters. There is no other explanation for his curious movements.'

" 'I agree,' Conreid stammered. 'They move back and forth to confuse us, but every Rebel battalion seems to be moving toward South Africa, toward Pretoria.'

" 'Will this Captain Klaus talk if they torture him?'

" 'That . . . would be difficult to say. He is a brave soldier, as his record shows, but virtually any man will crack under the right amount of pressure.'

"Bruno settled back in his chair. 'So your brilliant strategy has failed us, General Conreid. You assured me you could find Commander Malone and her Battalion Twelve and crush her soundly. Instead, you tell me we've been handed a crushing defeat, losing fifty valuable tanks and their support vehicles.'

"Conreid nodded, having some difficulty finding his voice for the moment. 'Somehow, they were expecting us at a particularly difficult spot to defend. The survivor who radioed me said it was deep jungle, and that land mines had been well placed in the most strategic and damaging areas.'

" 'Your tanks were drawn into an ambush.'

" 'It would seem so. Schultz was a brilliant field commander, and I'm at a loss to explain it. I can only offer this, and it will seem a weak excuse. The woman, Malone, has virtually no air support; thus she stays in the deepest jungles where our air superiority is of no use. If we could have put the Hinds on top of her, this disaster would not have happened. Colonel Walz had air recon over the area and he found no trace of an entire Rebel battalion in Botswana or Angola. We found out where Battalion Twelve was from a Zulu mercenary. Walz could give us nothing at all.'

" 'Then it would seem I have incompetent men directing our aircraft and our armored divisions,' Bruno told him, as his anger multiplied. He leaned forward and slammed his fist on the desk.

"Conreid flinched, but said nothing, as Bruno fixed him with a steely-eyed stare. 'You have failed me miserably, General. I will not tolerate failure. You can't even win a skirmish with a woman in command of our enemy. She appears to be a far better tactician than either you or Colonel Walz. I find I'm surrounded by incompetence, by idiots! In the days of the great Nazi regime under Adolph Hitler, both of you would be shot for failing our cause. Hitler would not have tolerated this!'

" 'I understand, General Field Marshal. I simply did the best I could, devising the best plan feasible to destroy an army that will not come out in the open to fight. The woman stays hidden, leaving us with no choice but to ferret her out of her jungle hiding places. I could think of no other way without cover from our airships. We had to go in after her, to halt her march on Pretoria.'

"Bruno's jaw clamped. 'Instead, you lead our men and matériel to total destruction!'

" 'I cannot deny it. I have served you and the New World Order as faithfully as I knew how. Until we were confronted by this elusive woman and her battalion, I enjoyed a great many successes in the name of our cause. But Malone does not fight with military strategy. It is as if she always does the thing we expect least from a well-trained army. I can offer you no other explanation.'

" 'What the hell will stop her from marching all the way to Pretoria, General?'

"For the first time, Conreid smiled, albeit weakly. 'If she gets this far, she will be forced to come out in the open, even if she does make it across northern Botswana. She must then face the Kalahari Desert in the south. Her tanks will break down in the sand. We can direct air strikes on her until she has been wiped out, down to the last man.'

" 'But what if she suddenly turns east into Zimbawe, following the rivers the way she has in the past?'

" 'She and General Raines and his other battalions will still have to cross the Transvaal. When they do, we will blow them off the face of the earth. There will be no places to hide from our bombers and rockets, and our antiaircraft gunners will knock their Apaches from the skies.'

"Bruno wondered, tapping a finger on his desk. What was happening now was all too much like events that had happened before in Europe many years ago. The weakling United Nations Secretary General, Moon, had branded him a neo-Nazi fanatic and a major threat to world stability. Bruno had raised a massive army to realize his dream of reviving the Third Reich in the post-apocalyptic world. He had formed an elite Minority Eradication Force in Switzerland, and had had almost 250,000 veteran troops to prepare for war against Ben Raines and other SUSA armies. After several months of bloody fighting, Bruno had called for a meeting in Geneva. There, he had made his racial position clear—the lands he controlled would be his empire forever, and he vowed to fight to the death to defend it, an empire where he would allow no Jews or blacks or any other minorities. By then, his army had risen to almost three million men. And it was in Geneva where Bruno had related that his scientists were developing a serum that caused infertility, which he planned to introduce to the drinking water supply in Africa and Asia, to thin the world's minority populations.

"When the talks grew ugly, Bruno's men staged an attack and captured President Blanton, but with a motive, to fake his rescue and win global sympathy. Ben Raines exposed his plan before he could put it into action. Since, he and Raines had become sworn enemies.

"Bruno had given Raines an ultimatum: Be out of Europe in twenty-four hours, or all-out war would commence. Bruno had no choice but to back up his threat and attack when Raines ignored the ultimatum. Bruno's empire, called the New Federation, all but collapsed. He was driven back across Germany, with high casualties, heading for Russia. But Raines cut him off and Bruno was forced to stage his own suicide, leaving his second in command, General Henrich, to show Raines a body said to be that of Bruno Bottger. While this delaying tactic was going on, Bruno took a hundred thousand of his men and escaped to Africa, to start over. All this because of Ben Raines—being forced to quietly rebuild a powerful army, equipped with the best weaponry on earth while in hiding in Pretoria, biding his time until he was ready.

"And now, Raines was coming after him again. And again, it seemed nothing could stop him.

"Bruno spoke to Conreid. 'Tell Colonel Walz I want a meeting tonight. Inform General Ligon. Perhaps now it is time to put our germ and chemical weapons to better use from the air. We will see if General Raines and his battalions are fully prepared for a new type of war.'

"Conreid seemed relieved. 'I will summon Walz and Ligon. I agree. The time has come to put everything to the ultimate test. We cannot withstand any more huge casualties or our weapons stock will be seriously depleted. We have superiority in the air, or so we believe. Let's test the Rebels in the skies.'

"Bruno pored over his maps, then studied recon reports, as few as they were, even though they were probably grossly inaccurate. He had given up letting others plan what his New World Order armies would do, deciding he could devise his own defense and counterattacks.

"Rudolf Hessner looked on from a chair across the desk,

as did Colonel Walz, General Ligon, and General Conreid, who had arrived only moments ago for the meeting.

" 'They'll come from three directions,' Bruno said, talking to himself as much as the others. 'One fork will come from the west, across the southern tip of Nambia, either along the Atlantic coast or across Great Namaland.' He pointed a finger to a spot on the map.

"Colonel Walz nodded. 'We can see them coming from the air. Namaland is fairly open. Not many places to hide tanks or APCs and our radar will pick up their aircraft. We can set up antiaircraft batteries west of Johannesburg. We'll put them in deep bunkers so they can't be taken out by smaller rockets.'

" 'Good,' Bruno said, moving his finger to the Republic of Botswana. 'I know Ben Raines . . . the way his mind works. He'll send a force of some kind across the Kalahari, probably with strong air support, fighters and helicopter gunships. Here is where we'll meet him head-on in the skies, with tank battalions to back us up.'

" 'A very good idea,' General Conreid said. 'We can put a few antiaircraft cannons in fortified sand pits near Serpwe, where there is enough rock to protect them. Sending tanks out into the Kalahari will be something he won't expect; however, our Minsks can do well in sand or snow.'

"Bruno looked at Colonel Walz. 'Can we give this area enough air support, Colonel?'

" 'Of course, General Field Marshal.'

"Now Bruno turned to General Ligon. 'The Kalahari would be a good place to drop nerve-gas bombs. We know they are impervious to our anthrax agents. Mustard gas, and tear gas, will force them into protective gear, which will slow them down significantly in the desert heat.'

" 'I agree,' Ligon said. 'Our inventory contains well over five hundred mustard gas canisters, and over twice that many of the tear-gas bombs. If we drop the right number of both on the forces coming across the Kalahari, they will suffer immeasurably in the desert heat.'

" 'I want the bastards to suffer,' Bruno hissed, returning to his map. 'Now all we have to do is prepare our defenses and plan for attack in Zimbawe.'

" 'Napalm,' Colonel Walz suggested.

" 'Yes, I like the idea of using napalm there,' Conreid agreed quickly.

" 'It will set the jungle ablaze,' General Ligon agreed. 'If we score direct hits they will be cooked alive, and then we can go in and mop up with tanks and infantrymen.'

"Bruno looked up. 'Make these preparations, gentlemen. And be sure of one thing. If any of you fails to carry out his assignment, I will personally see to your execution.'

" 'Do not worry,' General Ligon said as he got up from the table. 'Our chemical weapons will not fail if they are delivered properly.'

"Colonel Walz nodded when he stood up. 'Rest assured they will be delivered correctly by my aircraft, General Field Marshal Bottger. I will not fail you.'

"General Conreid got up last. 'I will redeem myself for what happened in Angola. This, I promise you.'

" 'Then get started,' Bruno said evenly, looking around the group with hooded eyes. 'This will be the final defeat of all Rebel forces.'

" 'We intend to make certain of it,' Walz said, turning on his heel to be let out by Rudolf.

"One by one his officers filed out of the room, leaving Bruno alone with myself and Rudolf. Rudolf came over to the table with a question on his face.

" 'Keep a close eye on General Conreid,' Bruno said, keeping his voice low.

" 'Do you suspect him of treason?' the muscular Rudolf asked, frowning.

" 'Perhaps. Perhaps he is only a clever fool. I may have been blind to his shortcomings. Report his every movement to me, and if he makes a mistake in these preparations, or if he talks to anyone who may be suspicious, I want to be informed.'

"Rudolf smiled, a chilly smile. 'Then, if you wish, I will kill him for you and make him suffer a terrible death.'

"Bruno shook his head. 'If he is a traitor, or even merely a fool who has led our soldiers to their deaths, that is exactly what I have in mind for him.'"

Perro Loco gave the American a steady gaze. "So tell me what happened?"

"General Raines was ready for us. He destroyed Bottger's armies. As I told you before, I was lucky to get out of Africa alive. He anticipated our every move, almost as if he knew what we were going to do before we did."

Loco walked back to the window. "We will show him a very different kind of war. Contact President Osterman. If we form an alliance we will have him trapped on two sides, from the north and the south. Just make sure your President understands I will be in charge of all military actions in Mexico. I will brook no interference from her in my plans."

When Ortiz had the connection made, he nodded and Mendoza took the microphone. "This is Arnoldo Mendoza. Let me talk to President Osterman. I have news from Perro Loco."

Twenty-eight

Claire Osterman gathered her inner circle of advisers around her following her talk with Arnoldo Mendoza and Perro Loco.

She sipped from a cup of herbal tea, trying to stay on her new health regime since Herb Knoff and even the usually imperturbable Harlan Millard had shown uncommon pleasure in her new body.

As usual, Harlan was being a worrywart. "I just don't know if we can trust this Perro Loco guy," he said, his forehead wrinkled in frown lines. "After all, what do we know about him?"

General Bradley Stevens, Jr., cleared his throat impatiently. "Goddamn, Harlan!" he said in his hoarse drill sergeant's voice. "What the hell do we need to know about the son of a bitch other than the fact he says he's got fifty thousand troops massed at Mexico's southern border an' he's willin' to attack in the next few days?"

Claire cocked an eyebrow and glanced at Herb Knoff for his input.

He shrugged, phlegmatic as usual when discussing matters of military strategy. He only became really interested if it seemed he might get the chance to do someone bodily harm personally, or when he was in bed with the now shapely and more youthful-looking Claire.

"I agree with the general," he said, stifling a yawn. "It seems pretty obvious he's planning on attacking Mexico with or without us, so we really have very little to lose by promising him we'll try to keep Ben Raines and the SUSA busy on this end—which *we* plan to do anyway." He looked around the room. "I can't see any downside to this arrangement."

Claire nodded. "Nor can I. If the dumb Mexican is stupid enough to believe everything I tell him, he deserves to be disappointed when we shitcan his ass."

"Actually, Claire, I believe he's a Nicaraguan, not a Mexican," Harlan said, causing everyone in the room to laugh.

Harlan looked flustered. "But, Claire, we don't even know if he's gonna be able to take command of the Nicaraguan Army like he says he can."

"I don't give a shit if he's from outer space, or if he will be able to take over the army down there. But as long as he can cause enough trouble down south to get Mexico or Nicaragua to ask Raines for help, that'll give Raines that many less troops to send against us once I take over as President of the USA."

Herb Knoff cocked his head to the side and looked at Stevens. "Speaking of which, how're we doing in that regard, Brad?"

General Stevens pulled a cigar as thick as a sausage out of his pocket and stuck it in his mouth. " 'Bout as good as we can expect, given the short amount of time we've had an' the limited number of personnel available to us. We've managed to hook up with most of the ex-Blackshirt regiments, an' a lot of the FPPS boys are on our side too. In the last two days we've managed to sabotage two airfields and put one entire base out of action by contaminatin' the water supply with . . . um, fecal material."

"Fecal material?" Harlan asked. "You mean . . ."

Stevens laughed. "You got it, Harlan, shit. The whole damn base is fightin' over the latrines 'cause of the dysentery they got from it."

"Any word on our assassination team?" Claire asked Herb.

He shook his head. "Nope, and I'm afraid that's bad news.

If they'd been successful, we'd've heard from them by now. I think we have to consider that particular mission a failure."

Claire shrugged. "It was a long shot anyway, but at least the bastards'll lose some sleep now that they know I'm damned serious about getting my old job back."

Stevens pursed his lips around the cigar butt. "You know, we might give it another try, if you don't mind possibly losing a helicopter or two in the attempt."

"What do you mean, Brad?" Claire asked, leaning her elbows on her desk as she glared at him.

"One of those airfields I mentioned happens to have a couple of Blackhawk choppers on it. We might wanta send 'em down to Indianapolis and fire a couple of missiles at Warner and General Winter. If we hit 'em, good enough, an' if we don't, hell, it don't never hurt to fire a couple a shots over the enemy's head just to keep 'em too busy duckin' to fire back at you."

Claire slapped her hand down on her desk. "Capital idea, Bradley. Why don't you take care of that right away?"

Stevens pulled a small notebook from his pocket and made a note. "I'll see that it gets done within twenty-four hours, Madame President, and I'll also work on getting a couple of jets to go after Raines's base in Arkansas."

"Okay, then. Gentlemen, this meeting is adjourned until tomorrow at the same time when perhaps we'll have some good news from the general."

As the three men got to their feet, Claire said, "Hold on a minute, Herb. I have a few additional things to go over with you."

"Yes, ma'am."

He followed Stevens and Millard to the door and closed it behind them. When he turned around, Claire already had her blouse unbuttoned, showing she was wearing no bra.

"Come back here to my private office, Herb. Talking about killing Otis always makes me horny as hell," she said, walking through a door on the far side of the room.

"Seeing you like that does the same thing to me," Herb said, undoing his shirt as he followed her through the door.

She stood next to the bed and slipped out of her shirt and skirt, posing naked in front of Knoff for just a moment before climbing beneath the covers.

When Herb hesitated, she smiled seductively. "Hurry up, lover. We're wasting valuable time."

Herb grinned. "Don't tell me to hurry, Claire. I know you like it much better when I take my time."

"Yeah," she said, leaning back with her arms behind her neck. "Like the old song says, 'I like a man with the slow hands . . .' "

Twenty-nine

Perro Loco sipped coffee as he sat in the rear seat of the Lear Jet as it sped toward Managua, Nicaragua. The jet, though almost twenty-five years old, was still pristine, having been maintained to the highest standards by the drug lord Loco's men had liberated it from.

"Is everything set up?" he asked Paco Valdez.

"*Sí, comandante.* Our friends in the newspapers have been reporting your fears of a Mexican strike against Presidente Montenegro in Nicaragua. They have been calling for him to appoint you as Ambassador at Large to try and head off such an attack."

"And Montenegro?"

Valdez shook his head. "He knows our accusations are bullshit, but with the people so afraid, he has not publicly said so. It is my understanding he is looking for some way to keep from having to give you any official authority, in fear you will try to take over the government."

Strunk, sitting a couple of rows forward, laughed out loud. "The bastard's right to be afraid, 'cause that's exactly what's gonna happen."

"How about Eduardo? Has he made it here yet?" Loco asked, referring to his helicopter pilot who'd been sent ahead the previous week with an old Huey gunship with Mexico markings on it.

Valdez nodded. "*Sí.* He radioed he had no trouble flying over Guatemala and Honduras. The fuel dumps were exactly where the rebels told us they'd be, and he reported he is now less than twenty miles from Managua and is ready to attack the Presidential Palace on our command."

"And the stolen DEA missiles we have fitted to his helicopter?"

Valdez shrugged. "We have no way of knowing if they will operate as they are supposed to. After all, they are fifteen years old and we have no one who can check them."

Strunk turned in his seat. "It won't matter if he actually manages to kill Montenegro or not. Once the attack is made and blamed on Mexico, Montenegro will have no choice but to appoint you to the government."

"That is correct, *comandante,*" Valdez added. "After you're proven right in your accusations against Mexico, the people will be screaming for you to be their new leader."

Loco nodded. "Yes, but it will be much easier if that old lady Montenegro is dead and out of the way. He is a coward and will be hard to convince to commit the Nicaraguan troops in a war against Mexico."

Strunk raised his glass of scotch whiskey. "Then let's toast Eduardo and hope he blows the son of a bitch to Hell and back."

"When are you planning to order the attack?" Valdez asked.

"Day after tomorrow. I will meet with Montenegro and again warn him of my fears for his life, with plenty of reporters present, and then the next day when the attack occurs, I will be ready to assume my proper place in the government of Nicaragua."

"By then, General Juan Dominguez will have our Belizian troops massed on the border with Mexico, ready to move northward and take the Mexicans' attention away from events in Nicaragua," Valdez said, rubbing his hands together in cheerful anticipation of finally putting into practice the plans he and Perro Loco had been making for several years.

"What about Honduras and Guatemala?" Strunk asked as

he stood up and refilled his scotch at a bar in the front of the cabin.

"I have been assured by the leaders of those countries they are ready to join us if I gain control of the Nicaraguan Army. They have no love for Mexico and even less for the United States."

"And they are tired of getting the rest of the world's leftovers. They hunger for the respect and wealth only Perro Loco can give them," Valdez added.

Strunk took a deep draught of his drink, then smiled. "Do they have any idea what your true plans are for their countries?"

Loco laughed. "Of course not, *amigo*. Would they agree to join me if they thought that soon they would also be under my control?"

"Once we have control of Nicaragua, Honduras, and Guatemala, we will have over fifty thousand troops at our disposal to use against Mexico. They will not stand a chance against us," Valdez said.

Loco interrupted. "Enough of this talk. I must ready my speech to the newspapers and the Congress about the unfortunate attack upon the peaceful peoples of Nicaragua by the imperialists of Mexico."

Two days later, newspaper reporters and camera crews from the two Nicaraguan television stations gathered outside the Presidential Palace in Managua for a news conference scheduled for ten o'clock in the morning. President Humberto Montenegro was going to speak to the country about his plans for the upcoming year, and whether they would include the well-known rebel leader Perro Loco.

At nine A.M., Eduardo Cortes lifted his helicopter from the airfield at La Crus, Nicaragua. He glanced through the Plexiglas windshield as the commander of the airfield, Colonel Santiago Gomez, waved him off. Eduardo smiled. All

Gomez had wanted for the use of his field was a promise that Loco would promote him when he came to power. Eduardo knew Loco would not forget the colonel, for he never forgot a traitor, even when they worked in his favor. Eduardo knew the colonel was not going to be happy to be remembered by Perro Loco.

At nine-thirty, Eduardo Cortes banked his ancient Huey around the ten-story Bank of Central America building, and headed down the main street of Managua at an altitude of two hundred feet and a speed of 180 miles an hour.

"Listo!" he shouted over his shoulder to Pablo Sandoza, who was strapped to a fifty-caliber machine gun on a post in the open hatchway door of the Huey. The World War II gun was almost as old as the helicopter, but was still capable of firing over a thousand rounds a minute and causing almost indescribable damage to whatever it was aimed at.

"I'm ready," Sandoza screamed back, trying to make himself heard over the *whup-whup-whup* of the blades and the whistle of air streaming in the open door. He reached forward, jerked the loading jack of the machine gun to the ready position, and swiveled the barrel to point forward and downward.

As the Huey hurtled toward the Presidential Palace, Eduardo remembered Loco's orders. "Kill as many of the reporters and media people as you can, because nothing so inflames the press as when some of their own are killed while covering a story. But try to avoid the cameras as much as possible. We want the picture of a Mexican helicopter mowing down innocent civilians to be on every news feed in the world by the evening newscasts."

Eduardo glanced at the screen in the middle of the instrument panel of the chopper, wishing it had a Heads Up Display so he wouldn't have to take his eyes off piloting to fire the twin twenty-caliber machine guns under the fuselage. Of course, the Huey was built and flying long before HUDs were invented, so Eduardo shrugged, vowing to do the best he could under the circumstances.

At the sound of the screaming turbines of the Huey, the crowd below all turned and looked up, most shading their eyes against the morning sun as the ship dived toward them.

Only at the last minute did they realize they were under attack and start to panic and try to run away. It was much too late for that, as the Huey screamed toward them at almost sixteen thousand feet per minute.

Eduardo thumbed the fire-control switch on his yoke, and the twin twenties began to chatter their song of death seconds before Sandoza did the same on the big fifty in the rear doorway.

Men and women in the crowd were literally blown to pieces by the thousands of rounds of molten lead pouring at them from the Huey as it flew by less than fifty feet off the ground.

In a belated reaction, the Palace guards began firing their rifles and machine guns at the Huey, but they were inexperienced in shooting at aircraft and all failed to lead the big bird enough.

Eduardo jerked the yoke and swung the Huey in a sweeping circle, lining up his missile sights on the second floor of the Palace, where Loco had told him Montenegro's quarters were.

Just before he thumbed the switch, Eduardo fancied he saw a shadow of a man standing at the windows overlooking Montenegro's balcony.

"Eat this, you *bastardo*," Eduardo screamed as he pushed the button and watched twin trails of exhaust arch toward the building. He banked as sharply as he dared and pushed the throttle to its maximum position to get out of range of the blasts, so as not to be blown out of the air by his own missiles.

Seconds later, his face distorted by several Gs of centrifugal force, Eduardo heard an immense explosion behind them and felt the aircraft jump forward and shudder as if a giant hand had flicked it aside. Struggling with all his might, he managed to keep airborne, and when the Huey's flight was stable, he twisted in his seat to see what he'd accomplished.

The entire Presidential Palace, what was left of it, was in flames, and the second floor had collapsed and was a smoking ruin of charred and blackened bricks and steel. No one in the place could possibly have survived.

"We did it!" he shouted to Pablo. "We did it, *amigo!*"

When he heard no answer, he twisted around and looked at his friend. Pablo was hanging lifeless in his shoulder harness, his hands still on the fifty-caliber machine gun. Twin holes in his forehead had blown the entire back of his skull off.

"You gave your life for our leader, Pablo. I will make sure Perro Loco knows of your sacrifice," he whispered to the spirit of his longtime friend.

As he passed over the eastern city limits of Managua, Eduardo plucked the microphone off the instrument panel.

He depressed the thumb-switch and began talking in a pre-arranged code on a set frequency. "This is Messenger. The telegram has been delivered. I repeat, the telegram has been delivered."

After a few moments and a burst of static, a voice answered. "Was the head of the household there to accept it?"

"*Sí,*" Eduardo said, remembering the shadow in the window. "Absolutely!"

Thirty

A week later, Ben Raines and his team, which now included by unanimous agreement Harley Reno and Hammer Hammerick, gathered in his office at his command center at Fort Hood, Texas.

On his desk in front of him he had a newspaper spread out, its large headlines reading, "Nicaragua, Guatemala, and Honduras Declare War on Mexico."

Ben shook his head. "How could a helicopter fly all the way from Mexico, crossing Guatemala, Honduras, and half of Nicaragua without being seen, and without having help from the other countries involved?"

Mike Post, his Chief of Intelligence Services, gave a short laugh. "It couldn't, and it didn't, Ben," he said, flipping some satellite photos onto the desk.

"Our analysts say they tracked the chopper from somewhere in Belize a couple of days prior to the hit on Montenegro's palace. That Huey didn't come from Mexico, it came from Belize, and it landed several times in both Honduras and Guatemala, so they had to be helping whoever sent it."

"And I'll bet the son of a bitch who sent it is the same man who was declared the de facto leader of Nicaragua, Perro Loco," Coop added with disgust in his voice.

Post nodded as he filled his pipe with black tobacco. "That seems a pretty safe bet, Coop."

Ben glanced at Mike. "Any way we can show these pictures

to Jean-François Chapelle, the Secretary General of the U.N.?"

"Sure," Mike answered with a shrug. "In fact, both Cecil Jeffreys and Secretary of State Blanton have had extensive meetings with Chapelle telling him just that."

"And?" Ben asked.

"He says all he can do is pass the information along to both Mexico and Nicaragua, but it's his understanding that it won't make much difference. Montenegro was an extremely popular figure in Nicaragua, as is this Perro Loco now, and everyone has seen the pictures on every television network in the world of a helicopter with Mexican markings blowing the shit out of the great man, as well as a couple of dozen media reporters."

"So the die is cast?"

Mike nodded. "There is little we can do to prevent an all-out war between Mexico and its southern neighbors. Hell, even Belize, though not officially at war with Mexico, is lending covert assistance to the rebels."

"Has President Diego Martinez of Mexico asked for our help?" Coop asked.

Mike shook his head. "Blanton has unofficially offered it if it's needed, but so far Martinez seems to think they can hold the others off alone."

From a corner chair where he sat next to Anna, Harley Reno looked up and said, "Bullshit!"

Ben grinned. "No, Harley, don't hold back. Tell us what you really think."

Harley returned Ben's smile. "I said, that's crap. Hammer and I've been all over the country down there, and the Mexican Army is fat and lazy from years of no conflict and relatively peaceful times. Their command is top-heavy, too many generals and not enough grunts to get the job done. They're gonna get their butts kicked, mark my words."

Ben glanced at Hammer. "You agree, Scott?"

"Yes, sir," Hammer answered. "Harley's right. The Mexican Army is way outclassed by the Nicaraguans. They might do all right against Honduras and Guatemala, whose forces are little more than peasants that've been given guns they don't know how to use for the most part. But the Nicaraguans have been fighting steadily for the past twenty years. First against each other, then against the U.S. in the bad old days when we supported the right-wing death squads."

Harley nodded. "Every kid down there is taught to handle a rifle before he can walk. Hell, five- and six-year-old boys can field-strip an AK-47 and put it back together in the dark."

"So you think we'd better plan on providing some help to Mexico?" Ben asked.

Both men nodded.

"I agree," Ben said. "I only hope it's not too late when Martinez decides to ask for it."

"Ben," Coop said, "we could save some time by having our battalions mass on the Rio Grande. We could have them there and ready to move out and when Martinez finally realizes he needs us, we'd be ready."

"Good idea, Coop." Ben turned to Corrie. "Corrie, get on the horn and get me Ike McGowen from Batt 2, Jackie Malone from Batt 12, and get Buddy and his Special Ops Battalion 8 up here as well."

"Yes, sir," Corrie said, bending over her radio and beginning to make the calls.

"You think three battalions will be enough?" Mike asked.

Ben shrugged. "I hope so. It's all I can spare right now until I make sure that Otis Warner can hold on to his position and keep his word about negotiating a peace. I don't dare pull the others off the border with the USA until I'm sure that little fracas is over."

"Speaking of that," Jersey said, "have you heard anything else about Claire Osterman, Mike?"

"We've been monitoring the airways around the clock, looking for that peculiar whistle the Unitel scramblers she's using make, and we've had a few hits."

"Yeah?" Ben asked.

"Uh-huh. Of course, the scrambler changes the voices so we don't know for sure if it's really Osterman or someone pretending to be her, but there have been some messages back and forth between her and Perro Loco, as well as between some bases in the USA and wherever she's located."

"You think Otis Warner is cooperating with her?"

Mike shook his head. "No, there's no chance of that. In fact, we have some preliminary intel that she sent a team of assassins to try and kill him."

"Then the traffic between Osterman and other USA bases means she still has some support among the military," Ben said.

"Of course she does," Mike said, puffing on his pipe. "A lot of people were pissed off when Otis Warner took over and sued for peace. The military in the USA doesn't want to lose its job, or its perks. If Warner's not careful, she's gonna hand him his ass in a can, and you can bet some general is gonna tie a bow around it for her."

The two T-34 trainer jets took off from the air base at Gatlingburg three hours before dawn and assumed a south-by-southwest heading. The two-man jets were designed to train young pilots and not primarily as fighter or bomber aircraft, but they were capable of carrying a couple of small missiles, and each had a twenty-caliber machine gun mounted on each wing. Relatively slow, they flew at just under 400 miles an hour, and would only have enough fuel for one or two passes at the base in Arkansas if they wanted to be able to make it back to Tennessee.

For the first hundred miles, they flew below five hundred feet so as not to alert SUSA radar of their presence or of their point of origin. The SUSA had owned the skies in the recent war against the USA, but since the peace process began, the number of flights had been curtailed to save precious gasoline, which was needed for civilian use.

Lieutenant Jimmy Bodine was at the helm of the first jet, and his friend from flight school, Tim Bundick, was flying the second. They flew alone, not needing a navigator for the short flight to Arkansas.

Bodine flicked his com switch. "Raven One to Raven Two, you copy?"

Bundick answered back, "Raven Two, I copy."

"We're thirty minutes out. You take the housing units, and I'll target the officers' buildings. Over."

"Roger that, Raven One. Good hunting, Jimmy."

"You, too, Timmy."

An alert air radar warning operator at Fort Chaffe Army Base in Fort Smith, Arkansas, saw the twin blips on his radar when they were two hundred miles out, the maximum range of his unit.

Bill Young glanced at his watch: 0500. *Damn, thirty minutes before reveille. The lieutenant is gonna kill me if I wake him up an' this is nothin' but a ghost echo*, Young thought.

He shook his head, remembering his training. "Damn, gotta do it," he mumbled to himself as he picked up the phone.

Lieutenant Carl Aycock fumbled sleepily for the phone, stifling a yawn as he answered, "Yeah?"

"Lieutenant, it's me, Bill Young over at radar."

Aycock looked at his alarm clock. "This better be important, Young," he snarled.

"It is, sir. I got two spooks on radar, about a hundred and fifty miles out and approaching at three hundred fifty miles an hour."

Aycock sat up straight in bed. "No ID beacon or radio call advising us of friendlies in the neighborhood?"

"No, sir."

"Sound the alarm, Young. I want a full alert and I want it yesterday!"

"Yes, sir!"

As the two jets dived at the base, coming in low out of the morning sun, men were running toward AA batteries and machine-gun emplacements, some still pulling up pants and buttoning shirts while the large Klaxon horns around the base blared their warnings.

Lieutenant Aycock had just run from the door when the first bomb hit the Officers' Quarters. The explosion lifted him off his feet and flung him forward as if a giant had flicked him with a finger. He rolled frantically on the tarmac to put out the flames on the back of his shirt. As he sat up, a leg landed next to him and bounced once before settling on his lap, slowly leaking blood onto his khakis.

Aycock's eyes widened. Then he leaned to the side and vomited on the cement.

After sounding the alarm, Bill Young got on the radio and began to send out a Mayday under-attack signal. "This is Fort Chaffe radar control. We are under attack by unidentified aircraft . . . repeat, we are under attack by unidentified aircraft."

Before he got an answer, a bomb exploded in the Operations Building and Bill Young was engulfed in flames a split second before he was blown through the wall and out onto the ground. He had time for one quick breath before the flames melted his lungs and seared his eyes shut forever.

By the time the T-34's had made two bombing runs, the AA guns were going full force and the air was full of flak and smoke.

"Raven One to Raven Two, time to boogie, partner. The dance floor's gettin' too crowded."

"Roger that, Raven One, meet you on the other side," Tim

Bundick answered as he jerked the nose of his jet around and pointed it at the sun.

Lieutenant Jackie Johnson glanced at his copilot, Blackie West, in the P51–E they were flying over Louisiana when the radio crackled to life. "Eagle One, this is base calling Eagle One."

Johnson flicked the mike switch. "Eagle One here."

"We got two bogeys attacking Fort Chaffe. They need assistance."

"Roger, Base. Any ID on the bogeys?"

"All we know is they're tail burners," the base contact said, meaning the attackers were jets.

"Shit!" Blackie muttered. He knew they stood little chance against jets in the P51–Es, but being Marines, they were going to try anyway.

"Eagle Two and Eagle Three, you copy that?" Johnson said, keying in the frequency to his wing men on either side of his craft.

"Eagle Two, I copy."

"Eagle Three, I copy."

"We'll circle around to the east and try to come at them out of the sun," Johnson said, not adding that that was about the only chance they had if the jet pilots were any good at all.

As they approached Fort Chaffe, Johnson got another call. "Eagle One, be advised bogeys headed east at three hundred and fifty knots and ten thousand feet."

Johnson looked at West. "Only three hundred and fifty knots? Either they're small jets or they're trying to conserve fuel for a long trip back."

Blackie nodded, his teeth showing in a grin. The P51's could cruise at 380 miles an hour and hit almost five hundred in an attack dive. "Either way, that means we got a chance," he said as he reached over and armed the air-to-air missiles under the P51's wings. "Let's go huntin', podna."

Within thirty minutes, the three Eagle patrol planes had the twin jets in sight below them. Johnson had his patrol flying at twenty thousand feet to conserve fuel and to come at the bogeys from an angle they wouldn't expect.

He saw a puff of black smoke from the tail burners below as they accelerated. "They've seen us. I'll take the one on the left, Eagle Two, take the one on the right, Eagle Three, you're backup in case one gets away."

"Roger that, good luck."

Johnson pushed the throttles to the maximum forward position as he pushed the nose over the top and they fell like a rocket toward the jets in the distance.

Blackie West leaned forward, his eyes glued to the radar-missile tracking screen, his fingers on the button, ready to fire as soon as the radar locked onto the jet's hot exhaust gasses.

Eagle One was still two miles back when the radar gave a shrill screech. "We got lock!" West said as he punched the button.

The P51 shuddered as if in orgasm as the missile shot from its wing, arching down in a curving path toward the jet below.

The jet, as if sensing its doom, wiggled its wings and jutted back and forth like a kite in the wind as the ATA missile bore down on it.

Seconds later, the jet was engulfed in a giant fireball and Johnson had to veer off to keep from flying through the debris.

Eagle Two wasn't as lucky, and its missile passed by the second jet as it made a sharp upward turn and hit the afterburners.

The jet completed the loop and came out of it on the tail of Eagle Two, its 20mm cannons spitting bullets at the P51.

Eagle One was out of position to help, but Eagle Three

was ready and dived at the pair, its engines screaming at full throttle.

Just as the wing of the P51 known as Eagle Two shredded and came apart, the missile from Eagle Three entered the tailpipe of the jet and blew it out of the sky.

Eagle Two pinwheeled down like a duck with a broken wing, two parachutes blooming as the pilot and copilot ejected safely.

"Eagle One to base. Send a whirlybird, we got two down on the ground at . . ." he hesitated and then read off their coordinates.

"Roger that, Eagle One. Medevac is on the way. Good shooting, guys."

Thirty-one

Perro Loco took the phone from Arnoldo Mendoza when he indicated Claire Osterman was on the line.

"Buenos dias, Madame President," he said, struggling to keep the sarcasm out of his voice.

"Good morning, and congratulations, Comandante Perro Loco. I hear you're now the head of the Nicaraguan government."

"Actually, I'm the head of the Nicaraguan military, but in my country it amounts to the same thing," he answered. "I am now in a position to begin my part of our bargain, Mrs. Osterman. My Nicaraguan troops are already joined with those of Honduras and Guatemala and are making their way toward the southern border of Mexico. We plan to cross the border within two days."

"Do you anticipate any heavy opposition from the Mexican military?"

"No, not at first. The Mexican Army is very sparse and ill-equipped in the southern portions of the country. The provinces of Chiapas and Oaxaca and Guerro will be easy to take. I don't think we will face any serious opposition until we near Veracruz and Mexico City."

"Will they be able to hold you without asking Ben Raines and the SUSA for help?"

"I doubt it. It is my plan to pick up both matériel and men as I cross Mexico. The military there is not as loyal as it should be, and will tend to fight for whoever will pay them the most money, especially the generals."

"My intelligence sources tell me Ben Raines has ordered several of his battalions to gather along the border with Mexico, but until Presidente Martinez asks for his help, he is powerless to act."

Loco shrugged, though Osterman couldn't see him. "It is of no importance. I have studied this Ben Raines and feel that if he dares to join the fight, I will be able to defeat him."

There was a pause. Then Osterman said in a low voice, "Don't make the mistake of underestimating Ben Raines, *comandante*. He may be a son of a bitch, but he's a damn good commander, and he's never yet been defeated in battle."

"There is a first time for everything, Madame President," Loco answered curtly. "Now, when can I expect you to make your move against Raines from the north?"

"I'll need at least two more weeks before my forces are strong enough to forcibly retake my rightful position as head of my country. Immediately after that, I will resume my war against the SUSA and Ben Raines."

"That is good," Loco said. "It will take me that long to make my way up Mexico to Mexico City. At that time, Martinez will surely ask Raines for help . . . He will have no choice if he wishes to remain in power."

"Until then, Comandante Perro Loco. Good luck."

"You also, Madame President."

Perro Loco was as good as his word. His forces from Belize under the command of General Juan Dominguez crossed the border, and immediately took control of the province of Quintana Roo and the Yucatan Peninsula before heading northward toward Campeche and the Laguna de Terminos.

General Jaime Pena, whom Loco had appointed as supreme commander of the combined Guatemalan and Honduran and Nicaraguan forces, crossed the Guatemalan border at Piedras Negras and began his march across Chiapas toward Villahermosa where he planned to join forces with Dominguez and his group.

Their plans of action were markedly similar, and very effective. They would move to surround the isolated Army and air bases, and then give the commanding officers the choice of annihilation or joining their forces. Once the officers contacted Mexico City and were informed there would be no last-minute rescues, in most cases, the generals and captains turned their men over to Pena and Dominguez.

The soldiers were told they would be well paid and their families would be left alone if they fought with the Nicaraguans. If they chose to resist, they and everyone in their villages and towns would be murdered. Left with little choice, and feeling abandoned by their own leaders, the soldiers readily switched allegiance and Perro Loco's armies swelled in both numbers and amounts of equipment and matérial while sustaining virtually no losses themselves.

Villahermosa was to be the first real test, and the soldiers there were backed up by the Naval force in the province of Tabasco at the port city of Paraiso. President Martinez had ordered the only serviceable aircraft carrier in the Mexican Navy to stand offshore in the Bay of Campeche and give air support to the beleaguered Army base at Villahermosa on the banks of the Gryalva River.

Since Villahermosa was only thirty miles inland, the planes would have no trouble making the trip to defend the Army base from the air.

While still twenty-five miles away, Pena and Dominguez met to decide their strategy in the upcoming fight for Villahermosa.

Pena, who was the senior officer, spoke first. "Juan, our most pressing problem is going to be the air support from the carrier in the Bay of Campeche," he said as both men leaned over a table in the command tent with a map of the region on it.

"I agree, Jaime."

"Do we know what kind of planes the Mexicans have?"

Dominguez opened a notebook and leafed through several pages of intel reports before finding the correct one. "Here it says they are for the most part surplus S-2's from the United States World War II fleet."

"S-2's?"

"Yes. Two-seater trainers used for carrier landings, twin props, limited ordnance other than 20mm canons on the wings and perhaps a few small bombs. No missile capabilities I am aware of."

"So our tanks will be safe unless they suffer a direct hit from the bombs?"

"That is correct, but on the other hand, with no jet engines, it will be hard for our Stinger handheld missiles to bring them down also."

Pena nodded. "Yes, that is true. So, let's send in the tanks and jeeps with the fifty-caliber machine guns as our advance guard, telling the gunners to concentrate on the airplanes while the ground troops take care of the base defenses."

"That is a good plan, Jaime," Dominguez said, wagging his head. "We may lose a few infantry, but after all," he said, grinning and spreading his arms, "they are much easier to replace than tanks and helicopters."

The battle was joined just after sunup, the tanks having moved into place during the predawn darkness when they were safe from the S-2's which had no night-vision capabilities.

The Army base at Villahermosa was completely surrounded by the Pena/Dominguez forces, with tanks and jeeps with machine guns occupying the high ground on all sides of the base. As the infantry moved in under cover of the tanks' big guns, the machine-gunners concentrated their fire on the propeller-driven planes from the carrier in the Bay of Campeche.

Out of seventy-five S-2's that assaulted the ground troops, less than twenty made it back to the carrier. The rest were brought down by a combination of withering fire from the machine guns and the inexperience of the Mexican pilots, some of whom flew into the ground while trying to strafe the infantry. One flew low enough to be shot out of the sky by a soldier with an AK-47, an unheard-of event.

By midafternoon, the soldiers on the base ceased firing and a jeep with a white flag flying pulled out onto the main road. The commander of the base, General Boliver Munoz, was standing next to the driver as it approached General Pena's command tank.

"General Pena, I wish to surrender my command," Munoz said without preamble as the jeep rolled to a stop in front of the tank.

Pena stuck his head out of the turret. "An unconditional surrender?" he asked.

Munoz hung his head. *"Sí.* I only ask that my men be treated as prisoners of war and accorded the rights they deserve."

"General Munoz," Pena said, his lips pursed. "Here are *my* terms. Your men will agree to fight with my army and pledge their loyalty to me and to Nicaragua, or I will order the torching of every home in every village within fifteen miles of the Army base."

Munoz sputtered. "But . . . but that's preposterous!"

Pena glanced into the tank beneath him and nodded once. The fifty-caliber machine gun sticking out of the front of the tank chattered to life, cutting Munoz's body to shreds and blowing him off the back of the jeep to land in a pool of blood and guts in the dirt of the road.

Pena addressed the driver, whose face was blanched pale and whose eyes were wide with fright. "Go back to the base and present my demands to whomever is second in command to General Munoz. Tell them you have one hour to decide. Then I will level the base and kill everyone within fifteen miles of this place. Do you understand?"

The driver, too frightened to speak, nodded rapidly as he ground the gears of the jeep and whirled it around with spinning tires and headed back toward the base.

"Radio the troops and tell them to stand down for one hour. I have a feeling this battle is over," Pena said as he ducked back into the interior of the tank.

It didn't take the troops an hour to decide. In less than thirty minutes, they began to march off the base, their hands on their heads, their officers leading them.

A colonel with a name badge reading *Villareal* was at the front of the line.

"I see you have more good sense than General Munoz had," Pena said to him from the top of his tank.

Villareal nodded. "Yes, sir. My men are ready to follow your orders, for the sake of their families and the people of the province of Tabasco."

Pena smiled. "Now, let their be no mistake, Colonel. If even one of your men betrays our trust and fails to fight for us, I will be forced to send a contingent of men and helicopters back here and carry out my promise to destroy every living thing in this province. Do I make myself clear?"

Villareal nodded, his jaw muscles bulging as he clamped his teeth together.

"Tell your men, Colonel. The lives of everyone they leave behind depends on them. Just one traitor among them will mean the deaths of thousands of civilians."

Perro Loco meanwhile had sent his helicopter and air force planes to the area over Chiapas, since the jungle there was not amenable to ground troop activity and the roads were too poor for easy movement of tanks, half-tracks, and troop-transport trucks.

"My plan," he explained to Strunk and Valdez, "is to form a pincer movement up through southern Mexico. The ground forces, led by Dominguez and Pena, will move the heavy armor and artillery up along the eastern part of the country, which has better roads and less jungle, while the western, more wild and mountainous jungle areas will be cleared by helicopter and air force units."

Strunk shook his head doubtfully. "But, *comandante,* airpower alone has never been enough to subjugate a population unless it was followed up by infantry."

"That is normally correct, Jaime," Loco said, a bland smile on his face, "but this situation is somewhat different. All we need to do is to cut off the supply routes from the main Army headquarters in Mexico City to the western bases, and the soldiers there will have nothing to fight with and no one to shoot at with their rifles. That is the mistake the Americans made in Vietnam. Instead of going for the head of the country, Hanoi, they wasted time and men on the outer provinces. I do not intend to make the same mistake. Once I take Mexico City, the outer provinces will fall into line or they will have to learn to eat dirt."

Thirty-two

Ben Raines called his battalion leaders to meet with his team in his office to discuss the war in Mexico being waged by Perro Loco's troops.

General Ike McGowen sat directly across from Ben, and as usual had one of his breast pockets stuffed with cheap cigars and the other with candy bars. He was commander of the 502 Brigade, had been a Navy SEAL in his younger days, and was Ben's oldest and best friend. Broad-chested, with an ample paunch and wide shoulders, he was a big man. Doc Chase was always after him to lose weight, but it was a losing battle. Ike had tried every diet known to man . . . all without success. The truth was he liked to eat, and he wasn't about to deprive himself of anything he truly liked to do.

Sitting next to Ike was Jackie Malone, the commander of the 512 Brigade. Jackie was movie-star pretty, but one of the toughest women Ben had ever known. She was strong on discipline, but never asked the men who served under her to do anything she wasn't prepared to do herself. Any man in her brigade would gladly give his life to protect her. She'd been severely wounded a couple of years ago, but had fully recovered now, and Ben was glad to have her back.

The man next to Jackie was Buddy Raines, Ben's son. Ben hadn't raised Buddy. In fact, he hadn't known of his existence until a few years ago when Buddy showed up in a Rebel camp. Buddy's mother, who called herself Sister Voleta, had hated Ben and eventually had become insane. In an aborted attempt on Ben's life, she'd been killed by Ike McGowen. In his early twenties, Buddy was one of the youngest of the brigade commanders, and had charge of the 508 Brigade, which consisted mainly of Special Ops troops. He received no special treatment because he was Ben's son, and had earned his position by hard work and an instinct for Special Ops work.

Doc Chase and Mike Post from Intel, along with the rest of Ben's team, sat at the back of the room, waiting to see what Ben had to say.

"Is it too hot in here for you, Ike?" Ben asked.

Ike shook his head, sleeving sweat from his forehead. "No, why?"

"I notice you're sweating."

"The fat bastard's always sweating," Doc Chase opined from the back of the room.

Ike gave him a dirty look over his shoulder. "It must be a thyroid condition," he said. "If our medical team was worth a shit, it would've already been diagnosed and treated."

"Thyroid condition my ass!" Chase said, laughing. "It's called a surplus of adipose tissue, you hog. I've told you for years you need to shed some weight before your heart stops and you drop like a stone."

"Doc, I keep tellin' you it's not fat, it's muscle . . ." Ike began, until Ben interrupted them both.

"Okay, guys, save it for later. We've got some serious business to discuss."

Jackie leaned forward, her face lighting up with anticipation. "We going into Mexico, Ben?"

Ben shuffled the papers from Intel Mike had given him. "Well, we certainly are going to need to, sooner or later. Martinez is getting his ass kicked by Perro Loco's generals."

"How bad is it, Ben?" Buddy asked, unwrapping a piece of gum and sticking it in his mouth. No one on Ben's team had ever seen him without gum in his mouth.

"Bad. General Pena and Dominguez have taken over the

base at Villahermosa as well as the Navy yard at Pariso on the coast."

"Villahermosa's the largest base south of Mexico City, and the Navy yard at Pariso is the main supply route for the entire lower half of the country. That means he's cut off all matériel supply routes to the southern bases," Ike said, unconsciously reaching for a candy bar in his shirt pocket.

Doc Chase leaned forward and whispered, "You eat that and I'll shoot you in the back of the head."

Ben glanced down to hide his smile as he answered, "Yeah, and Perro Loco's smarter than we gave him credit for. He's not even bothering to waste his time on most of the smaller bases, which Martinez had pretty well dug in waiting for his attacks. He's hop-skipped over them and is full-on heading for Mexico City."

Buddy nodded, smiling grimly. "Sure, it's brilliant. Just like with a snake, cut off its head and the body dies. If he takes Mexico City, the other bases won't have any leadership, and since he's also cut off their supplies, game over."

"Exactly," Ben said.

"So, when's Martinez going to ask for our help?" Jackie asked.

"He's not ready to go public with an admission that he can't handle Perro Loco. That would be political suicide."

"So, political suicide is better than ending up on the end of Perro Loco's bayonet," Ike said, putting the candy bar back in his pocket and glaring at Doc Chase.

"He has, however, said that if we wanted to send in a Special Ops battalion, he wouldn't object."

Buddy nodded. "He's no dummy either. If we can manage to slow Perro Loco down and keep him away from Mexico City, that'll give Martinez time to get his southern troops organized and moving north on Perro Loco's flanks and rear. If Martinez can catch Perro Loco's troops in a pincer movement, far from their own lines of supply, he's liable to win the whole shooting match and we won't hog any of the credit."

Harley Reno held up his hand, like a child in school who knew the answer to a question. "Permission for Hammer and me to go along, Ben?"

Buddy looked over his shoulder at Harley, his eyebrows raised. "Uh, I've pretty much got my own team . . ."

"Why do you ask, Harley?" Ben asked.

"We just got a shipment of new toys from an engineer friend of mine down in Corpus Christi, Texas. He's managed to fit our Berettas and Uzis with silencers. These are some primo gadgets, and he sent two hundred of each of them as a special favor to me. If we're gonna be doing some Special Ops exercises deep in Mexico, they might come in real handy."

Buddy chewed his lip in thought. "You say these silencers work well? The last batch we had wore out after only one clip. Couldn't depend on 'em worth a damn."

"Not these. With these suckers all you'll hear is the firing bolt clicking back and forth."

Buddy took in Harley's six-and-a-half-foot height and broad shoulders as he considered his request to join his Special Ops team. But it was the eyes that convinced him. They looked like snake eyes, flat and cold as ice. Hammer was only a shade smaller, and looked just as deadly. Buddy nodded. "It's okay by me, Ben, if you can spare them."

Jersey and Coop immediately jumped to their feet. "Hey, no fair, Ben. If Harley and Hammer go, we all go," Jersey said, giving Harley a look. "That's what the term *team* means."

Harley smiled and nodded. "Great," he said.

"Wait a minute, Ben . . ." Buddy began.

Ben held up his hand. "Of course, Buddy, the final say-so is yours. But I want it understood, if you take the team along, they'll be under *your* command, just like the rest of your Special Ops people." He cut his eyes to Jersey and Coop.

"And there will be no hotdogging or solo missions. Do I make myself clear?"

Jersey, Coop, Anna, Beth, and Corrie all stared at Buddy, their faces blank. "Of course, Ben," they all said at once.

Buddy laughed and held up his hands in surrender. "Yeah, right. Okay, it's all right with me. Hell, you got the best team in the Army so I'd be a fool to turn them down."

"Corrie," Ben said, "get with Mike and figure out some radio frequencies for you to monitor so he can keep you up to date on any fresh intel we have."

He glanced at Ike and Jackie. "You two get your units loaded and ready. We're gonna put you right on the border with plenty of transportation for a fast move when Martinez finally realizes he can't win this war without us."

"Yes, sir," they said in unison.

"Doc," Ben said, "get the troops loaded with whatever vaccinations they need for Mexico and load up the med teams with lomotil and antibiotics." He smiled. "You can't fight if you're spending all your time in the latrines."

"Why don't you come along too, Ben?" Buddy asked.

Ben shook his head. "I'd love to, but I can't. One of our Army bases in Arkansas, Fort Chaffe, was just attacked by a pair of jets."

"What?" several of the participants in the meeting asked at once.

Ben nodded. "Yeah. The jets were old and out of date, and it's my guess they were sent by Claire Osterman to make us think Warner couldn't be trusted."

"What's he say?" Ike McGowen asked.

"He says they didn't know anything about it and he certainly didn't authorize any attacks against us."

"You believe him?"

"Yeah. I'm convinced he wants peace as bad as we do . . . worse, since they were getting the worst of it. I think Claire Osterman is behind this and until this Osterman mess is straightened out, I'm gonna need to be here to monitor the peace process and try to keep Otis Warner in control and on track up there."

"Is he in serious trouble?"

"I don't know. Our intel says he's having some trouble with some of his bases and some of his military, but we just don't know how deep the rot goes. And until we do, I'm gonna stay here and keep an eye on things."

"What if Claire regains control of the USA?" Buddy asked.

"It'll be bad. She won't rest until either she wins or we do. It'll be a fight to the death for both countries. And, to make matters worse, we'll be fighting a war on two fronts, which no country in history has been able to do and win."

Ike McGowen got to his feet. "Hell, then we'll just have to make some new history, Ben. It won't be anything new to us."

Jackie stood up. "Two fronts or not, we're not going to let you down, Ben. We're gonna kick ass and take names."

Thirty-three

"How're we doin', boys?" Claire asked.

Herb Knoff, General Bradley Stevens, and Harlan Millard were sitting in her office for the usual breakfast staff meeting.

Stevens answered first. "All in all, not too bad. We hit Raines's base in Fort Smith, Arkansas, and did extensive damage before our jets were shot out of the sky."

"Any repercussions?"

"Not yet. So far, Raines still believes Warner didn't have anything to do with the raid."

Herb sneered. "Hell, Raines knows that chicken-shit Warner wouldn't have the balls to do something like that."

Claire nodded. "I believe you're correct, Herb. I think we're wasting our time trying to put a wedge between Warner and Raines. We should be directing all of our energies to regaining control of the government."

Millard and Knoff glanced at each other, neither daring to remind Claire it'd been her idea to hit the Arkansas base in the first place.

"So, Brad, what are your ideas on that?"

"We've had no trouble recruiting personnel so far. In fact, most of the military is behind us, either overtly or covertly."

"So, why aren't we in control?"

Bradley spread his arms. "Equipment, primarily. Warner and troops loyal to him control most of the high-tech gear and weapons. About all we have besides side arms are a couple of helicopters older than I am and some half-tracks and

HumVees. We don't have any tanks, or artillery, or fighter aircraft worth a damn."

"Well, gentlemen, it's about time we made our move. Perro Loco is well on his way to Mexico City, and if we're not leading this country by the time he takes it, I'm afraid our deal may be off and he may decide to make a separate peace with the SUSA."

"What do you want to do, Claire," Harlan Millard asked.

"We need to make our presence known. Where is the largest airfield near here?"

Bradley Stevens thought for a moment. "That'd be at Oak Ridge, just north of Knoxville. It's got everything we need, except long-range bombers. It's primarily a fighter squadron and helicopter repair facility, so there's plenty of aircraft around for the taking."

"And how many men do we have we can absolutely count on?"

"Between five and ten thousand, but they're scattered over the entire state at several small bases. We've kept them in place so as not to draw attention to our movements."

"The time for stealth is over, Brad. I want to take that base and get those aircraft. Once we have the planes, we can get the other equipment by using the attack helicopters in surprise raids on other bases that have what we need."

"What about troops, Claire?" Millard asked.

"I think they'll be glad to join us when they see that we're not going to take any shit from the SUSA or anyone else. Soldiers don't want peace, they want war. And, by damn, I'm gonna give 'em war."

Johnny Roy Lumpkin glanced up from his magazine to see a HumVee approaching the gate in front of his guardhouse. He looked at his watch. Three in the morning. *Who the hell could that be?* he thought, stifling a yawn as he walked to the door of the vehicle.

He saw two men in BDUs sitting in the front seat and six men in the rear.

"What's goin' on, fellahs?" Johnny Roy asked, a pleasant expression on his face. "Out on night maneuvers?"

The driver, whose name tag read *King,* said, "Yeah, an' we're told to report to the officers' quarters. Where might that be, boy?"

Johnny Roy frowned. "It's right over there," he said, pointing to a building on the edge of the base, "but I'm gonna have to see some orders 'fore I can let you on base."

"Sure," the man sitting next to King said, "here are our orders." He held his hand out and pointed a black revolver with a silencer on the barrel at Johnny Roy's face.

"What . . ." he said just before a .38-caliber bullet punched a hole in his forehead and blew out the back of his skull. He dropped like a stone on the concrete.

King didn't bother getting out of the car to raise the barricade, but accelerated the HumVee right through it, turning the steering wheel until the vehicle was pointed at the officers' quarters building in the distance.

Thirty minutes later, all fifteen staff and administration officers in the building were dead and King had his pistol in the back of a staff sergeant who was leading them to the pilots' barracks.

Unlike enlisted men's barracks, the pilots all had individual rooms, so they had to be gathered one at a time and brought to the mess hall under guard. Once they were all there, King paced in front of them as he talked.

"My name is Colonel James King," he said. "I'm a member of the Blackshirt Squad, so you know I mean what I say."

The group of pilots, most of whom were barely out of their teens, all nodded. They'd heard of the Blackshirts and knew they were badasses it was best to stay away from.

"We work for President Claire Osterman, who was illegally removed from office last year. The man who replaced her is a traitor named Otis Warner. Right now, he is selling out our country to the SUSA by negotiating a peace that will make us weak forever."

King stopped his pacing and faced the group. "We don't intend to let that happen. We do intend to take this country back for its rightful leaders. My question to you is, will you fight with us to see that happen?"

One of the men stood up. "If we join you, does that mean the war will start again?"

King nodded. "Yeah, it does. So your choice is join us and fight and fly, or resist us and go back to your farms and chicken ranches and live under the rule of the SUSA the rest of your lives."

The man who spoke said, "That's no choice, Colonel. We joined up to fly and fight, and as far as I'm concerned, that's what I plan to do."

The remainder of the men stood up, all nodding their heads and looking at each other.

"All right. Your first test is to help us take this base over. We need control of the aircraft and the armaments. It'll be up to you to help us determine who we can trust to be with us on this."

King looked over his shoulder and nodded, and the men with him began handing weapons out to the pilots.

By dawn, the base was secure and under the command of Colonel James King. Only about ten percent of the enlisted personnel had refused to go along with the change in command, and were in the brig under guard.

King went to the communications room and had the radio operator contact Claire Osterman's office in Gatlingburg.

"President Osterman, Colonel James King here. Mission accomplished. The air base at Oak Ridge is under our command."

"Well done, Colonel King," Claire said, glancing over her shoulder from the phone in her bedroom at Herb Knoff in bed and winking. "General Stevens will be in touch later with further orders."

She hung up the phone, slipped her nightgown off her shoulders, and crawled under the covers. "Herb, it's time to celebrate."

Herb grinned as he reached for her. "Yes, ma'am," he growled.

Thirty-four

Captain Raul Benavidez steered his Apache helicopter gunship over the jungles of Chiapas. Gunner Jesus Lopez sat in the front seat, reading his targeting display.

A Mexican military base at San Fernando was their first objective. Orders had come from Comandante Perro Loco to strike this installation quickly, taking the poorly equipped Mexican Army at San Fernando by surprise as the *comandante's* ground troops began their march up the western regions of Mexico toward Mexico City before sweeping across northern Mexico to take the SUSA.

"Do you see anything?" Raul asked.

"Nothing yet," Jesus replied. "No radar signals are being picked up by our sensors."

"Their radar may be down."

"Don't count on it. According to the *comandante* they have radar and five UH-1 choppers at San Fernando. The old Hueys can be deadly fighting machines, if the pilot and gunner know what they are doing."

"Those stupid Mexicans may not know how to fly them," Jesus said. He was a Honduran, with a strong dislike for anyone from Mexico.

"They will have SAMs," Raul assured him. "We'll be dodging rockets if they pick us up on their radar."

"You worry too much, *capitán*."

"I worry in order to remain alive."

"Mexican radar in Chiapas will be very old. It will not

see this Apache. This is why the Americans spent so much money on them forty years ago, before the big war."

Raul glanced out a side window of the chopper, scanning the jungle while he worked the collectives with his left hand, the throttle with his right. "I hope you are right, Jesus. Remember what is in our orders . . . Do not destroy any of the UH-1's on the ground. Comandante Perro Loco says we will need them to fight our way across Mexico, and we are instructed not to hit any fuel tanks."

"I understand, *capitán*. I will not shoot at anything unless it shoots at us."

"Do you see anything now?" Raul asked again.

"Nothing. It is late in the afternoon and the lazy Federales may be taking their *siestas.*"

Raul wondered if the Mexican Army was expecting them. The security surrounding their operation had been tight . . . but was it tight enough?

"We should have a visual sighting of San Fernando any time now," Jesus said, speaking loudly into his headset to be heard above the drone of the Apache's rotor.

They must be *idiotas,* not sending out radar signals."

"They are Federales. Most of them have not been paid in months because the Mexican government is bankrupt. They do not care."

"Then we will teach them a lesson," Raul declared, dropping the Apache to six hundred feet. A second helicopter in their formation, a Hind, descended to the same altitude, a ship flown by a German mercenary named Klaus Hafner, a former Nazi who had escaped General Raines's attacks on General Field Marshal Bruno Bottger's forces in Africa. The Hinds were old Russian-made choppers with limited capabilities. Five of them flew in a V-shaped formation behind Raul's Apache.

"There!" Jesus shouted into the microphone. "There is the San Fernando military base."

"Why aren't they shooting at us?" Raul wondered.

"Because they are lazy Mexicans, *capitán*. I will send them a rocket. Turn east, toward those adobe walls."

An air-to-ground Sparrow rocket hissed away from the Apache when Jesus activated its triggering mechanism.

Jesus grinned. "Wake up, *estupidos federales!*" he cried. "Your *siesta* is over."

The slender missile left a vapor trail in its wake as it plunged downward, toward the walls of San Fernando.

"We're going in," Raul said. "Blast them to pieces with machine-gun fire. It is time to teach them the lesson you promised them."

"It will be my pleasure, *capitán*," Jesus said, readying the twin fifty-caliber Gatling guns.

The chatter of machine guns filled the cockpit.

Jesus chuckled softly. "What good is a lesson to a dead man?"

The ship hung close to the treetops of the Chiapas jungle while bullets poured into the Army base at San Fernando. Raul could see men scurrying from the barracks below. Some were half-dressed and appeared to be buckling on their weapons as if they had in fact been taking *siestas*.

Two older-model Huey helicopters sat on landing pads cut from the jungle. The *comandante* had said there would be five. Raul wondered where the others might be.

"Commence firing, Capitán Hafner!" he shouted into the mouthpiece.

"Where are the other choppers?" Hafner asked. "I can only see two."

"They may have been sent back to Mexico City," Raul replied impatiently. "Just make sure you do not damage the ones on the ground."

More machine-gun fire banged from the Apache's guns. Below, Mexican soldiers began to fall, their bodies dancing dances of death as the large-caliber bullets shredded their flesh.

Raul tipped the nose of the gunship down, reducing their altitude to four hundred feet. He was worried that no rockets had been fired at them. Was it possible, as Jesus said, that the Mexicans were taken completely by surprise during the afternoon *siesta?*

Raul saw Klaus Hafner beginning a low pass over the fortifications at San Fernando in his Hind, his machine guns spitting forth a hail of lead.

Raul wondered why the Mexicans were not firing back at them now. Capturing the outpost at San Fernando was going to be very easy, he thought.

"I see something!" Jesus cried.

"What is it?"

"Aircraft moving toward us. Two, or maybe three. They are flying very low, *capitán.*"

The hair on the back of Raul's neck stirred as he had a sudden thought. Perhaps the Mexicans were not so stupid after all. *What if we've flown into a trap?*

Sweat pooled under his armpits as he quickly looked back and forth, searching the skies for signs of any other surprises that might be awaiting them over the jungles below.

The dark shapes coming toward them were almost invisible against the greens and yellows of the jungle foliage. Probably painted with camouflage so as to blend in, Raul thought as he gripped the throttle and collective with hands suddenly slick with sweat.

"Captain Hafner," Raul spat into his microphone. "I've got bogies at six o'clock low . . . repeat bogies at six o'clock low."

A burst of static was followed by Hafner's German accent. "I see nothing. You must be mistaken . . ."

"Look again, you fool," Raul shouted. "They're camouflaged. Use your radar . . . now!"

Thirty-five

Captain Klaus Hafner suddenly had two blips on his radar screen, both flying very low over tropical forest reaching the walls of San Fernando. "Damn," he muttered, "where did those bastards come from?"

Flying at the rear of the formation, he spoke into his radio as he gripped the M24's stick with the throttle wide open.

"Captain Benavidez! I have two of them on my screen. Two airships. Choppers, probably Hueys from the way they're moving. Activate rocket ignition when you can confirm a hit."

"They are too low!" a voice replied from another M24 Hind flying outer wing in their V-shaped formation. "I have no fix. Repeat. I have no fix."

Klaus knew the Hueys were capable of quick maneuvers and dangerously low flight, if the pilot knew what he was doing. It was hard to bring one down from the air with the older Soviet rockets they had on board the M24's, small missiles with an out-of-date guidance system relying solely upon heat, often misfiring at a vapor trail or following the wash of a turbine engine instead of the flying ship itself, allowing smart pilots to make sharp turns to avoid their rockets. While the Soviet-made rockets were excellent for ATG, air-to-ground, firing, they stacked up poorly against the more advanced rockets with computerized guidance systems. Most frustrating of all, the Hueys somehow made false echoes on radar screens, causing rockets or cannon fire to go wide.

"Let them have a taste of machine-gun fire," Klaus commanded, flipping switches on his twin-mount M-60 machine guns. These big guns required visual targeting, a difficult task while flying an M24 in hot pursuit, and the M-60's frequently jammed due to rust in this humid tropical climate. Comandante Perro Loco knew about the problems aboard the Hinds, and still he ordered them into battle with the Apaches as if pilots under his command and their Hinds were expendable. And as the war began, it seemed no one in the high command cared about equipment disadvantages, or badly needed repairs to planes and helicopters. Many of the air wars they fought now were like suicide missions.

The chatter of machine-gun fire came from a ship to Klaus's left as they sped over the dark forest below. Klaus's altimeter read less than four hundred feet, and the approaching Hueys appeared to be even lower, making them far more difficult targets for machine guns, cannons, or rockets. At this altitude and speed the bulky Hinds handled like a school bus rather than a flying machine. Hafner was sweating as he used all of his skill to keep the chopper in the air and on course. Flying like this, he had little chance to fire his machine guns accurately, but triggered off a few rounds just to let the Hueys know he meant business.

But with one Apache gunship in this squadron, Klaus felt the sheer weight of superior technology would give them the advantage. Silently, he prayed he wouldn't be one of the M24's shot down during this engagement. Yet he had to stay out in front of the formation to show Captain Raul Benavidez he had courage in battle. He could not lag behind. His pride would not allow it. His arm muscles began to knot and burn with the effort it took to keep the Hind flying level. *Damn,* he thought, *this humid jungle air is like flying through water.*

"One of the blips has turned around!" It was Benavidez's voice over the radio. "It is coming back toward us . . ."

"I don't see it!" the third pilot in their formation said. "Give me a mark! I can't pick it up on my screen!"

Klaus recognized the terror in Diego Ponce's voice, despite heavy static through his headset, a common failing of Hinds when the humidity was high, which caused all manner of electrical quirks in the guidance systems and in their radios.

"Something has been fired! I can see its burn trace. Go down!" Klaus said, feeling his palms grow even wetter with sweat on the controls.

"It's a rocket!"

"Evade, evade now!" he screamed into the microphone, jerking back on the collective at the same time he tried to twist the throttle for even more speed, praying the Hind wouldn't turn turtle on him or clip the jungle trees, which seemed mere feet below his tires now.

All members of the squad sent their M24's down to low altitudes to escape the missile, while the Apache flown by Captain Benavidez remained at five hundred feet.

Klaus took a quick glance at one of the other M24's when it nosedived out of formation, swooping down toward the jungle.

"I'm getting something on my warning system . . ." Lieutenant Ponce scarcely got the words out of his mouth before his chopper exploded, sending an aftershock across the jungle below them and setting some of the trees on fire.

Klaus watched Ponce's helicopter gunship go down in a ball of flames, coming apart as it spiraled toward the earth, leaving a plume of smoke and flames in its wake.

"Fire! Fire! I've got a target!"

Klaus fired one of his rockets. A finger of orange flame marked its passage away from his chopper.

Klaus watched the rocket shoot away from his gunship with his heart in his throat. Diego Ponce was already among the dead from this helicopter engagement, and the fight had only begun. He wondered how many more of his comrades would die.

"I'm hit!" a crackling voice shouted. "One of my rotor blades is . . ." His cry ended with a terrific explosion off to

Klaus's right. Another Hind burst into flames, flipping nose-over-tail amid an inferno. Oddly, the helicopter's machine guns were firing as it went crashing into the treetops below. Then one of its unlaunched rockets detonated, blasting trees out of the ground in a rapidly spreading circle.

Klaus took a deep breath. He saw a Huey making straight for the squad's formation, a suicidal move for a helicopter pilot at this altitude.

Klaus fixed his targeting sights on the Huey and pulled a trigger on a rocket. The swish of burning fuel made a faint sound above the staccato of his rotor. A fiery vapor trail left one launching tube. Then the Huey gunship suddenly disappeared on his screen. It was not possible, and yet he had seen the blip vanish himself.

"Where is it?" he cried, just as the rocket he launched went sailing into a black hole in the rain forest.

"It is gone! I don't see it," Raul exclaimed. "A big chopper cannot simply vanish like that."

Klaus's rocket ignited a stand of trees, brightening the sky briefly. He had missed the Huey completely and it did not make any sense, how an airship could be there at one moment, and then disappear entirely in a matter of seconds. It was not logical, he thought. Did these Mexicans have some kind of new weapon, making their aircraft invisible? Or were their pilots simply that good at the controls?

"I'm hit!" a slurred voice screamed, as one of the choppers to Klaus's left disintegrated in flames, twisting out of the sky in looping arcs. The Hind went out of sight, exploding upon impact, setting more trees aflame.

A split second later Klaus saw a flash of light off to his right. A Hind was struck by a rocket and it went down like a flaming ball of heavy metal, dropping straight down into the forest with a bang.

I am going to die today, Klaus thought. *How is this possible, against only two enemy helicopters?*

"Captain Benavidez!" a voice said. "We are flying over

batteries of antiaircraft guns. They are shooting rockets up at us, and cannons are spitting lead all over the jungle below."

Klaus looked beneath his gunship. The trees were alive with winking lights scattered among the flames from the burning Hinds that'd crashed, and the distant boom of cannons could be heard above the whine of his turbines and the hammering of his rotors through the air. Muzzle flashes illuminated the pathways of cannon and machine-gun shells, and bright orange tracers lit up the sky in winking fingers of death.

"I am hit. Going down!" Klaus did not recognize the pilot's voice. Their squad was taking a terrible beating . . . It was almost as if they had been lured into a nest of ground-to-air rocket launchers and antiaircraft gun batteries.

Something struck the underbelly of his chopper, followed by a pain so intense Klaus let out an unconscious yell, leaving him gasping for air. A horrible burning began in his left foot, shooting up his leg. His boot went flying past his face, slamming against the roof of his gunship cabin. The chopper tilted crazily, driven out of control by the impact from a cannon shell.

Blood sprayed the cockpit, splattering the Plexiglas windshield, and in dim lights behind the control panel, Klaus noticed that his lower left leg was missing, blown off just below his knee by a Mexican cannon. Air pressure fell in the cabin and a map, clipped to a visor above his head, was sucked out of a hole in the M24's steel-plated floor. An involuntary scream came from his throat.

He closed his eyes, gritting his teeth, fighting back the pain racing up his leg. And now he had no foot with which to control the rudder or the speed of the tail rotor. He felt the chopper begin what felt like a ground-spin, although his altimeter said he was still three hundred feet in the air. His mind would not function properly due to the pain, and his vision was blurred, his forehead and eyes smeared with blood from his shattered leg.

Another M24 broke into pieces far to his right, blanketed by flames and smoke. Klaus's radio crackled, but there was no voice from the pilot being shot out of the skies, only static as his last message never made it to his squadron leader.

The drum of antiaircraft guns became a rhythm from the dark forest, pounding, blasting away as Klaus's Hind began a slow descent he could not control. His mind calmed as he realized he was going to die over this godforsaken country, fighting for a man he hardly knew, for a cause he didn't understand.

"Son of a . . . !" Another pilot attempted a radio message in the last seconds of his life, before his chopper was hit by a hail of cannon fire.

Klaus's life flashed before him, his childhood in Germany and his enlistment in the New Federation Army headed by a blond giant named Bruno Bottger. Bottger had made so many promises to his new recruits, promises of a better world and an easier life for all who followed him.

Then the collapse of his Nazi-style regime, after a bitter war across Europe. Everyone believed General Field Marshal Bruno Bottger was dead, until he surfaced a few years later with his New World Order, headquartered in Pretoria, South Africa, proclaiming he had millions of followers and a better-equipped army to fight against Democratic tyranny.

Klaus Hafner had wanted to believe in this New World Order, as so many others had.

His M24 circled closer to the earth, out of control because he had no foot to guide it. Sheets of pain ran up his thigh to his belly, and he felt sick to his stomach.

Using the stump where his foot should have been, he placed bare bone and bleeding flesh on a rudder pedal and twisted the throttle. The pain almost caused him to black out when exposed, shattered bone pressed down, stabilizing the rudder.

The turbines responded with a roar, lifting the Hind just in the nick of time before he crashed in the jungle. Klaus ignored the white-hot pain in his stump of a leg to keep pressure on the rudder pedal.

He saw jungle underneath him.

"I am going down!" someone shrieked into his headphones, a voice frightened by hysteria he could not recognize.

I will not *go down,* Klaus promised himself. *I will stay in the air, no matter what.*

An M24 to his right blew apart, pieces flying, chunks of metal sucked into the downdraft of his rotor blades.

"Oh, no!" he gasped, feeling his gunship shudder in midair when something struck the tip of a swirling blade.

He fought the controls with all his strength, but with a nagging sensation that he was losing consciousness due to the loss of blood from his ruined leg. The Hind would not obey his commands when he tried to steady it.

It happened beyond his control, when a fragment of a torn M24 sheared off one of his rotor blades. The Hind flipped over, flying upside down, fluttering like a duck shot by hunters until it was driven into the jungle. Klaus Hafner was killed instantly.

Thirty-six

Raul Benavidez turned the Apache toward the approaching Huey choppers as two of the Soviet-made Hinds in his chopper squadron plummeted into the Mexican jungle rain forest below them. His support squad was going down in flames. His radio crackled with distress messages.

"Fire when you have a target locked on, Jesus," he said into the headset. "We'll head straight toward them."

"*Sí, capitán,*" Jesus replied, focusing his HUD on a tiny display. "I have one now."

"Fire a rocket," Raul cried.

Jesus pressed a small red button and a missile sped away from the Apache.

"This will be one dead Mexican pilot," Jesus said as the rocket's vapor trail raced toward a flashing symbol on his radar targeting system.

Seconds later, a fiery ball exploded above the treetops west of San Fernando.

"Got him!" Jesus shouted.

"Find the other one!" Raul demanded, keeping the Apache low, so dangerously close to the roof of the jungle Raul could see leaves and branches waving in the prop-wash of his Apache.

"I have him," Jesus said. "Wait until I have a fix on his position."

Raul watched the first Huey go down in a tangled mass

of metal, crashing into the jungle surrounded by flames. "Do not wait too long, Jesus."

Another rocket hissed away from the Apache.

"Adios, estupido mexicano," Jesus said.

The second UH-1 became a flying inferno. Pieces of the aircraft tumbled into the palm trees . . . Raul could hear the distant roar of exploding aircraft fuel as the chopper fell apart in midair.

"Bueno," he whispered into his microphone, glancing over his shoulder to see how many of the Hinds in his squadron had been lost.

Only two remained in the sky behind them.

"We will fly back over the fortress at San Fernando," he told Jesus. "Strafe them with machine-gun fire. Make certain no one is left alive before we go down . . ."

Bodies lay all over the compound. Blood mingled with white caliche earth inside the walls. The Apache and a lumbering Hind occupied empty space between a pair of disabled Hueys and six armored personnel carriers.

Captain Benavidez surveyed the carnage around him, a satisfied grin on his face.

"We have taken San Fernando," he said to gunner Jesus Lopez. "Radio the *comandante.* Tell him the good news."

"Should I tell him we lost four of our Soviet choppers?" Jesus asked.

"It will not matter. Tell him we have captured two of the American Hueys and six APCs."

"He will not care that we lost four gunships?"

"They were old. Out of date. We had no spare parts for them."

"And the men who flew them?"

Raul chuckled. "Perro Loco has no love for mercenaries who fight only for money. He uses them, but he does not trust them. The Soviet ships were expendable, and so were the men who flew them."

"But isn't it true that we all fight for the money, *capitán?*"

"Of course, Jesus, but we also fight for the cause of our great leader. Comandante Perro Loco understands this. Send him the message. We have won a big victory today. I know he will be pleased."

A Mexican soldier lying near the door of an adobe barracks groaned, digging his fingers into a pool of blood spreading around him.

Raul drew his Colt .45 automatic pistol and walked over to the wounded Federale.

"Are you in pain, *bastardo?*" he asked, jacking a round into the firing chamber.

The young Mexican looked up with pain-glazed eyes.

Raul shot him in the head. The echo of his pistol filled the walled compound at San Fernando.

Covering his progress with the pistol, he made a quick inspection of the small compound. Crates of fifty-caliber machine-gun bullets rested in an abandoned bunker. The Federale garrison was a storehouse for ammunition.

But when he entered a shadowy warehouse he found the best news of all. Two dozen American-made rockets lay beneath a piece of canvas.

"Now we can arm the Apaches and the Comanches," he whispered softly. "Mexico City will be ours."

He strolled back out in the sunlight, ignoring the dead Federales scattered around the compound. He strode over to the Apache while Jesus was raising the *comandante's* new headquarters at the Presidential Palace in Nicaragua.

"Inform the *comandante* that we have captured two of the UH-1's and thousands of rounds of machine-gun shells. But tell him the real prize is more than twenty of the American Sparrow air-to-ground rockets."

"More than twenty?" Jesus asked, waiting for an answer to his radio call to Belize.

"Two dozen. With these rockets, and the other Apache and Comanche gunships, we will take Mexico City with light casualties."

Jesus grinned. "Perro Loco will be very happy to hear of our victory."

Raul nodded. "There are antiaircraft batteries to be recovered out in the jungles, and ammunition. All the Federales have fled. The only Federales left alive are the wounded. We must find them, and execute them. Those were the *comandante's* orders."

"*Sí, capitán,*" Jesus said as a voice crackled on his radio. "It has been a good day, even though we lost all but one of our Russian helicopters."

Raul gazed at smoke coming from parts of the jungle around the compound. "I never liked Klaus Hafner anyway, or any of the other Germans. I did not trust them."

Jesus's attention was drawn to the voice on the radio, a voice Raul recognized as belonging to Jim Strunk.

"What do you have to report?" Strunk asked.

"A victory," Jesus replied. "The military compound at San Fernando has fallen. We captured two of the UH-1 helicopters and two dozen Sparrow rockets, along with many cases of machine-gun rounds and six armored personnel carriers."

"I'll inform the *comandante,*" Strunk said, his voice fading when static interfered with the radio signal. "Ground troops will be there before dark to help collect the booty. Eduardo will be with them to inspect the Hueys, to make certain they can fly."

"*Bueno,*" Jesus said.

Raul watched the crew from the remaining Hind walk toward them with drawn pistols hanging at their sides. It had been a good fight, helping the armies of Perro Loco prepare for the coming attack on Mexico City.

A cry of pain came from the headquarters building in the center of the compound. He marched toward the sound with his pistol.

Entering a darkened adobe room, he found a young Federale trying to reach a radio transmitter, crawling across the dirt floor leaving a trail of blood behind him.

"Idiota," Raul snarled, aiming for the back of the Mexican soldier's head.

Three loud explosions filled the room. The Federale was flipped over on his side, blood spurting from three wounds to his back.

"No radio messages to Mexico City," Raul told the dying soldier. "They will find out what happened here soon enough, only by then it will be too late."

The Federale groaned and lay still, gasping for each breath, reaching for a wound in his belly.

"What was that?" Jesus cried, rushing through the door with his pistol drawn.

"A fool," Raul replied. "He was trying to make a call on the radio."

"He is still alive," Jesus observed.

"Not for long," Raul promised, walking over to the soldier until he stood directly over him.

He aimed down at the Federale's head, pumping two more shots into the man's face.

The soldier's foot twitched with death throes. Then he lay still.

Raul turned to Jesus. "Have the men put fuel in the UH-1's and the APCs. The *comandante* said a ground force will be here within a few hours. Everything must be ready to head northward toward Mexico City."

Thirty-seven

Colonel James King accompanied his pilots on a tour of the hangars at the Oak Ridge airfield. When they entered the main hangar, he lined the men up in front of him and sat on the edge of a table.

"President Osterman has asked that we proceed to do what we can to help her regain control of the government that was illegally stolen from her." He stared at the men around him, trying to gauge their reaction to his next words.

"That means, gentlemen, we are going to have to attack the government's headquarters in Indianapolis."

He paused as the men looked at each other, some with frowns, others with what looked to be anticipation on their faces.

"I need to know right now if any of you are going to have trouble with fighting against troops who used to be your allies and friends."

A murmur passed through the crowd of pilots as they spoke softly to one another. After a moment, a man with lieutenant's bars on his collar stepped forward.

"Permission to speak freely, Colonel."

"What's your name, son?" King asked.

"Lieutenant Hawk, sir, Robert Hawk."

"And you are?"

"I'm the squadron commander, sir."

"Go ahead, Lieutenant."

"Well, sir, we haven't had a lot of time to discuss this

among ourselves, but it seems to me that if the present government officials took over the command illegally, that is, without a vote of the people, that's the same as a coup."

King nodded.

"And if that is the case, sir, then we have an obligation to try our best to restore the Commander in Chief to her previous command. Isn't that right?"

"That's exactly right, son." King stood up, thinking this was going better than he'd hoped. "In fact, you men are in the same position as some of your great-grandfathers were in back in the 1800's, when brother often fought against brother to insure the perseverance of the Union, of the very United States as we know it today. Those men who are fighting for the present government have been lied to from the very beginning. They've been told Claire Osterman is dead, when in fact those very same leaders are the ones who tried to assassinate her in order to take over the country."

The pilots glanced at one another and nodded, clearly believing everything King said.

"Now, you men may or may not agree with President Osterman's decision to continue the war against the SUSA, but until she is removed from office in a legal election, she is still your Commander in Chief, and as such you took an oath to defend her policies with your very lives if need be."

Several of the men stood straighter and said, "Yes, sir," under their breaths.

"So, are we all in agreement on the necessity for action to restore her command to her?"

Now all the men spoke up in unison. *"Yes, sir!"*

"Good. Now, Lieutenant Hawk, why don't you and your men show me what we have available to do the job?"

Hawk nodded and motioned for King to follow him to the area of the large hangar where a collection of helicopters were stored.

He stood in front of four dark green helicopters off to the side by themselves. "We have four McDonnell Douglas

AH-64 Apaches, sir. The Apache is the most sophisticated helicopter ever built. It's armed with six Hellfire missiles that can lock on to and destroy any known tank, and for softer targets it has 2.75-inch rockets and an extremely accurate 30mm Chain Gun. It is equipped with night-vision target-acquisition-and-designation systems to enable it to fly and fight in all weathers, day or night."

King nodded. These were going to be extremely useful against Indianapolis. "And what else do we have?"

Hawk walked a bit farther into the hangar. "We've got about ten Bell AH-1 HueyCobras. They were developed from the old UH-1 and were one of the most feared weapons back in the Vietnam War. They're kinda dated now, since they have no bad-weather or night-fighting capability, but it's still a devastating weapon in the daytime. It's got a 20mm Gatling gun beneath the nose, and can be fitted with either Target On Wire antiarmor missiles, cannon pods, or rocket pods beneath its stub wings."

King nodded and glanced at the side at an array of ten smaller helicopters off to the side.

"What are those?" he said, pointing.

"Those are McDonnell Douglas OH-6 Defenders," Hawk answered. They're used mainly as light scout choppers, though they can be fitted with a Minigun for strafing troops and light personnel carriers. They're too slow for major battles, but are great in the field when they're aren't any other choppers available."

"Great," King said. "Now how about airplanes?"

"They're in the next hangar, sir," Hawk said, leading the colonel through a side door and across two hundred yards of tarmac toward a much bigger hangar.

When they entered the hangar, King's eyes lit up. "Jesus," he said, staring at the array of aircraft in front of him.

Hawk stood next to several short jet-powered planes. "These are Vought A-7 Corsair IIs," he said, then grinned. "Better known as SLUFs."

"SLUFs?" King asked.

"Yeah, it stands for Short Little Ugly Fuckers," Hawk said, laughing. "Originally designed as a carrier-borne light attack aircraft, it has a huge bomb load and is very effective against both ground troops and buildings."

King nodded, his attention wandering to a group of planes farther inside the hangar. "What are those?" he asked.

"Those are the pride of the Air Force," Hawk said, "probably the best close-support aircraft ever designed. The Fairchild A-10 Warthog. Heavily armored and very maneuverable at low level, it carries both guided missiles and a 30mm cannon. It was the mainstay in the Gulf War of thirty years ago." He shook his head. "Pilots loved it. Several of 'em came back with half their wings shot off and tails missing, and they still brought the boys home alive." He patted one on the fuselage. "This is my favorite of all."

King smiled. "How about that?" he said, looking at a huge helicopter in the corner.

"That's an old Boeing CH-47 Chinook. It's too big to fit in the helicopter hangar so we stored it here. It can carry fifty troops and twelve tons of support equipment for 'em and drop 'em anywhere you want 'em to go."

King rubbed his hands together. "All right, gentlemen," he said to the group of pilots that had been following them through the hangars. "Get some rest this afternoon, and we'll meet at 2100 hours in the officers' mess and formulate a battle plan for President Osterman."

"When do you plan on staging the attack?" Hawk asked.

"Just as soon as we can arm these machines and get some troops up here for support," King said.

"We're also gonna have to have someplace nearer to Indianapolis to refuel the choppers," Hawk said. "Most of 'em only have a range of two hundred and fifty to three hundred miles."

"How far is it to Indianapolis from Oak Ridge?"

"About a hundred and fifty miles, but they're gonna need

some fuel for maneuvers, especially if we face any resistance."

King nodded. "I'll coordinate with President Osterman and General Stevens. There are a couple of old National Guard bases not too far from the government's headquarters." He thought for a moment, then snapped his fingers. "I'll get a couple of squads of Blackshirts up here and we can transport them to one of those fields the day before our attack. If they can take the field, the Chinook can carry enough avgas in drums to refuel the choppers on their way in."

Hawk nodded. "Sounds like a plan to me."

Three days later, the plan was set. Forty Blackshirt troops equipped with assault weapons were loaded into the CH-47 Chinook helicopter, along with 22,000 pounds of avgas in fifty-five-gallon drums and a handful of aircraft mechanics to see to the refueling when the time came. It'd been decided after consultation with Stevens and Osterman to have the Chinook make its assault at dusk on the morning before the attack, giving President Warner less than twelve hours to react in case word of the taking of the Guard base leaked out. The National Guard base they'd picked was at Terre Haute, Indiana, less than fifty miles from Indianapolis.

Stevens picked Saturday evening for the assault and dawn on Sunday for the final attack on the government's base. He'd grinned when he told Claire of the plan, saying, "Remember Pearl Harbor? No one's on their best on Sunday morning, especially when we're negotiating a peace and not expecting an attack."

The Blackshirts were under the command of Lieutenant Colonel Johnny Walker, an ex-Ranger in the Special Forces who was trained in assault techniques. His men were all in black, with black grease paint on their faces. Twenty of his

en were armed with Browning sawed-off shotguns, the
ther half with M-16's. His plan was simple. The pilot was
 radio he was having engine trouble and would request
ermission to make an emergency landing at the Terre
aute field. Since it'd been practically abandoned when the
overnment took over the base in Indianapolis, there would
nly be a skeleton crew stationed on the base, and most of
hose would probably be in town since it was Saturday
ight.

Pilot Tommy Windsong, a young Navajo warrant officer,
eyed his mike and said, "Tower at Terre Haute . . . tower
t Terre Haute. This is Chinook 7624 declaring an in-flight
mergency. Mayday! Mayday!"

"Got ya on the scope, Chinook 7624. What's the prob-
em?"

"Engine oil pressure is falling rapidly and I'm losing my
ydraulics. I need to put this can down fast!"

"Advise Chinook 7624, Indianapolis field is only fifty
niles north. They have emergency equipment on standby.
Advise you try there."

Windsong put as much sarcasm in his voice as he could.
"Listen, son. These whirlybirds have all the glide charac-
eristics of a rock when the engine quits. I say again, I need
o land now!"

There was a pause and a burst of static before the controller
came back on. "Bring her in, Captain. Wind's nor-noreast at
en miles, visibility is six miles. Happy landing, sir."

Windsong smiled and made an O sign over his shoulder
with his thumb and index finger to Colonel Walker, who was
standing just behind his seat.

Walker turned to his men and pumped his fist up and down,
signaling them to get ready. "Lock and load, gentlemen," he
said over the intercom into their headsets. "We've been in-
vited to the dance."

"Time to kick some ass!" an unidentified voice responded,

making Walker smile. It was the kind of spirit he liked in his men just before battle. It meant they were loose and ready.

The Chinook settled with a gentle bump on the tarmac in the middle of the airfield, and before the rotors began to slow, Walker had his men out of the chopper and running toward the tower. Since the field wasn't in current use, there were no emergency vehicles to shed light on the field and the men were practically invisible in the semigloom of dusk.

Private Sam Donally shielded his eyes against the reflection off the tower glass as he tried to see what was going on with the Chinook out on his field. He keyed his mike. "Chinook 7624, please advise present condition."

"Hang on, tower, I'm checking my gauges as we speak," Windsong replied, playing for time. "The engine temp is down but I'm still having trouble with the hydraulics."

"Do you want me to radio Indianapolis for assistance?" Donally asked, suddenly remembering he hadn't asked the pilot his mission or for his clearance codes in the excitement of the emergency.

"No," Windsong replied, "I think it's just a plugged hydraulic line. I may be able to fix it myself."

"By the way, Chinook 7624, I need to log the clearance code into my book. Would you give it to me?"

The door behind Donally burst open and a black-faced man stood there with a shotgun cradled in his arms. He pumped the lever with a loud metallic sound. "How's that for your clearance code, sonny?"

Donally raised his hands, his mouth suddenly dry and his stomach feeling as if he'd been kicked in the balls. "It'll do . . . it'll do," he croaked.

The man stepped aside and Walker walked into the tower and picked up the mike. "Mission accomplished, Chinook. Stand down."

Then he pulled a .45 automatic out of his holster and stuck the barrel against Donally's forehead. "We're not going to have any trouble out of you, are we, son?"

"No, sir!" Donally said.

"Good. Now tell me how many men you have on base and where they're stationed."

Thirty-eight

Lieutenant Colonel Johnny Walker had his squadron of helicopters fly into the Terre Haute Air National Guard base from several different directions and all at extremely low altitudes. He'd received the week's flight control codes from Private Sam Donally, who'd become very cooperative with a .45 aimed at his head, just in case the air traffic controllers at the Indianapolis base happened to be alert enough to notice the increased air activity on Saturday night.

Only two of the pilots had been questioned over the radio, and the controller had evidently accepted their stories about flying night maneuvers to get their air time up to standards to receive their flight pay.

Once all the pilots and Blackshirt Special Ops men were present, Walker had a pre-invasion conference in the officers' wardroom. He stood at the front of the room with everyone else gathered in the folding chairs scattered around in a semicircle.

"Some of you pilots who've flown into Indianapolis might already know this, but bear with me. A lot of the Special Ops boys have never been to the main base."

He perched on the edge of a desk with one hip and began his talk. "When President Osterman set up the new governmental headquarters, she chose Fort Benjamin Harrison on the outskirts of Indianapolis. At the time, the base boasted the largest indoor building in the country. Though only three stories aboveground, the main administration building has three underground bunkers that were built to withstand a nuclear blast. In the old days, back in the seventies and eighties, the base served as a repository for all the paper records of the Armed Services, as well as the center that processed all the payroll checks for the Army, Navy, and Marine Corps. The building was built to enormous standards, with halls wide enough for several jeeps to pass each other without crowding. It is my understanding that the new leaders of the country utilize the underground bunkers for most of their work and only lower-level administrative staff are housed aboveground."

One of the pilots, a young man with barely enough fuzz on his face to be shaving, raised his hand. "Sir."

Walker nodded. "Yes, go on."

"I was wondering if you expect many civilian casualties in the upcoming attack."

Walker smiled and shook his head. "No, not at all. That's one of the reasons we planned the attack for the early morning hours on a Sunday. Virtually none of the civilians will be on duty, and those active duty personnel will be at their lowest manpower and hopefully at their lowest level of alertness."

The young man nodded, evidently relieved he wouldn't be expected to slaughter too many of his fellow Americans.

"Now," Walker continued, "the topography of the land surrounding Fort Benjamin Harrison is mainly flat, with only gently rolling hills and a few shallow river valleys in the area. That means we won't have much cover on the way in, but it also means we can fly low and slow and not have to worry about flying into the side of a mountain."

He stood up and motioned to Lieutenant Robert Hawk to come forward. "Now, I'm going to be in charge of the commandos in the Chinook, and we'll be coming in on your tails after we're told you've taken out all the AA batteries and as much of the ground resistance as you can. Since I'm not a pilot, I'm going to let Lieutenant Hawk, your squadron commander, set the battle plan for the air assault. Lieutenant Hawk."

Robert Hawk stepped to a blackboard on the front wall, where he'd drawn a rough schematic of Fort Benjamin Harrison. "Since we've managed to get within fifty miles of the base and we'll all have full tanks, we're going to come in from the four points of the compass, with an Apache leading each of the four assault teams. They'll be followed by two each of the HueyCobras and two each of the Defenders, which have been fitted with Miniguns and will come in last for mopping up and strafing of any ground troops that will be on the move. Since the Apaches are the only machines with night-flying capabilities, the others will follow in V-formation behind them, using the Apaches' lights as guides to keep the correct altitudes and positions."

"Sir," one of the pilots said, "that leaves two each of the HueyCobras and Defenders left."

Hawk nodded. "Yeah, those will accompany the Chinook in on its approach to protect the ground assault troops, just in case the fort manages to get any aircraft in the air."

"What about our objectives?" the man asked.

"Primary is the ground-emplacement AA guns and any other defensive weapons or troops. Secondary is to destroy as much of the aboveground admin building as we can. Colonel King has asked that, within reason and safety, we avoid as much as we can damaging valuable aircraft on the ground, as we're gonna need those later when we go up against the SUSA."

Another of the pilots addressed Walker. "Sir, do you think forty men will be enough to hold the base after we take it?"

Walker nodded. "Yes, I do. Once we've taken control of the admin building and taken out the new leaders, we will issue a radio announcement that President Osterman has retaken her rightful position as head of the government and she will order all the troops to stand down. Without anyone to lead them against us, I don't feel we'll have too many problems. In addition, Colonel King will be arriving within hours of the assault with several hundred additional troops loyal to President Osterman, so there shouldn't be any difficulty whatsoever."

He stepped forward. "If there aren't any additional questions, hit the sack, men. We'll be getting up at 0500 and be ready for takeoff at 0600. I want to hit the base just before shift change at 0645, when the guards have been on duty for an entire shift and their alertness will be at its lowest ebb. Good night, and good hunting tomorrow."

At 0630 on Sunday morning, Private Sloan Wilson shook his head and rubbed bleary eyes as he sat in the radar room in the control tower at Fort Benjamin Harrison. He'd been on duty for seven and a half hours, and hadn't seen so much as a blip on the green radar screens lining the tower. To make matters worse, the coffee machine was on the fritz and he was having trouble staying awake.

He gave a last look at the screens, slipped out the door to the tower, and ran down the steps to the officers' mess below. He knew the Officer of the Day wouldn't mind if he borrowed a quick cup of coffee.

Sure enough, the lieutenant on duty was fast asleep, his head lying on folded arms on his desk, softly snoring.

"Jesus," Wilson whispered to himself, shaking his head. "Must be nice to be an officer in this man's army." He stepped to the coffee urn and poured himself a cup. He took a quick sip and smiled. *Hell,* he thought, *even their coffee is better.*

With a quick glance over his shoulder, he eased out the door and climbed back up the stairs. He sat at his console and leaned back in his chair, enjoying the last cup of coffee before he was relieved and went to his bed for some much-needed shut-eye.

As he relaxed, a movement on the screens caught his attention. "Goddamn," he muttered, spilling his coffee on his lap as he jerked forward. The screens were full of tiny white blips coming from all directions. "Shit!" he exclaimed, thumbing his microphone and almost yelling, "Unidentified aircraft, this is the tower speaking. I need your security codes at once!"

A thumping vibration and a blinding white light made him look up, just as a dark shape over a searchlight came straight at the tower.

Wilson had time to notice the winking lights as the Apache's M230 30mm Chain Gun lit up the sky. Several hundred rounds of the 30mm shells shattered the glass of the tower and literally shredded Wilson's body, throwing him backward over the chair and out the other window. He was dead before his body hit the ground thirty feet below.

Private Bobby Tupelow was dreaming of his girlfriend, who awaited him at his apartment, as he dozed at his anti-aircraft battery on the outskirts of Fort Benjamin Harrison. A chattering staccato of gunfire drove all thoughts of romance from his mind and jerked him awake in the seat between the twin barrels of his guns.

Blinking his eyes and trying desperately to come fully awake, he jerked the loading lever, which would fill the firing chamber with the fifty-caliber slugs the gun fired. Before he could sight, much less pull the trigger, an OH-6 Defender helicopter swooped out of the morning sun, which was just peeking over the horizon, and let go with its 20 mm Minigun. The shells sheared one of Tupelow's barrels off and ricocheted around his compartment, tearing through his body and setting his ammunition off in a blinding, shrieking explosion that could be heard for miles around the base.

Otis Warner was jolted out of his bed in the first basement level by an explosion that rocked the entire admin building as an Apache hovered two hundred yards to the west and fired first a Hellfire missile into the second-story, and then followed quickly with four 2.75-inch rockets into the side of the building. The walls of the second story disintegrated, collapsing half the third story and bringing the entire west side of the building down in tumbling rubble.

Warner looked back and forth, trying to come awake and think what he should do. Racing in his pajamas to the bedside phone, he picked it up to warn the troops of the attack, only to find no dial tone. *The damn thing must've been knocked out by the explosion,* he thought. He jerked his closet door open and began to pull on pants and shirt, not bothering to take the time to remove his pajamas. He stepped into shoes without socks and ran for the door to his bedroom. Jerking it open, he noticed plaster falling from the ceiling, but no visible cracks. *Thank God,* he whispered to no one, and began to run down the hall, not really knowing what he was going to do but feeling a desperate need to get out from under all the tons of concrete over his head.

General Joe Winter ran from his door, seconds behind Warner, holding a Browning shotgun in his arms. It'd long been rumored he slept with the gun, but actually it leaned against a wall next to his bed.

"Warner," he yelled when he saw the President running down the hall.

Otis stopped and looked back over his shoulder. "What the hell's going on, General?" he screamed, covering his ears as another explosion rocked the building.

"We're under attack," Winter shouted, almost adding "you idiot," but clamping his lips shut just in time. "Come on, follow me to the emergency exit!"

Warner reversed himself and ran shakily down the hall after Winter, huffing and puffing as he tried to clear plaster dust from his eyes.

Winter stopped before a thick metal door and quickly punched numbers into a pad on the wall. The door clicked open onto a long tunnel, emergency lights along the ceiling casting a gloomy glow in the darkness.

"Let's go, Mr. President. This will take us a quarter mile

away from the building and come out in a safe area," he said, adding under his breath an inaudible *I hope.*

Winter pumped a shell into the chamber of the shotgun and took off down the hall at a lumbering run, slowing so as not to leave the President behind.

Soon, with the tunnel shaking and quivering under multiple explosions, they were at the end of the passageway. Again, Winter punched in a code on a keypad and a metal door slid open, revealing a flight of stairs leading upward.

Winter led the way, slowly opening yet another metal door at the top of the stairs. He eased the door open and peered out, his shotgun held at the ready. Finally, after a few moments, he gestured for Warner to follow him and he slipped out the door.

Warner found himself in a concrete bunkerlike room, about ten feet by ten feet, with a cement floor and no windows or furnishings.

Winter twisted a dead bolt on the door and again checked to make sure there was no danger. "Okay, it looks clear," he said over his shoulder. "Follow me, and keep your head down and don't stop running until I tell you."

He disappeared out the doorway, and Warner took a deep breath, crossed himself, and ran after Winter.

Twenty yards away, across an open stretch of dried brown grass, was a building with a sign over the open door saying "Motor Pool." Winter darted through the open doorway and ran straight for a HumVee parked in a line of jeeps and APCs.

He jerked the driver's door open and motioned for Warner to get in the passenger side. Firing up the engine, he said, "Put your seat belt on, Mr. President. This may be a rough ride."

He floored the accelerator and the HumVee shot out of the motor pool building, skidding through a turn as Winter headed for the east gate, the nearest one to their position.

Overhead, Malcolm Salsbury gave a twist on the throttle of his HueyCobra when he saw the HumVee throwing up a dust cloud as it sped toward the exit gate to the base. He tilted the nose down and flicked his eyes to his Heads Up Display as the vehicle became centered on his targeting scope. He keyed his microphone and said, "Squad leader, I've got a HumVee heading for the gate at speed. Can't see occupants. Should I take it out?"

Lieutenant Hawk answered, "Is the vehicle making an aggressive move or firing on the choppers?"

"No," Salsbury said with a laugh, "he's haulin' ass tryin' to get out of the action."

"Then let him, Malcolm. We're not hear to kill people, just to retake the government."

Malcolm flicked off his HUD. "Aye, sir," he said into the mikc. As he banked away from the car, he gave a mock salute. "You are one lucky fucker, whoever you are."

The Apaches hovered over the admin building, pouring Hellfire missile after Hellfire missile into the structure until there was nothing left aboveground except a huge pile of smoking, burning rubble.

The HueyCobras used their 20mm Gatling guns on the AA emplacements until they were bent and twisted piles of scorched metal that looked like they were the work of some New Age sculptor, while the Defenders swooped and bent and dipped over the compound, strafing with their 20mm Miniguns any APCs that dared to try and bring troops into the battle.

All in all, since it was a Sunday morning and most of the troops not on guard duty were still in town sleeping off hangovers from Saturday night, there were surprisingly few casualties, with only a few scattered bodies littering the grounds.

Less than an hour into the fracas, Hawk radioed for Walker to bring his Special Ops Blackshirts onto the base. Moments later, the big Chinook could be seen lumbering in over the airfield, then hovering a few feet above the ground as it discharged its cargo of commandos like a dog shedding fleas.

Two hours later, it was all over. The base was secured and

all personnel not dead were captured and confined in a couple of hangars with the Special Ops troops keeping guard.

Walker shook Hawk's hand. "Good job, Lieutenant," he said. "As soon as you refuel, I'll need your men to fly a perimeter guard around the base at, say, ten miles, just in case someone gets the bright idea of trying to retake the base."

Hawk grinned and saluted. "Aye, sir. I'll rotate the men so they each have a little time to unwind and get some coffee and grub down."

Walker nodded. He liked a man who thought of his troops' welfare. It was the mark of a good officer.

After Hawk left, Walker turned to his executive officer, Lieutenant Bonner. "Cliff, have your men finished sweeping the underground bunkers?"

"Yes, sir. We found several secretaries, a couple of minor functionaries, and some . . . women."

"Wives?" Walker asked.

Bonner grinned and waggled his hand back and forth. "Maybe, or maybe just good friends."

Walker nodded. "Any sign of General Winter or Otis Warner?"

Bonner shook his head. "No, sir."

"Shit! President Osterman is going to be really pissed!"

Bonner shrugged. "He could be buried under all that wreckage of the aboveground structure," he said, though his voice showed he didn't really believe it.

Walker frowned. "No, I'm not that lucky. Oh, well, I might as well call Colonel King and let him know the bad news. Maybe he'll volunteer to pass the message along to Osterman."

Bonner laughed. "You ever know a senior officer to stick his neck out like that?"

Walker returned the grin. "Hell, no. How do you think they got to be senior officers?"

Thirty-nine

The Boeing/Bell CV-22 Osprey slowed in the predawn hours after passing over Mexico City on the way toward the forward elements of General Dominguez's and General Pena's troops. The CV-22 was a medium lift, multimission, vertical/short-takeoff-and-landing (VSTOL), tilt-rotor aircraft developed by Boeing and Bell Helicopter Textron to be used for long-range Special Operations missions, especially for combat assault and assault support.

Since it had the attributes of both a transport airplane and a helicopter, it was ideal for placing Buddy Raines and his Special Ops Brigade team deep into Mexican territory.

As the mission-ready light over the cargo compartment door changed from red to green, Buddy leaned over and said to Harley Reno, "I'll take my group out here, in front of the advancing forces, and then have the pilot leapfrog over them and let your team out to their rear. That way we'll have 'em pincered between us."

Harley looked down the cargo compartment, which was six feet in height, five feet, eleven inches in width, and twenty-four feet, four inches in length. "Good. I'll be glad to get out of this bird, it reminds me too much of a coffin."

Buddy stuck his hand out. "Good hunting, podna."

"You, too, pal," Reno answered, shaking his hand. "I'll have Corrie keep in close touch with your radio operator so we can coordinate our strikes."

Buddy stuck his thumb up and turned to his men. "Mount

up, gentlemen," he said as the rotors on the wing tilted and the big Osprey settled to the ground like a helicopter, hovering two feet off the caliche dirt of the Mexican desert.

Buddy opened the door and jumped to the ground, followed by his Special Ops team. As soon as the last man stepped out, Harley leaned over and pulled the door shut.

He signaled Coop, who banged on the wall behind the pilot to signal him they were ready for takeoff. As the Osprey rose in the air, then began to move forward as the rotors tilted again on the wings, Coop shook his head. "Damn, this thing can't seem to make up its mind whether it's a helicopter or an airplane."

Anna scooted over on her bench to make room for Harley to sit next to her, causing both Jersey and Coop to look at each other and smile. Anna's infatuation with the big redhead was becoming more obvious every day.

Soon, the Osprey again settled to the earth and Harley, Hammer, Anna, Corrie, Jersey, and Coop piled out and immediately spread out forming a defensive perimeter as the plane took off again.

Coop noticed Harley had grabbed a four-foot-long box painted Army green and had it under his arm. "What ya got in the box, Harley?" he asked as they squatted in the field, looking outward for any signs of hostiles.

Harley grinned. "An M-60 machine gun fixed with a leather strap."

Coop raised his eyebrows. "You mean like Rambo used in that old movie *First Blood?*"

Harley nodded. "Yep. Never know when a little firepower might come in handy."

"A little firepower?" Jersey said from next to Coop. "You can stop a tank with that thing."

Harley just nodded. "Yep."

Hammer stood up after seeing they were unobserved. "Let's go, people. Time to get under cover until dawn, when we can see to reconnoiter the area."

Hammer led them at a dogtrot until they found shelter under a grove of mesquite trees near a small stream that was little more than a trickle.

"Break out your MREs. No tellin' when we'll get to eat again," he said.

Anna took out a pouch of navy beans and ham hocks with corn and twisted the pack so the self-contained chemical reaction would heat the bag. Then she sat next to Harley, with her back against the bole of a tree.

"Harley," she said.

"Yes, Anna."

"Tell me about yourself. Are you of Swedish or Norwegian descent?"

He chuckled quietly as he ripped open a packet that said Swiss steak and mashed potatoes. "Neither. My ancestors were all Indians."

Anna looked at him like he was teasing her. "With red hair and blue eyes?"

He nodded. "There's a tribe of Indians in northwest Mexico called the Tarahumarra. They live over near Torrleon on the edge of the desert. All the men and women have red hair and green eyes, and the men are almost all over six feet in height."

"How did they get those characteristics?" she asked.

He shrugged. "No one knows for sure, but it's said that the Tarahumarra are direct descendants of the Nordic people brought over by Eric the Red and his fellow explorers."

"But, Harley, your eyes are blue."

He stared at her for a moment. "I'm glad you noticed, Anna."

Her face blushed a fiery red as he continued. "That's probably because I also have some Karankawa in me."

"Karankawa?"

"Yeah. The Karankawa lived along the Texas coast of the Gulf of Mexico, and are best known for being cannibals."

"Huh?"

He nodded. "But that's really not fair. They didn't eat people for fun, only the hearts and brains of enemies they'd captured, in order to get their wisdom and strength. Hell, almost all of the Native American tribes did the same thing."

"But how did they mix with your Tarahumarra?"

"Again, no one knows, but the best guess is Spanish slave traders used to cruise the coast of Texas and capture the Karankawa to make slaves of them. Naturally, they'd be taken back to Mexico, where most of the Spanish gold and silver mines were. Those that escaped, joined and later bred with the Tarahumarra."

"Do you ever eat your enemies, Harley?" she asked, smiling gently at him.

He stared deep into her eyes. "No, Anna, only my closest friends."

She dropped her eyes to her navy beans, her face again flaming red.

Parts of the old Pan American Highway ditches were overgrown with vines, and in places the asphalt was pockmarked by craters from RPGs made years before, when the big war raged across most of the world. Since then, there had been only sparse traffic on the long, badly damaged highway. The Mexican people, like most of those of the Third World, had suffered far more from the destruction of the old way of life than had the more developed nations. With the new struggle for survival and the destruction of much of the wealthier nations' infrastructure, there had been precious little money for foreign aid.

Buddy Raines led a squad of his Special Ops Brigade through the jungles of the Mexican state of Oaxaca, flanking the highway that once linked North America with the Panama Canal and Central America. His troops carried silenced Beretta pistols and the so-called Mini-Uzi 9x19mm machine guns with forty-round magazines.

They were placing "Bouncing Betty" land mines wherever an unsuspecting group of Comandante Perro Loco's ground forces was expected to march toward Mexico City. The Bouncing Betty came up three feet in the air before it exploded, sending shrapnel into anything and everything within a forty-foot area, one of the deadliest mines ever developed for warfare.

Perro Loco's troops were marching on Mexico City under the command of Generals Juan Dominguez and Jaime Pena.

Presidente Martinez of Mexico had promised Ben Raines that no one would molest his SUSA Rebels, so long as they kept it a limited conflict. General Dominguez's troops were said to be moving north with tanks, APCs, and several thousand of Perro Loco's infantrymen from both Belize and Nicaragua and Honduras to try to take the Mexican capital. The untended Pan American Highway was the only route through primitive jungle states like Chiapas, Oaxaca, Guerrero, and Michoacan to Mexico City from the south. There were no other roads suitable for heavy equipment.

Buddy Raines knew the Belizian rebels had to use the virtually abandoned highway to get their tanks and heavy artillery northward to the Mexican capital. He was preparing a welcome for them and the troops that would be walking alongside them.

Buddy led his handpicked force of a dozen trusted specialists along the dark, mosquito-infested jungle trails running beside the highway. No motorized traffic moved past them in any direction. The gasoline refineries across southern Mexico had been knocked out during the war, and fuel was at a premium in this part of the hemisphere.

Sergeant Chuck Flood, dressed in camouflage with his face blackened like the others, came over to Buddy, his Uzi hanging from his shoulder on a thin leather strap.

"We've got 'em out, sir. Not using any patterns, like you told us. They'll have to sniff them out one at a time to find all of them. Maybe as much as half the column will be in our trap before they realize what's happening to them. When they try to get off the road, they'll hit our Bouncing Bettys in most of the ditches."

"Recon says the lead battalion is only a few miles south of us. Captain Storm says they should be crossing the first mines in an hour, maybe less."

Sergeant Flood nodded.

A woman wearing an infantryman's cap came running up to Buddy as he was talking to Sergeant Flood.

"They're coming," Corporal Crisi Casper said, out of breath as she gave her report. "Two miles. Moving slowly, but I don't think they suspect anything."

"Have they got dogs out front?" Buddy asked.

"No. No dogs."

Flood grinned. "Then they should hit the land mines with the APCs and tanks without any warning." He glanced up at the sky. "I sure as hell wish we had some air support for this operation."

"That would give us away," Buddy said. "Better to let them wander into the middle of our minefields without suspecting anything."

"They don't suspect anything," Crisi said. "They act like this is a parade of some kind. Some officer is riding out in front in a jeep mounted with a fifty-caliber popgun. He acts like they're headed for Disneyland. He was smiling when I saw him."

Buddy looked south. "Tell Captain Storm to get everyone off the roadway. We've laid better than five hundred land mines on this stretch, including the old Claymores. We'll pull back into the jungle and see how many of Perro Loco's soldiers and tanks get blown to bits in the next couple of hours. It's good to know they don't have scent dogs to guide them through. The trap is set now."

"I'll inform Captain Storm," Sergeant Flood said, taking off at a jog.

"What do you want the rest of us to do?" Corporal Casper asked.

"Get back off the road, a hundred yards or more. Scatter out and wait."

"Wait for what, sir?"

"When things start blowing up along this highway, we'll call for an Osprey and get the hell out of here. It'll take Perro Loco's soldiers a couple of days to clear a way through this jungle for their heavy stuff to get around the mines we've laid along this road."

"These Central American rebels may call in their own air support, sir."

"Suits me just fine," Buddy said.

"It suits you?"

"It sure as hell does. We'll see how well Comandante Perro Loco's air force does in the skies . . . We've got two rocket launchers."

A thundering explosion came from a bend in the roadway and pieces of heavy iron flew into the air, along with a thick column of smoke.

"Bingo," Buddy whispered to Captain Storm from their hiding place in the jungle. "Something . . . a tank or an APC, just hit a mine and their fuel tank exploded."

A huge ball of swirling flame rose above the canopy of the rain forest.

"They're right in the middle of the minefield we set for 'em," Storm said.

Another explosion prevented Buddy from agreeing with the captain out loud.

"Damn," Corporal Casper said when another ball of fire boiled into the sky.

"That had to be another fuel tank," Buddy said as he put his fieldglasses on the bend in the Pan American Highway. "A Betty doesn't make that much noise."

"A Claymore don't either," Storm remarked. "We've g 'em right where we want 'em now."

"Spread out," Buddy said, adjusting the focus knob on h binoculars. "Their foot soldiers will be coming from all d rections in a minute or two."

"We can't hold off so many," Storm said.

"I know," Buddy replied. "I'm going to radio for the O: prey to pick us up. We've done all we can do with very limite resources."

Gunshots rang out from the south.

"Who are they shooting at?" Crisi wondered.

"Shadows," Buddy told her. "When things start happenin, fast on a battlefield, you see ghosts."

A third explosion shook the ground underneath Budd: Corporal Casper, and Captain Storm.

Buddy grunted, still unable to see anyone moving throug; his field glasses. "Must have been a munitions truck. Prett dumb of General Dominguez to put a truck full of explosive near the front of an advancing column."

"They don't have a West Point in Mexico," Storm said a the sound of the explosion faded.

"Spread out," Buddy said again.

"I'll call in the Osprey. Before long these trees are gonn: be crawling with Perro Loco's rebel soldiers."

"Here they come now," Crisi said, pointing south.

Buddy could see shadows moving through the jungl: southeast of the highway.

"We'll take out as many as we can," Captain Storm said as he pulled back the loading lever on his Uzi.

Buddy nodded. "Give the Osprey fifteen minutes. It': coming from Tampico. Move north along the road and we'l meet at the bridge."

Captain Storm slipped off into the jungle. Corporal Caspe: moved behind a tangle of vines, walking east.

Two more explosions in rapid succession told Buddy tha: a land mine had destroyed two vehicles.

"Welcome to southern Mexico, General Dominguez," he said under his breath, returning the field glasses to his face as he searched the jungle.

Private Julio Villalobos lay in the ditch beside the Pan American Highway with his M-16 resting on his chest. He was having trouble breathing.

Julio's friend, Gulliermo Costas, came crawling toward him with both legs blown off below his knees.

"What . . . happened, Julio?"

"Land mines. Someone put mines along this road. They knew we were coming."

"I am dying, Julio. I have no feet."

Julio wasn't all that sure of his own injuries. "I cannot get any air," he said. "Something went down in my lungs when the tank blew up."

"Por favor, please give this watch to my sister, Julio. It belonged to my father."

"I am not sure I can stand up, *compadre."*

"But you must give it to her. It is all I have. Take the twenty *pesos* from my pocket and give it to her also. She has four children."

An earsplitting blast shook the jungle beyond the ditch where Julio lay. "I cannot move, *compadre.* Put the watch and the money in my pocket."

A chunk of iron track from an old Sherman tank came tumbling into the ditch beside Julie and Gulliermo, landing with a thud a few yards away.

"What is happening?" Julio gasped.

"We are being attacked," Costas groaned. "I am dying because I have no feet."

The chatter of machine-gun fire came from the north, farther up the road.

"Please give the watch and the money to my sister," Costas pleaded.

"I am not sure I can stand up. I do not know what is wrong with me."

Costas crawled over to him. He looked down at Julio lower body. *"Dios,"* he gasped.

"What is it?" Julio wondered, feeling nothing other than a strange floating sensation.

"Madre de Dios. Where are your legs, Julio?"

"My legs?"

"They are not here . . . There is only blood."

Julio tried to wiggle his toes. "I cannot feel anything," he said.

Three explosions in a row echoed down the line of tanks and trucks stopped along the highway.

"Your legs!" Costas cried. "Julio! You have no legs and have no feet!"

Julio closed his eyes, thinking of their small village in the mountains in Honduras where his wife and children waited for the money promised by Comandante Perro Loco. "I must have legs," he said, unable to raise his head to see for himself. "No one can live without legs."

Costas started to vomit, gagging up the meager contents of his stomach.

Julio began to dream of a ripe banana, along with a piece of breadfruit. He closed his eyes and dreamed of better days until the dream became lost in a fog.

Forty

Crisi fired into a mass of moving bodies, her Uzi making low-pitched *phfittt* sounds through the new silencers as the forty-round clip emptied, jumping in her hands, spitting out its deadly loads.

Screams of pain came from the forest.

"Nice shooting, Corporal," a soft voice said.

She turned around and found Sergeant Barry Brown standing behind her with a handheld rocket launcher.

"Thanks," she said, ramming another full clip into the loading chamber.

"We'll have company in the air pretty soon," Brown said in his typically understated way. "I can't wait to see how many of the bastards I can knock down."

"You enjoy this, don't you?" Crisi asked, as the rattle of automatic-weapons fire surrounded them. South of their position men were shouting, and the roar of engines filled the rain-forested hills.

"Damn right I do," Barry said.

"I suspect you'll get your chance to enjoy a great deal more of it," she said, hunkered down behind a tangle of vines when the whine of stray bullets sizzled overhead.

"I hope so," Brown whispered, his eyes turned up at blue sky above the treetops.

Above the din, Crisi heard the hammering of a helicopter's rotor blades.

"Here they come," she said.

"I hear it. Just one. By the sound, it's a Kiowa or an OH-(
Defender. This is gonna be too easy. An OH-58 Kiowa is too
slow to dodge a Hellfire missile, if you aim just the righ
way. I'm gonna knock it down."

His expression changed. He rested the launching tube or
his right shoulder.

"Jesus, Barry. You've been at this too long. You're getting
a kick out of this."

"I'm killing an enemy of the Tri-State Coalition. It's wha
I'm paid to do."

"Does General Raines pay you enough so that you like
what we are doing?"

"Yeah. But I'd do it for nothing. Since the war I haven't
had anybody to shoot at."

Brown squinted into the sights. The sounds of battle raged
all around them.

"There it is," Brown said. "A Kiowa, and the jerk at the
controls is flying a straight line at just the right altitude for
me. He should grab his ankles, bend over, and kiss his ass
good-bye."

"We don't have much time," Crisi reminded him. "Buddy
said he's calling in the Osprey to take us out of here. We've
got less than fifteen minutes to do as much damage as we
can before we pull back to the bridge."

"It won't take me long," Brown said, frozen next to the
trunk of a coconut palm with the launcher held fast against
his shoulder.

He flipped the sight up on top of the long, tube-shaped
rocket launcher, aimed, and grinned through gritted teeth as
he pulled the triggering mechanism.

A whooshing sound followed a trail of white vapor toward
the tops of the trees.

Crisi watched the helicopter without firing off any more
Uzi rounds at the enemy. There was something about having
Barry Brown standing behind her that made her nervous as
hell. Brown was a psycho . . . a good soldier, but a crazy

son of a bitch who enjoyed killing. She'd been on Special Ops missions with him before, and always felt unclean afterward, as if she'd swum in a swamp.

The Kiowa's pilot must have seen the vapor trail of the missile headed toward him, for he jerked the nose of the helicopter skyward, evidently trying to avoid the deadly rocket. It did him no good, for the chopper exploded, tilting at an odd angle when the Hellfire missile struck its underbelly. Fire and smoke engulfed the body of the aircraft just as it came apart in the air. The main rotor went straight up as it was torn from the driveshaft by the rocket, continuing to spin in the air like some child's toy launched at a July Fourth picnic.

"Adios, you dumb son of a bitch," Brown said, his eyes glittering wildly as he loaded one more rocket into the tube. He chuckled. "It's easy to kill a stupid son of a bitch at the controls of one of those old things."

Crisi felt gooseflesh pimple her skin. There were plenty of war-crazed mercenaries in Ben Raines's army, but none any worse than Barry Brown. He made Anthony Perkins, the lead actor in the old movie *Psycho,* seem almost normal.

The chopper began to spin crazily in a loose downward spiral, what was left of it, until it finally crashed on top of a squad of Mexican soldiers in the jungle below, causing inhuman screams of anguish and pain as a giant fireball ignited trees for hundreds of yards around.

"I wonder if the pilot shit his pants," Barry said while he watched huge clouds of oily smoke cascade toward the sky, ignoring the shouts and screams of dying men as if they meant nothing to him.

A spray of AK-47 fire from the roadway sent Crisi and Barry ducking lower for cover.

"They spotted you," she said needlessly.

"Give 'em a little dose of lead," Brown replied, still watching the sky in spite of the bullets shredding jungle vines and leaves all around them. "I hear another big bird coming ou way."

Crisi swallowed hard. It was one thing to be on a team with good professional soldiers. But when you had a killing psycho in your unit, everything changed. Some of these old warriors like Brown never left a battlefield in their minds . . . They were still fighting the conflict inside their heads, and nothing would change them.

"It's an old Huey . . . probably a UH-1," Brown said. "Easiest damn ship to knock down there is. Slower than my granpaw's piss on a cold morning."

"I'll cover you," Crisi said, just before another land mine went off near the highway. Seconds later a man was shrieking in agony.

"I wonder if it blew his balls off," Brown said, sighting into the rocket launcher. "Sure does sound to me like he's in a lot of pain."

"Dear God," Crisi whispered, suddenly feeling sick to her stomach. Barry Brown was a madman. She had a fleeting thought that if she ever became like that, she hoped someone would put a bullet in her brain.

"Here it is," Brown said, when the noises from the chopper were almost directly above the jungle canopy. "Watch this, baby doll. I'm gonna show you how to kill a stupid pilot and turn an old Huey into scrap metal."

The dark outline of a helicopter appeared over the treetops, its rotor swirling leaves and undergrowth below while the staccato of machine-gun fire moved along the Pan American Highway from the south. A lone figure could be seen in the open hatchway of the chopper, leaning over a fifty-caliber machine gun, looking for targets to kill.

Brown fired a rocket. "It's a heat-seeker," he said with what might have been pride in his voice. "Watch this. See how quick it goes down."

Crisi didn't want to watch what would happen next, but

he was drawn to the missile's vapor trail during a brief lull
n the shooting.

The missile headed straight for the helicopter's big turbine
exhaust pipe, darting into it like a mouse headed for home.
The green-painted chopper came apart with a thunderous
roar. Scraps of metal exploded outward in a huge fireball
and then began falling toward the jungle, spinning a sparkling
in late afternoon sunlight like confetti at a parade.

"Got the bastard," Brown said.

Bits of the main rotor swirled into the treetops as flaming
fuel fell like yellow rain on the Oaxaca forest, igniting the
green palm leaves like old newspaper.

"Ain't that pretty?" Barry asked.

"Beautiful," Crisi replied, swallowing a mouthful of bitter
bile.

The regular rhythm of machine-gun fire came from all
sides now. She knew if she didn't get away from this creature,
she was going to shoot him in the head.

"It's time to pull back for the bridge," Crisi said, putting
another clip into her Uzi. "We sure as hell don't want to
miss that Osprey."

"I wouldn't mind," Brown said in a distant voice, still
watching the last pieces of the Huey crash into the jungle
along the highway. "I could stay here the rest of my life and
shoot down helicopters."

"You've only got two Hellfires left," Crisi observed. "We
need to start moving toward that bridge."

Brown stood up. "All right. I don't hear any more birds,"
he said, clearly disappointed.

"Let's go, Barry," Crisi cried above the hammering of machine guns and the explosion of another Bouncing Betty
somewhere to the south.

"They must be low on helicopter fuel," Brown said, scanning what he could see of the skies. "Otherwise, they'd have
sent more than two birds for air cover at the front of this
attack squad."

"Get down, Barry!" Crisi said. "They're shooting at anything."

"Screw 'em," Barry said, with a distant look in his deep blue eyes.

Crisi was about to reach for Barry's wrist when his body jerked backward.

"Barry!" she yelled. "Get down!"

Sergeant Barry Brown from Fort Worth, Texas, turned his back on Crisi. She saw a huge hole in the back of his camouflage shirt.

"I'm shot!" Brown stammered. He began to sink to his knees next to the palm tree.

A piece of flinty white bone jutted out of the hole in his back. Blood pumped from his wound, keeping time with the beat of his heart.

"Oh, no," Crisi sighed, watching Barry slump to the floor of the jungle with his rocket launcher pinned underneath him in a growing pool of blood.

She crept over to him. "Barry? Can you hear me?"

Brown's eyes were glazed.

"I can't carry you all the way to the bridge," Crisi said. "We don't have any medics."

Brown's lips moved, but no sound came from them.

"Jesus, Barry. I told you to get down," Crisi said, her eyes filling with tears. She didn't like Barry Brown, but he was a member of her squad and she'd known him for years, since General Raines formed the Special Operations Brigade with a select group of soldiers.

Off in the distance another series of explosions announced the ignition of more Bouncing Bettys.

Crisi knew it was time to get the hell out of there before Comandante Perro Loco's troops began scouring the jungle for the soldiers responsible for this ambush.

She looked down at Barry. He was still alive.

He turned distant eyes glazed with pain on her. "Don't let them take me, Crisi," he mumbled through lips covered with loody foam. "You got to do it for me, girl, I can't feel my rms."

She agreed. The only merciful thing to do was to end his uffering.

Crisi drew her silenced Beretta, rolled him to the side vhere he wouldn't see it coming, and quickly fired three bullets into Sergeant Barry Brown's brain . . . She wouldn't allow herself to think about what she was doing.

She slipped away from the tree and made her way toward he bridge where the Tri-State Osprey would pick them up nd get them out of southern Mexico.

At least for now, the Mad Dog's assault on Mexico City ad been halted.

It was an odd sight, an airplane with engines that tilted upward, the Boeing/Bell V-22 Osprey, a VSTOL, vertical-akeoff-and-landing plane for combat search and rescue.

The sweet sound of the tilt-rotor, hybrid fixed-wing aircraft illed Crisi's ears as it came down on a stretch of old asphalt ighway north of the bridge.

A demolitions team was set to blow the bridge after they ook off.

Buddy Raines came over to Crisi.

"The only team member we can't account for is Sergeant 3rown," he said.

"He's dead," Crisi told him. "Took a bullet in the chest and it broke his spine."

"I don't suppose one casualty is all that bad," Buddy said as he gazed south along the empty highway. "It could have been a helluva lot worse."

She left out the rest, that she had killed Sergeant Brown to spare him any more suffering. She felt sure there was nothing else she could have done.

The Osprey settled onto the roadway.

"Get aboard that V-22, Corporal Casper," Buddy said. "We

need to get the hell out of here and pick up Harley Reno's team before they're cut off."

"Yessir," she mumbled, stumbling toward the plane, shutting everything else from her mind.

She was, after all, a soldier.

Forty-one

Harley Reno had shown Ben Raines's team how to plant the Bouncing Bettys and Claymore mines so they'd do the most damage.

"You bury them in a large pattern like this," he said, drawing a > in the caliche with a stick. "That way, the entire column is inside the pattern before the point man sets off the top mine. When it explodes, the men in line behind him will scatter to the sides, causing them to set off the other mines alongside the trail."

"In other words," Coop said, "You get more bang for your buck."

Harley nodded. "Exactly. Now, in about twenty-four hours, they're gonna run into the stuff Buddy Raines and his men set out. When that happens, a lot of the more undisciplined troops will turn around and run like hell for the rear lines to get out of danger. That's where we come in. We're gonna be waitin' for 'em with mines and machine guns."

Coop shook his head. "The poor bastards will feel like rats in a trap."

"Yeah," Hammer Hammerick said, his voice and face showing no sympathy, "war is hell, ain't it?"

Within twenty-four hours, Harley and his team had planted several hundred mines. The Bouncing Bettys, which were primarily antipersonnel mines, were buried alongside the Pan American Highway, where troops were likely to be walking. The older Claymore mines, used for vehicles and APCs, were dug into the road itself to catch any HumVees or jeeps or APCs heading back southward.

After planting the mines, Harley had the team dig in, placing them along a ragged line stretching across the highway just north of a wooden bridge over a deep canyon. He'd rigged the bridge with explosives.

"Once we've done as much damage as we can, or if the numbers become too overwhelming, we'll retreat back across the bridge and blow it. That should slow 'em down enough for us to get airlifted out of here."

Coop noticed Anna watching Harley with adoring eyes as he spoke. Well, he thought, he couldn't blame her too much. The man certainly knew his stuff.

By midafternoon the next day, they began to hear distant explosions from the area where Buddy and his team had been dropped off. Soon, several helicopters came roaring overhead, heading for the area to give tactical air support.

Harley walked along the line of his troops. "I figure in about three, four hours we'll start seeing the first of the troops as they decide it's too hot up there and head back here. If you can stand another MRE, it's time to eat it. You're gonna need some carbos in your body when the fightin' gets goin'."

General Juan Dominguez was riding in an open-topped HumVee about fifty yards back from the head of his column of troops when the first mines went off. He could see the Bouncing Betty throw its tomato-sized can five feet in the air before it exploded, cutting four men almost in half with its load of razor-sharp shrapnel.

"Vamos! Rapido!" he screamed. "Let's get the hell out of here . . . now!"

His driver jerked the steering wheel of the HumVee to the side and moved the vehicle off the road in a sweeping U-turn. The right front tire rolled over a Claymore mine that'd been set off from the road for just such a reaction.

The front of the HumVee was lifted off the ground and blasted to pieces in a giant fireball that consumed Dominguez before he knew what had happened. All the men in his car were killed, along with fifteen troops that'd been walking alongside it.

Men began screaming, both in pain and fear, and hundreds of troops and vehicles turned around and began running for their lives back the way they'd come. Some dropped their weapons in fear, others running off the road into the nearby jungle, hoping for safety there.

When he was radioed the news of Dominguez's death and the trap set up ahead of his troops, General Jaime Pena called for a general retreat until he could call in air support to destroy the ambushers.

He watched in horror as the first two helicopters on the scene were shot out of the sky by GTA missiles. Grabbing the radio, he shouted angrily, "Goddammit, send me some pilots who have combat experience. We're blocked here until you get me some help!"

The air traffic controller at the Villahermosa base they'd taken over said he'd send some Apaches right away. "They won't be so easy to kill," the man said.

General Pena told his squad commanders to pull the men back five miles or so until the Apaches arrived.

Hammer Hammerick climbed down from the tree he'd been in, watching the horizon through his binoculars. "They're on the way, Harley," he said, putting the binoculars in a leather case and picking up his Mini-Uzi. "Looks like the dance is about to begin."

Harley nodded, his lips pulled back in a savage grin. "Good. Let's see if we can't strike up the band."

Within a half hour, the advance troops and jeeps and APCs reached the line of mines the team had planted. Explosions began to blossom along the Pan American Highway like deadly flowers, sowing seeds of death and destruction among the scattering troops. Vehicles could be seen lifted and blown into scrap metal along with bodies tossed in the air and torn apart like rag dolls.

When the screaming, running, shouting men neared Harley's line of defense, he stood up from behind a fallen log and held his Uzi out in front of him. It began to jump and chatter in his hands, spewing 9mm messengers of death among the running men.

The rest of his team followed suit, not bothering to aim, just spraying the Uzis back and forth like garden hoses into the mass of soldiers racing toward them.

The line of advancing men stopped under the onslaught, some dropping to the ground and returning fire, others turning tail and running back the way they came into the certain death of the Bouncing Bettys.

Explosions and fireballs and gunfire mixed with the screaming, shrieking, and shouting of men wounded and dying to produce an almost unbelievable din of destruction.

The smell of cordite, gunpowder, blood, and excrement wafted on the air like some malevolent fog to burn the noses and eyes of Harley's team, until they were forced to begin to draw back from the carnage.

"Pull back to the bridge!" Harley shouted as he bent and opened the box at his feet.

As Coop and Jersey and Corrie and Anna began to withdraw, Coop looked back over his shoulder to see Hammer standing next to Harley, his Uzi bucking and jumping in his hands as he ejected clip after clip and continued firing into the crowd of men still coming at them.

Suddenly an armored half-track with a fifty-caliber machine gun on its turret pushed through the soldiers, bearing down on Harley and Hammer.

Coop grabbed Corrie by the shoulder. "Get on the horn and get that Osprey down here as fast as they can make it. We don't have much longer."

"What are you gonna do?" she asked as she unlimbered her radio set.

"I'm gonna join the party. It looks like the last dance is about to begin."

He ran back to stand next to Harley and Hammer just as Harley pulled out his M-60 machine gun and draped a cartridge belt over his shoulder.

Harley jacked the loading lever back and held the large gun at waist level, aiming it at the half-track that was bearing down on them.

As the 9mm shells from Coop's and Hammer's Uzis bounced harmlessly off the half-inch armor plate of the big vehicle, and its fifty-caliber machine gun began to target them, chewing large chunks of wood out of the trees around them, Harley let go with the M-60.

After the silenced firing of the Uzis, the explosion of the M-60 was deafening. Harley's arm muscles bulged as they tried to control the recoil of the big gun. It jumped and bucked and shook as it pumped hundreds of shells per minute at the half-track.

The helmet of the soldier manning the machine gun on the half-tack disintegrated under the impact of dozens of slugs from Harley's weapon; then the thick glass in the front windshield of the tank shattered and exploded inward as Harley's bullets stitched a line of pockmarks down the front of the half-track.

The vehicle began to waver, turning back and forth as the driver ducked to avoid the ricocheting slugs as they entered the inner compartment of the half-track. One of the bullets must have hit the ammo inside, for suddenly the vehicle exploded with a mighty roar, its sides buckling outward like a tin can that had been stepped on, greasy black smoke pouring from the wreckage.

Coop grabbed Harley's shoulder. "Come on, big guy, Corrie's got the Osprey on the way. Time to go home."

Harley's finger eased off the trigger, his chest heaving as

he tried to catch his breath after fighting the big M-60's reco
his eyes lit with a fierce light.

Hammer punched his shoulder. "Harley! Get your ass i
gear, son, time to boogie."

Harley nodded and followed Coop and Hammer as the
ran for the bridge and safety.

Once they had cleared the end of the bridge, Corrie de
pressed a button on a small black box she was holding an
the bridge exploded, collapsing into the canyon below.

When the three men got to her, she shouted, "Raines an
the Osprey are on the way. We got to hurry. They say a coupl
of Apaches are headed this way and the pilot doesn't war
to have to duke it out with them."

Anna ran up and threw her arms around Harley. "Are yo
all right?" she shouted.

Harley draped his arm around her shoulder, walking besid
her. "Yeah, just another day at the office," he said as the
headed for the pickup spot.

Forty-two

General Jaime Pena jumped to attention when Perro Loco, followed by Jim Strunk and Paco Valdez, entered the Commanding Officer's office at the Mexican Army base at Villahermosa. Pena had pulled his troops back to this location after the disaster on the Pan American Highway.

"Buenos dias," Pena said, saluting smartly.

Loco gave him a look, his eyes flat as he sat behind the desk in the office.

"General Pena, would you ask your second in command to come in, please."

"Certainly, *comandante.*"

Pena stepped to the adjoining door, which led to the officers' wardroom, and called, "Colonel Gonzalez, would you come in here?"

A tall, swarthy man with a handlebar moustache, and a knife scar on his right cheek that coursed down his face to the corner of his mouth, entered. He nodded at Perro Loco and stood at attention, his back to the wall.

"Now, General Pena, please be so kind as to explain to me why you failed in your mission to take Mexico City," Loco said calmly.

Pena looked from Strunk to Valdez, who were standing behind Loco on either side.

"But, *comandante,* there is only one serviceable road northward through this miserable country, and it was heavily mined and defended." He spread his arms wide. "I needed more air support, but the Mexicans had ground-to-air missile and shot the few helicopters I had at my disposal out of th air."

Loco nodded, then glanced at Strunk. "Jaime, how mucl does a helicopter cost?"

"Several millions of dollars, *comandante.*"

"And an APC or a HumVee?"

"Many thousands of dollars, *comandante.*"

"And a portable mine detector?"

Strunk smiled, shaking his head sadly. "Only a few hun dred dollars, *comandante.*"

"Why did you not think that the road might be mined General, and take appropriate precautions? Surely, losing a few men with mine detectors would have been preferable to losing . . ." He bent his head and studied a sheaf of papers on the desk. "Two helicopters, four APCs, three HumVees and four hundred and fifty-six soldiers, not to mention General Juan Dominguez."

Pena, sweat beginning to bead on his forehead and run down his cheeks to drip off his chin, lowered his head. "We moved so fast, *comandante,* I did not think the Mexicans would have had time to mine the road."

Loco sighed heavily. "That is the truest thing you've said today, General," he said. "You did not *think!*"

"I am sorry, *comandante,*" Pena said, his eyes on the floor in front of him.

Loco slipped a .45 caliber automatic out of his pocket and aimed across the desk.

Pena glanced up, his eyes widening and his mouth opening to protest as Loco fired. The pistol exploded and the bullet entered Pena's forehead, snapping his head back and blowing the back of his skull out, showering the wall behind him with blood and brains. Pena's body collapsed in a heap in front of Loco's desk.

Loco cut his eyes to Colonel Gonzalez. "What is your first name, Colonel?"

Gonzalez swallowed, the scar on his cheek pulling the corner of his mouth up in a caricature of a grin. "Enrique, *comandante.*"

"Enrique Gonzalez, you are now promoted to general and will be in charge of our forces in Mexico. Is that satisfactory?"

Gonzalez glanced at Pena's body on the floor, trails of smoke still rising from his empty skull. He nodded rapidly. *"Sí, comandante."*

"And you are aware of the penalties for failure?"

Gonzalez continued to nod, unable to take his eyes off Pena's corpse and its right foot that was still twitching. *"Sí, comandante."*

Loco stood up and holstered his weapon. "Good. Then let us go to the communications room and contact President Osterman of the United States. I fear we are going to need some of her more modern equipment to take Mexico City."

President Claire Osterman hung up the phone after over an hour's discussion of how Perro Loco's forces had been stymied on their journey toward Mexico City due to lack of air support and stronger than expected resistance from the Mexican forces.

"Jesus," she said, "God save me from Central American desperadoes who think they're generals."

She looked at her team of advisers arrayed before her. General Stevens, Harlan Millard, and Herb Knoff were sitting in chairs in the Commanding Officers' quarters of Fort Benjamin Harris in Indianapolis.

She winced as rumbling sounds and vibrations shook the ceiling. "Herb, can't we quiet that infernal noise?"

He shook his head. "Madame President, you ordered the removal of the wreckage of the building overhead yourself. The bulldozers cannot do that without making some noise."

"All right, all right," she said testily. She was still pissed off that Otis Warner and General Joe Winter had been allowed to escape the attack on the fort the day before.

"How is everything going with my resuming command of the country?" she asked Stevens.

General Bradley Stevens, Jr., nodded. "Very well, Madame President. The Armed Services have all acknowledged your right to continue as head of the government, and the rank and file of the Army is behind you one hundred percent. A few of the officers whose loyalty was questionable have been replaced with men I can trust, but overall, it's going just fine."

"And the country?"

"A massive propaganda campaign has been undertaken," Millard said. "All of the media are cooperating, as usual. We are informing the people that the coup attempt to overthrow you was orchestrated by Otis Warner with the complicity of Ben Raines and the SUSA. In the absence of any voices telling them otherwise, I think they'll buy it."

"Good," she said. "Now we have two things to do in addition to restarting the war against the SUSA. One, we have to transport some equipment to Perro Loco down in Mexico. He has control of the Navy base at Pariso near his command at Villahermosa. General Stevens, we need to send a transport ship down there with some helicopters, tanks, APCs, and whatever else he needs. I'll leave the coordination of that to you and your men."

"Yes, Madame President."

"The second thing I've got to do is get him some help with his soldiers and command structure. He's just too damned stupid to run a war."

"How do you propose to do that, Claire?" Millard asked.

She glanced at a folder on her desk which read Top Secret, Intel, on the cover. "I have here an intel report on Bruno Bottger."

"Bruno Bottger?" Stevens asked. "I thought Raines killed him in Africa a few years back."

She shook her head. "No, as it turns out, Bottger escaped

to the island of Madagascar. He stayed there for a year or so, recovering from wounds he'd received in his escape. Then he made his way to South America. Intel has found out he's used his vast fortune to hire an army of mercenaries with the idea of reattacking Ben Raines at some point in the future."

Stevens shook his head. "I don't know, Claire. Getting involved with Bottger will be risky. The man is a zealot and a Nazi. He will be very tough to control."

"That's the beauty of it, Brad. We won't have to control him. He hates Ben Raines so much he'll jump at any chance to get revenge on him. I plan to get him and his mercenary army to join Perro Loco by promising him unlimited access to our weapons and technology. I'll also promise him he may have Mexico as a prize for his new Nazi state if he manages to conquer it."

"But Claire," Millard protested. "You've also promised Mexico to Perro Loco."

"Yes, I have, haven't I?" she said, a smile curling her lips. "Well, in the event they are successful, they'll just have to fight it out to see who ends up on top down there."

Stevens nodded, seeing where she was headed. "Yeah, and after they've weakened each other fighting it out, we'll step in and take over from whoever's left."

Claire grinned. "Brad, you're a man after my own heart."

Forty-three

Bruno Bottger sat on his terrace overlooking the ocean on the Ilha de Sao Sebastiao, a small island two hundred miles south of Rio de Janeiro. He gently rubbed oil into the burn scars on his face, trying to keep the shiny skin supple so it wouldn't crack.

Rudolf Hessner, his trusted bodyguard, stepped onto the terrace with a bottle of beer, frost droplets gathering on the glass in the humid sea air.

Bruno took the bottle and took a deep draught.

"Is the pain bad today, Herr Bottger?" he asked, a concerned look on his face.

Bruno gave a short laugh. "The pain is always the same, Rudolf. It is a constant reminder of the debt I owe Ben Raines."

Rudolf sat across a small glass table from Bruno. "Have you decided what to do about the American President's offer?"

Bruno looked at Rudolf. "I do not fully trust the woman, Rudolf, but if we take her offer of help, it will cut years off my timetable for retaliation against Ben Raines."

"But Herr Bottger, you would have to share command with the Nicaraguan, Perro Loco."

Bruno snorted through the holes in scar tissue that used to be a nose. "If I cannot outsmart a little brown man, who is not much better than the blacks that are taking over the world, then I do not deserve to lead the New World Order."

"So, you've decided then?"

"Yes, Rudolf. It is time to avenge myself against Ben Raines. This time I will not stop until he is dead!"

Otis Warner and General Joe Winter sat in Ben Raines's office, along with Raines, Mike Post, and General Ike McGowen.

"I tell you, Mr. Raines, Claire Osterman *is* going to start another war with the SUSA. The woman is obsessed with killing you and your country," Warner said.

"But Mr. Warner," Mike Post said, "your country is severely weakened by the beating you took last year. We just don't think it'd make sense for her to resume hostilities now."

General Winter shook his head. "You don't understand, sir. Claire Osterman cares not one whit for the USA or what's best for the people. She is a madwoman who is only concerned with her pride. She will do anything, sacrifice anyone, and risk everything to bring down Ben Raines. It is like an illness within her. The hatred is eating her alive and the only cure, in her mind, is to defeat Ben Raines."

"But, General Winter, you and I both know she has no chance of doing that with her present resources," Mike continued. Ben Raines interrupted. "I agree with General Winter, Mike. Claire is not the type to give up, or to ever do what is rational. Hell, look at the way she joined forces with Perro Loco."

"But Ben," Mike argued, "Perro Loco's army is a joke. You stopped him in his tracks with less than thirty people."

"Nevertheless, Mike, I've got a gut feeling we haven't seen the last of Claire Osterman, or of Perro Loco, and my gut is rarely wrong."

In the next book in the Ashes series, *Warriors from the Ashes,* Ben Raines finds that his gut feeling was correct. He is faced with fighting a war on two fronts. From the north, Claire Osterman resumes the USA's war against the SUSA, while from the south, Perro Loco's army, invigorated by the infusion of thousands of mercenaries under the command of Bruno Bottger and fresh equipment from the USA, manages to take Mexico City and move northward toward the SUSA's southern borders.

Realizing that no country has ever won a war fighting on two fronts, Ben must use all of his knowledge and bravery to combat the massive forces arrayed against him.

William W. Johnstone
The *Mountain Man* Series

Complete Your Collection of
THE EAGLES SERIES
By William W. Johnstone

__#2 **Dreams of Eagles** $5.99US/$7.99CAN
0-8217-6086-6

__#4 **Scream of Eagles** $5.99US/$7.50CAN
0-7860-0447-9

__#5 **Rage of Eagles** $5.99US/$7.50CAN
0-7860-0507-6

__#6 **Song of Eagles** $5.99US/$7.99CAN
0-7860-0639-0

__#7 **Cry of Eagles** $5.99US/$7.99CAN
0-7860-1024-X

__#8 **Blood of Eagles** $5.99US/$7.99CAN
0-7860-1106-8
